PATCHWORK FAMILY

BOOK III

JAMIE'S JOURNEY

M.H.P. Rosenbaum

BLACK BEAR PRODUCTIONS

Published by Black Bear Productions
815 Simon Greenwell Ln., Boston, KY 40107
mhpros@hughes.net

Cover art by Rivkah Walton/studio-rw.com
Book Layout and Cover Design
by Maggie Pagratis/Custom-book-tique.com

For my children, my succor and my inspiration.

CHAPTER 1.

SATURDAY, FEBRUARY 21, 1953

"Today I am a man," The Boy said. "The Boy" is how he thought of himself. It was what the men in the concentration camp had called him, *Der Yingl* in Yiddish. He had been told that, at his circumcision on the eighth day of his life, Rabbi Metzger had lifted him up and proclaimed, "His name in Israel shall be Chaim." But Rabbi Metzger had also been The Boy's own Tati, and Tati and Mamme had called him Hymie.

The Boy looked over the edge of the pulpit to the synagogue's congregation, with his own American family sitting in the front row. Most Americans had a hard time pronouncing "Chaim," with its throat-scraping beginning that sounded like someone hawking up a gob of spit, so they called him Jamie.

He started the bar mitzvah speech he'd been preparing and practicing for months, but inside he was thinking, *I'm thirteen years old; I'm a bar mitzvah, with the responsibilities of an adult Jew. I'm not a boy any more. I should be Hymie to myself again.*

He put aside his speech notes. "My name is Chaim," he said, looking down at the front row, his family filling the high-backed wooden pew. "In Hebrew, *chaim* means 'life.' And my family name was Metzger, 'butcher.' My old life was butchered by the Nazis, and now my name is Jamie McAlister. The name 'James' comes from the Hebrew name 'Jacob,' which means 'supplanter,' one who takes the place of another. The last name I have now means something like 'child of the protector.'"

His brothers and sisters were glancing at each other uneasily; they knew this wasn't the speech he had memorized. Mom caught his eye and nodded encouragingly, but Ruby Jones's dark face beside hers looked worried. Elsewhere in the congregation, people were shuffling a little. *I'm losing them.*

"I'm trying to say," he went on desperately, "that I was given a new life after the concentration camp, that after all that death and suffering, I've come to a safe place." That made people settle back more comfortably. But they snapped into tension again when he said, "Too safe, it makes me feel too safe. Because we're never safe, we never will be safe. Less than two weeks ago, our new president, Eisenhower, refused to grant clemency to Julius and Ethel Rosenberg, who've been condemned to death supposedly for spying. But does anyone here doubt that they would not be facing execution if they were not Jews? Does anyone think it's safe to be a Jew, even in America?"

Now a low murmur arose in the congregation; some people were glancing at the rabbi as though hoping he would intervene. Mom was still looking supportive, but her hand was wound so tightly in her purse strap Jamie could see the reddening bands of her flesh from here.

Jamie sighed and went back to his prepared text. "I would like to thank my teachers…" The congregation relaxed, though Mom's hand was still in its painful grip on the purse strap.

Afterwards, eating Ruby's sponge cake and the special little tub of tapioca pudding she'd brought for him in the social hall beside the

5

sanctuary, Jamie was still shaking in reaction. He hated to talk, even in ordinary ways; he liked to retreat into silence, to shield himself behind it. And he hated to be touched, to have all these people shaking his hand and patting his back and even pinching his cheek.

It was a little easier to bear when his adopted family congratulated him. His older brother, Laurence, put an arm around his shoulders, ignoring Jamie's reflexive flinch. "Man," Laurie said, "I'm glad I'm a Catholic, and didn't have to give a Confirmation speech." He leaned in to say softly into Jamie's ear, "I know that was hard for you. You done good." Laurie gave Jamie's shoulder a playful squeeze and let go.

A couple of people Jamie didn't recognize stared at the young Negro half hugging the bar mitzvah boy. The rabbi noticed and hurried over to speak to the strangers in low tones, shifting them aside from Laurie and Jamie.

From long practice, Jamie put them out of his mind and turned to his sisters. Celia and little Joy, both with Dad's Scottish features and Mom's dark Italian hair and eyes, grinned at him companionably. They were guiding blonde Beth in this unfamiliar place, and moved her toward the cake table just as her biological brother, Rob, came bounding in from the direction of the boys' bathroom. He gave Jamie a friendly swat on the arm as he passed. "I'll get yours, Bethie," he said, heading for the table. "Punch and cookies, too, or just cake?"

Then the milling crowd stilled and fell silent as the rabbi invoked the blessings on wine and Sabbath challah bread in sonorous Hebrew. Jamie closed his eyes and let the sound sink into him. *I know these prayers, I know them in my bones,* he thought. *Why don't I ever say them?*

He thought back to his conversation with Dad last night on the long-distance phone; Dad was down in Florida, at the Pensacola naval technical training school. "I'm so sorry I can't be with you,

6

son," he'd said. "Now that this business in Korea is winding down, everything's in flux. I hope to be with you all soon."

Hearing Dad's voice, even at a distance, always calmed Jamie. Dad had found him in the French orphanage where he'd been sent after World War Two ended and Jamie's concentration camp was liberated, when he was only four. With that voice, and his quiet, steady strength, he'd coaxed Jamie out of the space under the orphanage porch where he hid when strangers visited, and out of the place inside his head he retreated to when anything unexpected happened.

When Dad's leave was up, he'd asked Jamie—in the fractured mix of German, Yiddish, French, and a few words of English they'd cobbled together to communicate in—whether he wanted to come home with him and be part of his family. "I don't belong there," he'd said. "I don't belong anywhere."

"If you don't belong anywhere, then it doesn't matter where you are," Dad had said with that patient rationality Jamie found more reassuring than the sometimes overbearingly emotional attempts at comfort from the orphanage nuns. "Come with me, and then that's where you'll belong."

Last night Jamie had said on the phone, "I thought becoming bar mitzvah, all the studying I've done this year, learning the Torah portion in Hebrew—I thought being more Jewish would make me feel more like I belonged somewhere. But..." He fell silent, unable to say more.

Dad had let the silence stand for a while, then said, "You're only thirteen, son. You've lived horrors most children couldn't even imagine. Don't be so hard on yourself. You'll find who you're meant to be, and we'll all help you. I'm proud of you for doing this, and I love you."

Now Jamie was sorry he'd eaten the sponge cake; it felt like clay in his stomach. *There's too much food,* he thought, panicking a little. In the camp, when the American soldiers arrived to free them, they'd handed out chocolate bars, and fatty meat from cans, and cheese and hard crackers. Some of the others, frantic with hunger, had died from gobbling the food. Not Jamie: Jamie had been hiding, watching, waiting for it to be safe.

Now, seeing all the food piled on the buffet table made his stomach clench. The smell nauseated him; the lingering taste in his mouth revolted him. The din from fifty people chatting and laughing in the big room hurt his ears. The movement of all the bodies in their colorful clothing circulating around the room made his head spin.

He was terrified he might faint. If that happened, if he lost consciousness, if he fell on the floor, he'd be out of control of the situation. All these people would immediately gather around, staring at him, exclaiming over him. They wouldn't step on him, of course they wouldn't, but even so… He sank onto a folding chair but he still felt unbalanced, as though he might fall off it. His palms were sweaty and his temples pounded.

Then he heard Mom's voice, low beside him. "Do you need to leave the room?"

He managed to nod. She put a hand on the inside of his arm, hidden but holding firmly as she helped him to his feet. They walked slowly toward the door. People spoke to Mom and she answered, her voice light and cheerful, but she never stopped moving toward the door.

Finally they got out into the synagogue lobby. Mom helped him to lie down on an upholstered bench along one wall. "Rest a minute, Hymele," she said, using the nickname Mamme used to, that he'd told her about after one of his nightmares. "You did very, very well today. There's no reason to force yourself to do any more."

8

He closed his eyes and felt her shift back to sit by his feet. She put her hand on his shoe: touching but not touching. *She knows what I need,* he thought, letting himself relax. The noise from the nearby room full of people didn't bother him any more; even if strangers came up to them, she would shield him.

Some immeasurable time went past, then she said, "Here's Ruby with the car. Let's go home, my darling."

Crowded with the others in the station wagon, Jamie tried to calm himself. *This is my family now, this is my reality. Buchenwald is gone; I'll never see it again. That terrified child is gone; I'll never be him again.*

He wondered, if he repeated it often enough, whether it would start to feel true. Because he did see the concentration camp, every day of his life: looming ominously in his memory, realer and more present than the world around him.

Clear in his mind, as always, was the iron gates of the camp. They stood athwart his mind, blocking whatever lay behind them, what he couldn't see—didn't want to see. There were just the looming gates, with the motto across the top: *Jedem das Seine.* Quoting it, he said now, "You get what you deserve," and turned his head to gaze at the Pennsylvania farmland sliding past the car windows.

CHAPTER 2.

THURSDAY, MARCH 26, 1953

Jamie shifted around, feeling his sleeping bag zipper chafe against the scars on his back in the narrow space. He was in the long cabinet under the eaves in the attic, the place he hid in when he had to be alone.

A fine sleety rain peppered the roof inches above his face, increasing his sense of protection and safety. *No footsteps up there,* he thought, not even sure where the notion had come from. But once, on a summer evening, a squirrel had leapt onto the shingles overhead and he'd scrambled frantically out of the cabinet, heart pounding with a fear he didn't understand.

He hurriedly put that memory away and went back to thinking about the Rosenbergs again. *All the protests, all the important people in Europe objecting, the physicists saying the Russians would have gotten the A-bomb anyway—none of it matters. They're going to be electrocuted. They're going to die, and it's because they're Jews.* Other people had been arrested on suspicion of espionage for no other reason than that their names were also Rosenberg and they worked at government facilities. *Is it happening here, the hatred and the persecution? Will they be coming for us again?*

Jamie forced his mind back to the announcement in the papers today, that everyone had been talking about at school. Dr. Jonas Salk had invented a vaccine against polio. They were only beginning field tests, but early results looked promising; if it worked, polio could be wiped out. Jamie tried to picture what it would be like: the girls wouldn't have to wear white gloves when they went to Hershey Park; the boys wouldn't have to avoid touching things like the safety bars on the roller coaster. Maybe they could swim in Laurel Lake even when it was really hot.

Maybe there wouldn't be kids in wheelchairs and leg braces with wasted, deformed limbs trundling down school corridors. Maybe nobody would ever again have to spend life confined in one of the futuristic-looking steel capsules called an iron lung. *All because of a New York Jew at the University of Pittsburgh. Will that make them not hate us so much?*

Next to Jamie's head, his wind-up alarm clock went off. *Have to leave,* he thought reluctantly, silencing the rattling buzz and opening the cabinet door. When he'd first come to this house, a terrified, malnourished five-year-old, he'd felt lost in the huge rooms and quiet, spacious hallways. There were only nine people in the whole place—three adults and six kids. In the orphanage in France, there had been that many in his dorm room. In the camp barracks, there were hundreds, crammed in flank to flank. Here he had a bedroom all to himself.

They had seemed to think they were doing him a favor; the other boys—Rob and Laurie—shared a room, and so did Celia and baby Joy. The only other kid in a single room was Beth, and she was blind so she needed to be in a space she could control. Jamie had wondered whether they thought he had some kind of crippling condition, too. Except he never felt in control in his room; he felt lost and abandoned, startling at every sound and peering into the shadows for half-sensed ghosts.

Dad, who'd found him in the orphanage and befriended him and brought him here, soon went back to sea. Mom, who was a psychologist, always wanted him to talk about the past, when Jamie

11

couldn't even stand to think about it. Ruby's brown face had frightened him at first, until her unfailing kindness let him hesitatingly relax. But she always wanted him to eat; her constant attempts to cook dishes that would appeal to him oppressed his spirit, and his stomach rebelled against the richness and the abundance of them.

And all of them—the adults and the kids—constantly wanted to touch him, petting and hugging and kissing his cheek. At first he ran from them, then he flinched away; now he just froze, waiting for them to stop. He held himself to their embraces as he might have held a wound to a cauterizing flame: he knew it was necessary for him to live, but it hurt; God, it hurt.

So when he'd been in the family for a couple of months and had fled to the attic away from them and had found this cabinet, he'd scrambled into it without thinking about it and closed himself in the darkness with his heart pounding and his breath gasping as though he'd been chased there. After a while he'd pulled out the dusty old curtains stored there and hidden them behind a trunk, leaving only the ancient cotton sleeping bag to lie on.

They hadn't noticed he was gone the first time, or the second. But the third time he sought the refuge of the cabinet, he'd heard after a while the sound of his new American name being called, increasingly frantically, and the thumping of doors downstairs. When he could hear through the eaves that the calling voices had gone outside, he'd levered himself out and crept out of the attic area, through the music room, and downstairs to the second floor and his own room. Mom had found him there, hiding under his bed.

He'd closed his eyes and lain as still as he could when she came into the bedroom, but he could sense when she'd found him. He forced his eyes open and met hers peering in at him. She'd withdrawn her head then and dropped the dust ruffle; in the gap between it and the floor he could see her knees shaking. After a minute she got to her feet and he'd heard her go to the door and call, "He's here. I found him. It's ok." Then she'd sunk down to sit on the floor by the bed.

"We were so frightened," she'd said softly.

"Sorry," he'd whispered. English was still new to him, but he didn't think he could have said more in any language at the moment.

She'd sat there in silence while the afternoon faded to dusk. When it was almost too dark to see, he'd found it in himself to say, "I hided."

"Where?"

"Here."

"No. This was one of the first places I looked. You weren't here the first time."

She didn't sound angry, but Jamie was terrified.

Eventually she'd said, "It's all right. You don't have to tell me. Just, if you hide there again and you hear us calling, come out, okay?"

"Okay," he'd said.

In the years since, they'd worked out some ground rules: don't lock or block himself in, don't squirrel food away, only stay an hour a day. And his hour was up for today.

With an easy stealth born of long practice, he crept to the attic door and listened. No one was practicing on the spinet in the music room, or fooling with Mom's old Spanish guitar. He eased the door open, closed it softly behind him, and slipped down the stairs to the second floor landing. He paused at the turn, listening for voices.

There were none in the second floor hall beside him, but from the kitchen below he could hear Ruby's voice. "... need to get these

13

potatoes peeled," she was saying. "And those beans aren't going to string themselves."

"He'll be along." Beth's voice, calm and confident. "I'll start on the beans."

My turn to help with dinner, he suddenly realized. *Along with Beth tonight. Ok, that'll be ok. Let's go, Hymie.*

He took a breath and moved toward the voices.

CHAPTER 3.

SATURDAY, JUNE 20, 1953

J amie couldn't believe it. The rabbi was talking about the week's Torah portion—today of all days. The first part was all about women's vows, and how they didn't count unless they were allowed by her father or husband. Then there was a long piece about the Israelites purifying themselves after slaying the Midianites.

But Jamie's mind kept churning over what he'd read in the paper this morning, the account of the Rosenbergs' execution. *He went on the first jolt of electricity, but it took three tries to kill her. They say smoke came out of her head. Smoke...*

He wrenched his thoughts back to the present, shifting in the wooden pew and choking down his rising gorge. *Why is he talking about this ancient stuff? He usually uses the Torah portion to comment on current events. Why is he...*

Babylon. He just said the word "Babylon." Jamie'd learned when studying for his bar mitzvah that Jews had historically used the name to mean the Diaspora, life in exile, the societies that forced them into ghettos and persecuted and murdered them. *It's code; he's talking about the Rosenbergs after all.* The thought brought him no comfort. *He's afraid to speak openly. The rabbi himself is afraid. Does he think there'll be... what, pogroms? Will they rise up against us to kill us, like it says in the Passover Haggadah?*

Smoke... The image of smoke came back to him, rising from Ethel Rosenberg's head with its neat, dowdy hairstyle. Then another flash: smoke rising from a charred Torah scroll. *I never saw Mamme's hair. She kept it covered, always.* Where did that thought come from? He ruthlessly pressed it back down into the ferment in his mind, forcing the seething to still, making himself calm. *Nothing, there's nothing, I remember nothing. Besides, if there's a pogrom, if it starts here, I'll be safe. I have a gentile name, a gentile family. They'll hide me.*

On that thought, he was filled with a shame so deep he thought he might die from it. The only way he could bear it was to go cold, to freeze thought and feeling and muscle and bone. He would have stopped his blood and breath if he could have willed them to stillness.

He knew nothing more of the service until he felt Mrs. Epstein's hand tugging his jacket sleeve. The Epsteins knew not to touch him, ordinarily; they must have been trying to get his attention for a while. He pulled his arm away and followed them to the pillars at the entrance of the building, where Rabbi Samson stood, brow furrowed. "Are you all right, son?" he asked.

If I don't answer, they'll all start fussing. "Fine," he forced through his stiff lips.

The adults looked at each other over his head. Whatever they communicated, it ended when Mr. Epstein heaved a sigh. "Let's get going, then," he said.

There was absolute silence in the car all the long drive from Lancaster back to Pine Springs. Silence in Jamie's head, too. Silence.

He bestirred himself when the car pulled into his driveway. "Thanks," he croaked, "for the ride." He got out of the car and started up the walk to the front door.

But instead of the Epsteins' car backing out, he heard the thud of another door slamming, and other footsteps on the walk. By the time he pushed open the heavy white door, Mr. Epstein was close behind him.

Ruby was just coming into the hall. "Jamie, I heard the car..." She stopped short at the sight of Mr. Epstein. "Is something wrong?"

"Is Mrs... er, I mean, Dr. McAlister here?"

"No, sir, she's still at Rolling Meadow seeing her Saturday patients. She should be home in an hour or two if you'd like to leave a message?"

"I don't suppose Commander McAlister..."

"No, he won't be getting leave till later this summer. Has something happened?" She said the last to Jamie.

Mr. Epstein answered. "No, it's just—he seems a little... upset."

Jamie stood frozen between them, feeling Ruby's sharp gaze and Mr. Epstein's worried one.

"You go on into the kitchen, child," she said. "I'll fix you something hot."

"Not hungry," he managed.

"Just some broth," she said. Then, when he didn't move, she said firmly, "Kitchen. Now."

He forced his feet forward, leaving the low murmur of their voices behind him. The kitchen was empty, the others' lunch dishes half done in the sink. He slid onto the breakfast nook bench and thought longingly of his cabinet in the attic.

A thin curl of steam rose from the saucepan on the stove. *Steam, not smoke.*

The front door closed and the sound of the Epsteins' car pulling away filtered through to the kitchen. Still, it was several minutes before Ruby came into the room. *Bet I know why.*

Sure enough, she said as she poured the soup through a tea filter into a heavy ceramic coffee mug and handed him the broth, "I just called your mother. She'll be back as soon as she can rearrange her schedule. Till then, she says you can be alone if you have to, but she doesn't want you to go to your hiding place now."

He nodded and immediately lurched up and headed for the back stairs, still cradling the hot mug in his cold hands. He felt a twist of—guilt? Shame? He wasn't sure what exactly the feeling was—at the soft, sad breath Ruby exhaled behind him, but whatever it was didn't slow his flight to his room.

In Celia and Joy's room across the hall, the girls were talking over the sound of Julius LaRosa singing on Celia's record player: "My heart will find no home/ Anywhere I wander, anywhere I roam." He shut his hall door against it, put the mug of broth down on his nightstand, then crossed the room to use the bathroom. Through its adjoining door into Rob and Laurie's room, he could hear them laughing.

"How about this one?" Rob giggled. "Why did the moron tiptoe past the medicine cabinet?"

"So he wouldn't wake the sleeping pills," Laurie scoffed. "Gosh, first time I heard that one, I laughed so hard I fell out of my crib. Here's a new one, though…"

As he left the bathroom, Jamie shut that door behind him to muffle their voices, too. *Mom will scold them if she hears them telling those,* he thought. *She's so touchy about calling people names, even in jokes.* He sat on his bed, scooting up against the headboard and putting his head down on his raised knees, arms clasped about them.

After a long while, a thin thread of memory rose like smoke, a voice laughing: *"So the men of Chelm carried the boulders back up the mountain so that this time they could roll them down again and save labor."*

But he would have said it in Yiddish, he thought, and flinched away from the thought. *I'll have a nightmare tonight, I just know I will.* His nightmares were not like the other kids': fantastic monsters to be gently laughed away or mundane fears and anxieties to be salved and reassured into tameness. Jamie's monsters were real, and his fear never went away. Or his rage. Unless he could stay in the silence.

He raised his head, pushed his glasses up onto it, and scrubbed his hands over his face, banishing the ghosts in his head. There was a thud from downstairs.

The front door. Mom's home. Jamie straightened his back. He knew what came next: she would come in and sit with him. She would ask him if he wanted to talk. He wouldn't answer. After a while, she would put her arms around him. He would let her.

It's supposed to help, I know it's supposed to help. Maybe it even does. Just put up with it, Yingl, Boy. Then he corrected his inner voice. *Hymie, I'm calling myself Hymie from now on. So, Hymie, let her help you.*

But when Mom or Ruby held him, he couldn't seem to breathe right. Their soft arms, their pillowy breasts—he felt like he might suffocate. Dad wasn't like that; when Dad was around, and Jamie started to shake or freeze, Dad would hold him hard in sinewy arms against a hard-muscled chest. That was almost as good as being in his cabinet. He couldn't move, there was no space around him—nobody could get at him, and he didn't have to do anything. But he could still breathe.

Mom tapped on the door and came in. Her face was loving, compassionate, understanding. There was no smoke coming out of her head. *I wish Dad was home.*

CHAPTER 4.

SATURDAY, AUGUST 15, 1953

The Epsteins' car pulled away and Jamie made his way up the walk, enjoying the muggy air. Everyone at the synagogue had been exclaiming to each other about the heat and humidity, as if it didn't get this way every August in central Pennsylvania. But Jamie never minded summer weather. *Heat is life; it's cold that kills.*

He pushed into the front door and stopped just inside. Rob and Celia were there, arguing over some comic book. He felt a rush of wry affection for them. *Children. They're only a couple of years younger than me, but what do they know?*

"Don't you both read enough trash already? Don't you ever want to do anything worthwhile with your time?" He meant it to be funny; the others all teased each other constantly, and laughed while they did it. But as soon as the words were out of his mouth, he knew he'd gotten it wrong again. *I hurt them,* he realized, but he didn't know how to make it better.

There was a shadow at the top of the stairs. Their big brother, Laurie, stood there. "Cissy, give me the comic," he snapped. "You'll get it back when the two of you stop acting like five-year-olds. As for you," he said to Jamie over Celia's head as she obediently brought him the comic, "what made you think you're so great? You might read a lot, but what have you ever done that's so 'worthwhile'? Just go to your room and get out of sight instead of making life miserable for the rest of us."

Jamie fled past them to his room and closed himself in. He perched on the end of his bed, rocking back and forth in despair. *You did it again, Hymie,* he told himself. *He's right, you always ruin everything. You never know what to say or how to act; you're never normal. He's right to send you away.* Jedem das Seine; *you get what you deserve.*

The Rosenbergs didn't get what they deserved.

Stop with the Rosenbergs already. You don't fit in any better than they did. You're like a spy in their midst; you don't belong.

No, they love me.

They think they do. They wouldn't if they really knew you.

They know me, he insisted to himself, but the thought felt hollow. Long ago, when he'd first come here, there'd only been one voice in his head: the one that warned him to stay hidden, not to risk letting anyone see who he really was. In those days, he paid attention to how the others felt so he wouldn't fall victim to any emotional shifts—their anger, or the affection he felt must be false. But gradually the second voice, the one that said their feelings were real and must be acknowledged, arose and grew stronger. *When Laurie talked to me that way, it's because he thought I was trying to hurt the others, and he thinks it's his job to keep everybody safe. Even me...* Jamie cut that thought off ruthlessly. *No, he doesn't even like me, he can't care about* me *that way.* The reassurance of the second voice felt hollow. He needed to hide in the silence now.

Through the adjoining bathroom, he could hear Rob and Laurie's voices. He crept to his door and peered into the hallway. The girls' doors were closed; the coast was clear. He scooted down the hall and up the attic stairs. Just past the turn, he froze; Ruby's voice came up from the kitchen. "I need some help down here."

21

It's Rob and Celia's night to help. I don't have to go. He felt uneasy, though; bringing in the groceries after a shopping trip wasn't technically part of helping with dinner. Then he heard two sets of feet tromping down the steps. *Ruby has enough help with them. I'd just be in the way.* He went on up to his cabinet.

In bed that night, he tried not to fall asleep. At dinner, everyone had acted as though nothing had happened. Rob and Celia talked about the stupid comic and the others chattered away about their own concerns. Mom asked Laurie about his friend Tommy. *That's right, his friend's family moved to Chicago today. That's why he was so crabby.* But Laurie carefully never glanced toward Jamie.

Now he felt a pressure on his chest that had nothing to do with the steamy weather. He knew what that meant: he would have a nightmare tonight. He hadn't had one for a long time; not even the Rosenberg executions had sparked one as he'd feared. Mom said to try not to be afraid of them; they were his mind's way of dealing with the past he couldn't bear to remember, and the fears and frustrations of his present life. *Easy for her to say. She doesn't have to live through them.*

That's what they felt like: living things over again. He knew it was futile to resist slipping into unconsciousness, but he fought against sleep anyway.

He focused on the sounds of the others getting ready for bed.

Laurie brushed his teeth—he always made more noise spitting and gargling than Rob did.

Celia and Mom spoke softly in the hall, then Celia and Joy's door clicked closed.

Mom had already been in here to say goodnight to Jamie; now she hummed a little as she moved down the hall to her and Dad's room at the end.

The big house fan in the attic over his head thrummed.

The little window fan in his room whirred.

Outside, the summer crickets scritched.

Across the hall, a door opened.

"Always with the books. Think they're better than everybody else."

Mrs. Albrecht. But she's always nice to me—why does she sound so mean?

"Sitting there in that big apartment with the nice view while we're stuck here in the back. What are they, royalty? A rabbi, he says. Whatever that means."

Footsteps now, hard, booted feet. Across the hall, a door clicks closed.

"This way, Hymele, quickly now, sha, sha, shepseleh, don't make a sound." Mamme's voice.

Tati's hands pulling him out of bed, slinging him over his shoulder like a sack. Jamie stretches his hands toward his shepseleh, his stuffed lamb, but it is already out of reach.

Through the little door half hidden in the pantry, down the narrow back stairs to the building's cellar. Mr. Schulz, the janitor, helping Tati push Jamie up through the coal hole.

"We'll be at my cousin's," Mamme says. "Please keep everything safe for us till this is over."

"Of course," says Mr. Schulz.

Jamie is lying crushed on the floor of someone's automobile, blankets over his head; he can't breathe. "Too late, we waited too long," Tati is moaning.

"Cousin Yankel will hide us," Mamme says.

Jamie used to hide in the garden, behind the potting shed or under the shrubbery lining the apartment building's courtyard. "I'm coming to find you," Mamme would call gaily.

They'll find us. They will. They did.

Jamie is choking. He can't breathe. He forces vomit back down his throat. *"Sha, sha, shepseleh, Hymele," Mamme is saying, stroking his brow.* No, it's Mom. Mom parroting Yiddish she's heard him cry, Mom wiping his face. The girls are there, and Ruby. Rob comes in.

They all talk at him, pet him; Ruby brings him warm milk. Finally, Laurie is there, apologizing, saying that he lied when he said Jamie was worthless. *He thinks this is his fault. He imagines I'm someone I'm not, someone better.*

Laurie presses Jamie's shoulder with his hand; Jamie tries not to shrug it off. Laurie lends him a book, *Go Tell It on the Mountain.* "About a kid having a hard time because people hate who he is. He's not a Jew, he's a Negro. Seems like kinda the same thing, though," he says.

They drink warm honeyed milk together and eat shortbread cookies. The sweet, soothing liquid on his throat, the solid but undemanding nourishment of the cookies, the equally solid but undemanding presence of his brother: Jamie calms down and comes back to the present.

Mom held Jamie from behind, propping him against her soft chest. It felt too soft; Jamie didn't trust it.

Still, the milk was real, and the book from Laurie. They could see him well enough to see he'd be comforted by those.

"You're safe here, with your family that loves you," Mom said. She's said it before.

Jamie might actually believe her.

CHAPTER 5.

THURSDAY, SEPTEMBER 10, 1953

"You think you're smarter than everyone else?" Mrs. Andress snarled.

"No," Jamie answered. "I just think I'm smarter than you."

Half an hour later, he was on his way home, suspended from school for three days because he refused the principal's demand that he apologize to his teacher. Jamie had sat slumped before Mr. Dickerson's desk for what seemed like hours while the man loomed threateningly over him and Mrs. Andress raged in the background. He'd kept his eyes on the sunny playground outside the window and his mouth firmly shut. He was amazed at himself, that he'd dared to talk back. He'd keep silent now, though. *Just keep mum, Hymie. What can they really do to you?*

But it wasn't the people in the room that worried him, it was the ones he actually cared about. Ruby was the only one home at this time of day; she'd come to pick him up when Mr. Dickerson called. Now, from his usual place in the back seat of the station wagon, as far from Ruby as he could get, Jamie could still see her face in the rear-view mirror. Her mouth was tight, her expression grim, but she didn't try to make him talk about what had happened.

I was going to stay out of school for Rosh Hashanah tomorrow, anyway, he thought, trying for smug satisfaction. He couldn't quite manage it. *What are they going to say? What is Dad going to say?*

Dad was finally home for good, now. Oh, he'd go to his job at the Navy Depot every day, of course, but there'd be no more sea duty for him, no more two-week leaves when they'd just be getting used to having each other around again by the time he'd have to go.

Laurie had gotten into some kind of trouble with him at first. They'd evidently worked things out, but it took a while and things were still a little shaky—they were super polite to each other, walking softly so as not to break their fragile peace. *Laurie's used to being the oldest guy in the house: not "the man of the house," exactly, but the one Mom and Ruby rely on, the one the rest of us listen to. It was hard on him to have Dad suddenly take over.*

That wasn't a problem for Jamie. He never wanted to be in charge. He just wanted to go his own way… and still find everything safe and secure when he got back. He felt confident that Dad could make that happen.

God knows, Mom and Ruby are both strong in their own way. But they're soft. Strong and soft, like foam rubber, maybe. It would be hard to break or tear them, but easy to squish them. And if they screamed, their voices would be high and helpless.

He shook his head, wondering where that last thought had come from. The older he got, the more he felt besieged by the voices in his own head, almost as though someone else were thinking his thoughts. Or maybe the thoughts were there all the time and he was only intermittently aware of them, as though he wandered in an alien landscape lit by flashes of lightning.

The Pontiac turned into the driveway. Ruby had left the folding double garage doors open, so she pulled directly in. "I called your mother before I left," she said. "You're to wait in your room."

Jamie nodded. Halfway out of the car, he paused. "Thanks," he said. "For getting me."

Ruby looked across the seat back at him and nodded. Her face had softened a little. "I'll bring you up some iced tea," she said.

She remembers that the punch stuff the other kids like is too sweet for me. Their eyes met in mutual understanding and he got on out of the car.

In his room, he sat in the window seat, iced tea glass sweating softly onto the sill beside him, looking out at the distant hulk of South Mountain and wondering just how much trouble he was in. He knew Mom would be supportive in front of the school officials, but she didn't like it when he turned his sharp tongue against adults. *She'll be disappointed, at least,* he thought resignedly.

But when there was a soft knock and the door opened, it was Dad standing there, straight and imposing in his service blues. Wordlessly, Jamie shifted to make room for him on the window seat.

They sat knee to knee in silence while Jamie drew patterns in the condensation on his tea glass. Finally Jamie croaked, "She was wrong."

"Tell me," Dad said.

"She said that when you're on a bed, you spell that "l-y-i-n-g," but when you say something that's not true, that's spelled "l-i-e-i-n-g.""

Dad snorted softly. "But couldn't you tactfully—"

"I tried," Jamie interrupted. "I said, 'Excuse me, ma'am, I think there's a mistake here.' She said, 'No, there isn't.' She didn't even look, Dad! And she wouldn't look when I brought her the dictionary. She just said, 'Your grade stands.' I said, 'I don't care about the grade,' (though I do, really) 'I just thought you'd like to know you made a mistake.' Then she got really mad and said, 'You think you're smarter than everybody," and I said, 'I'm smarter than you, anyway.' That's when she sent me to Mr. Dickerson and he said I had to apologize and I wouldn't. I couldn't, Dad, I just couldn't! She was wrong! And she didn't care that she was wrong!"

Dad caught the glass as Jamie's shaking hand almost knocked it over. He leaned to set it over on the dresser and then took Jamie's cold hand in both his warm ones. "Of course you couldn't, son. I understand."

"You do?"

"Of course. Maybe you could have chosen your words better, but I do understand you couldn't just stay silent."

"Mom says pick your battles."

"Well, she's right about that. Have you picked this one?"

Jamie thought it over. "Yes," he said finally. "Yes, I have." *Giving in on this would be unbearable.*

Dad gave a sharp nod. "Let's go, then," he said, getting to his feet.

"Now?"

"If not now, when?"

"You're supposed to wait till the suspension's over and come to the school with me so they can—"

Dad leaned forward, setting his hands on Jamie's shoulders. "'Attack where your enemy is unprepared, appear where you are unexpected.'"

"That sounds like a quote."

"Sun Tzu, *The Art of War.* You should read it; you may need it some time."

Back at school, standing ramrod straight in front of the school secretary's desk, Dad looked ready for battle. His neatly brushed hair shone as golden as the brass buttons and gold braid on his navy blue—nearly black—jacket with its colorful rows of ribbons and decorations. He tucked his stiff-brimmed, braid-encrusted hat under his left arm as he said firmly, "Commander Sean McAlister to see Mr. Dickerson."

"Er, do you have an appointment?" she said, looking out of the sides of her eyes at Jamie.

"I do not. However, I am here on a matter of some urgency and importance, and I believe he will want to speak with me before I take formal steps."

"Formal... um, a suspension is usually—"

"I am not here about the suspension." Jamie kept his jaw from dropping with an effort; the secretary was less successful. Dad went on, as though oblivious to their reactions, "I am here to register a formal complaint of anti-Semitism on the part of my son's teacher."

The secretary's gaze flickered past them toward the door of the principal's office. Dad turned to follow it. The man who'd looked so threatening to Jamie earlier that day looked pathetic now, in his shapeless brown suit and sloppily knotted tie and his face the color of soft cheese. "Anti-Semitism?" he exclaimed in a tone that started at outrage and ended in a squeak.

"Mr. Dickerson," Dad said, steaming toward him with Jamie in his wake, "Sean McAlister. Thank you for agreeing to see me."

Mr. Dickerson, who'd agreed to no such thing, spun like an unmoored boat as Dad sailed past him into his office. Dad turned and looked back at him with a mildly puzzled look, as though he couldn't understand why the principal was still stranded in the doorway. Jamie slid in after them, exhilarated and terrified.

"... classic anti-Jewish stereotype," Dad was saying.

"But it's true," Mrs. Andress shrilled. "They really do think they're smarter than the rest of us."

Mr. Dickerson blanched and flapped his hands at her as though he could shoo her into silence as Dad sat back with a grimly justified expression.

"And besides," Mrs. Andress rattled on, "this one doesn't even have any friends. I knew the minute I saw him he was going to be trouble. I can always tell, on the first day, which ones are…"

"'The first day'?" Dad repeated incredulously. "I've commanded thousands of men in the past twenty years, madam, and I assure you there is no way to measure a man's worth on an initial superficial encounter. And what does his having friends have to do with anything? The fact is, you took an immediate dislike to my son because he is a Jew—"

"Not just because he's… that," Mrs. Andress insisted.

"Can't we just agree to disagree?" Mr. Dickerson interposed feebly.

Jamie sat and looked out the window. The playground was still sunny, Mrs. Andress was still raging, Mr. Dickerson was still trying to control the situation; everything was as it had been earlier, except now Jamie wasn't here alone. Now there was someone to defend him.

A man in a uniform. My father.

Chapter 6.

Saturday, November 7, 1953

Jamie lay on his bed listening to the wind howling in the bare branches of the larch trees outside his window, staring at nothing in the gray afternoon light. *You ought to get up and do some homework,* he chided himself. But for once he didn't feel like it.

It didn't matter what he did in school these days, anyway. Since the scene in the principal's office, Mrs. Andress had pretended Jamie literally wasn't there. She never called on him in class or even looked in his direction. She marked his multiple-choice quizzes according to her answer key, impersonally; so far there had been no more issues with whether her required answers were correct. But his essay questions and papers came back uniformly graded "C" with no comments. Last week he'd put in a line of nonsense syllables on the second page and her silence proved his suspicion correct: she wasn't even reading them.

In a way, it was a better outcome than he had expected that day when he sat in Mr. Dickerson's office, shaking in reaction at his own temerity at having dared to be so openly rude to a teacher. Only his outrage at her refusal to recognize the fact that she was simply wrong about a simple point of English spelling had let him overcome his fear of authority figures. Accepting mediocre grades seemed a small price to pay.

But he was beginning to feel invisible, as though he really didn't exist. There was a time he would have welcomed that feeling:

invisible was safe. Lately, though, it grated on him, ate away at his gut, sitting there day after day being ignored. Something had shifted in him, and he no longer felt simply safe in hiding. He needed to be acknowledged, to feel he had a place in the world. In any case, his family wouldn't let him not exist, he knew.

The folks will have six fits when your next report card comes in, he thought resignedly. He knew there'd be more meetings and confrontations. *Too bad I'm stuck all day with the same teacher. If I were in high school, like Laurie, it would be different. He doesn't seem to be having such a great year, though.*

Laurie had been gloomy and out of sorts since school started in September. He spent most of every evening studying, and hours on weekends, which he'd never had to do before. Jamie had tried to ask him about it once, but Laurie had given an irritated growl and waved him away. Later, he'd come around to Jamie's door with the new book of Salinger short stories by way of silent apology, but there was still something off about him.

I thought things would be easier for him with Dad home because Laurie wouldn't have to feel like he had to take care of all of us so much. Jamie sighed and turned over to face the empty bed beside his. *No point in worrying about it; it's all I can do to take care of myself.*

There was a knock on his door and, at Jamie's word, Mom came in. *Uh, oh. She's got That Look on her face. Mom with a plan: head for the hills.*

Jamie pulled himself up to sit against his headboard as Mom perched on the mattress beside him. "How are you today, sweetie?" she asked brightly. "Having a little rest?"

Jamie snorted. "Just come out with it, Mother. Have you signed me up to head a Unicef collection for starving refugee kids in Europe, or am I just supposed to babysit Beth and Joy for the afternoon?"

32

Mom laughed. "Am I that transparent?"

"As a plate glass window."

"Well, it's nothing so major as a Unicef collection—that's a good idea, though, by the way—but it's a little more involved than looking after the girls for an afternoon. It's Laurie."

"He's having trouble in school this year, isn't he?"

Mom tilted her head to one side and smiled at him. "You're so quiet, but you don't miss much, do you? Yes, he's upset because he got two C's on his midterms."

"What? But he studies all the time! What were the C's in?"

"Biology and algebra. He's going to get help from Dr. Barrett in biology, and study more with his new friend, Linda, but the algebra... your dad thought, since you've been studying that on your own, you might be able to help him."

Jamie ruthlessly tamped down the little thrill of excitement the idea kindled in his chest. "Laurie would never go for it," he said. "He hates taking help from anybody, and especially from me. He doesn't even like me."

"Oh, honey, Laurie loves you."

"Yeah, sure, I know. He doesn't like me, though. And he's sure not going to like this idea."

"Let's go down and see, shall we?"

In this mood, she's relentless. She'll keep after me till I say yes. There was that little flicker in her eyes just now, though... "He's already said no, hasn't he?"

Mom huffed impatiently. "I think he was about to, yes, but I'm sure your father's made him see reason." Jamie rolled his eyes. Mom gave a little grimace, then leaned forward and smoothed back a lock of Jamie's hair without actually touching his skin. "This could be a way for you two to get to know each other a little better, too. It'll be common ground."

Defeated in the face of her unrelenting optimism, Jamie swung his legs over the opposite side of the bed and got up. "If he really doesn't want to, it won't work," he warned.

"I'm counting on you to help him want to," she said, beaming.

"Great. All right, lead on."

But when they walked into the study, what Dad was saying drove Jamie's misgivings out of his mind.

Dad was standing by the fireplace, looking at the tiled hearth, talking to Laurie, who was sitting on the couch.

"There," he said, pointing downward. "My head did that. He'd knocked me down because I got cut from the football team. I'd told him I just wasn't big enough, and he punched me in the face and stood over me, sneering. 'How big are you now?' he said. For grades that didn't meet his expectations I'd get the belt. That didn't leave any marks on the room, just on me."

Jamie gasped. *But Dad's so strong. He's always in charge, always the master of every situation. How could he have been… a victim?*

Jamie's head was spinning. The world turned upside down. *It sounds like he didn't even fight back,* one of the voices in his head said scornfully. The other voice countered scorn with scorn: *Of course he didn't fight back! Use your head, Hymie. It was his father. What was he supposed to do? But if he could go from that to who he is today…*

Jamie was vaguely aware that the conversation in the room was going on, but he couldn't follow what they were saying. Dad was talking to him, now, though. "So, Jamie, did your mother tell you my idea? Laurie's not too sure about it, but maybe you two could talk it over."

Jamie walked forward to where he could see Laurie's face and hitched his hip onto the arm of the couch. *Will he let me do this? I really want him to let me.* "Yeah," he said. "I could—I mean, I saw you were having a hard time. I wanted to say something, but I thought you'd be mad."

Laurie didn't look mad, though. He actually looked a little embarrassed. *This is hard for him*, Jamie realized. "Maybe I would've," Laurie said, turning his head a little away and looking at Jamie sideways. "But that would've been stupid. Could you give me, say, half an hour a night?"

An unaccustomed feeling surged through Jamie, leaving him feeling a little lightheaded. *I'm not invisible; he sees me. He sees who I am, and it's ok with him*. I'm *ok with him*. "Sure," he said. "And an hour a day on weekends?"

Laurie groaned theatrically. "Slave driver! What have I let myself in for?"

Jamie followed his lead, keeping it light. "Oh, never fear, I'm going to have a field day with this. You won't know what hit you." He grinned, and his brother grinned back.

Mom and Dad went on talking to Laurie, but Jamie tuned out again. *This is it. This is me not being invisible. I can do something here; I can help Laurie. Look what Dad did with himself, even though he was hurt when he was young. He made himself strong; maybe I can be strong. I stood up to Mrs. Andress. Being smart is good.*

"C'mon, Teach," Laurie said. He *said that like he liked me*. Jamie smiled as they left the room together.

CHAPTER 7.

SUNDAY, DECEMBER 6, 1953

Jamie wasn't sure sometimes whether he actually liked music. Like his brothers and sisters, he had music lessons; for him, it was piano. Some of what he played, particularly Bach Inventions, with their almost mathematical progressions and clever interweaving of notes, gave him a deep satisfaction, a sense of completion. Other compositions disturbed him in ways he didn't understand.

Tonight the family had gathered in the living room to listen to the radio; the great conductor Arturo Toscanini was leading the NBC Symphony Orchestra in Beethoven's *Eroica*. Mom had explained that Toscanini was in his eighties; there might not be so many more chances to hear him conduct.

As soon as the first dramatic chords sounded, Jamie knew this was going to be one of those pieces that gave him trouble. The strings seemed to thrum through his gut, and when the horns came in he thought his heart would pound out of his chest.

This is stupid, he thought. *Get a grip on yourself, Hymie. This is one of the most famous and beautiful works of classical music in the world. Nothing to get worked up about.* He took a deep breath and tipped his head onto the back of the long couch where he sat beside Ruby, and tried to see in his mind's eye the patterns that the sounds he was hearing would make on a page of sheet music.

Gradually, a strange sensation came over him. He seemed to be hearing the notes before they sounded in the room. He opened his eyes and sat up straight. *I know this piece.* But he'd never consciously heard it before tonight. He usually avoided Beethoven's works, with their disturbing passion that roiled his emotions in uncomfortable ways. But the unusual rhythms and clashing chords he was hearing only echoed the ones he could feel agitating his mind and vibrating in his limbs.

Why should that scare me? he wondered. But it did. *I'm ok here,* he reminded himself. *Mom and Dad even got me transferred out of Mrs. Andress's class this semester. They'll keep me safe, there's nothing wrong.* Still his heart rattled like a ringing alarm clock.

Fighting panic, he looked around at the family. Mom and Dad were on one of the twin settees in front of the fireplace, closest to the speakers of the radio and hi fi set that lived in the cupboard beside it. Mom's eyes were shut, her head nodding slightly in time to the music. Dad was gazing at the lit Hanukkah menorah in the bay window beyond the settee opposite them. Every now and then his fingers would twitch as though he wanted to conduct the unseen musicians himself.

Across from them on the other settee, Celia and Beth cuddled with their arms around each other's waists. Celia's free hand toyed with her own dark hair, winding and unwinding it around her finger, but Beth was utterly still, her face glowing in its corona of tumbled gold.

Beside the bay window, Laurie sat in the big armchair, intent face turned downward, leaning forward, hands clasped between his knees. Rob, on the floor at his feet, had his face buried in his arms on his upturned knees.

Between them and the long couch, Joy perched on the ottoman, jiggling and twitching a little. Her back was to Jamie, but he could imagine her face in its usual curious, slightly impatient half-frown.

Looking at them all calmed Jamie a little; the familiarity of them and their constancy anchored him. He sat back into the couch with a little sigh. Beside him, Ruby shifted, grazing the back of his hand ever-so-lightly with the back of her own work-roughened one. It might have been accidental—when he looked over at her, he saw her eyes were fixed on the fire—but there was the slightest loosening of the set of her lips: not a smile, but a tiny signal of sympathy.

Silence fell into the room. Joy immediately jumped up. "That was nice. Now let's—"

"Shh!" admonished voices all over the room.

"That was just the first movement, sweetie," Mom said. "There are three more."

"Three more! But that one was so long!"

"Shh!" people hissed again, just as the adagio began. Joy stood poised as though ready to leave the room. She looked toward Rob in appeal but he, head up now, gestured at her to sit down again. After a second, the music seemed to catch hold of her and she did.

The haunting plaint of the oboe over the swaying strings reminded Jamie that this movement was called the funeral march. That thrumming sensation along his nerves and sinews deepened into dread. A cold sweat broke out on his forehead. From the corner of his eye he saw Ruby's hand reach toward him. He flung himself away from it, forward onto his knees on the floor in front of the couch, arms wrapped tight around his middle.

He screwed his eyes shut but, eyes open or closed, the iron gates were there before him, and the sounds of an orchestra playing Beethoven were pouring out of a loudspeaker, punctuated by screams and a repeated meaty thudding noise.

Someone turned off the radio, so that the loudest sound in the room was his own gasping breath. Jamie opened his eyes a slit and saw Mom's knees on the carpet beside him. A little wider, and he could see the feet of the others, gathering around. Then Ruby's scuffed oxfords planted themselves beside him.

"Children, come on with me now," she said. All the feet reluctantly scuffled away, leaving only Mom's knees, and her voice.

"It's all right, Hymele," she was saying. "You're all right, you're safe here with us. Can you feel the carpet? Come on, put your hand down and feel the carpet."

It was warm and nubbly and rough under his fingertips; he could feel crumbs from where Rob had been illicitly eating graham crackers without a plate this afternoon. It felt like nothing that had existed behind those iron gates.

Mom's fingers reached forward and took a pinch of Jamie's shirtsleeve. She shook it a little, bringing his eyes up to her face.

"Can you tell us where you were?" she asked.

"Us"? Then he saw that Dad was still in the room, standing grave and attentive behind Mom. He'd changed out of his uniform after work, but Jamie could still sense it like an aura around him, power and security and threat all at once. The tightness in his chest eased a little more.

"The music," he croaked. "I heard it before. They were playing it—there, in that place."

Mom and Dad both nodded, understanding what place he meant.

Then Dad said hesitantly, "I heard there were inmate musicians at Buchenwald, but I didn't realize there was an orchestra big enough to play a symphony."

"Maybe… I don't know," Jamie said. "There were loudspeakers. But sometimes there were people playing. I saw them. I saw—" He choked again.

"You saw?" Mom prompted.

"They were playing. I was little, the men told me to stay in the barracks but I wanted to see, I came out and peeked between their legs and I saw, but I didn't get it, I didn't realize until now..." He coughed and fought back his rising nausea. "The other sounds, what else I could hear," he whispered. "The guards were beating someone and the inmates were playing to cover up the sound. That's where I was, that's what I remember." He slumped back onto his heels. "And don't tell me I'm safe," he said to Mom. "I'll never be safe."

Dad cleared his throat, calling their attention back to him. "They've torn it down, you know," he said. "The gates and a couple of the buildings are still there, but all the barracks have been destroyed. Some people think they shouldn't have, and they're making a memorial out of what's left, but the building where they hid you, that's gone. There's nothing there but weeds. I've seen pictures: just a flat, bleak space. Empty."

Mom took up the thought. "And the guards who did the beating and the killing, they're gone, too. They're dead or in prison or in hiding. Yes, there's still evil in the world, and danger, but those particular people can't hurt you now, and that particular place will never hold you again."

Jamie leaned forward until his forehead rested on the crest of Mom's shoulder. He could smell her perfume, and the oil in her thick hair. Her fingers came up and lightly carded through his hair. They breathed in sync for a moment, then he said, "I have to go. Ok?"

"Not too long, all right?"

He nodded. She pulled back, releasing him. He got shakily to his feet. Dad stood right there in front of him. He leaned into him, too, and endured a brief one-armed hug. But right now he needed to get away more than he needed comfort.

Jamie left the room and used the downstairs bathroom; after he washed his hands, he rinsed his mouth out and splashed water on his face. He started up the stairs, holding onto the bannister rail with both hands like an old person or a cripple, only his determination to gain his attic cabinet lending his shaky knees strength.

But when he finally got to the third floor, Robbie was in the music room, fiddling around with Mom's guitar. Jamie suspected that Rob had guessed where Jamie's hiding place was, they'd run into each other up here so often, but neither of them ever said anything about it. Still, Jamie didn't feel he could go on through the door into the attic area with Robbie sitting right there watching.

He turned back toward the narrow staircase.

"Wait," Rob said. "I was just going to play a record. There's this song called "Hound Dog," by Big Mama Thornton. I don't know if it's your kind of thing, but it's like a whaddayacallit, an antidote, to that highbrow stuff that got you all shook up."

Jamie hesitated. His younger brother's face was earnest, though his fingers twitched uncertainly over the surface of the guitar in his lap. A fine drizzle splatted futilely against the window. The room was warm, and smelled of guitar wax and adolescent boy.

"Don't go," Rob urged him. "Stay."

Jamie stayed.

CHAPTER 8.

FRIDAY, JANUARY 15, 1954

"*vitzivanu l'hadlik ner shel Shabbat.*" Jamie stood for a second as he ended the blessing over the Sabbath candles, hands still over his eyes. *It should be a woman doing this. I remember, her voice, her—* When Jamie had told the family after his bar mitzvah that he wanted to start celebrating the Jewish Sabbath on Friday nights, Mom had offered to learn to do this candle ritual, just as Ruby had learned to make the braided Sabbath challah bread. But Jamie wanted to stand here—hands over his face, having lit the candles and passed his hands over them in the ancient way and covered his eyes—to stand here himself, in his murdered mother's place, and say her prayer, and make her gestures.

"Olly olly oxen free!" a voice yelped.

Jamie jerked his hands down, shock and outrage snapping his spine straight. *That new kid, the one they want to bring in here with us.*

The others were glaring at the kid. "What?" he said innocently, green eyes wide in his light-coffee-colored face. "Isn't he playing hide and seek?"

Mom was the only one who wasn't glaring. "David," she said patiently, "these are Jamie's special prayers, we explained that to you. He covers his eyes during this one because that's the tradition. It comes from not wanting to do work on the Sabbath, and lighting the candles counts as work, so—"

David shifted impatiently. "Are we going to eat or what?"

"When Jamie's finished," Mom said firmly. "Jamie, go on, darling."

Jamie breathed deep, centering himself the way Mom had taught him years ago, and brought his attention back to the ritual. He blessed the silver goblet of wine, sipped from it, and set it going from hand to hand around the table, ignoring David when he pretended to gulp it and rolled his head to one side as though he were drunk.

Celia brought the copper bowl and pitcher of water from the sideboard, fancy linen towel over her arm, and held them while Jamie did the ritual hand-washing.

"Did he go to the john or something while we weren't looking? I thought we washed our hands before dinner." David smirked.

"David," Mom admonished him.

Jamie uncovered the challah, broke off a chunk as he said the blessing over bread, and tossed bits of it to the others the way Mrs. Epstein's father had taught him to do.

"Play ball!" David crowed.

Dad spoke for the first time. "David, please stop," he said mildly. "We all like to make jokes, but this is not the time. I realize this is making you uncomfortable, but I'd like you to sit quietly and respect his customs."

Jamie finished the prayers as quickly as he could and they started passing the food around. But the only one who ate less of Ruby's roast chicken and potatoes than David was Jamie. His stomach was in knots, and his chest felt sore, as though someone had punched it.

As for David, he kept giggling and goofing around, singing "Book-a-ta, book-a-ta," which Jamie recognized as a parody of the beginning of most Hebrew blessings. When David began to accompany himself by beating on his plate with a drumstick, popping his lips like a drumbeat and spattering gravy all over, Dad said with a crack of command in his voice, "Settle down, David."

David glowered, dropped his drumstick, and started to shove his chair back. Mom said, "You are not excused, young man. Keep still and eat your dinner."

The kid slumped back to the table and sulkily picked at the food.

When Laurie and Joy, whose turn it was to help tonight, cleared the table and brought out the brownies, David muttered, "Do I have to eat dessert?"

"No," Dad said. "You may be excused. I'd just like you to understand—" But the kid had already lurched out of the room.

Mom sighed. "Remember, everyone, I warned you this was going to be difficult when I told you David would be visiting. Try not to make your minds up about him too soon. He's testing us, trying to see where the boundaries are for his behavior. Please, just give him some time. I really think he might be a good match for us. Just be patient, please. I'd better go talk to him." She left the room, shoulders slumped.

"So much for Mom reading to us tonight," Laurie said gloomily, jabbing at his brownie.

"There'll be other Friday nights for reading aloud," Dad said.

One of Jamie's secrets was that he didn't really enjoy the Friday night readings. The others seemed to love sitting in the living room by the fire, the only other light the small lamp by the big wing chair in the corner, listening to Mom read.

She read well, with different voices and a lively rhythm; that wasn't the problem. The problem wasn't really the stuff she read, either, though the fantasy stories the others liked left him cold, and the current choice—C. S. Lewis's Narnia series—had a heavy Christian symbolism that made Jamie itchy. He liked the Shakespeare she sometimes read better, and Heinlein's science fiction best of all.

But the real problem was that he simply didn't enjoy sitting and listening as a story slowly spooled out. When he read, he devoured the text, sometimes reading entire books at a sitting. What he was reading would inhabit his whole mind for as long as his eyes could focus on a page. Listening to reading aloud left too many gaps, too much space for his mind to drift elsewhere and to see things he'd rather not think about. So he'd play music in his head (not Beethoven, never Beethoven), or think about mathematical problems.

On the other hand, those Friday evenings by the fire gave him a way of being with the family that didn't demand he actually interact with them. He could revel in the comfort and the coziness and not have to speak to anyone. He resented David for taking that away tonight.

Tonight he played a little chess with Laurie and then fooled with the piano for a while, but he was relieved when Mom came down because it meant they weren't talking in his room any more. Mom gave another "Give him time" speech, then Jamie went on up to bed.

David was sitting up on the second bed that had lain empty for so long, arms around his knees, head buried on his arms. It resembled the way Rob had sat listening to the *Eroica* that time, but Rob had looked natural doing it. On David, the pose looked like just that to Jamie—a pose, a bid for sympathy or attention. He ignored it and moved into the bathroom to change into his pajamas.

When he came out, David had pulled the covers over himself and huddled on his side with his back to Jamie's bed.

Jamie felt a twinge of uneasy sympathy. He tamped it down and got into bed. He snapped off the lamp beside him and muttered the *Shema*.

"What's that mean?" David asked in a sulky tone.

"'Hear, oh Israel, the Lord our God, the Lord is one,'" Jamie answered.

"Why don't you just speak English? Are you some kind of foreigner?"

"I'm a Jew. I say the prayers my parents said, in Hebrew, language of Scripture. I know Mom explained that to you."

"Your parents are dead," David said flatly. "She explained that, too."

"And your mother's dead, and your father's in prison for killing her; she told us that when she first told us you'd be coming here."

"She talks too much."

"Keep your damn mouth shut if you can't be nice about her. She's been nicer to you than you deserve."

"You don't like me."

Jamie bit his lip. "You haven't given me much reason to like you."

"She likes me. She likes me better than you."

"No, she doesn't."

"I know. Nobody likes me." Now the kid sounded tearful.

Jamie was confused, and resented feeling confused. *What does he want from me, anyway? I don't have anything to give him.*

"Just go to sleep," he said. There was silence in the room. Jamie watched the dim gray shapes of snowflakes falling outside for a long time before his eyes dropped closed, but David didn't speak or move again.

CHAPTER 9.

SATURDAY, FEBRUARY 20, 1954

I hate David, Jamie thought. *The others all think it's wrong to hate, but I don't see why. This kid is ruining my life.*

David came every weekend now. He'd learned to keep quiet during the Sabbath prayers on Friday nights, and Jamie himself spent Saturday mornings at services, and the others all went to church on Sunday, but the remaining weekend hours he had to spend around David seemed endless. His presence on the second bed in Jamie's room was so oppressive Jamie couldn't even read while he was there, and Mom had told him sympathetically but firmly that he was not to sequester himself in his cabinet while David was in the house. Even watching TV, the kid couldn't seem to keep still, fidgeting and poking at the TV room knick-knacks and keeping up a running commentary on whatever was on.

He was affecting the others, too. Laurie was always hovering around looking anxious and making well-meaning suggestions that never seemed to lead to anything. The girls petted and cossetted him like a new kitten, then were taken aback when his mercurial temper led him to scratch at them—verbally or by wreaking some minor destruction. Rob would go off by himself to enjoy his music; if he was lucky, David wouldn't follow after and pester him to play something else.

Was this what it was like for everybody when I came into the family? Jamie wondered. *We were all little then, Joy was just a baby, but how did the others feel about me?* Jamie himself had been too overwhelmed at the time by the numbing avalanche of new sensations—new country, new language, new people—to think about them. *But we're a family now, a whole family. We don't need him.*

The family was settling itself around Jamie, who sat in the big armchair pulled in front of the fire. David had planted himself front and center, staring at Jamie. *He's not in the family yet, though. And if I have anything to say about it… but they never listen to me.*

You never speak to them, the other voice in his head said.

Now David spoke to him. "I don't get it. Your birthday was Wednesday, Dr. Mac said. So how come you get two birthdays?"

Jamie just rolled his eyes. *He knows very well why, Mom explained it all.*

But Beth said, in her patient way, "The Jewish calendar is different, David. It goes by the moon instead of the sun, so there aren't as many days in the year. We're celebrating on Jamie's Hebrew birthday instead of his… what's the word? It's not 'Christian,' exactly."

"Secular," Laurie supplied.

"Right, his birthday on the secular calendar, the regular everyday one, because it's on Saturday so I can be back from my boarding school and you can be here, too."

That's not why. Well, for Beth, maybe, but not so HE can be here. As it is, I'll have to hide all my presents till he leaves tomorrow. The day after David had acted up at the Sabbath table, he'd taken the book the folks had given Jamie for Hanukkah and scribbled all over it with black crayon. They'd bought him another one, and Mom had had a long talk with David that had left him red-eyed and subdued, but the whole event still rankled Jamie.

Half his presents tonight were books, too, which suited Jamie just fine. A book of Sholom Aleichem short stories and Wittgenstein's *Philosophical Investigations* looked the juiciest. Ruby had embroidered him a fancy white silk yarmulke with gold thread, Joy had written him a poem. Beth and Rob had clubbed together to "buy" him a tree in Israel, sending money to help in the reforestation of the Holy Land.

Jamie leaned out of the chair to wad up the discarded wrapping paper littering the carpet and spotted a scroll tied with ribbon still lying there. *What's this? Another poem?* Then he saw David's face, expectant and a little sly. *Good grief. What now? Is it going to explode?*

Jamie lifted it gingerly and caught Dad's eye. Dad took a deep breath but nodded encouragingly. He also shifted slightly on the settee so he was subtly closer to David and poised to stand up quickly.

Reassured, Jamie slipped the scrap of red silk off the coiled paper and unrolled it. It was a crayon drawing of a book. It was colored dark blue, with crooked yellow letters that ran across the top and curved at the end to fit in the last few. "Union Home Prayer Book," it said. It was a drawing of Jamie's siddur, the prayer book he used on Friday nights. *This is an apology,* he realized.

So what? It's that easy, just a little drawing and his making fun of my religion and ruining my book can just be all forgiven? But it wasn't just "a little drawing," he knew. David could hardly read and write; it was one of the problems Mom was working on with him. For him to have reproduced the title and spelled it right, he had to have sneaked the book out of the sideboard, probably more than once—and when no one else was around, judging from the looks on everyone's faces.

Jamie let his glancing eye touch David, almost flinching as though it were an actual touch, as though David might be hot, or freezing cold: as though looking at David might hurt him. The kid was yawning elaborately, tapping his spread palm over his open mouth, eyes scrunched up. But between the slitted eyelids, he was watching Jamie.

Jamie drew his feet in, crossed his ankles, bit his thumbnail. "Thanks," he said. David's hand froze in place over his mouth. "It's nice," Jamie went on, to make him stop staring. "I, uh, I appreciate it."

David's hand went down to his lap. It was shaking ever so slightly. "It's nothing," he shrugged. "You can throw it out if you want."

A bolt of pity slammed through Jamie's heart. "Of course I'm not going to throw it out. I told you, it's nice."

Like one of those little wooden figurines that bobbed from side to side on a fulcrum, David switched positions completely. "It's 'nice'? Is that all you have to say? I worked and worked on it. It's terrific!"

"Ok, it's terrific."

Immediately, the green eyes welled up. *Crocodile tears,* Jamie thought, remembering an expression of Ruby's.

"I knew it," David said. "You hate it."

Jamie sighed and knuckled his glasses up the bridge of his nose. "You know what I hate? I hate conversations like this. Thanks for the present. Thanks, everybody. Listen, I have homework to do." He scooped up his presents, not really caring if the books crumpled David's drawing a little. As he shuffled out of the room, Dad put a hand out and briefly pressed his shoulder. Jamie nodded and kept moving.

That night in bed, Jamie was almost asleep when the voice came in the dark. "Did you really like it?"

"I said I did."

"You say a lot of things."

Jamie propped himself on an elbow to peer across the shadowed space between them. "That's not true. I hardly say anything."

There was a silence, then David said in a wondering voice, "You're right. It just seems like you do, 'cuz when you do say something, it's so... sort of, sharp, I guess."

Jamie sank back down on his pillow. Just when he thought it was safe to relax, the voice came again.

"I don't mean to piss you off."

Jamie sighed. "I know. I don't mean to—whatever it is I do to you."

There was a soft giggle, then silence settled over the room.

Chapter 10.

Saturday, March 14, 1954

Jamie and Ruby never talked much when he helped her with dinner or the weekend chores. That was all right with Jamie; he found the steady rhythm of chopping vegetables or washing windows restful, and felt the undemanding, silent competence of the woman beside him as sympathetic rather than distant.

Last night, David had created a fuss over Mom's birthday presents. He'd drawn another picture, a peacock feather with a misspelled caption, and threw a fit when Mom wouldn't say it was a better gift than everyone else's.

The others had been puzzled and frustrated, but Jamie found himself feeling a reluctant empathy, growing in spite of himself. He remembered what it was like, being the new one, being the stranger and afraid he wouldn't measure up, afraid he'd be cast out even as he despaired of finding a place among these people who seemed so alien to everything he'd ever known.

As David fled the room and Mom went after him, Jamie rubbed his temples. Obviously there'd be no reading again tonight. They'd be in his room; he couldn't go there. He certainly didn't feel like watching television. Celia and Beth had already cleaned the kitchen.

Then Ruby had wordlessly held up a new skein of yarn, her eyes soft on his. Settling back onto the long couch, he'd lifted his hands to take it while she wound it into a ball.

Today they were turning mattresses and changing bed linens, turfing out the grumbling occupants where necessary so they could finish before the Epsteins picked Jamie up for services. As they finished in Celia and Joy's room, Ruby broke the silence.

"There's just your room left. We can do it after you get back. Go on and get ready for church, child."

"We call it services, Ruby, you know that."

"Doesn't seem respectful enough."

Jamie huffed a laugh and shook his head. "Anyway, I'm not coming straight back. I'm supposed to meet the girls at the library in Carlisle. I've got time to finish now."

Jamie stripped his own bed while Ruby worked on David's. He had just wrestled his mattress into its new position when he heard her gasp. She had pulled David's mattress half off the box spring. There on the taut muslin surface lay the big carving knife from the matched set in the kitchen block, its curved blade glinting even on this gloomy day.

How did that get there? Jamie thought stupidly. Then he looked at Ruby's face, or what he could see of it over the hands she had clasped over her mouth. *David. He put it there himself, of course. He—* Jamie's thoughts skipped back to the family meeting the night Mom had told them David would be coming here. *He saw his father stab his mother to death. He saw it. When he was three. He was three.*

"He was three," he said. Ruby's hands had dropped to clasp at her waist, but her eyes were still on the knife. "He was three," Jamie repeated. "He was just little. The knife looked big to him, of course it did, but it wasn't. You can't stab somebody with a knife like this."

Ruby shook her head. "We can't have this," she said.

"He's scared," Jamie said. "He might wreck a book, but he'd never hurt anybody. Not anybody here, anyway." *Why am I defending him? Just because I know I'm right about the knife.*

But Ruby said, "I have to call your mother."

Robbie's voice came from the hall. "Jamie, your ride's here."

"Go on, child," Ruby said. "I'll handle things here."

Jamie looked again at the knife and sighed, shoulders sagging. "I'll put this back," he said, picking it up. He turned and left the room, and the house, and the whole situation.

By the time a distracted Mom drove him and the girls back from the library, the situation had crystallized, hardening in the way he always felt powerless to stop. Other people made decisions and Jamie could only stand and endure.

But he was sulky and resistant when Laurie called them into the TV room. Mom disappeared into the study with David, who had a manic grin on his face that didn't fool Jamie for a minute.

In an hour Mom and David were gone, back to Rolling Meadow. Jamie noticed Laurie was having as hard a time choking down Ruby's tomato soup and grilled cheese sandwiches as he was. *He wanted him gone, too. So why aren't we happier?*

"I don't get it," Joy said. "What's everybody so upset about? Did David do something?"

"No, he didn't do anything," Jamie said.

"He's got some problems," Laurie added. "Don't worry, Mom'll work it out."

"So he'll be back next weekend?" Joy appealed to Ruby.

Ruby's eyes met Laurie's, then Jamie's. "I don't know, child," she said.

I do, Jamie thought. *We're never going to see him again.*

Dad walked into the room, and the look on his face told Jamie he was right.

"Dad?" Rob said, voice quavering.

Dad's hand fell on his shoulder; Jamie could see the strong fingers clench as Dad squeezed his little brother reassuringly. His face was still set in stern, sad lines, though.

"I think David needs a little more time before he's ready to join a family," Dad said.

"He was only three, Dad," Jamie said.

Dad's eyebrows drew down in puzzlement for a minute, then straightened as he understood. "I know, son," he said gently. "Just like you, when your world ended."

That took Jamie aback; he hadn't thought of it quite that way. "The knife was too big," he said. "You couldn't…"

Laurie cleared his throat, interrupting. When Jamie looked, Laurie slewed his eyes toward the young ones, watching big-eyed.

Jamie swallowed and fell silent. He could see in Dad's face that he didn't need to finish the sentence, anyway.

Dad sighed heavily and sank onto the bench next to Celia. He glanced at Ruby, then around the table at each of them until he came around and looked back at Jamie. "You are my children," he said. "Your welfare comes first."

Jamie felt a strange double pang, of comfort and loss at once. He bent his head back to his plate. "He was only three," he said under his breath.

CHAPTER 11.

THURSDAY, JUNE 4, 1954

Dad had hit Laurie. Just cracked him across the face, twice, forward and back. He'd actually knocked him down. Jamie wasn't even sure what Laurie had said that set Dad off; they'd all been clustering around Mom, comforting her because she was upset that they'd finally decided for sure that David wasn't coming back. Laurie had leaned over and said something quietly to Mom—Jamie had caught only the words "colored kid"—and the next thing anyone knew, Laurie was on the floor, and then he was gone out the door into the night.

Everyone else stood frozen around Mom, sitting on the hassock, tear-streaked face bone white. Then Dad covered his face with his hands, groaned, "Oh, God," and fled to his study. Joy burst into tears; Celia reached to comfort her, her own face starting to redden and tear up.

Robbie was breathing as though he'd run a race. "What about Laurie?" he quavered. "Isn't anybody going to go after Laurie?" He made a move toward the front door.

"No," Ruby said from her usual place on the end of the long couch by the entryway. She reached out to stop Rob and pushed him gently back towards the others. "Let it be. He'll come back in his own time."

"What if he doesn't?"

"He will."

"He will," Beth said. "This is his home. Where else would he go?'"

Not good enough, Jamie thought. But he said nothing and allowed Ruby to shepherd him upstairs along with the others. They, in unspoken accord, trooped up to the music room. Jamie could hear their low voices as he shut himself into his room, thinking longingly of his cabinet in the attic, unreachable now with all of them between it and him.

He wasn't sure which was making him feel worse: the flash of violence or Laurie's departure. Of a piece, of course, but they felt like two separate catastrophes.

At first he focused on Dad, or rather the stranger who'd seemed to inhabit Dad's body. *A man in a uniform, but not a protector this time: violent, powerful. What happened to turn him into that? His father beat him, he said. Is that coming to the surface? Is he going to start hitting us now?* The thought didn't frighten Jamie; it desolated him. *I don't want him to turn into that. I don't want him to be the enemy. I want him back. I want my Dad.*

Unaccustomed tears stung the backs of his eyes, so he shifted to think about Laurie. *Why did he run? Why didn't he fight back, or maybe die? I would have died, right there in the living room.* The other voice in his head, the one he seldom heard any more, put in, *You didn't die before, Hymie. You hid so you could live. If Dad turns on you, you'll hide and you'll keep living.* The other part of him thought, *Is that what Laurie's doing?*

The only answer he could get from either voice was, *Maybe.*

Eventually he fell into an uneasy sleep, still in his clothes on top of the bed. He woke in the dark, feet uncomfortable in his heavy shoes, teeth furry, drool on his face. He was halfway to the bathroom before he realized there was already someone in there. He moved silently to the door and listened.

The first voice he heard was Dad's, soft and rumbling. "Almost there," he said. "Just let me button your pajama shirt and we can get you into bed."

Then Laurie's, sounding confused and young. "My dirty clothes… Mom'll be mad, I don't want Mom to be mad."

"It's all right, sweetheart," Dad said. "I'll take care of it. There you go. Come on, my honey…"

The voices faded as they moved into the other bedroom. Jamie waited until he heard the door click, meaning Dad had left, then crept across the bathroom and looked through. Laurie's form was motionless under his heaped quilt, but in the dim light from the window, Jamie could see the glint of Robbie's eyes as he raised his head. Jamie nodded to him and closed the bathroom door.

When he'd finished getting ready for bed and slipped back into his room, he found Dad sitting on his bed in the dark. Jamie stood still for a long moment, then came on and slipped under the covers on the opposite side. The silence stretched between them.

What's he doing? Then it came to him. *He's waiting for me to do something. But what could I possibly do to make this any better?* Jamie felt as though he were stepping forward into an ocean, not certain whether a wave might sweep him under or the ground under his feet suddenly break off and drop him into the depths. *Just a little step. Just try it, Hymie.*

Jamie lifted a hand and moved it toward Dad, trembling at his own daring, testing the boundaries of his own safety. *He needs me to reach out and touch him. And I can do it. I can trust that it really will be ok. He made things better with Mrs. Andress. The way he always does. But now he needs my help, mine. It's like Mom always says: people can go off the rails, but still come back. Don't shrink away, reach out.*

His hand kept inching forward gingerly, as though he were about to touch something that might bite. He lowered it onto Dad's hands, which were folded—no, clenched—on his own knee. *His big navy ring is gone,* Jamie realized. *The one he cut Laurie's cheek with.* He hadn't remembered that detail till now.

At Jamie's touch, Dad released a puff of breath and his hands loosened slightly. "I'm so sorry," he whispered.

"It's ok," Jamie answered.

"No, it's not."

"No, it's not. But you'll make it better." *How do I know that? Because he's already made it better for Laurie, from what I heard in the bathroom. And because he's here, now.* "You'll make if better," he repeated.

"By God, I will," Dad said. His hands turned under Jamie's and he clasped it. "I want to kiss you goodnight."

Keep moving forward, Hymie, just one more step. "Ok."

Dad pressed his lips briefly to Jamie's forehead, then got up and pulled Jamie's covers up over his shoulder. He went out and there was some rustling and clicking that Jamie read as Dad going into the girls' rooms. Then he heard the parents' bedroom door at the end of the hall open, and Mom's soft voice: "Sean?"

"Oh, Lassie," Dad said, and started to cry.

"Hush, hush, *Carino,*" Mom murmured as their door shut behind them.

It was a long time before Jamie slept again.

Chapter 12.

The house was still quiet when Jamie got up in the morning. Ruby came out of her apartment while he was halfway through his bowl of cornflakes.

"School's out," she said, "did you forget? I'm making French toast when the others get up, if you want to wait."

"No, I didn't forget. I'm going to the library," he said.

She stood there, watching him eat.

"It's ok," he said finally. "Dad and Laurie, I mean. They worked it out, I guess."

"I know," she said. "Didn't know whether you did." She took her hands out of her apron pockets and brushed them together briskly. "You want orange juice?"

"No, thanks, my stomach's a little sour."

She nodded and let him be.

He spent the morning poring over an old scientific journal article by Alan Turing on artificial intelligence. He walked home under a lowering sky, hoping he'd make it before the rain started again, feeling cleansed and refreshed from immersing his brain in the coolness and clarity of mathematics and science. He turned up the walk at the end of the road, wondering what Ruby would have for lunch, and stopped dead.

There was a dog tied to the boot scraper by the front door. A big dog. It was the kind of dog some people called a German Shepherd; other people called them Police Dogs. *Schäferhund.* The word came back to him. Then the fear.

He sank to his knees, holding his arms bent up around his neck. *They're trained to bite the neck,* he remembered. *And the ankles, so you can't run.* He huddled further into himself, wrapping himself in a ball on the chilly concrete of the barracks forecourt—*No, it's the front walk, I'm home,* he told himself. But he couldn't uncurl.

He heard a thud and some exclamations, shouting. *The guards? No, it's Celia.* "I said, 'Take him away!'" she yelled.

Then another voice, another girl, coming closer. "But he's gentle, he wouldn't hurt a fly. You can't be afraid of him, look, just hold your hand out—"

"Get him *out* of here!" Celia screamed.

Then Ruby's voice, "Young lady, take that animal away this instant."

Nobody disobeyed Ruby when she took that tone. There was a huff and a disgruntled mutter, but the footsteps—the two feet and the four—pattered past Jamie and disappeared. Ruby and Celia started toward him, which meant the door was clear.

Jamie leaped up and hurtled past them into the house, up the stairs, down the hall, up the second stairs, through the attic, and threw himself into the cabinet under the eaves as though the hounds of hell were after him.

When he came out, it was mid-afternoon. The rain had started while he was hidden under the eaves; the sound had helped calm him. The house was quiet, so he felt safe going downstairs to find something to eat, but when he got into the living room he found Mom there in the armchair by the fireplace, with Celia cuddled in her lap as though she were ten instead of thirteen. She'd been crying, but she got up as soon as she saw Jamie and stepped toward him a few feet.

"Jamie, I'm so sorry," she said. "That girl, that Rima, I just started being friends with her. I told her not to bring her dog here, but she thought it would be ok if she left it outside. As soon as she told me, I said she'd have to take it away, but it was already too late. I'm really, really sorry."

Jamie shrugged. "It's ok," he said. I really like that word, 'ok.' It covers such a multitude of possibilities. And once you've said it, you usually don't have to say anything else.

Maybe not this time, though. Mom and Celia were still watching him worriedly. *I'd better give them something.* "They lived better than we did, the dogs. Their houses were nicer, and cleaner. And they ate better. Even when they didn't have bites of us."

Mom put her hand over her mouth and Celia's eyes got big. *Not funny, I guess.* "They're all dead by now, too, right?" he said to Mom.

"Yes, that's right."

"So it's ok." And he went on past them through the dining room and into the kitchen. Ruby had left onion soup on warm on the stove, and a sardine sandwich wrapped in waxed paper.

He ate it all, so he didn't have much appetite for Sabbath dinner a couple of hours later.

That was just as well, as it turned out. Laurie and Dad trying to outdo each other with apologies for last night's upset would have killed his appetite in any case. During dessert, Laurie started talking about how he sometimes felt like a stranger in the family, as though he didn't really belong.

Fat lot he knows about not belonging, Jamie snarled to himself. He's been here all his life that he remembers. He doesn't have a past that keeps jumping out and attacking him. Everybody here loves him; he doesn't have to cope with hate looks...

Don't be ridiculous, the other voice said. People he doesn't even know give him hate looks. You don't have to cope with that; you're safe as long as you don't let them see you. But people here can see you. Talk to them.

They wouldn't understand. But as he thought that, he looked around at the Sabbath table: the starched white cloth, the good china and silver, the braided bread Ruby baked every week, the burning candles. *They did this for you. Ever since you said you wanted it, they've gone to all this trouble to give you something that was important to you. Tell them how you're feeling. And remember last night, how Dad came to sit with you.*

So Jamie told them. He talked about the way he sometimes felt like an outsider. Because Laurie had been talking about being black in a white family, Jamie stuck to talking about being the only Jew. But he knew he felt separate on a deeper level than that. *I can't deal with all these feelings the way they do; I can't even tell what I'm feeling half the time. Maybe I'm like those artificial intelligences Turing wrote about in that article I read this morning: I'm self aware, more or less, but there's something crucial missing. I wonder whether I'll ever find it.* The other voice in his head chimed in: *You won't if you're afraid to actually look for it.*

The others had been talking, chiming in with their own feelings of alienation, and now were standing up, starting to clear the table. *Sha, shut up, both of you,* he told the voices.

Chapter 13.

Jamie stood in the doorway to the larger spare room, staring in at the borrowed hospital bed taking up the central space, with the usual twin beds pushed to the walls. The little woman in the bed hardly made a noticeable lump under the quilt. It could almost have been just rumpled covers, except for the harsh rasp of her uneven breath. Laurie slumped in the chair beside her, sleeping uneasily.

His mother, Jamie thought. *He gets to have his mother back, if only for a little while.* He was glad for Laurie that they'd found his dying birth mother, really he was.

And he was glad he'd been able to help with the algebra tutoring; Laurie'd ended up with a B+, thanks to Jamie. *That was something I could fix, anyway. But it's over now, he doesn't need me for that any more.*

Jamie felt irrationally rejected by that fact. *Stop it,* he chided himself. *You're glad you could help, and you don't begrudge him his mother, even if you'll never see yours again.* He wasn't convincing himself, though.

This was just what he'd thought that night at the Sabbath table: he didn't feel things the way normal people did. He'd gone to Mass with the others the day Laurie was going to meet his mother, to show solidarity. Everyone else had seemed to find some solace and security in the service; certainly Laurie had. But Jamie was only conscious of the grisly crucifix hanging at the front, and the incomprehensible

Latin only further alienated him, and he was sure people stared when he sort of crouched forward in the pew while the others knelt.

Still, I did manage to speak to him afterwards, and encourage him, and even take his hands. That's better than I would have been able to do once, right?

The front doorbell rang. "I'll get it," Joy called, pelting down the front hall from the TV room.

That'll be Linda. Laurie's friend—his girlfriend, if Jamie was any judge of the way they looked at each other when she came for their regular Saturday biology study sessions—had been invited to have dinner with them for Dad's birthday celebration tonight.

Laurie stirred, pushed himself up in the chair, rubbed his eyes, and focused on the figure in the bed before him. She was stirring, too, just the barest disturbance in the covers. Linda's voice floated up from downstairs, greeting Joy. Laurie leaned over and kissed his mother's head, then turned toward the doorway and spotted Jamie.

"Linda's here," Jamie said unnecessarily, hoping it would look as though he'd just come to tell Laurie that. *I don't want him to know I was watching him. He'd take it the wrong way.*

"Thanks," Laurie said, moving across the room toward him. Jamie stepped out of the doorway so Laurie could get past without touching him. But they were standing within two feet of each other when Laurie caught sight of Linda coming up the stairs, tanned from weeks in the Adirondacks with her parents. So Jamie saw the change that came over Laurie's face to match the look on hers: the light in his eyes, the smile. And he saw the way the tension in Laurie's shoulders seemed to drain away. "Hey," Laurie said to her, "come and meet my mother."

Jamie nodded at Linda and slipped off to his room.

Dinner that night was a subdued affair; Laurie's birth mother was dying, after all. At first, people tried to act cheery, but Dad gently put a stop to that. "Just being here with all of you for my birthday is celebration enough," he said. "I'm just happy to be alive, and to be with my family. Laurie's poor mother upstairs never had that pleasure."

"Why didn't she, Dad?" Beth asked. "Why did she throw—I mean, what made her leave Laurie at Rolling Meadow?" Her face was tight, her voice constricted. Robbie was watching her the way he did when she was too close to the top step on the staircase and he was afraid she'd fall down.

They'll never find their natural parents, Jamie realized. *There were no clues, the way there was for Laurie. They'll never know why they were abandoned.*

It was Laurie who answered Beth's question. "I asked her about that when she first came here," he said. "Her husband, my father, had died while she was expecting me. Then, after I was born, she was sick and couldn't work. We both were starving. She put me in that basket and left it at Mom's work so that somebody would take care of me. She was trying to save me."

Mothers try to save you, Jamie thought. *Mine did.* He dredged up the snippet of memory that had come to the surface in that nightmare last year: his parents snatching him out of bed with the Gestapo in the hall outside their flat; his mother asking the building supervisor to look after their things "till this is all over"; the ride in the dark on the floor of the taxi. *What happened next? Where did they go?*

Ruby was bringing in Dad's cake, with forty-six candles on it. Everyone laughed and joked about what a blaze they made, but Jamie stared at the flames, transfixed.

The Torah scroll, he realized. *At Cousin Yankel's shul. The SS burned it. Tati tried to save it; I saw him beating his hands on it, burning himself, from where I was hiding behind the* aron, *the ark. But Mamme tried to save me. "Hide!" she yelled, "Hastair!"* The Hebrew came back to him, and her choked, terrified voice. It was what Cain said he'd do with himself

66

after God banished him for killing his brother. They never spoke Hebrew ordinarily; it was *lashon ha-kodesh*, the holy tongue. *She knew the Nazis would understand Yiddish, though—it's too much like German.*

At the time, he'd understood her without thinking about it. He'd remembered the loose floorboards behind the ark that Cousin Yankel had shown them. It was meant to hide the Torah from marauding Gentiles, but the soldiers' descent on them had been too sudden for that. It was just big enough to hide Jamie, though: just big enough for a three-year-old.

The family now was singing "Happy Birthday" but Jamie was still stuck in that hole. *That's why I feel safe in the cabinet. But I wasn't safe in that hole under the floor, not really.* His hand went to the spot on his chest that held a small round scar. It all came back to him now. *There was a nail in the floor, and every time they stomped on it, wrecking the shul, it pierced me. But I didn't cry out. The dust was choking me, the heat from the fire was stifling me, I could hear Tati praying, Mamme screaming, but I kept quiet. I knew I had to keep quiet.*

Still, they had found him. They had ripped up the boards and pulled him out. Hands were under his arms, pulling him up, pulling him out. Jamie struggled, his arms flailing; he screamed for Tati, but the hands were firm. Firm, not harsh. Steady, inexorable, but not cruel. He waited for the blows, waited to be thrown down and kicked and dragged away, but before that could happen, the hands shifted around his back and pulled him against a broad, firm chest. It was now, not then. He was here, not there.

"I've got you, son. I've got you. I won't let you go. You're safe now," a low voice murmured in his ear. The arms held him close, kept him from falling.

Sometimes fathers save you, too.

CHAPTER 14.

MONDAY, SEPTEMBER 20, 1954

Jamie woke up feeling sluggish and logy. Thunder rumbled in the distance, rain sheeted down the window, the soggy air was warm and stale. It felt late. *Did my alarm fink out again?* He rubbed his face with both hands, then reached toward his nightstand for his glasses. The covers pulled and refused to give; there was a weight holding them down. *What the...*

It was Mom, sitting on the bed beside him. She'd been staring out the window, but as he craned around to gape at her, her eyes met his. *Oh, God.* "Mom? Mom, what's wrong?"

She shifted back to loosen the covers and took his hand. "It's David," she said.

Jamie didn't have to ask, but he did anyway. "Is he dead?"

"Yes, he's dead."

He dropped his head back on the pillow and stared at the ceiling. *Dead. That annoying, volatile, insecure kid is dead.* "He did it himself?" It was the only thing that made sense, of a grim sort.

And "Yes," Mom said. "He'd gotten in a fight with another boy and beaten him badly, put him in the hospital. They put David in the secure facility; nobody called me when it happened. By the time one of my nurse friends tipped me off yesterday, he was already in the system. I spent hours trying to get in to see him... and then it was too late." There were no tears as she spoke, but Jamie could see she'd been crying. The sight struck him in the chest and he lashed out.

"Don't you people have any security?" he snarled. "What did he do, steal pills from the nurses' station? Strangle himself with a bed sheet? Run his head into a wall? Wasn't anyone watching him?"

Mom answered sadly but calmly, not provoked by his tone. "No, they weren't watching him properly," she said. "They saw him as an aggressor, so to their minds he was only a danger to others, not himself. He managed to steal a bobby pin from a nurse, then he sharpened it on the grout between the tiles in the bathroom. It must have taken him hours, all that time I was outside, trying to get to him—" Her voice hitched, then she went on, "He cut his throat with it."

Jamie exhaled hard. "You'd have to really want to die to do that."

"Yes," she said. "He'd given up hope."

Hope, Jamie thought. *Who needs hope? He should have just kept on. I kept on.* A deep, unfocused anger began to fill his chest. He resolutely tamped it down, pushing it back into the depths.

Mom was still talking. "… back into therapy?" she said. "Just to help you over this rough spot—"

"'Rough spot'? *Rough spot?* He's dead, you know. He's not coming back for the happy ending. You really think my going and blabbering about my *feelings* to that idiot in your office is going to make me feel all better?"

"Of course not, I don't mean to minimize the situation, but to help you deal with the—"

"Yeah, because your 'therapy' really worked so well to help him, didn't it?

He'd never made Mom cry before. She'd shed tears of sorrow and sympathy when he was in pain, but never because he'd deliberately hurt her. *This must be how Laurie felt, the night Dad hit him because of what he'd said to her.* But Dad wasn't here, and Jamie couldn't run out of the house the way Laurie had. So he escaped his own way:

he shut down. He could feel himself stilling, shrinking in on himself, going cold.

After some time Mom said, "You don't need that place you hide in, really. You hide perfectly well in the open. Lucky you."

She got up and turned for the door.

No, wait, he cried inside. *Come back!* But all that came out was a strangled little whimper.

It was enough. She paused with her hand on the doorknob, then came back to his bed and sat down again, taking a tissue from his night table and blotting her eyes with it. "I'm sorry," she said. "I shouldn't have said that. I know that's how you survived, keeping quiet and hiding. I think it's why standard therapeutic techniques never seemed to help you; they depend on your being able to talk about what happened to you and how you feel about it: exactly what you can't do. I still hope you'll be able to some day, but it's not fair to put my sense that I failed David into expectations on you."

She brushed her knuckles lightly over the arm he had folded across his stomach and he forced himself to loosen it and turn toward her. She pulled him into her arms. *I knew she would.* She was warm and soft, enfolding and encompassing him. It felt to him like penance, holding still in her embrace. *She needs this, it's the least I can do after making her cry.*

After a while she let him go with a sigh. "It's all right," she said. "We'll keep trying. I love you, sweetheart, and I know you love me."

She patted his cheek and left the room. Jamie had to use the toilet, and his mouth was thick and sour from sleep, but he stayed on the bed, knees drawn to his chin, wondering what was wrong with him. *Other people like it when their mothers hug them.*

Other people's mothers. He thought about Laurie's mother, who had died in his arms. She'd given him up because she couldn't feed him; she'd given him up to save him. Mom would do anything to save him, he knew.

And his own mother? He remembered the night they'd fled the apartment. He remembered her desperate cries to him to hide when the Gestapo came to the shul. *Strange, how that thought came easier now, once he'd relived it in his mind.* But after that, there was nothing. *Did she try to save me? Where did she go? Why can't I remember what happened to her?*

He remembered what happened to Tati; his father had died of typhus, in a welter of suffering and stink, in the cramped, cold barracks, leaving little Hymie alone among strangers. But hard as he tried, Jamie couldn't remember what happened to Mamme.

He didn't think about David at all.

Chapter 15.

Thursday, October 7, 1954

The cantor was singing *"Kol Nidre,"* the chant in Aramaic that ushered in the Jewish Day of Atonement, Yom Kippur, with a prayer to be released from all vows for the year. Studying for his bar mitzvah, Jamie had questioned the new rabbi. Why should people expect to be released from promises? It was just past the Jewish New Year, Rosh Hashanah, ten days before. What kind of way was this to usher in a new year? The answer had been complicated and historical and abstract, and hadn't come near what was really bothering Jamie.

The tune was haunting, beautiful; it uplifted his heart and made the hairs on his neck prickle. It ought to be about something less dry and legalistic than the formal requirements of vows. *That's what Christians like to claim about Judaism,* he thought defensively. *That it's just about nitpicking rules, superficial and rigid.* But Jamie knew better. His religion, his Jewishness, was something that happened deep in his gut. Since he'd started observing some of its laws and customs when he turned thirteen, he'd felt a grounding, a centering, that years of therapy had failed to bring him.

This Reform American service was far from the scraps of memory he had from Before: the congregation, his adopted family among them on this highest of High Holy Days, stood rigidly in pews listening to the cantor, dressed as for church; most of the service was in English. *They might as well be Protestants,* Jamie thought a little scornfully. In his head, he saw flashes of a smaller, more modest sanctuary, with women hidden behind a screen and men wandering about and talking in low tones, joining in the prayers when Jamie's *tati* sang out the cues, praying in Hebrew, singing with the cantor. Still, there was a link from that experience to this, and it nourished Jamie's soul.

Then came the *Unetanne Tokef*, the ancient prayer that was repeated on the New Year and the Day of Atonement:

"On Rosh Hashanah it will be inscribed and on Yom Kippur it will be sealed… who shall live and who shall die; who will die at his predestined time and who before his time; who by water and who by fire, who by sword, who by beast, who by famine, who by thirst, who by war, who by plague, who by strangling, and who by stoning. Who shall rest and who shall wander…"

He hadn't let it in before. Before this Rosh Hashanah, he'd never heard it, so far as he could remember. It wasn't usually read in Reform congregations. He'd vaguely heard the Epsteins talking in the car on the way from Carlisle about people being upset that Rabbi Rosenbaum planned to include it, but he hadn't paid much attention. So when they'd recited it on Rosh Hashanah, he'd been thinking about the philosophy behind it, the hint of predestination; he'd been feeling bitterly superior that all these soft Americans were upset at the reality of inexorable death and the impossibility of resisting or even foreseeing it.

But tonight his heart felt roiled and opened by the Kol Nidre, like a field plowed ready for seed, and David came into it from where he'd been hiding. For as long as Jamie could bear it—a few seconds that doubled him over in the pew—he saw David: his bright green eyes filled with tears ("crocodile tears," he could hear Ruby say, but that didn't matter now), his restless artistic talent, his sulks and enthusiasms, his hunger for contact and his reckless rejection of it. Jamie finally let himself feel that David was gone.

The prayer finished, "But Repentance, Prayer, and Charity annul the severe Decree." *"But he was only little,"* he whispered. Beside him, Dad put a hand on his bent shoulder; on his other side, Laurie angled his body to shelter Jamie a little from the view of the congregation. Jamie straightened up and looked across Dad to meet Mom's eye; she gave him a small nod, filled with understanding and compassion. He understood the message she was sending: *I was little, too.*

When the service was over, he stood in the lobby by the cloakroom with the others, waiting his turn to get his coat in the milling crowd. A girl—another teenager—he'd never seen before was staring at him. He turned his shoulder to her self-consciously. She shifted to keep him in view. He'd been doing pretty well, standing in the press of people without panicking, but she was making him nervous. He looked at her out of the corners of his eyes; she was biting her lip and breathing fast. *She looks nervous, too.*

The girl had pressed her lips together and was edging toward him, looking determined now. Jamie held his ground, thinking he'd look like a fool if he dodged her. *Maybe I know her from somewhere and I just don't remember.* He doubted it, though.

She moved right into his space and stared at him uncertainly. She was still breathing hard; he noticed with some discomfort that her ample breasts strained at her blue sweater. He quickly shifted his eyes back to her plain but pleasant face. "Um," he started, "do I—"

But she broke in. "I just wanted to apologize."

"Uh, ok." This was standard procedure during the days between Rosh Hashanah and Yom Kippur, to restore all human relationships as a prelude to reconciling with God. Jamie himself had gone to each member of his family over the past ten days, sometimes with specific apologies for infractions small and large—to Rob, for having refused to move to the downstairs piano one day when the younger boy wanted to use the attic music room to work something out on the guitar he was teaching himself to play; to Mom, for having hurt her feelings over David—to others with a general request for forgiveness for anything he had done to offend them over the course of the year. He couldn't understand what this stranger was apologizing for, though.

His face must have looked blank, because she licked her lips and tried again. "For the dog," she said.

She's apologizing for her dog?

"I didn't understand," she went on. "Celia tried to tell me, but I didn't really get it till I saw you, what it did to you."

Jamie's cheeks flushed hot and his feet and hands went cold as he grasped what she was saying. *She saw me. She saw me crouching on the ground, afraid of somebody's pet. She saw me shaking and falling apart...* He started to back away, but banged into someone standing behind him.

Meanwhile, the girl—*Rima,* he remembered from what Celia had said—was staring at him with eyes gone wide in alarm. She reached out and grasped his hand; Jamie froze. "I just wanted to say I'm sorry," she said. "I didn't mean to—I mean, I don't think anything bad about you because..." She trailed to a stop and slumped miserably, her eyes on her feet. "Celia doesn't want to be friends with me anymore. I get that, I just didn't want you to think that I did that on purpose."

Her hand was warm in his. Her hair fell about her shoulders in dark, wiry curls. Her blue sweater strained; she was still breathing hard. She smelled of warm wool and slightly oily skin: a homey scent with no threat in it, only a tiny undertone of dog.

Jamie tightened the grip between them. "It's ok, Rima," he said. She looked up in surprise when he said her name. "I know you didn't mean any harm. I'm sorry I upset you. Is the dog ok?"

Her uncertain smile widened to a grin. "'Is the *dog* ok'?" she repeated. "What, you think you hurt his feelings?"

Jamie snorted. "I'm sure he's very sensitive."

"Yeah, he cried for an hour, then he went and wrote in his diary about how bad he felt. He says to tell you he's sorry, too."

"Tell him I forgive him, but I don't ever want to see him again."

"But you wouldn't mind seeing me again?"

Caught out of the silly banter, Jamie stared at her. *She wants to see me again?* He dropped her hand and narrowed his eyes suspiciously.

"Just to talk," she said. "I mean, I don't mean talk about… you know, stuff that upsets you. I just mean you seem interesting. You're a couple of years younger than me, but you're in advanced algebra with me, and—I don't know, maybe we could be friends?"

The crowd had thinned out around them; people were opening the synagogue's front doors, letting in gusts of chilly air, calling holiday greetings. Celia spotted them standing there together and started toward them, looking worried. Ruby was right behind her, Jamie's jacket over her arm. "Sure," Jamie said hurriedly. "We could be friends. Just—"

She backed away, waving her hands, but she was smiling. "I know, I know, just not the dog. He's not a little lamb, you know; he never follows me to school."

"Well, that's all right, then."

Chapter 16.

Sunday, December 19, 1954

Jamie had never been to a Hanukkah party before; there weren't many Jewish kids in the area, and there were none his age. His family had observed the holiday last year, at his request, with candle lighting and small presents. Ruby had made potato pancakes, but they were nothing like the ones Rima's mother was serving tonight. Ruby's were made with mashed potatoes, golden-crusted but dense and soft inside. Mrs. Shapiro's, which she called latkes, were crispy all through, with separate shreds of potato visible in the patties.

The Shapiro Hanukkah menorah was different, too. Where Jamie's family's was polished brass with old-fashioned branching arms curving from a central stem, Rima's family's was angular and modernistic in some kind of dark-turquoise-finished metal with brass edging: from Israel, Rima said. And there were jelly doughnuts as well as latkes; that was evidently a custom from Israel, too.

But they prayed the same blessings and sang the same songs. Then they played with the little four-sided tops called dreidels. Jamie recognized the Hebrew letters on them, but Rima had to tell him what they stood for—*Ness Gadol Haya Sham*, a Great Miracle Happened There—and what their values were in the game, but when they started spinning the tops for the pot of gold-foil-wrapped chocolate coins, another memory hit Jamie in the back of the palate. *"Rozhinkes mit mandlen,"* he said.

"Gezundheit," one of the other kids joked. Rima glared at the kid, but Mrs. Shapiro nodded at Jamie approvingly.

"That's right, Jamie," she said. "Raisins and almonds: that's what they played dreidel for in the Old Country. There's a famous song."

Now the other kids were all staring at him. "I thought you were Jewish?" one of the girls said. "How come you don't know anything?"

"He knows stuff," another girl said. "It's just weird stuff."

Jamie excused himself and locked himself in the bathroom. He stayed in there till he was afraid they'd notice and start banging on the door asking how he was. When he came out, the party had moved down to the rec room on the lowest floor of the tri-level house. "Earth Angel" was playing on the hi-fi, kids were dancing, and nobody paid much attention to Jamie as he slipped around the shadowy edges of the room to wedge himself back into a deep upholstered club chair.

After a while, Rima came over and pressed a cold Coke bottle into his hand. "Don't you want to dance?" she asked. The others were slow-dancing to "You're Nobody Till Somebody Loves You," arms draped around each other's necks and waists. At the panic on Jamie's face, she wrinkled her nose at him. "Don't worry about it," she said, and perched on the arm of his chair.

She seemed to be watching the dancers, and Jamie pretended he was, too, but he was really focused on Rima's generous haunch in her tight tweed slacks, almost brushing his arm. He shifted his Coke to his other hand and took a sip just as she jumped to her feet again. "Let's play Spin the Bottle!"

Now Jamie was acutely aware that the others were all a year or two older than he. He'd heard of Spin the Bottle, and knew it had something to do with kissing, but he wasn't sure how it worked. Gingerly, he lowered himself to the floor to sit in the circle with the others. One of the boys set an empty Coke bottle in the center of the circle and the game began.

Jamie was increasingly horrified, watching. He didn't even know these people; how was he supposed to kiss one of these girls, assuming that's what each couple was doing as they disappeared into the storage closet? *Maybe they're doing something else, something I don't even know about. What will I do if the bottle lands on me? There couldn't be anything worse.*

But there could be, as it turned out. The bottle spun to a stop with its neck pointing at Jamie like the barrel of a gun… and the girl who'd spun it nudged it with her foot so it moved to the guy next to him, and everyone laughed as the two of them hopped giggling and snorting into the closet. Jamie went cold, frozen and staring at his own feet as he sat cross-legged on the linoleum floor.

He heard more talking and laughing somewhere, but he sank away from it. Before he got too far, though, there was a hand on his arm, tugging insistently. He focused his eyes and saw the bottle was pointing at him again. It was Rima pulling on his sleeve. *She's going to help me get out of here. Bet she's sorry she ever asked me,* he thought as he got to his feet.

But she was pushing him toward the closet, and then into it, and closing the door, and then she was kissing him. He could hear Prince, the German Shepherd, rustling and whimpering a little on the other side of the wall, in the laundry room where Rima had shut him in for the evening. *He can smell her… and me,* he thought uneasily.

Then the immediate sensations of Rima drowned out thoughts of the dog. Her breasts were soft against him, but her arms were surprisingly strong around his neck, and her mouth was both soft and hard, yielding and insistent, and—was that her *tongue?* It was, right there in his mouth, sliding around as though it belonged there.

Jamie was fascinated and terrified, repelled and yet... there was a stirring in his groin and a thrill in his belly. Part of him wanted to run away and part of him wanted to stand here and do this forever. But she was already lifting her head and loosening her arms. She gave him a conspiratorial grin, opened the closet door, and rejoined the others. After a minute, Jamie followed.

The rest of the party passed in a blur for Jamie. Ruby came to pick him up—she'd been at an Intercultural Council meeting with her friend Mrs. Hodge—and he thanked Mrs. Shapiro and ran out of the house to the station wagon as though he were fleeing a burning building. When he got home, he went straight upstairs to get ready for bed.

He had lurched into the bathroom and was clinging to the sink, gazing unseeing at the mirror, before he noticed that Laurie was there, using the toilet. He gently shouldered Jamie aside to get at the sink and looked sidelong at Jamie while he washed his hands.

"You ok?" he asked.

"Fine, I'm fine," Jamie said, trying not to croak.

"Coulda fooled me," Laurie said. "No, seriously, man, you look about like that woman must've who got banged up when that meteorite slammed into her house last month. Did something happen at your party?"

One voice in Jamie's head said, *Freeze him out, make him go away.* The other voice countered, *He's right, you do feel like you've been hit by something from outer space. Maybe he could help.*

"Do you make out with Linda?" he asked baldly.

Laurie's jaw dropped, then his mouth softened. "Yeah. Yes, I do," he said. "Is that what's happened? It's not that something fell on you, it's that you fell for someone?"

"Not exactly. I mean, I don't really know her."

"But?"

"We played Spin the Bottle, and she, you know, she kissed me. I guess what they call French kissing. I mean she put her, uh… "

"Tongue?" Laurie said helpfully.

Jamie swallowed and looked away.

"Listen," Laurie said. "Kissing is great, being close to somebody you really like is great. But Spin the Bottle—I mean, it would maybe be better to keep it to someone you want to be with, not just because of some game."

"But what if it's both?"

"You care about this girl?"

"I don't know." Jamie was horrified to hear a whine in his own voice. *I'm showing him too much.* He busied himself with toothbrush and paste. He couldn't seem to get the cap off the tube, then suddenly it popped off and rolled under the sink.

Laurie bent and retrieved it. "Thanks," Jamie said. "I mean… thanks."

Laurie clapped him on the shoulder. "Any time, little brother," he said. "Any time."

Jamie brushed his teeth as though he were scrubbing a tile floor. After a minute Laurie said, "Well, good night then."

Jamie nodded.

Chapter 17.

Thursday, February 17, 1955

Jamie stood in Rima's back yard, hands braced lightly on the wire mesh fence around Prince's pen. The big shepherd was asleep, sheltering from the drizzle under the overhang fronting his doghouse. *He's just an animal,* Jamie told himself. *He's not a demon or a monster. He's been trained to be gentle.*

Behind him, he heard the house kitchen door open and close, then the tattoo of light rain on an umbrella, coming closer. Rima stepped up and held the umbrella over both of them, pressed close to his side. In the pen, Prince stirred and yawned, ears pricked forward though his eyes were still closed.

"He's not even a good guard dog," she said softly, as though she'd read Jamie's mind. "Once when my mom was alone here, a couple rough-looking characters pulled up and started trying to get her to let them resurface the driveway or something. The one guy had his arm resting on the open window of their car. Mom said, 'You better not get out; I can't always control the dog if he thinks I'm in danger.' Princie jumped up and started licking the guy's arm. Mom said they laughed like hell before they drove away."

Jamie sighed. "I understand intellectually that he won't harm me," he said. "It's why I'm standing here, trying to get used to him, to the idea of him. It's my gut that's scared."

He turned back toward the house with her. Her brow was wrinkled, her lips pulled in over her teeth. He waited for her to come out with whatever she was worrying over. They made their way through the back door and into the Shapiros' shiny modern kitchen, slinging their damp jackets onto the Formica countertop and the open umbrella into the stainless steel sink, before she spoke.

"Listen, Jamie, I'm not trying to be a smart alec here, or poke my nose in where you don't want it, but I can't figure something out. You've been here, in America I mean, since you were little, right?" Jamie nodded cautiously. Rima traced a damp sneaker toe around a diamond in the patterned vinyl floor. "So," she said slowly, still looking down, "why do you still get so… squirrelly about stuff that happened before? I mean, I get that it was, like, horrible and all, but shouldn't you be getting over it by now?" Jamie thought his face was frozen, but it must have showed something, because she looked up and gasped at the sight of it. "I don't mean anything bad by it, it's not a criticism," she said. "I was just… wondering. Oh, never mind, please, sorry I said anything, it's really not my business—"

Jamie put a hand out to stop the spate of speech. He took a few deep breaths, gathering his thoughts, then said, "When I came here, when Dad brought me here, it was like running in from a storm and slamming the door shut behind me. All that stuff that happened Before was outside, and I was safe inside, hidden. But… I don't know, lately it's started leaking, or something. Starting with my bar mitzvah, the past has been coming back to me, the gates are opening, and I can't hide any more; I have to deal with it—for the first time."

The umbrella in the sink rolled a little and Jamie reached to stop it, glad of the excuse to stop talking. But that let Rima see that his hand was shaking. She moved forward to put her warm hand over his. He turned, and then they were kissing. Jamie sank into the sensation in relief. *No talking, no thinking, just this, just these sensations, this softness.* He let it wash over him. For a moment he felt as if he was drowning, but he held his breath and hung on.

83

That night, sitting in the birthday armchair throne for the tenth time since coming to this house, he wished he'd thought to ask for Rima to be included; it was his fifteenth, after all, a milestone of sorts. *It's a school night, though, and her parents are pretty strict about that.* His birthdate in the Hebrew calendar this year wouldn't fall until March, which felt too weirdly off from his regular life. *Besides, that will be a weeknight, too.*

Jamie sighed and returned his attention to his family's presents. Most people had given him books, as usual—a collection of Bradbury short stories and Einstein's latest looked the most promising. Still, he couldn't help being intrigued by a largish flat box on the bottom of the pile. It was neatly wrapped, but the heap of frizzed up ribbon was subtly off: crimson rather than the scarlet of the balloons on the paper. It must be either from Rob, who wouldn't have noticed, or Beth, who couldn't see.

She'd cut her week at boarding school short to be here for his birthday, which made Jamie a little uneasy. She was a gentle, loving little soul, older than her twelve years, who seemed content to sit quietly near him if they were alone in a room together: playing the piano or reading Braille or simply sitting with the sun on her face. Celia was bracingly unsentimental, but she could be bossy; Joy's perpetual high spirits and occasional fits of melancholy could be wearing. But his middle sister had never plagued or irritated him, which left him feeling oddly wrong-footed around her, as though he were waiting for some demand or revelation that would find him wanting.

So he reached for the flat package, saying, "Now Beth's."

She smiled and answered, "I hope you like it. Mom said you needed new ones. The woman at the store said this was the most popular style these days."

By now he had the paper off and was lifting the lid. The gray and white stripes seemed to pierce his brain before his eyes could make sense of what they were seeing. Somewhere in the distance, Joy exclaimed, "Pajamas!"

"They felt very soft and nice," Beth said uncertainly, picking up on Jamie's silence.

Jamie felt Mom's hand on his shoulder, then saw her other hand come forward and replace the lid on the box. That freed him to say, "Thank you, Beth." But he couldn't say any more.

Ruby cleared her throat and then clapped her hands. "Well, if anyone wants more cake, now's the time. And I could use some help in the kitchen."

"It was my turn last night," Joy complained. "Yours, too, right, Laurie?"

"I don't mind," Laurie said mildly, moving through to the dining room.

"Well, I do. It's not fair, and Jamie hasn't finished—"

"Joy May," Dad broke in. "How about I teach you some of those chess openings we talked about? Come on into the study."

Finally, there was no one there but Jamie and Beth and Mom. Mom said, "Talk to Beth, Jamie," and left the room, too.

"What did I do wrong?" Beth's voice was very small.

Jamie clamped down on the nausea roiling his stomach and willed his pounding heart to slow. "Not your fault," he said. "You couldn't know. It's just—they look like what we wore, the gray stripes."

If it had been Celia, or Laurie, or any of the others, really, there would have been a spate of apologies. From Beth there was only silence, which let Jamie say after a while, "They are soft. Or, they look like they are, anyway, I didn't actually touch them."

Beth huffed a little impatiently. "I don't get how something can *look* soft. Ruby explained to me about stripes a long time ago, but I

85

don't understand color, either. Robbie told me once that red is a warm color, but my winter coat is blue, which he says is a cool color. Now there's something about this mysterious thing called 'color' that makes you hate my present."

"I'm sorry," Jamie said. They both laughed a little at the thought that Jamie was the one apologizing.

"They won't let me return pajamas," Beth said then. "But if I save my allowance for a couple of weeks, maybe I could get you—"

"No," Jamie said with sudden decision. "I'm going to wear them."

"You are?"

"Yes. It's not going to be that my birthday present turned into concentration camp uniform; the camp uniform turned into nice soft pajamas that my sister gave me."

"Thank you," Beth said.

"You're welcome," Jamie responded, and they laughed again. In the doorway to the hall, Mom was beaming.

"I'm going to call Rima," Jamie said. As he passed Beth on the way to the hall telephone, he let his hand drift across her shoulder. She touched it just as lightly, with the tips of her fingers.

As he moved by Mom in the doorway, he wryly quoted an old Cagney movie: "Top o' the world, Ma!"

CHAPTER 18.

SATURDAY, MAY 7, 1955

The sun beat down on Jamie's head and glared off his glasses, the edge of the bleacher bench he sat on bit into his thighs, but he was content: Rima was beside him, her hip in madras plaid Bermuda shorts pressed to his, her breast in its cotton t-shirt just brushing his upper arm. At his other side, his little sister Joy jiggled impatiently, whispering "C'mon, c'mon," as the runners on the track below toed into their starting blocks and assumed their four-point "set" positions.

The starter's gun sounded. Laurie seemed to get off well, his upper body still almost horizontal as he pushed forward for maximum momentum, but there were other runners between him and the audience, so Jamie couldn't see him clearly at first. A blond guy was running almost in tandem with Laurie in the next lane; *Tank Lebo,* Jamie remembered.

He was the one who was so racist and obnoxious when they were in elementary school. Funny how you can't tell by looking at people who's decent and who isn't. Or can you? He does have that Aryan, Master-of-the-Universe look. But would I think that if I didn't already know he was a jerk? That would be playing into the kind of prejudice people like him have against Negroes.

Lebo's fair hair was darkened with sweat around his face—a handsome face, if a little slack-jawed. The muscles in his pounding legs clenched and loosened with his strides, his upper arms bulged as he swung them and his chest heaved with the effort of breathing as he strove to pass Laurie, now more visible as he gradually pulled ahead of Lebo. Jamie tried to shift his attention back to Laurie, but somehow his gaze seemed fixed on the other boy. Lebo puffed his chest out as they approached the finish line as though he could will it to break the tape, but Laurie was the one who hit it.

"And once again, folks, it's Laurence McAlister, County High's own version of Jesse Owens, winner of the Hundred Yard Dash," the announcer's voice boomed over applause and cheers, loudest from the seats around Jamie where the rest of the family had now leaped to their feet. The announcer—one of the gym teachers whose name Jamie couldn't remember—went on, "The ref just gave me an official time of ten seconds, only six-tenths of a second off the world record for high school runners. Second place goes to Roland "Tank" Lebo at ten point one; would have been almost a photo finish, if we had one of those fancy cameras. Michael Burba, with a finishing time of ten point nine, takes third place. Congratulations, boys, great sprinting! Now, folks, if you'll turn your attention to the curved part of the track where the contestants are lining up for the half-mile run…"

Jamie let his attention wander. They would stay for the other events out of politeness, but now that Laurie's part was over, so was Jamie's interest. Still, he watched as, beside the track below, Laurie had almost reached the entrance to the locker rooms, surrounded by teammates slapping his back and punching his shoulder enthusiastically. Tank Lebo hung back alone, clenching his biceps and looking disgruntled.

Rima shifted, calling Jamie's attention back to her. She was craning her neck around, looking at the surrounding bleachers.

"Where's that girl, what's-her-name, Linda? I'd've thought she'd be here to see her boyfriend run. If you were in some kind of contest, I sure wouldn't miss out on watching you."

Is she saying I'm her boyfriend? The thought gave Jamie a little thrill, along with a stirring of uneasiness. To cover his confusion, he answered sardonically, "Any event I compete in is likely to take place entirely in the contestants' heads: nothing much to watch. As for Linda, she and Laurie broke up, I think."

"Really? I thought they were, like, the ideal couple. What happened?"

"I don't know. Some kind of spat. He's been down in the dumps about it."

"And you haven't asked him what happened?"

Jamie shrugged. "Not my business. Anyway, we don't talk about stuff like that."

"You don't talk about what's going on in your lives? I always thought that would be the whole point of having brothers or sisters, having somebody to talk to about that kind of thing."

"That's because you're an only child. You idealize what it would be like to have siblings. Anyway, boys don't talk about re-e-e-la-a-a-tionships." He drew the last word out in a simpering tone.

Rima slapped at his forearm. "Oh, you. I don't think that's true at all. I think it's just that you don't like talking about how you feel, or how other people do, either."

"Maybe," Jamie shrugged. "Who just won that last race, anyway?" He turned his eyes back to the track.

"No idea," she said. "I'm more interested in you." Her voice was now low and sultry; her hand crept forward to clasp his.

Jamie, confused and surprised at the sudden shift in topic and tone, turned his face toward her. Without warning, she leaned forward and caught his lips with hers in a brief but sound kiss.

After a few seconds, he jerked back. "Rima," he hissed. "My family's here."

She laughed, but there were spots of embarrassed color in her cheeks. "Sometimes I forget you're younger than me," she said. "You're so smart, and in some ways you're really sophisticated, then you do something like go all ape over a simple kiss and I remember you're just a kid."

"It's not that," he protested. "I'm just a more private person."

"Well, then, let's go somewhere private," she murmured into his ear.

Before he could respond, she was standing up, still holding his hand so he was dragged up after her, and stepping over Celia on her far side. "Gotta see a man about a dog," she said.

"And Jamie has to go with you?" Celia asked incredulously.

"Sure. Protect me against the unwanted advances of all those hunky, sweaty boys down there," Rima said blithely.

Jamie gulped and followed her.

Chapter 19.

Dad's usual Sunday morning pancakes had been particularly lavish today, swimming in maple syrup, with blueberries in them and whipped cream instead of plain butter on them, in honor of Mother's Day. The family had insisted that both Mom and Ruby sit at leisure while the rest of them put brunch together, including the platter of paper-thin lox, the smoked salmon Dad had shipped in from Philadelphia that stood as a savory in place of sausage or bacon since Jamie had decided to stop eating pork. There had been a cheese omelet, too, and a big bowl of cantaloupe and honeydew balls sprinkled with ginger and cloves.

So the kitchen was a mess, and it was Laurie and Jamie's turn to clean it. "I'm glad we're going out to dinner tonight," Laurie said as he filled the omelet pan with water to soak while Jamie scraped the pancake griddle. Outside, a warm drizzle spotted the window over the sink. "Maybe I'll go out running when we finish here," Laurie mused. "The rain'll keep me cool, and I've got nothing else to do this afternoon."

Thinking of his conversation with Rima yesterday, Jamie ventured, "Why don't you have anything else to do? You don't seem to be spending time with Linda these days. I guess you guys broke up?"

Laurie had filled the sink and begun swishing their juice glasses in the suds. "I guess," he said gloomily. "I'm not even really sure how it happened. We were arguing about her girlfriend Sydney and I told her I thought Sydney was a bad influence on her and she got sore."

Jamie started pouring boiling water over the glasses in the drain basket, careful not to splash on himself or Laurie. He was equally careful as he said, "She didn't strike me as the kind of person to junk a relationship just because she disagreed with you about something."

Laurie's mouth quirked wryly. "You're right, she's not. I wasn't being quite honest with you. I didn't just disagree with her, I told her I wanted her to stop seeing Sydney."

Jamie gaped. "I don't know much about girls, but I could have told you that would get you in dutch with her."

"Don't let Mom hear you say that," Laurie warned.

"Say what?" Jamie asked, confused.

"'In dutch.' Isn't that some kind of slur, like 'gyp' is about gypsies, or 'jew him down.'"

"Is it? I never thought about it. Anyway, don't change the subject, which is you getting in trouble with Linda."

Laurie, now working on the silverware, nodded. "It was like the *Titanic* and the iceberg. I could see I shouldn't say it, but somehow I couldn't stop, and once it was out, there didn't seem to be anything I could do. It's how I really feel."

"That's important to you, how you feel, isn't it?" Jamie turned back from putting a freshly dried glass in the cupboard to find Laurie staring at him.

"Isn't that important to everyone? Don't you?"

"I don't think about it much. Thinking, that's what I care about. If I think something's a certain way, that's more important to me than what I feel about it."

"Wow," Laurie said, dropping the last handful of silverware into the basket and starting in on the greasy, syrup-smeared plates. "That explains a lot."

Jamie stiffened. "Why I'm so weird, you mean?"

"Weird? No, I don't think you're weird. I meant about why we're so different. It seems like sometimes we just don't understand each other. I really love you a lot, though. I hope you know that."

Jamie lowered his eyes from Laurie's earnest gaze, shivering with embarrassment and uneasiness. *I ought to say something, to say it back to him, but I couldn't do that in a million years. I wish I could go up to my cabinet.* He hadn't hidden there since he'd gotten involved with Rima, but he thought of it with longing now. *It would be so peaceful, with the rain on the roof, not too cold or too hot...*

Then Laurie's hand on his arm brought him back to the kitchen. "I didn't mean to get you all shook up, there, sweetheart."

With an effort, Jamie pulled himself together and turned back to start drying the plates he'd just rinsed. Laurie, however, didn't go back to working on the pots and pans.

"When David died, so soon after my mother," he began in a low voice behind Jamie, "it really made me think—you know, life, death, what does it all mean?" His tone was lightly dismissive, but that didn't fool Jamie. He looked over his shoulder and met Laurie's eye briefly as he nodded.

Laurie came forward and started in on the omelet pan. "It was your doing, really," he went on. "When you started doing all that Jewish stuff, just because you decided you wanted to after your bar mitzvah, I saw that it was possible to change things in your life. Even if you'd never been a certain way, that didn't mean you couldn't start. You weren't afraid of looking foolish, you just followed your heart."

"My brain," Jamie said, dry-mouthed with astonishment. "It was my brain I followed."

Laurie chuckled and tapped him on the forehead with his finger as though he'd made a joke. "Yeah, ok, your brain, fair enough. Me, I'm a heart guy. And my heart said life's too short to go around trying to be some cool cat. I want the people I love to know it, and if people think that's not cool, or it makes me a fairy or something, too bad for them." Then he shook his head. "Don't tell the folks I said 'fairy.' Another word we're not supposed to use." He turned back to the sink.

He emptied it, swished it out with the sponge, squeezed the sponge and set it on the ledge to dry, all while Jamie stood there dumbly staring at him. Then he turned to Jamie, eyes soft. "I know this isn't your thing. You don't have to say anything back to me, or anything. I just want you to know that I love you, and that I think you're really great. When you helped me with algebra last year, I realized I didn't have to feel bad that you're smarter than I am with stuff like that; I could enjoy it, and feel good that you were willing to share it with me, and take all that time out of your own Saturdays to help me. And it's not just that you're so good at math. I started to see that when, for instance, you make those snide remarks of yours, you're being funny. Once I realized that, I realized you really have a sneaky sense of humor that I could appreciate."

He plucked the dishtowel out of Jamie's lax hands and dried his on it, then hung it over the edge of the sink to dry. "So the point is," he went on, "you can be sharp and sarcastic, and I can be soppy and soft, and we can still appreciate each other. And I know you love me, too, so don't worry about it."

Before Jamie realized what he had in mind, Laurie had reached out and pulled him into his arms. Jamie couldn't respond to the hug, even though it felt good—strong, like when Dad did it—but when Laurie pulled back a little and cupped Jamie's cheek in his palm, Jamie reached up and covered Laurie's hand with his own, holding it there for a second while he let their eyes meet.

Then he dropped his hand, and his gaze. Laurie left his in place for an instant more, then moved away, saying briskly, "Well, I'd better get cracking if I want to get a run in before the rain gets any worse."

"Yeah, catch you later," Jamie said. Laurie left and Jamie thought about going up to his cabinet, but the appeal had waned, so he made his way to the living room piano instead. *Nothing like a little Bach to get me back in balance,* he thought.

Chapter 20.

The temperature had dropped over the past couple of days, and the spring drizzle seemed perpetual. Jamie and Rob huddled in the portico in front of Bosler Library in Carlisle. Jamie turned up the collar on his trench coat, Robbie plunged his hands into the pockets of his waterproof jacket.

"Wish Dad would hurry up and get here," Jamie's younger brother said. His teeth were chattering a little.

It's not that *cold,* Jamie thought distantly, his mind still on the article he'd been reading. It was Alan Turing again; Jamie was still intrigued by the famous mathematician's early explorations into computers and the possibility of their becoming self-aware. He'd died last year, not quite 42 years old; there were rumors it had been suicide.

Why would someone that brilliant and successful in such fascinating work want to kill himself? It bothered Jamie to think that someone whose brain was so superior evidently might be brought down by factors or emotions that had nothing to do with intelligence.

Robbie had taken to hopping from foot to foot now. "What's wrong with you?" Jamie snapped at the thirteen-year-old, irritated at being distracted from his musing.

"Everything," the kid said sulkily. At least he stopped jiggling, though. He hunched his shoulders up around his ears. The rain was coming down harder now, bouncing in little spurts up off the steps in front of them. Across the street, some Dickinson students crowded into the archway covering an entrance to Denny Hall, laughing and jostling for cover.

"Aren't you happy to be graduating from eighth grade? I thought you were all hot to trot in high school?"

Robbie shrugged unhappily. "I got some of my tests back today. I guess I'll pass all right, but my grades won't be that great. Not like you and Laurie and Celia. Even Beth does better than I do in school, and she can't even see. And Joy: God, she leaned over me while I was doing English homework the other night, and she got the answers faster than I did, and she's only in sixth grade."

Jamie was a little shocked; he hadn't realized the kid was having so much trouble. He covered the shock with sarcasm so as not to embarrass him. "My heart bleeds," he said.

Robbie glared at him. "You don't have to be mean about it."

He didn't understand. Why can't I ever make myself understood? Jamie pretended to be interested in the hijinks of the students sheltering across the street so he wouldn't have to look at Rob and how he'd hurt his feelings. After a minute he chanced a quick glance back and saw the glare was gone, though Rob was still staring hard.

"You weren't trying to be mean, were you?" he asked wonderingly. "I just got it, Laurie's right: you think you're being funny."

Jamie bit back a sharp rejoinder and said instead, "I just meant you have other things going for you. Music, for instance. And sports—you're good at basketball."

"I almost didn't get on the intramural team this year, though. I might not get to play at County High. And I started off good on the guitar, but I'm sort of stranded now. I can't seem to get any better."

"That happens sometimes with an instrument," Jamie said. "It's like learning a foreign language; you can get to a point where you can't seem to get any easier with it, then all of a sudden your brain kind of lights up and you jump forward."

"Yeah?"

"Really."

Rob kept staring at Jamie, chewing on the inside of his cheek. Then he said, "You helped Laurie with his algebra last year. Do you think you could maybe help me a little, if I have trouble getting it next year?"

Jamie felt a flush of pleasure. "What's in it for me?" he said.

But Rob wasn't fooled this time. He grinned up at Jamie. "Eternal gratitude?" he said.

"Only to be expected. Try again."

"Um, Cool Daddy-o of the Year Award?"

"Not my style."

"How about I take over all your turns for helping Ruby in the kitchen?"

"Now you're talking," Jamie said, knowing as well as Robbie did that the adults would never allow such an arrangement.

"Great. So slip me some skin to seal the deal." Rob held out his palm and Jamie grazed his across it. Then, thinking of what Laurie had done in the kitchen last Sunday, he raised his hand and cupped Robbie's cheek with it.

As Jamie had done with Laurie, Rob raised his own hand and pressed Jamie's closer, but he also unselfconsciously nestled into the caress, leaning his head sideways and closing his eyes. Jamie held the position for a minute, feeling proud of overcoming his usual reluctance to touch anyone in sheer affection.

Then the racket from the students across the street penetrated his consciousness. They were hooting and wolf-whistling, and one of them shouted, "Look at the little queers!" Then he started singing in an exaggerated lisp, something about, "Whoops, we are fairies!"

Jamie pulled his hand away sharply; Rob opened his eyes, surprised and taken aback. He opened his mouth as though to question him, then the song registered with him, too. Brows knitted, he looked uncertainly from the catcalling group back to his brother.

At that moment, Dad's black and white Buick pulled up to the curb. Jamie ran behind Rob through the slackening rain and they both flung themselves into the car, Rob in the front and Jamie in back. Dad moved forward to the next alley and made a right to turn back towards Pine Springs; Rob craned his head back to look at the students, who were spilling out onto the sidewalk now that the cloudburst was over.

"Have a good day, boys?" Dad asked.

Instead of answering, Rob said, "Dad, what's a fairy? I mean, I get that it's some kind of guy who acts like a girl, but what does it mean exactly?"

Jamie cringed in his seat but made a little scoffing sound in his throat to indicate the subject was beneath his notice.

Still, he listened closely as Dad said, "It's a cruel term for a homosexual, which is a man who is attracted to other men sexually instead of to women."

They were back on High Street now, headed out of town. *He'd already gone around the block before he picked us up, so he could be on our side of the street,* Jamie realized. *If he hadn't done that, we'd have had to cross over and walk around the car to where those guys were standing.* He shivered.

In the front seat, Rob persisted, "But I don't get it. Why would anybody do a thing like that?"

"They don't decide to do it, son, it's just the way they're made."

"You mean on the inside? Their brains or whatever?"

"Of course on the inside. Their outer bodies are the same as any other man's."

"Well, then, I really don't get it. I mean, we learned in health class about, you know, how it works with men and women. But girls have…" Robbie, red-faced, ground to a halt and fell silent.

In the rearview mirror, Jamie could see Dad press his lips together, pondering. Then he said carefully, "There are other ways, other… mmm, openings that can give pleasure."

It took a minute for Rob to think about that, then he said emphatically, "Yuck. That's disgusting."

"Not to them," Dad said mildly. "Any particular reason you're asking about this now?"

Jamie couldn't have spoken at that moment with a gun to his head, but Rob didn't seem to have trouble saying, "Those guys on the corner, those students, they were calling us fairies. Jamie put his hand on my face and they just started whistling and carrying on and singing this stupid song. Why would they do that?"

"Because they're idiots," Dad said firmly. "And because anything outside their usual frame of reference frightens them. Pay no attention. And I don't ever want to hear you use that word, understood? No matter how 'yucky' you think it is."

"Yes, sir," Rob answered.

"Jamie?"

"Of course not. I mean, yes, sir." Jamie put his head back and watched the tops of the telephone posts seeming to slip by the car windows, and listened to the measured thwock of the windshield wipers.

I'll call Rima when I get home, he thought. *See what she's doing this weekend.*

Chapter 21.

Tuesday, July 5, 1955

Celia and Joy were sitting at the summer dining table in the screened porch; the table was strewn with old newspapers and pages cut out of magazines. A shoebox full of snapshots and a pot of rubber cement sat at Celia's elbow and a big open book lay in front of her, while Joy clacked a pair of shears and rummaged through the magazine pages. Jamie stood in the doorway from the kitchen and stared at them in silence.

Joy picked up a page that had what looked to Jamie like a poem printed in a broad border of purple flowers. Joy started to clip through the border.

"Don't do that!" Celia yelped. "She loves those flower borders."

"It's the poem that's important," Joy said defensively, but she put the scissors down and patted the cut she'd made as though she could heal it. Her shoulders drooped but she made one last try: "This is that Mother's Day poem. You said Mother's Day was next, and it won't fit with the snaps unless I cut it down."

"Facing pages," Celia said a little scornfully. "Ever hear of them?" She started arranging three or four Polaroid pictures on the left hand page of the book in front of her, trying different angles and order.

Jamie came into the porch. He stood there without saying anything, but Celia spoke as though he'd asked.

"It's a scrapbook for Ruby's birthday," she said. "We were *supposed* to finish it yesterday, but *somebody* just *had* to go swimming instead, and now if we don't hurry she'll be back from Philadelphia before we're finished."

"It was the Fourth of July!" Joy protested. "It's our patriotic duty to have fun on the Fourth."

"But you knew she'd be coming back today," Celia started, then dismissed her with a wave of the hand and turned to Jamie.

"What did you get her?" she demanded.

"Bottle of perfume."

"What kind?"

"Evening in Paris."

Celia wrinkled her nose and Joy said, "She doesn't wear perfume."

A familiar feeling of failure filled Jamie. "I didn't know what else to get her," he said.

"You could have come in with us," Joy said.

Jamie shrugged. "That's a girl present."

Celia snorted and Joy said, "Is there a rule or something?"

Tiring of the focus on his shortcomings, Jamie said abruptly, "What's wrong with her family, anyway?"

"Nothing's wrong, what are you talking about?" Joy protested.

But Celia nodded at him. "It is funny that she only sees them on her birthday and Christmas. Nowadays, with the Turnpike, it's only a two-hour drive. But she always comes back out of sorts when she does go. I don't know what it's about, though."

"She should just stay here," Joy declared. "Here's one for the Fourth," she said in an undertone to Celia, handing her a poem surrounded by fireworks sprays. Then she went on, "We're her real family, anyway."

Jamie and Celia both chuckled. "I mean it," Joy insisted. "*We* don't make her unhappy."

"Says the girl who kicked up a fuss about helping clean our room last week," Celia said.

Joy shrugged. "That's different. It's my right as a kid to gripe about chores. I might bug her sometimes, but I don't make her *miserable.*"

"Her family doesn't make her miserable, don't exaggerate." Celia started pasting corner mounts for the photos onto the scrapbook page. "Rima coming over today?"

"I guess," Jamie said.

"You don't know if your girlfriend's coming over?"

My girlfriend, Jamie thought. *Sounds so normal.* To Celia he said, "She's your friend, too."

Celia shrugged. "Not really. She hardly talks to me since she took up with you."

She hardly talks to me, either. It's just straight to the clinches these days. Guess that's normal, too.

They all turned toward the sound of heels clacking on the walk from the garage. Celia slammed the scrapbook shut and Joy tried futilely to cover the drift of magazine pages with her arms, but it was just Mom. They sighed and relaxed.

"Thought you were Ruby," Celia said. "You're home early."

"I had a meeting at the Carlisle Hospital," Mom said. "It wasn't worth it to go all the way back to Rolling Meadow this late in the day. Oh, is that the scrapbook you're making?"

She leaned over Celia's shoulder and opened the scrapbook. "This was such a nice idea," she said. "I like the way you're mixing photos and printed materials. She's going to love this."

"What's wrong between Ruby and her family?" Jamie asked.

Mom shook her head at him, still smiling slightly. "Sorry," she said. "That's Ruby's business."

"So there is something wrong?" Joy said.

Mom shrugged a little. "Like a lot of families, they had expectations, and Ruby had some different ideas for herself."

"So why does she keep going back there?" Jamie asked.

"They're her family, sweetie," Mom said, as though that were an answer. She patted Jamie's arm as she moved past him into the house. "Oh, hi, Rima," she said.

"Hi, Dr. Mac." Rima came out of the kitchen onto the porch. "Laurie said you guys were back here." She slipped an arm around Jamie's waist and leaned into him, nodding at the girls. "You making a scrapbook?"

"For Ruby's birthday," Joy said. Celia didn't look up.

"I think it's so sweet, how nice you guys are to the maid," Rima said.

"She's part of the family," Celia said, still not looking at Rima.

"I know, I know." Rima tugged at Jamie. "Let's go for a walk. You said you'd show me that old barn on your property."

Celia snorted and started slathering rubber cement on the back of a poem.

"Later, alligator," Rima said blithely as they left the porch and started toward the barn.

As soon as they were out of earshot, Jamie said, "Celia's never forgiven you for bringing Princie that day. I've told her I'm working on not being scared of him—did I tell you I patted him yesterday?—but she's acting so dumb about it..."

"She's not dumb," Rima interrupted. "Look, Jamie, I have a sort of confession to make."

Jamie felt cold. *She's going to tell me she just felt sorry for me, she's breaking up with me.*

But Rima said, "Celia's way younger than me, you know. And we don't really have anything in common. The truth is, I started talking to her in the library that day because I was hoping to get to know you."

Jamie stopped walking. "What? Why?"

"'cause you're smart and you're cute and you're nice and—oh, hell, enough talking." She grabbed the front of his shirt and pulled him into a kiss.

Jamie reflexively dragged them both behind the lilacs so they'd be screened from sight of the porch. *Enough talking,* he thought.

Chapter 22.

Sunday, September 26, 1955

Jamie stood in the door of the bathroom that led into Rob and Laurie's room. He'd wanted to talk, for once, especially to Laurie. Yom Kippur had ended at sunset. The twenty-four hours and more of fasting and praying had been, as usual, no physical challenge for Jamie, but this time the lightness and focus they gave him did not bring along with it that sense of mental and spiritual clarity he'd come to look forward to.

It's the Emmett Till business, he told himself. The fourteen-year-old Negro boy, who'd grown up in the North, had been beaten to death in Mississippi for being "fresh" to a white woman, and a jury had acquitted the men who'd done it without a second thought.

The horrendousness of the crime, the brutality of the beating, the senseless irrationality of the racism, had been enough to spiral Jamie into a series of nightmares. Mom had urged him into what she called "booster shots" of sessions with a counselor, but they'd been worse than useless.

Mrs. French kept prodding him to talk about his past so that, she said, they could explore the reasons behind his "obsession with discrimination" and his "irrational fear of persecution." When he'd been a child, he'd been both unwilling and unable to recall, even to himself, what had happened to him. Now that those dark realities were coming back to him, he thought he could try to communicate what they meant to him. But the woman actually thought he was exaggerating. The last straw came when she exclaimed skeptically, "Oh, come on; do you mean to tell me the whole time you were in that camp you never once had dessert?" Even Mom had agreed that his talking to the woman was useless after that.

But today something had happened that made him want to talk again. Several people in the congregation had come up to Laurie and apologized, not for anything they had done to him, but for the murder of Emmett Till. Jamie didn't know all of them, but he'd heard one, Mrs. Weissmann, refer slightingly to her maid as the *schwarze*, 'the black''; another couple he distinctly remembered staring with affronted expressions when Laurie had hugged Jamie at his bar mitzvah.

But there they were, apologizing as though they felt somehow complicit in what had happened halfway across the country, to a boy they knew nothing about except that he had dark skin. Jamie wanted to ask Laurie about that, about what it had felt like to him and whether he considered all white people responsible for Emmett Till—or all white Americans, anyway.

But he was too late. Laurie was already asleep. *Maybe tomorrow,* he thought, knowing the impulse would have disappeared by then. But Jamie still stood in the doorway, staring. Because Laurie wasn't alone in the bed: Robbie was with him, golden head just visible beyond Laurie's broad shoulder, Laurie's arm curved protectively around the younger boy as he nestled behind him.

Do they do that a lot? Jamie wondered. *Have they done it before? Is it just about being upset over Till?* And then, *Would they let me in?* He shook himself. *No, there's no room for me. And besides, I wouldn't want that. I couldn't sleep like that, all crowded next to somebody.*

You'll have to when you're married, Hymie, he reminded himself, then shook off the thought. Being married was some unimaginable state that would happen in the dim future to a future self he couldn't even picture at the moment. Laurie and Linda had gotten back together, but even they weren't talking about marriage yet. As he made his way back to the bed in his solitary room, he wondered, *Would I want to do that with Rima?* He thought of her warm arms, her lush breasts and fleshy hips, pressing against him all night.

He took a deep breath and shook out his shoulders. *No. I wouldn't be able to sleep like that. Besides, that would be like sex. That's different. What Laurie and Rob are doing isn't about sex, it's just... love.*

Pushing away the uncomfortable thought, he climbed into bed and said his prayers. He set his glasses on the nightstand and composed himself for sleep, stretching out comfortably on the crisp, cool sheets.

When he awoke deep in the night, the sheets were creased and hot, and wet with his sweat, though he lay shivering and curled in on himself. *Another nightmare, of course. But I must not have screamed this time; nobody else woke up. That's good.*

That's good, he repeated to himself as he made his way to the bathroom. He used the toilet, washed his hands and face, rinsed out his mouth. Back in the bedroom, he changed into fresh pajamas—the gray-striped ones Beth had given him—pulled his crumpled sheets straight, fluffed up his pillow. *I'm getting better,* he thought as he climbed into bed. *I don't need help every time, I can do this myself.*

He lay on his back, hands relaxed across his chest, concentrating on keeping his breathing slow and even while he focused on recovering his dream, the way Mom had taught him.

The usual. The camp, the barracks, the bodies pressed in around me, the sense of dread. The terror filtering in through the cracks in the wall boards along with the growing light of dawn: another day that might be the last day, another day of fear and pain and hunger. But this time there was something different—a flash of gold in the gloom. A golden head. A boy, or a man, leaning over him. "Come," he said in English. "I'm going to get you out of here."

In the dream, Jamie had slipped out of the packed shelf where he slept without disturbing the others, floating down to the filthy floor without effort, following his savior straight through the walls and into the free air. But the parade ground was not deserted in the early dawn; all the inmates, including the ones he'd just left behind in the barracks, were drawn up in ranks as if for roll call. The guards lined the platform before them; the gallows stood ready.

Jamie turned to the man beside him. It was Tank Lebo, in an SS uniform. "You said you'd take me out of here!" he cried.

"I am," the other replied calmly. "You don't belong here. You don't really belong anywhere, do you? So I'm going to set you free, and then you won't be anywhere—see?" He smiled delightedly and clasped Jamie's hand. "Trust me," he said.

"Yes," Jamie said, allowing himself to be led toward the platform. Then terror gripped him again and he tried to pull away. "No," he whispered. Then he screamed it: "No, I don't want to, I won't!"

He didn't realize he'd fallen asleep again till he woke up. It was Dad holding his hand, blond hair glinting in the light from the hall. "It's all right, son," Dad said. "You're here, you're safe. Your mother's coming; do you want to tell me what you dreamed meanwhile?"

"Just the usual," Jamie said, and hung on.

Chapter 23.

Saturday, November 6, 1955

Jamie tried to ignore the noise from the other boys' room; he wanted to study. *If I'm going to make it through high school in three years and get started with my real life, I need to be on top of things now. I can't be distracted.*

There'd been a lot of distractions from Laurie and Rob's direction in the weeks since the Till murder, though that event didn't seem to be the immediate source of the friction between them. Jamie wasn't sure what the source was, though, and not sure he wanted to get involved enough to know.

If this keeps up, I'll have no choice, he thought exasperatedly as the bickering in the other room rose to shouting. Silence fell suddenly, then a door slammed. Jamie got up to close his own door against whatever might happen in the hall, and saw Laurie stand irresolute for a minute and then disappear into Beth's room.

So Rob must be in their room, alone, he reflected, pausing before sitting down at his desk again. The notion that had come into his head on the night following Yom Kippur popped up again. *If there's a break between them, maybe there's room for me.*

He stood between the desk and the door to their shared bathroom with his weight on one foot, wondering whether he should go through. *What would I say to him, though? It's not like I usually go around asking how people are when they're upset.*

The decision was taken out of his hands when Robbie appeared in the doorway, as though Jamie's thoughts had conjured him. His hands were shaking and his pale face was blotched with red, though Jamie didn't think he'd been crying.

At Jamie's gesture, he came fully into the room, swiveled to face him, and said abruptly, "I want to know how you do it."

"Do what?"

"Not care about anybody."

Jamie sank back onto his desk chair, appalled.

Rob perched on the end of the empty second bed, frowning at Jamie's expression. "I don't mean 'not care,' exactly. I mean you never let stuff get to you. You're always so cool and, I don't know, together, sort of. Like nothing bothers you."

Jamie tilted his head to one side. "You mean like when I wake up screaming, covered in my own shit and vomit? That kind of cool?"

The blotches on Rob's face disappeared in a more general flush. "That's different. You can't help that."

"And you think I can help the other?"

Rob opened his mouth as if to speak, then left his jaw hanging as he thought over what Jamie had said. Slowly he closed it, staring down at his own knee and rubbing his forefinger over a small tear in his jeans. Finally he looked back at Jamie and said, as though it were a response to what had come before, "I hit Laurie tonight."

Jamie rocked back in his seat. "What do you mean, hit him?"

Rob huffed out a breath. "I mean I made a fist and punched him in the chest." He pressed a hand to his own chest, right above the heart. "He piled his books all over my side of the desk…"

"A punching offense if I ever heard one," said Jamie, only half joking.

Rob went on, heedless, "…and when I tried to move them, he shoved me out of the way! And that's just tonight. He's been awful to me for weeks."

"I have noticed he's been out of sorts," Jamie admitted cautiously. "I guess Mom would say he's been under a lot of strain."

"Well, so have I! He's not the only one who gets upset about stuff. Look at you, all the crap you've been through—I mean, actually been through, not just heard about it—and you don't act like that."

Jamie snorted. "First time I've been accused of being nicer than Laurie," he said. "The thing is, he lets himself feel things that happen to other people the way most of us only feel about ourselves. I don't know how he does it, or why, actually. I have trouble enough dealing with my own ghosts. But restricting my spleen-venting to cutting remarks doesn't make me Albert Schweitzer, you know."

"At least you don't go around shoving people."

"Or hitting them?"

Robbie flushed again. "I didn't know I was going to do that till after I did it. Can you feature that?"

"Yeah, I 'feature' it, all right. I have to sit on my impulses all the time, though. I can't afford to let myself do what I want to; that's why I seem so cool and unaffected a lot of the time."

"Why? What is it you'd want to do, if you could?"

"Kill," Jamie said honestly. "I'd hunt down everyone who ever hurt me or mine and kill them." He hadn't actually known he felt that until he'd said it.

Rob, though, seemed to think he was speaking metaphorically. He shrugged a little and nodded dismissively, still caught in his own drama. "Sometimes I'd like to kill Laurie," he said gloomily. "But I don't guess I will. Something has to change, though."

There's never going to be room for me between them. Jamie's thought was bleak. *Rob can't even really hear me.*

"Listen," he said. "I'm no peacemaker. Why don't you go talk to Beth? Let her be your UN ambassador?" He carefully didn't mention having seen Laurie go into her room earlier.

Rob looked startled. "But—but Beth is... I mean, I was always the one who took care of her." He rubbed his hands over his knees, thinking. "But yeah, I see what you mean. Yeah, it's worth the old college try, I guess." He pressed down on his knees and stood up.

At the door, he paused and looked back. "Hey, I didn't mean to lay a load on you," he said. "I didn't mean anything bad about, you know, you keeping stuff to yourself."

"No, I know," Jamie said. "Don't worry. I'm cool." He tried to think of something further to say, but Rob had already left.

CHAPTER 24.

FRIDAY, DECEMBER 9, 1955

It was both Shabbat and the first night of Hanukkah, so the table was awash in candlelight. Ruby had served her soft mashed-potato cakes with the roast chicken; Jamie had never had the heart to tell her they weren't authentic latkes.

Conversation at the table centered on Rosa Parks, the Alabama Negro arrested last week for refusing to give up her seat on the bus when the white section filled up. Jamie didn't quite understand the fuss; she wasn't the first black bus rider to do that, or to take the matter to court—a woman named Sarah Keys had gotten a favorable ruling regarding interstate travel just a few days before. But this Rosa Parks was soft-spoken and personable: attractive but not threatening. *I guess she'll make a good symbol for the fight against Jim Crow laws.*

Watching Laurie's eager face as the others discussed the implications, Jamie let his mind wander from the subject to the person across from him. Laurie had turned sixteen yesterday, and the birthday gift that had been the biggest success was Mom and Dad's paying for train tickets to Chicago next week so Laurie could visit his old grade school friend Tom Thumma. *Why's he so excited about it, though?* Jamie wondered. *He told me last year he hardly had anything in common with the guy any more.*

Depressed at this further evidence that he didn't understand people or the way they felt, Jamie pushed his chair back as the others got up to go into the living room. It was Beth and Joy's turn to help

114

with the dishes tonight; Jamie reached around them to take up the big brass Hanukkah menorah, its fast-burning candles already out, and move it to the front bay window where it would spend the rest of the week.

He set it on the broad sill and stood back, admiring it for a minute as the others filtered in and found seats. For a few days, at least, it wouldn't be competing with the Christmas tree. Once that behemoth was up in the other bay, the menorah would fade into relative insignificance. *Well, Hanukkah is a minor holiday,* he reminded himself. It still felt a little like being relegated to second-class status, though.

Jamie shook the feeling off and went to sit by Ruby on the long couch by the hall entrance as Dad lit the fire in the fireplace and Mom settled into the armchair in the corner, the reading lamp behind her shining on her dark hair as the other lights in the room were put out and the family hushed expectantly.

She was reading the final book of the Narnia series, *The Last Battle*. Jamie was glad the thing was finally going to be over. He was tired of the Christian imagery and the theological claptrap, though the others seemed to be enjoying it. This one in particular seemed heavy-handed and preachy to him, with an end-of-the-world plot and an extravagantly unlikely storyline.

Dad was sitting on one of the settees by the fireplace now, with his arm around Laurie, who was leaning against him. Rob sat at their feet; Laurie's long fingers were tangled in his silky hair. Whatever the crisis had been last month, they'd evidently resolved it. They'd gone to Dad with it, Jamie knew, and he'd told them about his history with his own brother, a brother none of them had known existed, that somehow helped Rob and Laurie get over their own problems. *Still no room for me,* he thought.

Then a word Mom had just read caught his attention. *Was that—yes, there it is again. There's a character called Emeth.* He could feel a fury build as she kept reading and it become clear this character was meant to be a virtuous pagan who thought he worshiped the demonic Calormene god but whose devotion was received by the Christ-like lion, Aslan. *How dare you?* he addressed the author mentally. *How dare you co-opt the Hebrew word for "truth" and give it to a character who's no doubt going to see the "light" before the end? We Jews are the ones who gave the truth to you Christians, and look what you've done with it, you bastard.*

Realizing he was working himself into an unreasonable frenzy, Jamie slipped out of the shadowy room and went into the hall bathroom to rinse his face and cool off. He still didn't feel like going back to be assaulted by more of the story, though—and that's what it felt like, an assault—so instead of heading back into the hall he slipped through the sliding door into the study.

There was no visible moon, but a lavender cast to the sky formed a backdrop to the snowflakes falling black against it. With the windows and the dim wash of light from the living room through the open study door to orient him, Jamie made his way to the couch in front of the fireplace in here—dark and cold, unlike the one in the other room. He wedged himself into a corner of the couch and pulled the afghan on the back down and around himself. From here, Mom's voice was just a soothing hum of undifferentiated sounds.

Why do I get so angry? The guy means well enough, I suppose. And it's fiction, and fantasy fiction at that—who cares what it says? Jamie thought about going upstairs to his cabinet, but it seemed like too much trouble, and would likely be too cold for comfort tonight. Besides, he didn't really want to be alone. *So what are you doing hiding in here, Hymie? Hoping they'll notice you're gone and come after you?* "Oh, please, Jamie, please come back, we miss you." *That's likely.*

Actually, they probably would if they knew you wanted them. You could try telling them. He shook his head. *They should know without me saying it.* That was unreasonable enough to shake him a little out of his anger and into a more generalized sadness, a familiar state that he sank into with some relief, curling up in the corner of the couch.

In an hour or so the lights came up in the other room and he could hear them all moving and talking quietly and saying goodnight as they made their way upstairs. *They don't even see I'm not there.* But after a few minutes, as the going-to-bed noises from upstairs tapered off, he heard footsteps coming back down.

Then Dad's voice came softly from the doorway. "Jamie? Are you in here?"

Jamie shifted and cleared his throat. That was all it took; Dad moved on into the room and sat on the other end of the couch.

After a while Jamie said, "I'm so angry. I'm angrier all the time, about things that happened longer and longer ago."

"You have a right to be angry," Dad said. "I understand that."

"You don't really," Jamie said miserably.

"What don't I understand?"

"How much I want to lash out, to hurt people, even people who haven't done anything to me. Maybe especially them… you. All of you."

Dad sighed. "Of course I understand that, honey."

Jamie said nothing, but his silence was loud.

Eventually Dad said, "Laurie says he told you and the others the story he and Rob heard from me, about my brother. What exactly did he say?"

"That one time after your father had been beating on you both, this brother we never heard of said you should make an alliance against him, or at least aside from him. He said your brother tried to hug you and you saw your father was watching and pushed him aside and didn't do anything to help him when your father whipped him for it." Jamie licked his dry lips and burst out, "Why didn't you ever tell me that? Why could you tell them the truth and not me? Did you think I wouldn't get it?"

Against the pale sky through the window, Jamie could see Dad's head drop to his hands. "In fact, you're the only one who could possibly understand the real truth," he murmured. "Laurie and Rob are too… innocent. They look up to me. I couldn't bear to tell them all of it."

So what am I, guilty? Jamie thought, then corrected himself: *No, tainted, that's what he means.* The idea gave him a bittersweet sense of communion with Dad. "'Show your enemy what you want him to see'," Jamie quoted, "'so he won't see what you don't want him to see.' Is that what you mean?"

Dad huffed a humorless laugh. "You took my advice and read Sun Tzu, I see."

"Yeah. But Rob and Laurie aren't your enemies."

"No. That makes it worse. I don't want them to really see me."

"You—you didn't tell them what really happened?"

"I lied to them," Dad said uncompromisingly.

"What part?" Jamie whispered, though he was starting to suspect the truth.

Dad turned toward him and reached for his hand. Jamie let him take it. "I've never told this to a living soul," Dad said. "Ruby knows, because she was there. And she told your mother. But I've never actually said the words, not to anyone." He took a deep breath. "Our father didn't whip Kevin. He made me do it." He started to cry aloud in short barking sobs.

Jamie was terrified. Part of him wanted to run away and hide, or at least get Mom or someone who was better at handling emotions than he was, which was almost anyone in the world. Another part of him exulted: Dad had told him something he hadn't told anyone else, not even Rob and Laurie. He trusted Jamie in this more than them. Most of him just felt an overwhelming pity, though.

But Dad started talking again. "No, I'm still lying," he said. "I'm trying to let myself off the hook with 'he made me do it.' He couldn't make me do anything. What he could do was hurt me if I didn't, so I chose to hurt Kevin instead. I'll never forget the look on his face when I picked up that belt, never as long as I live. My little brother. Oh, Kev. I'm so sorry."

Dad pulled a handkerchief out of his pocket, ghostly in the gloom, and held it over his face with his left hand while he cried and cried. With his other hand, he still held Jamie's tight. Jamie wondered uneasily whether he ought to do more, put his arms around him or something, but just that grip seemed to be enough.

The storm slowly ebbed. Dad's sobs dwindled to hiccups and gasps, and then to silence. His fingers tightened on Jamie's, then loosened. He patted his hand and his shoulder and took a deep breath. "Thank you, son," he said. "I know that wasn't easy or pleasant for you, but I needed to get it out and I appreciate your being there for me."

"But I didn't do anything. Shouldn't I get someone who can help, Mom or somebody?"

"Nobody can help," Dad said. "And you don't need to do anything. You've already done it. There's always a possibility in grief that our hearts will break in pieces, but there's also the possibility that they will break open. This is what life is for. Thank you for helping mine break open tonight." He pulled Jamie's head forward and kissed him on the forehead, then let him go and stood up. He yawned cavernously. "Boy, I could sleep for a week," he said. "How about you?"

"Me too," Jamie said.

Chapter 25.

The brother was here, actually here in the house. That's why Laurie had been so excited about going to Chicago: Mom had tracked down where the brother lived, with Ruby's help, and Laurie had gone to fetch him. He was shut in the study with Dad now; everyone else was in the living room, pretending to be interested in something else.

Jamie sat at the baby grand in the corner, but for once Bach didn't appeal to him. He sifted through the sheet music on the rack: "Unchained Melody." *Soppy. Goopy. Slush.* But even as he thought the scornful words, Jamie found his fingers starting to pick out the tune. His eyes followed along the lyrics: "Oh, my love, my darling... a long, lonely time..."

He let himself drift with the music, and suddenly the two men were in the room, red-eyed and smiling, and Dad was saying, "Children, this is your Uncle Kevin. I know you'll make him feel that he is welcome home."

Then everyone was smiling and joking and Ruby chivvied the two men off for breakfast as though they were ten years old. As the dining room door swung closed behind the three of them, Mom beamed at Laurie where he sat in the armchair by the window with Rob at his feet. "You did it," she said softly.

"I had help," he said, but he was smiling proudly. Rob punched him companionably on the knee, a wide grin on his face, too. The three of them gloated at each other while Jamie thought, *And why shouldn't they be proud? They really did something for Dad. Why didn't I think of that? Or why didn't they let me in on what was going on, at least?*

Judging from the pleased looks on their faces, the girls didn't mind only having found out after the fact that Laurie was going to go out and bring back Dad's brother. Joy was already bubbling over with questions about "Uncle Kevin" and plans to "reorient" him into the family. Celia and Beth kept her from dashing off to the kitchen to pepper him with questions while he ate breakfast. "Give them some time together," Celia said. "The two of them and Ruby were really close once, and they need to find their way back to that."

"Besides," Beth agreed, "I could hear in their voices that Dad and Uncle Kevin went through a pretty emotional hour in the study together. Let them calm down and have a little peace before we all start talking at them and pestering them."

"I wasn't going to pester them," Joy protested, but she settled back into her seat, reopening her book of Emily Dickinson poems.

Celia cleared up the clutter of her things for doing her nails, tucking her emery board and bottle of frost-pink polish into her flowered cosmetics bag and scooping up some stained cotton balls. "Come on," she said. "The sun is finally out. Let's get into that snow."

The others fell in with her suggestion enthusiastically. Jamie fended off their encouragement for him to join them, and soon there was no one in the room but Jamie and Mom.

"He told me how you helped him last week," she said without preamble. "He wouldn't have been able to do this today, I think, if not for that. He's been paralyzed with guilt for so long; you let him get it out, got him moving again."

Jamie felt something release in his chest, a tiny knot he hadn't been aware of till it was gone. Shrieks and cackles of laughter filtered in through the windows from outside.

"I'd better get out there," he said. "It's three against two, and Laurie and Rob never take the time to build their fort properly."

"Have fun," Mom said, getting up and heading toward the kitchen. Jamie almost changed his mind and went with her, but he suddenly felt shy at the thought of being with a stranger he knew such intimate things about, so he went on into the hall and started getting into his outdoor clothes.

Five minutes later, he was sorry he'd come out. Rob and Laurie, good-naturedly but implacably, shrugged off his suggestions about how to improve their "fort"—really just a drift that had formed over a fallen branch—and stockpile some snowballs. The girls were doing much better, using the corner of the garage for shelter; even Beth was able to score hits, Jamie's brothers were making so much noise. The boys' only advantage was that the girls couldn't throw quite as hard or far, so the boys could dance back out of range.

Then, to the boys' outraged dismay, Dad's head appeared around the corner right above Celia's, and he began a cannonade that drove the boys to ground. "We need to come up with a strategy," Jamie said, "and some tactics to implement it."

Robbie groaned. "This isn't a classroom, Egghead," he said. "I don't even know what the difference is between those two things, anyway."

Laurie's mouth opened, but before either he or Jamie could answer, a voice came behind them. "'Strategy without tactics is the slowest route to victory. Tactics without strategy is the noise before defeat.'"

Uncle Kevin had evidently come around the house from the other side and crawled across the yard to their tree branch-drift; he was crouched behind them, the front of his fancy camelhair coat plastered with snow.

"That's what *I* was trying to tell them," Jamie said, then, "You read Sun Tzu?"

Uncle Kevin gave a smile that was half a grimace. "It was required reading in our father's house." There was a pause while they returned a barrage from the girls and Dad, then Uncle Kevin said to Jamie, "What was your plan here?"

Jamie was torn between irritation that Rob and Laurie looked much readier to listen now that an adult was saying it, and pride that he was being asked for his opinion. "Well, their advantage is that the house gives them basically impregnable cover," he said. "Their weakness is that they're not strong throwers... but now Dad's there."

Uncle Kevin nodded. "I agree. But he's only one set of arms, against four of us. So..."

"So we have to lure them out from behind the house," Laurie said.

"Right." Uncle Kevin nodded as he lofted the balls he'd been forming while they talked. "And?"

"And build up our fort to be better protection," Robbie said, "and stockpile some ammo."

He and Laurie both gave Jamie embarrassed nods—it was what he'd been advising before Uncle Kevin appeared.

Uncle Kevin smiled knowingly at Jamie. "Ok, General," he said. "Let's get to it. *Gambattai!*"

The battle never did come to a clear conclusion. By the end of it they were just rolling around mashing snow in each other's faces. Dad surrendered when Rob managed to cram a freezing handful down the back of his collar and Uncle Kevin, red-faced with laughter and exertion, threw his hands up soon after and followed Dad into the house.

The others decided to build a snowman, but Jamie'd had enough. He stomped on the front step till he'd knocked most of the snow off, then went in and stripped off his soaked outer clothes in the vestibule. Even his socks were wet, and the lower legs of his chinos clung damply to his calves.

He'd have to go upstairs and change, but first he really needed to pee. He padded quickly across the hall in his bare feet and flung the downstairs bathroom door open. He was halfway into the tiny space before he realized someone was already in there—Uncle Kevin was just turning from the sink.

The sliding door to the study was open a couple of inches; Dad was on the other side of it, saying something about lunch.

It hit Jamie like a bolt: the story Laurie had repeated to him. They were around my age. Dad was there by the sink and Kevin stood where I'm standing and said they should be allies against their father and tried to hug Dad, and their father saw them from the study and…

He was in arm's reach of Uncle Kevin, of this familiar stranger, now, frozen. He watched the man's face change as he realized what Jamie was thinking of.

Dad's voice came from the study. "I said, do you remember Ruby's corn cakes? Kev? Kevin, are you all right in there?" He slid the door open, saw them there, and joined the frozen tableau.

Jamie broke it by gesturing mutely at the toilet. Kevin took a breath, then moved past Dad into the study. "Come through when you're done," Dad said.

When Jamie was finished, he opened the sliding door and heard Kevin say, "So he knows it all?"

"Yes," Dad said. "He's the only one of the kids who knows everything." He raised his voice a little. "Come in and join us, Jamie."

They were sitting on the couch, close together. Holding hands. Jamie lowered himself stiffly onto the smaller armchair by the fireplace and stared at them.

Uncle Kevin was glancing between him and Dad. Dad's face had that familiar patient, open, grave expression of his; Jamie knew he'd sit there like that for an hour if it took that long for Jamie to come out with what he was thinking.

Jamie wasn't conscious of thinking anything specific, actually, so he was surprised—and then horrified—at what came out of his mouth. "The *kapos,*" he said. Dad winced; Uncle Kevin looked puzzled. "At the camp," Jamie went on. "Jews, prisoners like us, they helped the SS. I was reading about it, about the trials they had after the war. They got extra food, better clothes. For that they would beat us, keep us in line." He stopped, choking.

Dad's eyes were closed now, screwed tight shut; Uncle Kevin's face was white. "No," he whispered. Then, louder, "Oh, God, no, Jamie. It wasn't like that. Listen to me, it wasn't! Your father was just a kid, and he wanted so much for our father to approve of him, we both did, it wasn't his fault…"

"Of course it was," Dad said harshly. "I should have been stronger." He tried to disentangle his hand, but Uncle Kevin held onto it.

Jamie found his voice again. "That's not what I meant," he croaked. He looked at Uncle Kevin. "You forgive him," he said.

"Yes, of course. I understand why he did it, what he had to fight. And I love him."

Jamie nodded. "I understand them," he said. "But I can't forgive them. I can't ever forgive them."

He saw Dad's fingers press Uncle Kevin's: a signal to let go. He got up and came and knelt in front of Jamie, taking his hands instead, gazing intently into his eyes. "You don't have to," he said firmly.

Jamie sighed and let go.

Chapter 26.

The others were making their usual fuss about Jamie's choice of birthday cake. "Is this dinner or breakfast?" Celia said, as she did every year.

"Leave him alone," Mom said, as she always did. "He gets to have what he wants on his birthday. We could all stand to have fewer sweets, anyway."

It's perfectly sweet enough, Jamie thought rebelliously, stabbing his fork at the yeasty, bread-like *kuchen* and dislodging one of its embedded raisins. He found the standard American-style batter cake with its coating of buttercream icing unbearably cloying. In fact, left to his own devices, he'd have skipped dessert altogether, but he knew that would cause more uproar than it was worth.

"Aren't you going to at least have some ice cream with it?" Rima asked from across the table.

She flinched when Jamie glared at her, and he tried to get a grip. *They just want you to be happy,* he reminded himself. *It's not their fault it's impossible to make you happy.*

Rima gamely kept a cheerful face through Jamie's present-opening in front of the living room fireplace, but Jamie could see that she was tense and uncomfortable—her body language mirrored his own. So when people were dispersing afterwards and she knelt to help him scoop up the discarded wrappings, he said in what he hoped was a natural tone, "How about showing me that passage you were telling me about in that calculus text."

Rima's shoulders immediately relaxed. "Sure," she said. "Is it upstairs?"

Two minutes later, they were pressed against the inside of the closed door to Jamie's bedroom, lips locked, tongues entangled. Jamie ran his hands down her sides, then grasped her hips and pulled her lower body closer to him. Rima arched up from the wood of the door, clutching Jamie's head by the hair. Jamie slid one hand down her leg, then up under the edge of her wool skirt, feeling the rough texture of her tights over her full, firm thigh.

Mom's voice came from the hallway outside. "Rima, your mother's here."

Jamie leaped away, gasping, as Rima called back in a creditably casual tone, "Thanks, Dr. Mac, I'll be right down." She tugged her skirt down, patted her thick, curly dark hair into place, gave Jamie a wicked smile, waggled her fingers at him, and disappeared.

Jamie backed against his desk, fighting to control his breathing. He bent forward with an arm across his thighs when Mom appeared in the doorway Rima had just left. They gazed at each other in silence for a minute, then she said mildly, "Leave the door open next time, sweetie."

"Sure," he croaked.

Jamie awoke the next morning with his heart pounding and a familiar stickiness in his pajama pants. He slipped the black silk yarmulke from his nightstand to his head and swiftly said the awakening blessing without touching his body. There was a confusing memory of a flash of blond hair in his head. He looked over toward the door where Rima had stood last night, sighed, and hauled himself out of bed to head for the shower.

Once shaved and dressed, he stood in the window gazing out at the rain on the larches by the back door as he recited the rest of his morning prayers. A stiff breeze tossed the bare branches and stripped the last dead leaves from the lilac bushes below. The drive to services would be tricky; Mr. Epstein would probably want to leave early.

Mom had said something about giving Jamie a driving lesson today, but it wasn't looking like the best weather for it. And Rima was supposed to come over, but she'd left so suddenly last night, they hadn't talked about what time. *And there are still Saturday chores to do,* he reminded himself. *Better get going.* He'd made up his mind back when he'd decided to start observing the Jewish Sabbath that he wouldn't try to opt out of the regular chore schedule, even though to follow the strict tradition he shouldn't be doing work on Saturdays; it was part of the compromise he'd made between his roots and his current life.

He was vacuuming the smaller guest room when Joy popped in front of him, waving her arms and mouthing, "Telephone," exaggeratedly. It was Rima. "I can't come today," she said. "Mom found out I haven't finished my English lit timeline project and threw a fit. If I get through it today, maybe I could come over tomorrow?"

"Sure," Jamie said.

"I'm sorry, Jamie, really."

"No, it's okay, I understand. School comes first. Listen, I have to get ready for services; the Epsteins will be here in fifteen minutes. Sometimes I feel like you're lucky your folks don't go every week, but I'm on the hook for it. See you tomorrow, maybe."

He got back from services just as a car pulled out of the driveway with Ruby in the passenger seat and her friend Mrs. Hodge driving. Jamie waved from under his umbrella and scurried into the house, changed out of his good clothes, and finished the vacuuming.

As he was storing the machine back in the lower compartment of the linen closet, Mom came out of her bedroom dressed in heels and holding her purse and gloves. "Oh, there you are," she said. "Listen, sweetie, this kind of day is why they invented the phrase 'rain check.' I really don't think it's a good day for a new driver to be on the road for the first time. But the girls and I are going into Harrisburg to see this Archibald McAllister House that's been opened to the public. Do you want to come?"

"No, thanks," he said. The prospect of gawking at some old, probably slave-built, mansion didn't interest him. *Besides, I'm not really a McAlister.*

Mom, misunderstanding, smiled indulgently. "The other boys weren't interested in looking at colonial architecture and old furniture either," she said. "Laurie's taken Linda to see *Carousel,* and Rob's gone uptown to Smith's to listen to the new records and look at sheet music. Will you be all right on your own?"

Jamie rolled his eyes and she laughed. "Ok, ok. You're a big boy—sixteen and a day, after all. Anyway, Dad's in the house if you need him, but he's holed up in the study working on a report, so you'll have to entertain yourself."

"Why God invented books," Jamie said, flapping a hand at her and heading back to his room.

He couldn't settle to reading though, not even the new Huxley novel Celia had given him last night. His day had gone from too many options to none at all. *But I'm virtually alone in the house; that almost never happens except for an hour on Sundays. I should take advantage of that somehow.*

He flopped over onto his back on the bed, sliding the Huxley onto his nightstand. *Who are you kidding?* he asked himself. *You know exactly how to take advantage of it.*

He got up, went through the bathroom into Rob and Laurie's room, and started gingerly searching through Laurie's nightstand. Baldwin's *Notes of a Native Son,* a few textbooks, a Heinlein novel, a tattered copy of Shakespeare's sonnets... *No, he probably wouldn't keep it out in the open, anyway.*

Jamie slipped to his knees and started to feel around under the bed. *Ah.* His fingers gripped slick pages, and he pulled out the *Playboy* Laurie's friend Tom had filched from his father for Laurie in Chicago. The cover slid into view: a blonde prone on a beach blanket with her bathing suit bra spread open under her; instead of the line of her top, her tan was lightened in the shape of the famous bunny. Jamie snorted at the conceit and scuttled back to his room with the magazine.

On his bed again, he set himself to studying as though for an exam. He glanced at the letters, leafed through the articles, but pored over a series of "Beach Sketches." When he got to the centerfold, a supposed "girl next door" improbably called Janet Pilgrim, he settled with serious attention.

The picture was posed as if from the point of view of the mirror over the vanity table she sat at. Her arms were crossed on the surface, her creamy ripe breasts pressed against them. She was wearing diamonds and holding a powder puff; her hair was blonde but her eyebrows were dark.

Who's that man silhouetted in the doorway supposed to be? Jamie wondered briefly, then went back to cataloguing the woman's charms. *Not like any girl I ever lived next door to,* he thought. *I suppose it just means she looks sort of wholesome, not like a hooker.* Not that Jamie really knew what a hooker would look like.

He followed Pilgrim's every curve with his eyes, then with an extended forefinger, as though he could actually feel the flesh. He focused hard, willing himself into the picture.

When a throat cleared behind him, he almost went through the roof. Clutching the magazine reflexively, he twisted around to see Laurie in the bathroom door, back from his movie with Linda and looking to relieve a little tension.

Before long they were side by side on the bed, propped on their elbows, going through the magazine together. *Two brothers,* Jamie thought. *Sharing a typical teenage boy experience. Why do I think we're not actually getting the same thing out of this, though?*

He was trying to think of a way to broach the subject, to find out what Laurie was thinking... or, more to the point, what he was feeling, when suddenly Ruby was in the room with the shaving soap Jamie'd asked her to pick up, snatching the magazine and ranting at them about the "filth."

Laurie tried reasoning with her; Jamie just curled in on himself, trying to escape the situation. Then she started blaming Laurie for "corrupting" Jamie; Jamie tried to contradict that, but she paid no attention. Then, to compound Jamie's utter humiliation, Dad came into the room and he and Ruby started arguing.

Finally, Ruby hissed at Dad something about his brother, Kevin, "being the way he is."

Dad said, "You think Kevin became homosexual from looking at pictures of naked women?"

She shifted her feet. "From thinking too much about this kind of thing, thinking the wrong way."

Laurie snorted at that, but Jamie was beyond irony. Part of him was thinking, *Dad's brother is queer?* and assimilating that into the rest of what he knew about them. Another part just wished he could magically transport himself into the upstairs cabinet and never talk to anybody about anything ever again.

Dad was saying, "I really don't think people 'turn' homosexual, Ruby. I know you don't agree with me, and most other people wouldn't either, but nothing 'made' Kevin the way he is but God, I'm sure of it. And it's normal for boys to be interested in girls' bodies, and vice versa, come to that."

Ruby wasn't having it. "This isn't proper to be talking about," she said.

She left the room eventually, and Dad kept talking to Laurie for a while, but Jamie couldn't listen. He stayed curled into a miserable ball when Dad kissed his head and went out, and when Laurie offered to leave the magazine with him, Jamie refused.

Finally alone again, he tried to sort out his feelings—*No, forget feelings, THINK!*

I was embarrassed about being caught at it, by Ruby and then by Dad, but there was something more than that. What was it? He'd been lying there by himself at first, staring at page after page of buxom female pulchritude, then next to his brother, listening to Laurie's breath speed up and sensing his body tense with excitement. He'd wanted to ask Laurie about what he was feeling, but Ruby interrupted them. *So what did I want to ask him? I think it was, why wasn't I excited? I was last night, with Rima.*

He thought and thought about it, but came to no answer.

CHAPTER 27.

FRIDAY, MARCH 30, 1956

A burst of laughter from the dining room made Jamie shift uneasily where he and Rima half-lay, half-sat on the living room settee. The others were coloring Easter eggs in there; ordinarily, Jamie would have joined them, but the parents and Ruby were out and this seemed too good a chance to have some time making out with Rima. He'd made a sarcastic remark about pagan practices, but Laurie had laughed in his face and pushed him toward Rima.

He still felt a little odd being out here with her instead of in with them, though. After all, Linda was helping with the egg coloring. *Not the same thing, Hymie,* he told himself. *She's... one of them.*

One of them? he mocked himself. *You mean, one of the people who helped you have the Passover seders this week?*

Still, there was something oddly relaxing about the way it obviously never occurred to Rima that they should be taking part in anything to do with Easter. Then he heard the garage door rumble; Ruby must be home. Jamie wasn't sure where he was with her since the *Playboy* incident, so he'd been avoiding her.

The chatter from his brothers and sisters in the other room sounded like they were having fun, and Ruby would probably be putting together some lunch, but when Jamie disentangled himself from Rima, he took her hand to lead her to the comparative quiet of the TV room behind the front staircase.

The couch in here was narrow and shabby, but it was solid enough. It didn't take long for Jamie to sink himself back into the sensuous oblivion of Rima's willing embrace. They had taken their make-out sessions up a notch since Jamie's unsatisfying encounter with the Playmate of the Month. Now, when Jamie slid his hand up under Rima's sweater, she reached behind herself and unclipped her bra to give him easier access.

Her own hands were all over him—all over him, except at the one place he both craved and feared her touch. It felt as though that would be some kind of irreversible step, as though for either one of them to venture below the waist would commit them to something neither seemed ready for.

His mouth had left hers and was traveling down her neck toward the V of her sweater collar when a shift in the distant sounds of the family told him they had finished with the eggs and were in the kitchen cleaning up. "They'll be coming looking for us," he said hoarsely. "They'll probably think it'd be funny to catch us like this."

"Let's go to my house," she said, pulling away and re-fastening her bra.

Sure enough, by the time they had their coats on, Laurie and Linda were in the hall. While Rima talked with them about some friend of Linda's, Jamie shifted his feet, hoping they wouldn't be roped into driving Linda home.

They were saved by Mom coming in the front door behind them; Linda evidently wanted to talk to her about this girl Sydney. Jamie could see that Laurie was relieved, too—they smirked knowingly at each other as Jamie hustled Rima out the door to Mom's standard "Drive carefully!" warnings.

But once they were in the car, Jamie almost wished Linda were with them. At least then there wouldn't be this thick silence that had developed. He masked his discomfort by exaggeratedly craning forward to gaze through the windshield. In fact, he was nervous to be driving in the rain after just a couple of lessons, even the short distance to Rima's house in Carlisle.

He actually couldn't think of anything to say. When they talked, it was usually about schoolwork, and nothing came to mind on that subject. "Um," he ventured, "how was Passover at your grandparents'?"

"Boring, they made me sit at the kids' table," she said. "I already told you that, Jamie."

"Oh, right, I forgot."

There was another silence, then out of nowhere she said, "Do you like me?"

"*What?* How can you ask me something like that?"

"I'm asking you."

He pulled up at a stop sign and looked across at her, but she had her head turned away. "Rima, what do you think I... I mean, we were just..."

"Yeah, we were just," she said. Her voice was thick with held-back tears; he prayed she'd keep holding them back.

Almost as though she'd heard his wordless plea, she took a deep breath, straightened around, and said in a clearer tone, "We spend most of our time together these days on second base, and don't get me wrong, I like it as much as you do, but we never seem to do anything else."

"What else did you want to do?"

"Don't make like a cube, Jamie. You know what I'm talking about."

He pulled up in front of her house and killed the engine. "Ok," he admitted. "I do know—in fact, I was thinking something along those lines myself a few minutes ago. But Rima, of course I like you. I wouldn't just—"

136

"I'm not just the town pump, you know."

"Rima! Why would you say a thing like that? You're the smartest girl I know! And you're classy, and pretty, and nice—"

Now she really was crying. "Nobody else thinks those things about me."

Jamie was bewildered; it seemed self-evident to him. "They don't?"

"Well, the smart part, maybe, for whatever that's worth."

"You called me 'cute' once. You think anyone else in the known universe thinks that about me?"

"So we're together because we're a couple of losers?"

Jamie's head was starting to hurt. "We're together because we like being together. Can't that be enough? For now, anyway? We're just kids, Rima, this doesn't have to be *Romeo and Juliet.*"

Rima found a crumpled tissue in her coat pocket and blew her nose, a long inelegant honk. It was one of the things Jamie liked about her, that she never put on airs and graces. He gave her a genuine smile.

She smiled back, snorting a little. "Some Romeo and Juliet we'd make," she said. "Look, Jamie, I know it was my idea for us to come to my house, but I'm thinking I'd just better go in by myself."

"Probably just as well," he agreed. "I should be getting back before Shabbat, anyway."

"Ooh," she said, "now that I think of it, I didn't smell Ruby's chicken roasting this afternoon."

"Good Friday," he said. "The goyim don't eat meat then. We'll be having fish."

"Fish and matzo, urgh," she said. "Want to see if I can wangle an invite for you here?"

"No, thanks," he said. "I should be there with them. Besides, it's only food."

"You're a sweetheart," she said, pecking him on the cheek, then jumping out of the car and dashing through the rain to her door before he could move.

"I am?" he said to the empty car. He thought of a novel he'd just read. *Forster was right. The Eternal Feminine leads us a pretty dance.*

Shaking his head, he started the car and headed home.

CHAPTER 28.

SUNDAY, MAY 13, 1956

A thunderstorm was brewing but had held off so far. The air was hot and heavy. Jamie lay on his bed reading *The Merchant of Venice*. The house was quiet, with Beth at Meeting and the others all at Mass, but Jamie was uneasily aware that he wasn't alone in it as usual. Laurie's friend Roscoe had come to stay for the month so he could finish out the school year here even though his mother and newly paroled father had moved to Chester.

You should talk to him, Hymie, he told himself. *You know how it is to feel that out of place.*

Roscoe had been hostile and combative, sneering at the creature comforts—the big house, the ample food, the books and records—and condescending to all of them as pampered and sheltered from the harshness of what he called "the real world." Except for Ruby: Ruby he avoided even making eye contact with, as though he couldn't acknowledge someone who didn't fit his neat, bleak vision.

But Jamie was drawn to him. He appreciated his mordant sense of humor, though it had a blunter edge than Jamie's own sardonic wisecracks, and he sympathized with Roscoe's cynical world view.

Roscoe and Dad had had a blowup at the beginning of the visit, when Roscoe had skipped Shabbat dinner and stayed out till all hours without telling anyone where he was. Laurie had helped them resolve it, in terms of Roscoe's uneasy relationship to Dad's

139

authority, but it suddenly occurred to Jamie that maybe it wasn't just happenstance that the triggering incident had meant Roscoe wouldn't be present for the Jewish Sabbath that night.

At the one night before last, he'd gone along with all the rituals, but he'd kept staring at Jamie. When Dad started talking about a Jew who'd helped found the NAACP back at the beginning of the century, Roscoe had scoffed dismissively, but he'd seemed familiar with the history of Jewish involvement in the civil rights movement.

Maybe there's a conversation opener. Jamie got up and made his way down the hall to the larger guest room, where he stood in the doorway. Roscoe was lying on one of the twin beds, idly tossing a tennis ball into the air and catching it again.

"Do you think Shakespeare meant Shylock to be a sympathetic character?" Jamie asked.

Roscoe tossed the ball a couple more times, then cupped it against his breast and turned his head towards Jamie. "Does everybody in this family talk about books every minute of every damn day?"

Jamie shrugged and twisted his lips. "Pretty much," he said. "For one thing, it seems like a safe way to get into things without getting too emotional. Though I wouldn't guess Laurie's too worried about that."

"First time he spoke to me, he started with *Uncle Tom's Cabin.*"

"Ah. Well, there I guess he'd want to not get too worked up."

"'Too worked up,'" Roscoe repeated scornfully. He started tossing and catching the ball again.

"So," Jamie persisted, "Shylock?"

"I ain't read no frigging *Shake-speeeer,*" Roscoe sneered.

"Bullshit," Jamie said. "I heard you Friday night. When I tossed the piece of blessed challah at you, you muttered, 'Hath not a Jew hands?'"

Roscoe flicked the tennis ball at Jamie, who flinched away and let it fall to the floor, where it rolled under the dresser.

"So, no, then," Roscoe said. "'S why you throw bread at people?"

"It's about not treating people at the table like mendicants... er, beggars."

"I know what the word means," Roscoe snarled.

"So stop pretending to be—well, a mendicant," Jamie snapped back. "Anyway, it's also tied in with the custom of handing bread to a mourner, so you don't want to do that at the Shabbat table. But I've read that some people say it's forbidden to throw the challah, so I guess it depends on your own custom. I got it from the Epsteins, the people who drive me to services on Saturdays."

"Why you have to get it from them?" Roscoe asked, sitting up. "Why not do what your real parents did?"

Jamie hesitated, chewing his lip, then stepped forward and folded back his shirtsleeve, thrusting his arm in front of Roscoe. Roscoe gazed at the numbers tattooed there, then up at Jamie. Their eyes held for a long, speaking moment.

The front door banged open. The others were home.

"Come on," Jamie said. "Time for pancakes. And since it's Mother's Day, there'll be extra treats."

Roscoe got up, cramming his feet into a pair of ragged sneakers, and followed Jamie downstairs.

Mom was standing at the hall mirror taking off her hat. "Hi, boys," she said cheerily. "Roscoe, if you haven't called your mother yet, you might want to do that now. It'll be half an hour or so by the time Sean gets changed and has the pancakes going."

Joy popped in from the living room. "Mom, where's that tablecloth with the daisies on it? Ruby wants me to use it 'cause it looks festive and spring-like, but it isn't in the drawer with the others and she's in her room changing."

"We hang it because it wrinkles so easily," Mom said. "Come on, I'll show you."

As they disappeared toward the dining room, Jamie said, "I better go with them; it's my turn to help today. You can call your mom on the upstairs phone if you want more privacy. In fact, the cord'll reach into Laurie and Rob's room if you want to close the door behind you; they won't mind."

Roscoe shrugged. "Not going to call, anyway," he said. "What's the point?"

"'What's the point'? To wishing her a happy Mother's Day? She's your mother, Roscoe." *Listen to you, Hymie, giving relationship advice.*

The look Roscoe gave him was poisonous. "What you know about it, honky?"

Jamie almost backed off. Then he remembered their moment of understanding in the bedroom, when he showed Roscoe his concentration camp tattoo. He held Roscoe's gaze with the same intensity they'd shared then.

"I know my mother ended up as a pile of ashes in a Nazi oven," he said, though he didn't know that, not for sure. Still, it felt true enough in the face of Roscoe's seeming indifference. "I don't know what your beef is with your mother; I don't pretend to know what troubles you've got or what your relationship's like. I only know your mother is still alive. Call your mother, Roscoe."

Roscoe's eyes flickered and dropped. He turned and trudged up the stairs, shoulders bent. Jamie stood and watched till he reached the top and turned right, toward the phone, rather than left to the spare room.

There was the sound of running water from the hall bathroom beside him. The door opened and Laurie came out.

"You heard," Jamie said, looking at his face.

"I heard," Laurie said, and squeezed Jamie's shoulder as he passed on his own way up the stairs.

Jamie turned to go help Joy set the table, an unfamiliar glow of satisfaction warming his belly.

CHAPTER 29.

SATURDAY, MAY 26, 1956

One of Rima's homeroom classmates was hosting the sock hop. Jamie didn't really know her, but he didn't much care. He felt he'd done his part by donning the ludicrously loud red and green argyle knee socks Celia had gleefully lent him; Rima had dyed macaroni sewn in patterns all over her white bobby sox. There'd be some kind of prize-giving later.

Meanwhile, Jamie was content here in the corner of the Mumper girl's family room, half hidden by a big potted philodendron, excavating for Rima's tonsils. *This is right,* he told himself. *This is normal. I'm supposed to feel this way.*

After their conversation in March, their relationship seemed to have turned a corner, though Rima still had occasional resurgences of anxiety over it. They had made that all-important move to below-the-waist petting, which seemed to further cloud the issue; Jamie was uneasy about it, and felt oddly distant from what they were doing sometimes, but it felt so good that he resolutely pushed his doubts aside.

Now he slid a hand up under Rima's blouse, pulling it free from her skirt waistband. Her bra was taut and full, heavily stitched, her breasts packed into it coming almost to a point. She thrust forward into his hand and moaned a little. The stirring in his groin felt reassuring, for some reason. He opened his eyes so he could peer through the thicket of Rima's dark, curly mane and remind himself

144

that she was not blonde. *A Jewish girl. A nice Jewish girl.* Not like Janet Pilgrim. *Or Tank Lebo.* Where did that thought come from? He closed his eyes again.

A theatrical cough came from somewhere to his left: Mrs. Mumper, standing there with an expression at once amused and disapproving. "Rima, we have plenty of chairs," she said not unkindly but firmly. "I think you'll be more comfortable in one of them than in Jamie's lap."

Rima, cheeks flushed, jumped up immediately, leaving Jamie to cross his legs and hunch over in an attempt to cover the evidence of his waning arousal. But Mrs. Mumper had already turned away and was briskly organizing a party to go up to the kitchen and carry down bowls of potato chips and Chex mix, and ice to replenish the washtub of Cokes in the corner.

A couple of guys looked resentfully at Jamie as he continued to sit at what must have looked like ease, but he really couldn't safely stand up quite yet, so he covered his discomfort with a feigned obliviousness that he suspected looked snooty. But any unpleasant interpretation was better than exposing his vulnerability, so he kept his legs crossed and his face indifferent.

After a while he was able to get up and dance a little with Rima, a song called "Heartbreak Hotel" by somebody with the unlikely name of Elvis Presley. The song was everywhere; Jamie'd heard it dozens of times in the past couple of months, but he still couldn't decipher many of the words. The gliding, mournful sound and the blood-pounding echo effects were stirring, though, and it was slow enough to let them shuffle around in a full-body clinch without attracting undue disapproval.

By the time he dropped Rima at home, it had started to rain. He grabbed a quick kiss under the overhang that ran across the front of her house, then her mother came to the living room picture window and rapped on the glass. Rima gave an exasperated sigh and waved him off as she let herself inside.

Jamie dashed back to the Pontiac, drove through the dark, slippery streets of Carlisle, and down the twisty rural road that led to Pine Springs. By the time he pulled into the driveway, it was pouring. He didn't have an opener with him for the new automatic garage door, so he left the car in the driveway and braved the few yards to the front door, holding the sport coat he'd worn for the party over his head.

In the front hall, he slung the heavily water-spotted coat on the closet doorknob and toed off his sodden shoes. Dad came out of the study and looked at Jamie's feet. "Nice socks," he said drily.

Jamie lifted his toes in their garish red and green and shook his head. "We didn't win," he said. "A couple of kids—or I guess she did them both, really—had socks with all this sort of embroidery stuff all over them, with those, what are they, sequins stuck on and hearts and flowers and little beads… must have taken her hours. I don't see the point, really. They got a five dollar gift certificate to Smith's, so they can buy a couple records each."

"Did you have a nice time, anyway?"

"I guess."

"You don't know whether you enjoyed yourself?"

Dad cocked his head to one side; Jamie stared at his socks. After a minute, Dad went back into the study, leaving the door open. Jamie followed almost immediately.

Dad had flipped off the overhead light and sat down on the old blue couch. It had been warm today; there was no fire, but Dad gazed at the empty fireplace as though he could see the flames of the past there. His desk lamp cast a soft glow over half the room and left half in shadow.

Jamie sat down on the other end of the couch. *Jump, Hymie,* he told himself, as he often did when there was something he had to deal with but didn't want to. He jumped. "I think there's something broken in me," he said. "I don't act right."

"It seems to me you act just fine," Dad said. Jamie huffed impatiently and Dad turned toward him and went on, "I understand what you mean. Yes, it's true that what has happened to you—what has been done to you—has affected you in ways that most of the kids your age, or American adults, for that matter, can hardly imagine. Those things have helped shape you into the person you are. Everyone's unique, of course, but you're a little farther out of the ordinary mold than most."

He reached across and gripped Jamie's elbow. "But *you are not broken,*" he said intensely. "You can use those ways in which you're different, your self-containment, your keen intellect and your ability to use it even in stressful situations, in positive ways. These are the gifts your travails have won you."

His words seemed to lodge in Jamie's chest, warming and loosening deep frozen parts there. At the same time, though, they were missing the spot that was most grating on him, that was scorching, not cold.

"I want to have sex," he blurted.

Dad sat back. "Whoa," he said, shaking his head. Then he said it again: "Whoa. I mean it. Hold up there, son. You're barely sixteen years old."

"How old were you?"

"That's not really the point, but I'll tell you. I was eighteen. I had run away from home a few months before, and some of my shipmates took me to a brothel. And there were a couple of casual contacts in the years after that. No one else after your mother, though."

Dad pressed his fist against his mouth for a moment, then said, "I will also tell you something that may seem old-fashioned, though: I wish I had waited. I wished on my wedding night that I could come to your mother with the same... purity she brought me—and I'm not talking about virtue just now, I mean purity of the experience, that we could share the wonder of that first time, with all the awkwardness and fumbling that novices would find themselves suffering, that we could be first and only for each other."

He leaned forward again and took both Jamie's hands in his own. "And I wish that for you, son." He looked keenly into Jamie's face and asked, "Is it Rima? Or just any girl?"

Any girl? "I don't know," Jamie said. "It just feels like, when I'm with her, there's something missing, and if it's not something wrong with me, then it must be something about what we're doing—or not doing. QED."

Dad smiled. "It's not a math theorem, Jamie. You can't parse out love, or even sex, like an equation."

"What should I do, then?"

"What does Rima think?"

"She's worried that we're going too far already. But she still likes what we do, I can tell."

"Why wouldn't she?" Dad said. "She's a normal girl, I'm sure she has normal reactions to physical stimuli." He linked his hands behind his neck and stretched his head back, looking up at the ceiling, then let out a gusty breath and let his hands flop back into his lap.

"This worries me, Jamie, I tell you frankly. And the reason is precisely that you are so adult intellectually, and you've seen so much of the horrors of the world, but emotionally you're—young, you haven't developed yet. I'm afraid you'll get yourself into a situation where you feel out of control, and you'll get hurt. And you can so easily hurt Rima, and that would make you feel terrible, I know."

Then he did a very odd thing. He leaned forward and picked up Jamie's feet, in their ridiculous garish socks, and hauled them into his own lap. He started rubbing them, pressing his thumbs into the pads behind Jamie's toes and kneading his arches with the heels of his palms.

After a second of shock and embarrassment, mostly thinking of how smelly his feet must be after a night of dancing and then squelching around in wet shoes, Jamie registered what this was doing to him physically. He felt as though binding cords were coming undone all over his body, leaving him limp as a stringless puppet and feeling as though he were floating. The tension the conversation had generated drained out of his shoulders and the skin over his temples.

"Where did you learn to do that?" he gasped.

Dad smiled wryly. "From a lady in a brothel," he said. "One I did not have sex with. In North Africa, after we lifted the siege of Malta. She told me I didn't need a woman, I needed to relax. Wise woman."

"I'll say," Jamie said fervently.

Dad finished the impromptu massage with a few long, firm strokes over the tops of Jamie's feet, then wrapped his hands around Jamie's ankles. "Two things I'd like to ask of you," he said. "First, may I tell your mother about this conversation? I'd like her advice and insight."

"So would I," Jamie said slowly, thinking about it. "But—could I maybe put a condition on it? You can talk about it with her, and tell me what she thinks, but I'm not ready to talk directly to her about it. It's just too embarrassing."

Dad smiled. "Sure, I understand, and she will, too."

"And the other thing you wanted to ask? Was it about using condoms? Because I remember our talk about that."

"Good, but that wasn't it." Dad's face got grave again. "I'm not going to ask you for a promise, because I know you take promises seriously, and I also know that things can happen in the heat of the moment that neither of you might intend. But I want to ask you to try very hard not to let anything… irrevocable happen without talking to me first. I promise you, for my part, that if you've really made up your mind to go ahead, I won't try to pressure you. But I'd like the chance to help you through what I'm afraid could end up being a trying experience for you."

Jamie didn't have to think about that one; a wave of relief went through him. "Yes!" he said so enthusiastically it made them both giggle. *Me, giggling?* he thought in disbelief. Then he said, "Talk about not being normal: I wonder whether there's any other guy my age on the planet who'd have a conversation like this with his father."

"Your mother says normality is overrated," Dad answered, lightly slapping Jamie's feet off his lap onto the floor.

"Lucky for us," Jamie said, getting up off the couch.

Dad turned off the desk light and they went out into the hall and up the stairs with Dad's hand on the back of Jamie's neck.

Chapter 30.

Jamie surfaced from a restless sleep to the sound of soft tapping on his door. "Come in," he said groggily, reaching for his glasses. As he slipped them on, he suddenly remembered what it had been like being fitted for his first ones, back when he was a little kid, new to America and everything else: how the world had suddenly taken on a clarity that seemed magical. "I can see the leaves," he'd said wonderingly to Mom.

Now here came Beth into his room; she would never see at all. *Don't kid yourself, Hymie,* he thought. *She sees plenty.*

"What's up?" he said, as much to orient her with the sound of his voice as anything.

She moved past him to the window seat and sat facing him. "Sorry if I woke you," she said. "It's just that I can't find Mom or Ruby or Dad. I heard you answer the phone late last night, and then get Laurie. He just came in an hour ago and went straight to bed. I thought you might know what's going on."

"It was Linda," Jamie said. "She was pretty upset. I think it had something to do with that friend of hers, that Sydney. Rima said Sydney's been acting weird, running out of classes and sulking in corners. Laurie took Mom and Ruby with him to Linda's. I don't know why they didn't come back with him, or where Dad is."

They sat in silence for a minute, thinking about it, then Beth rubbed her hands over her knees and stood up. "I'm going to fix myself some cinnamon toast," she said. "Want some?"

"Sure," Jamie said. "I'll be down in a few."

She'd made Ovaltine to go with the toast, he discovered when he sat in the breakfast nook after quickly washing and dressing and reciting his morning prayers. Sipping the hot, sweet liquid brought him back again to those first weeks in this house and the simultaneous feelings of safety and strangeness.

"Penny for them," Beth said.

"Hmm? Oh, just thinking about the first time I tasted Ovaltine."

Beth dipped a crust in her drink and slurped it into her mouth, spattering a few drops on the tabletop. Jamie reached across with his napkin and quietly blotted them up as she said, "You said something last night at supper about the first time you slept in a room by yourself, but then you seemed to think of something else and broke off what you were saying."

"I remembered that I did have a room of my own, Before." He could see from her face that he didn't need to explain when he meant.

There was a question in her look, though. "You really remember that far back?"

"Just flashes. That one came back to me a while ago, in a nightmare about running away from the Gestapo."

Beth stirred the crumbs on her plate with a delicate finger. "I don't remember anything from my Before," she said. "My whole life seems to have started with me and Robbie on the streets in Harrisburg, trying to keep warm and searching for things to eat."

"But trying to keep warm was worse, right?" Jamie said. "You get numb to feeling hungry, but when you're cold you can't think about anything else."

"That's right," she said. "The most wonderful thing anyone ever gave me was the winter coat I got after we came to live here."

"New clothes in general," he agreed. "They made me feel like... like..."

"Like it was possible to live, to do something instead of just having things done to you."

He stared at her in shock. "God, I'm really stupid," he said. "It never occurred to me that you would understand things like that. I think of all the rest of you as——"

"Soft?"

"I'm sorry." She shrugged and he went on, "I guess I get to thinking that, since nobody can understand everything that happened to me—hell, I don't myself—then nobody can understand anything. Roscoe set me a little straight on that, but evidently not straight enough."

"Laurie's friend? What do you mean?"

"When he stayed here last month. I don't know how much you saw, since you were still at school most of that time, but he was pretty hostile and angry at everybody."

"From what Celia told me, his father just got out of prison and his mother has a drinking problem."

"Right, but I don't think that was all of it. It's about his being black, and the crap most Negroes have to go through on a daily basis. You know, he was lurking around at David's funeral right after he and Laurie first became friends, and when he stayed here I asked him why, since he never met David. He said Laurie had told him about David after Mom went over there the day he died—how David's father was in prison like Roscoe's, and that then when Mom went

153

running off to try to take care of whatever was going on with David, Roscoe wondered what that would be like, to have someone do that for him. He came to the cemetery to see how we were all taking it, what it would be like to be one of us. But he thought David dying was like a sign that he wouldn't make it, either."

"Poor kid."

Jamie shifted around on the breakfast nook bench. "Sure. But the point is, I suddenly felt like I had more in common with Roscoe than either one of us had with Laurie, even though they're both black. Roscoe and I both know what a crappy place the world is, and how lousy most people are. We know it in our bones; Laurie only knows it from books. And I guess you know it, too."

Beth got up and started clearing the dishes. There were only a few, so Jamie didn't move to help her, just scrubbed some more at the smears of her spilled Ovaltine as she said, "I know what you're talking about, that's true. But I don't think I feel the same way about it. 'In spite of everything, I still believe that people are really good at heart.'"

"Anne Frank," he said, recognizing the quote. "But that was before they hauled her and her family off to Belsen."

"But until then, people had risked their lives to keep them hidden."

Before Jamie could respond, the door from the dining room opened and Mom and Ruby came in. They weren't wearing hats or gloves, but were just as they'd left after hastily dressing last night. Ruby went to the sink and took the breakfast dishes out of Beth's hands; Beth came back to the table as Mom slumped down on her own chair at the end. "Did Laurie get back all right?" Mom asked.

"A couple of hours ago," Beth said. "He went straight to bed."

"Good. He was exhausted. I sent him back and had him ask your father to meet us at the hospital. He dropped us off just now and went on to the Depot."

"Hospital? What's going on?" Jamie demanded.

"If it's all right for you to tell us," Beth put in.

"I think it is," Mom said. "Sydney's not my patient. But I would like you two to keep this confidential; it's not something to gossip about." They nodded and she went on, "She took an overdose of drugs last night. I don't know whether it was a serious suicide attempt or a cry for attention, but as I said to her father on the long distance phone, if she would go that far to get attention, then she really needs it."

"Will she be ok?" Beth asked.

"Physically, yes. They pumped her stomach and got her comfortable before we left. Emotionally—it depends on what kind of help she gets, and how much she can accept it." Mom turned in her seat. "Ruby, please leave that. The children can do it. You've been up all night, and did most of the work before we got to the hospital."

"I'm happier busy," Ruby said. "Anyway, I'm done now." She set the last mug in the dish drainer. "I think I will try to get some sleep, though."

"Would you like me to make you a cup of tea?" Beth asked. "Either of you? Or maybe some Ovaltine?"

"No, thank you, child," Ruby said, running a hand across Beth's shoulders as she passed on the way to her rooms. "I need rest more than anything."

"Me, too," Mom said, pushing up from her chair. "Are you two all right?"

"I'm fine," Beth said, getting up too and putting her arms around Mom. "Feeling lucky to have this family." Mom held her tight for a minute, then let go as Beth said, "I think I'm going to go up and read a little."

She went up the back stairs and Mom turned to Jamie. "How about you, sweetie?" she asked.

He knew she wanted to hug him, too, but the thought of it made him feel too vulnerable; she understood him too well. In his current mood, her embrace might even make him break down, and he didn't want to risk that. He did need to be touched, though. He suddenly craved touch the way inmates at the camp craved bread.

"I'm going to see Rima," he said.

CHAPTER 31.

WEDNESDAY, AUGUST 15, 1956

The attic cabinet was too hot to relax in, and Jamie was beginning to realize he'd just about outgrown his need for it, anyway. It was starting to feel more confining than sheltering. And in this weather, even the music room felt stuffy. Jamie had just gotten to the bend in the back stairs, heading for his room, when he heard a tinkling crash from the kitchen below, then Laurie's voice shouting, "God damn it to hell!"

Jamie dashed down to see what was wrong. Laurie stood in the middle of the kitchen surrounded by a circle of spilled liquid and broken glass. Jamie recognized the shards of the round-bellied yellow pitcher they had used for orange juice for as long as he could remember. "Oh, you broke the pitcher," he lamented.

Laurie gave a wordless snarl and Jamie looked at him in surprise. Then he realized that his brother was barefoot, standing there amid the splinters of glass and stickiness. "Sorry," he said. "Hang on a minute."

He edged around the spill to the closet by the basement stairs and got out the broom and dustpan. "Just let me get the glass out of the way before we worry about the juice," he said, sweeping a path through the worst of it.

Laurie gingerly made his way along the path and then over to the back door, where his discarded shoes and socks lay. Then he stood glancing back and forth between his sticky feet and the heavy brogans he'd worn to his summer job at the Navy Depot.

"Go on and get cleaned up," Jamie told him. "I'll clear up here."

By the time Laurie got back, changed into shorts and t-shirt as well as sneakers, Jamie had managed to corral all the broken glass and dump it into the garbage can beside the sink. He rinsed the juice out of the broom bristles and sluiced out the dustpan and put them both outside the back door to dry as Laurie fetched the mop and pail and set to cleaning the juice off the floor.

"I'm sorry I made that crack about the pitcher," Jamie said, sliding into the breakfast nook. "It was just that I was surprised, and it's been around so long. You didn't get hurt, did you?"

"No, not a bit," Laurie said. "And I'm the one who's sorry, growling at you like that. I was just mad about another spill I had to clean up today, and on edge about that; this one was just the frosting on the cake."

"You spilled something at the Depot?"

"Not me. A new lieutenant commander named Angstrom. He dropped his coffee in the hall and automatically decided I was the guy to do his scut work." Laurie finished the mopping, rinsed mop and pail and set them out to join the broom and dustpan on the back step.

"And you just went along with that?" Jamie asked.

"He obviously didn't know who I was, or rather, whose son I was," Laurie said, joining Jamie at the table and sighing. "I told myself I should be the bigger person, but to tell you the truth, I thought I'd get him back for his nasty attitude by getting him in trouble with his new boss."

"It didn't work out that way, I take it."

"No kidding. It was worse when he realized and got scared. I thought I was going to throw up; he was so smarmy and toadying, but I could tell he hated me more than when he'd thought I was just some no-account broom pusher." Laurie sighed again. "I know I should be trying to understand him, figuring out how to be more sympathetic. He just got posted there, hadn't even met Dad yet, trying to make a good impression and probably nervous about—"

"No," Jamie interrupted harshly. "You should crush him." Laurie's stare was shocked and fascinated. Jamie went on, "People like that are all the same. He'll just get worse if he's not slapped down. It's like the fascists in Germany: when they first started passing those laws restricting Jewish rights and making hateful propaganda, people shrugged it off and made excuses for it, said it wasn't that bad, wasn't worth starting a fight about. So millions died. You have to fight back before they crush you, because they will if they get the chance." Jamie's breath was short and his eyes were screwed shut.

He opened them when he felt Laurie's hand cover his fist where it pressed on the table. "Ok," Laurie said gently. "I see what you're saying. And God knows I don't think we should just cave in to bigotry. But if we can see them as human beings at the same time…"

"How can you do that when you're trying to flatten them?" Jamie pulled his hand out from under Laurie's.

"I'm not trying to flatten them, that's the thing. I'm trying to get them to stop. That's different. It's not about what I feel about what they're doing, it's what I want to get them to do."

"How can you separate them?"

Laurie sat back and pondered for a minute. "I guess," he said slowly, "I'm talking about keeping track of your feelings, being clear on what they really are. The feelings I got with this Angstrom character today, how lousy he made me feel, were separate from the feelings I have about prejudice and discrimination in general. If I let the personal feelings take over, then it'll be harder to do anything about the general situation, and it's more important to me to change the way things are than to salve my own hurt pride. And I'll never change that guy's attitude by beating him down. Maybe I'll never change it at all, but I have to try, even with a guy like him, because it'll get me closer to the result I want in the long run."

Jamie felt as though a gear had just slipped into place in his head, clicking cogs together that had been grinding each other before. "It's like me with Rima and sex!" he exclaimed.

Laurie gaped. "It is? How on earth?"

"I just realized something that's been confusing me. You may have noticed that Rima and I like to, er, get physical a lot."

"Hard not to notice," Laurie said wryly.

"I thought, a while ago, that I needed that the way inmates in the camp needed bread. I had a hunger for it. And I thought it meant I really wanted to have sex with her. But listening to you, I realized that's separate from the sexual attraction. It's the touch I need."

"Yet you pulled away from my hand just now."

Jamie felt himself flush. "I'm not saying I've figured out how to get what I need," he said. "And touching Rima is—I don't know, something that feels normal, that nobody would think twice about, and I don't have to think about it, either. It's just teenagers making out. That doesn't scare me. But what you just said maybe gave me a clue about where I'm going wrong. I have to focus more on the end result I want, and keep straight what that is."

"So what is the end result you're after?"

"Getting somebody to touch me without going up the wall like some kind of freak. The sex part is just a byproduct."

"So what's wrong with me touching you? Or Mom, or Dad?"

"There's nothing wrong with it, and I'm better about that than I used to be, right?" At Laurie's nod he went on, "But it's safer with Rima because she can't hurt me. I can't be vulnerable around you guys. You know what 'vulnerable' means: 'able to be wounded.' And when she touches me, it's not about my showing a part of myself, it's just being a teenaged boy. I don't love her, not really."

The two of them stared at each other a minute, somewhat aghast at what Jamie had just discovered about himself.

Jamie said, a little shamefaced, "I don't mean that I don't care about her. I do; she's great. But… it's not the same as with you guys. That's what I realized when you were talking about this jerk at the Depot; you can put aside your feelings about him because he's not really important to you."

Laurie smiled. "Well, I can't say I really understand the connection, but I'm glad if I was any help. And you've helped me, by the way, getting me to talk this out and figure out what I was feeling."

"That's one for the books."

"Don't sell yourself short, kiddo."

The back door opened and Ruby sidled in, arms loaded with grocery bags. "Why are those cleaning things on the step?" she said. "Did someone make a mess?"

The boys got up to take the bags from her. "I broke the pitcher," Laurie admitted.

"The yellow glass one?"

"It slipped out of my grip," he said defensively. "I'd just washed my hands; maybe they were still a little wet."

"Well, praise the Lord," Ruby said. "I've hated that pitcher for twenty years."

They all laughed and started putting the groceries away.

CHAPTER 32.

WEDNESDAY, SEPTEMBER 5, 1956

The high school cafeteria was the usual mob scene; the hundred or so students who had lunch this period made a noise that seemed out of proportion to their numbers, and the clatter of china and the clink of utensils brought the whole thing to a cacophony that made every meal a torment to Jamie. The smell and look of today's entrée—a supposed chicken à la king that looked like gray slime with strings of meat in it, poured over dry, crumbly corn bread, turned his stomach so that he couldn't even face the bag lunch Ruby had packed for him.

Across the table, Rima took a bite of the school lunch and twisted her face in disgust. "Let's get out of here," she said to Jamie in an undertone. He gladly got up and followed her out into the hot, sunny courtyard, then to the shade of the far side of a nearby equipment shed. Jamie knew Laurie ate out here sometimes, but Laurie had lunch second period, so Jamie figured they'd have the place to themselves.

They were hardly out of sight of the students eating in the courtyard when Jamie fell on Rima like a ravening wolf. She melted easily into his arms, pressing against him and moaning as he nuzzled her neck. Then he nipped at the place where her neck met her shoulder and she yelped a little, pulling away.

"What are you, Count Dracula?" she said, half laughing.

162

"I vant to drink your blood," he said in a fake Transylvanian accent.

"I think you really do, sometimes," she said. She took his hand and dragged him down with her as she sank to the grass and leaned against the wall of the shed. "You are kind of like a vampire or something; it feels like you want to get inside of me." Her face flushed. "Oh, that came out wrong."

He laughed. "I know what you meant," he assured her. He gazed out across the athletic field in front of them, then said, "Did you hear they buried him in his vampire cloak, Lugosi?"

"Yeah," she said. "Creepy."

"I don't know," he said. "Seems like it might be kind of nice, spending eternity all wrapped up, surrounded by something warm that had played such a big part in your life."

"Phooey," she said. "What a downer. Let's talk about something else. How are your classes this year?"

"All right so far."

"You still planning to apply for college a year early?"

"Yeah. I know it's weird, but sometimes I feel like I'm running out of time, like I have to get going. And anyway, most of my classes last year were boring. I'm too smart for them." He spoke matter-of-factly, not boasting.

Rima nodded, unsurprised. "Myself, I'm looking forward to being a senior this year; I wouldn't want to miss the fun. But I guess that's not your kind of fun."

"Speaking of my kind of fun…" He pulled her into his arms again and buried his face in her hair. After a minute she twisted her neck so that her mouth could meet his. He kissed her back, but soon went back to his earlier position.

He was sinking into a sensory-overload daze when she startled him by putting her hands on his shoulders and pushing back. "Jamie, what's wrong?" she said.

"Huh? Nothing's wrong. What do you mean?" This close, he could see the enlarged pores in her nose. A pimple was sprouting in the crease next to it. He didn't mind these physical imperfections; they reassured him about his own.

She was watching his face. "You're different lately," she said. "The way you touch me, the way you are when we're making out."

He felt a guilty pang. *I'm using her,* he realized. *I want somebody to touch me, to hold me. She thinks it's about her, but I'm not really thinking about her when I do it.*

She wrapped her arms around herself and stared down into her own lap. "I'm sorry, Jamie," she whispered. "I know what you want, but I'm just not ready. Jeez, I'll be eighteen on Rosh Hashanah, I shouldn't be such a wimp, but—"

"No," he said. "You're wrong. I'm not ready for that, either."

"Really?" She cocked a disbelieving eye. "Sometimes I think that's the only reason you really hang around with me, because you're hoping we'll go all the way."

"But it's the opposite!" he exclaimed. "I mean, you're sexy, sure, and I… I like the way it feels, but lately I'm realizing that the most important thing isn't the sex, that it's that you're someone I can hold, that I can be close to someone. That's what I'm looking for."

"What? But…." She digested that for a minute, then fisted her hands on her knees and said, "Are you saying that it doesn't matter who I am, that you're just looking for a warm body?"

"No, of course not. I thought we went through this in the car that day. I like you, Rima—and I trust you, too. I know you'd never deliberately hurt me."

She stared at him for a long minute. "But your family," she said. "They're the biggest bunch of touchers I've ever known. And I've seen them—Celia and Laurie and your mom and dad, all of them—reach out to you at one time or another. You almost always flinch away or freeze them out."

"Because it scares me when they do that," he admitted. "They'd never deliberately hurt me, either, but I could still get hurt because I... I care about them so much. I've had all the people I love taken away from me once already. When my family now touches me, unless I'm really feeling, I don't know, *needy,* I guess, I feel as if letting them get that close is dangerous, like the only way to be safe is to shut myself off. I don't feel that way with you."

To his surprise, Rima's eyes filled with tears: not sympathetic ones—the look on her face was devastated. "So you're saying it's ok when I touch you because you don't care about me that much?"

Jamie's automatic denial stuck in his throat. *She's right.* "But I do really like you," he croaked finally.

She turned her face away and patted his hand at the same time. He wasn't sure what to make of the mixed signals, so he just waited.

Finally she turned back to him. "Since literally the first minute I saw you," she said, "I've known you were... that you had..."

"That I was broken, half crazy, a mess?" he suggested harshly.

Now her face was full of compassion. "Stop that," she said softly. "That you had problems that are beyond the usual teenage dramatics. But I felt like you were worth the extra trouble it would take to get to know you." She shifted around till she was kneeling next to him, watching him so intently he had to look away.

She tapped the knuckle of a forefinger against the side of his jaw to bring his face around to her again. "And I was right," she said. "You are worth it. And I'm glad, really I am, that you trust me enough to let me close to you. But I admit I'm hurt that you don't—that you don't love me, I guess, the way I love you."

"Are you breaking up with me? I wouldn't blame you. I know I don't deserve you." *Jedem das seine.*

She sighed. "It doesn't have anything to do with deserving," she said. "I'm just not sure how I feel about all this. I have to think about it. Ok?"

He nodded reluctantly.

She pushed back onto her heels and stood up. "We better go," she said. "The bell rang ten minutes ago."

He shrugged, getting up too. "I'm only missing gym," he said. "I hate gym."

She shoved him toward the school building. "Well, I'm missing European History," she said. "And I'll be applying to college this year; I can't afford to screw up."

When they were almost at the doors, he said, "I'm not sure where we are now."

"Neither am I," she said. "You'll just have to live with it till I figure out how I feel about all this."

"Ok," he said.

Chapter 33.

For once, Jamie and Rima were together without engaging in their perpetual dance of approach and avoidance, kissing and quarrelling. They sat in the Shapiros' kitchen while Rima's mother darted around fixing supper, talking a mile a minute.

"So Israel's invaded Egypt, so what? Britain and the U.S. are having fits—a bunch of hypocrites, I say. What was Israel supposed to do? They have to have access to the Suez Canal if they're going to ship goods around to India and Africa. Here, Rima, finish grating these carrots, please."

Rima moved from the table to the counter and Jamie shifted to hook his feet over the rungs of her abandoned chair. "They have to stand up to Nasser, they can't let him keep them out, my piano teacher says," he agreed.

"Who's your piano teacher?"

"Mrs. Seixas."

"Seixas," Mrs. Shapiro said in a knowing tone. "Figures they'd be pro-Israel."

"Why?" Rima asked. "'Say-shass'—what kind of name is that? It isn't a Jewish name, is it?"

"Of course it is," her mother said, and spelled it for her.

"How do you know?"

"I just know," she said, voice muffled by the doors of the cabinet she was rummaging through. "It's Sephardic," she continued, emerging triumphantly with a box of raisins. "It's one of those names that's always Jewish, like Shapiro—though Mr. Beltzhoover at the market in Carlisle thought we were Italian when he heard it."

"The first rabbi born in America was named Seixas," Jamie told Rima, who looked unimpressed.

Mrs. Shapiro was still chuckling over Mr. Beltzhoover as she dumped raisins into the bowl of carrots. Jamie waited for her to add mayonnaise, the way Ruby would have to make it into a salad, but to his surprise she took the whole thing and poured it into a pot on the stove where a beef soup bone was simmering. "Tsimmis," she said to his inquiring look. "You've never had it?"

He shook his head. "Ruby grew up in Georgia," he said. "She's learned to make challah so I can celebrate Shabbat properly, and she's made a valiant effort at potato pancakes, but her cooking is really country Southern—minus the pork, these days."

"It's nice that your family does that for you," Rima said, "even if they don't really have Jewish food."

"'Jewish food'—you're actually talking about Eastern European food, aren't you?"

"Grandma Shapiro says we're Sephardic," Rima protested.

"Grandma Shapiro has delusions of grandeur," Mrs. Shapiro said. "Though I have to admit, when you say 'Eastern European' I want to make clear that the Shapiros are from Speyer, firmly in Bavaria."

"Mr. and Mrs. Seixas came from Germany, too," Jamie said.

"His family probably went there after the Expulsion of the Jews from Spain," Mrs. Shapiro said.

"When was that?" Rima wondered.

"Fourteen ninety-two," Jamie and Mrs. Shapiro said in unison.

"The year Columbus landed in America?" Rima exclaimed disbelievingly. "They never taught us that in school!"

"What they don't teach in that school would fill a book," Jamie said darkly. "That's why you have to read books."

"I read plenty of books, smart guy."

"Math and science, sure. And English lit, I know you read that. But what's the last history you picked up?"

"I don't have time to do *everything,*" she countered. "For one thing, I have a *very* demanding boyfriend."

"Who'll lend you a book about Jews in America by Harry Golden and some other guy. See how great I am?"

Mrs. Shapiro patted him on the shoulder. "A nice Jewish boy," she said. "Even if you were raised by goyim. How did that happen, anyway?"

"Mom!" Rima gasped.

Mrs. Shapiro flushed. "I don't mean to sound insensitive..." she faltered.

"No, that's all right," Jamie said, though his temples were pounding and his stomach clenched. *I'm going to make it be all right; I can talk about this.* "They sent me to an orphanage in France after—after Buchenwald. Dad visited the place when he was on leave, and something sort of clicked between us. Things were still pretty rough there, after the war, so they were happy to get rid of me."

Rima's hand slipped into his as Mrs. Shapiro said, "I apologize, Jamie. I didn't mean to poke up bad memories. I should have realized. I am sorry."

Jamie shrugged. "It's good for me to get used to talking about it, actually. And this is a good place to start: you and Mr. Shapiro have been so nice to me. And Rima, of course."

"Of course," Rima giggled.

It had been a while since Jamie had heard that sound from her. *Maybe she's figured out that it's ok to be with me, even if I am screwed up.*

"Would you like to stay for supper, Jamie?" Mrs. Shapiro said. "I know it's a school night, but you could go home right afterwards; I'd like to have you try the tsimmis."

"Thanks, I'd like that, too. Just let me call home, and then maybe Rima and I can set the table or something."

"Or something," Rima said playfully.

Mrs. Shapiro winked at Jamie as he led Rima out of the kitchen toward the phone in the hall.

Once they were out of earshot, he said to her in an undertone, "Is this all right with you? When I came over to return that book, I really wasn't trying to worm my way in. I know you said you needed time to think, so I've been trying to give you some room this past month…"

"No, I know," she said softly. "I appreciate your backing off a little, and I have been thinking about it, and what I think is that I really miss you."

"We could still be friends, even if—" he said, surprised to feel a slight surge of hope at the idea. *Things would be so much simpler if we just eliminated the sex stuff.*

But he also felt some relief when she said, "No, I miss being with you physically, too. It's not fair for me to push all the responsibility for that on you; after all, I've usually been the one to start it."

In his guilt and confusion about the whole business, he'd lost sight of that elementary fact. Her reminding him relieved his guilt a little, but added to his confusion. *We'll just have to keep trying to figure it out,* he thought as he reached for the telephone.

Then Rima said, "I would like to pull back a little on the physical stuff, though. Maybe go back to staying north of the Mason-Dixon line?"

"Good," he said. "That would be good."

CHAPTER 34.

THURSDAY, NOVEMBER 22, 1956

This year, Jamie managed to get all the way through Thanksgiving dinner without feeling sick or panicking over the surfeit of food. He'd done it by compartmentalizing the components of the meal, focusing first on the slice of turkey breast he'd forked off the serving platter, then on his small scoop of stuffing, then on a candied yam and a spoonful of green bean casserole. He'd ignored the mashed potatoes, the peas and onions, the rolls, even the cranberry sauce and gravy, as though they were pictures in a magazine or props on a stage set: nothing to do with him.

He watched Celia and Beth clear it all away with relief, glad it wasn't his turn to help in the kitchen. When they carried in the bounty of pies—pumpkin, pecan, apple, lemon meringue—he accepted a modest slice of pumpkin and then he was done.

Mom smiled approvingly at him as they all rose from the table. *Should have known she'd notice.* He gave her a diffident shrug.

The older girls and Ruby were clanking around in the kitchen; most of the others had headed for the TV room and the annual Packers/Lions football ritual. Jamie wandered into the living room and stood staring out the window. The day was already darkening, and the rain turning to sleet. Jamie shivered a little, just as glad that his and Rima's respective family obligations today meant he wouldn't have to venture outside. In the reflection in the glass, he could see

Mom behind him, pausing on her way through the room to gaze speculatively at his back.

Sighing, he turned around. "You want to talk to me," he said. It wasn't a question.

Her mouth twitched in a rueful half-smile. "Is it such an ordeal?"

"Can I take the Fifth?" He sank onto a settee as she settled on the facing one.

"I wasn't thinking of asking you anything that might incriminate you. I was just wondering how you managed during dinner. I know that in the past, all that extra Thanksgiving food has brought back bad memories of being starved and then suddenly inundated with GI provisions after the camp was liberated. What was different this year?"

"Something Rima suggested," he said. "She told me to just focus on one food at a time, whichever serving I was just about to eat, and not look at anything else or think about how much more there was on the table."

Mom crossed her legs and linked her hands around a knee, gazing off to one side. "That's excellent advice," she said. "Obviously, since it worked, but I think it would be a useful strategy for people with other kinds of issues around food, too."

Her gaze came back to Jamie and she put her feet flat on the floor again, hands sliding loosely into her lap. She tilted her head a little. "So you talked to Rima about those feelings? Shared some of those memories with her?"

Now it was Jamie's turn to look to the side. "I was trying to explain why I didn't look forward to Thanksgiving," he said. "It just kind of came out."

"I don't think that's a bad thing, Jamie. I think it's excellent that you feel safe enough with her to share that sort of thing." She took a breath as though about to say something else, then closed her mouth and looked down at her lap, twining her fingers around each other.

Jamie wasn't sure whether he felt gratitude at her tact or amusement at her subterfuge. Both, he supposed. So, though he felt nervous about broaching the subject with her, his voice took on a sardonic note as he said flatly, "We're not having sex."

She didn't pretend to be surprised at the seeming shift in subject. "Well, I have to say I'm relieved to hear it. Your father told me, of course, about the conversation you'd had. I'm glad if you feel ready to talk about it with me, but I really don't think you're ready for that level of intimacy."

"No," he agreed. "And neither is Rima." He pushed his glasses up and scrubbed his hands over his face. "I get confused, though," he admitted. "In the beginning, she was the one who always went straight to the clinch. I didn't want to talk, and that was ok with her, she didn't want to talk, either. But then, a few months ago, she asked me if that was all I wanted from her, like that was all she was good for."

There was a roar from the game watchers in the TV room. Jamie was distracted for a second, picturing it to himself.

Mom waited patiently as he brought his thoughts back to the subject at hand. "I tried to tell her that wasn't it, but after that we started... I mean, we got..."

"You stepped up the intimacy?"

He puffed out a relieved breath. "Yes." He gnawed a thumbnail, thinking it over, then said, "A few weeks ago, I got talking to Laurie about some things he's struggling with, separating how he feels about prejudiced people and the way they treat him from what it is he actually wants to change about them. You know, I'm not big on thinking about feelings, but it did make me kind of sort out that, with

Rima, what we do together is more, for me anyway, about a safe way of being touched than about sex."

"How do you mean, safe?"

He bit his lip, then blurted it out. "Normal." She still had a question in her eyes, so he went on, "Dad says I'm not... broken, that I'm different from a lot of people because of my experiences, but they give me—what did he call it?—the gifts my travails have brought me."

They both smiled as Jamie captured Dad's sober, measured tones when he spoke of something important. Then Jamie's mouth twisted down again. "But when I talked to Rima about it, about the touching thing, I hurt her feelings. I made her feel like I was using her, and not only that, but that I could stand her touching me when I can't sometimes with you guys because I don't care enough about her." He raised his eyes to Mom in appeal. "And in a way that's true, but I do care about her. I think she's great. I just don't know how to make her see it."

"What do you think she wants from your relationship?" Mom asked.

Jamie was dumbstruck. *What kind of selfish jerk are you, Hymie, that you never thought about that before?* "I don't know," he said miserably. "I don't even know why she wants to hang around me at all."

Mom shook her head at him. "Don't 'beat yourself up,' as they say," she said. "Just think about the question. And—I realize this is a revolutionary notion—talk to her about it?"

"About why she likes me?"

"About what she wants from you." Mom leaned forward. "And maybe about what you value in her aside from the physical." As he looked blank, she prompted, "Dinner today?"

"What? Oh!" he said, the penny dropping. "I could tell her how she helped me!"

"You could indeed." Mom sat back on the settee as the dining room door opened behind her.

Celia came in. "Oh, there you are," she said to the back of Mom's head. Then she caught sight of Jamie and stopped uncertainly. "Sorry, am I interrupting something?"

"No," Jamie said, getting up. "I was just leaving." He started for the stairs and the upstairs phone.

Chapter 35.

Sunday, February 17, 1957

"Rima, it's too cold to take my shirt off," Jamie said. She pulled away from him and propped her back against the door of Mom's Dodge Coronet. The ribbed plush of the upholstery had left marks on her bare arm. "But not too cold for me to take mine off," she said.

"It's my birthday," he said plaintively. *Stupid, childish thing to say. You're seventeen, not seven, for God's sake.*

But Rima narrowed her eyes at him appraisingly as she shrugged her cardigan back on and buttoned it up. By the time she had her coat around her, Jamie had wilted in more ways than one.

He was taken aback when she said, "I know why you do it, you know. Or rather, why you don't do it."

"Do what?" But he knew.

"I've felt under your shirt when we're making out. You don't want me to see your scars. Your back is covered with them, isn't it? They whipped you there, in that camp."

With a surge of fury, Jamie ripped his shirt open, popping several buttons that flew around the back seat where they huddled. "Yes," he snarled. "Want to see them? And here, this one on my chest, that's from a nail in the floor where I was hiding from the Gestapo. And the tattoo on my arm, you've seen that. Anything else you want to know about?"

He'd expected horror, pity, distaste, possibly tears; he hadn't expected her to be furious. "Is that what you think? That I have some sort of sick curiosity about what happened to you? Is that why every time we start to have any kind of meaningful conversation, you start groping me? To keep me from really seeing you?" She pounded her fist on the armrest in wordless frustration, then went on, "You survived, Jamie! That's what's important about what happened to you: you lived through it, and here you are. So live, already!"

Engrossed in their drama as they were, they jumped as though shot when someone pounded on the car window. Jamie's heart pounded even harder when he turned and saw the figure outside. *Uniform. Gun. Danger.* He sat frozen for a moment, then fell back to shield Rima, as though the very gaze of the soldier could harm her.

The pounding on the window came again, more insistent. Rima shoved Jamie off her and reached around him to roll down the window.

"You kids need to go make out somewhere else," Jamie heard through the drumming pulse in his ears.

"What business is it of yours?" Rima demanded. "This building is Dickinson property." They were parked in an alley across from the main campus, behind a featureless white cinderblock building known as "the potato chip factory" from some earlier incarnation.

"Never you mind," the soldier said. He was a kid himself, Jamie realized as his panic receded. "Just move along before I have to report you."

Rima still seemed disposed to argue, but Jamie'd had enough. He opened the door on the far side from the soldier, crawled awkwardly over Rima's legs to get out, pushed himself into the driver's seat in front of her, and fired up the engine.

"What is this place, anyway?" Rima was still asking as he slammed the car into gear and took off.

177

That night he dreamed. He dreamed of pain, of fear, of hunger: all the familiar chain of misery. But there was also bewilderment, and a deep sense of betrayal. He woke screaming, *"Tati! Ich vein mine Tati!"*

Mom was holding his hands, Dad was rubbing his back. The other kids hurried in, petting him, murmuring, bringing cold washcloths. Ruby appeared, bearing a glass of water: all the familiar trappings of comfort and reality. But for once Jamie couldn't stop crying, even after he was properly awake.

"I left him," he kept saying. "I left him, he's gone. But he left me first. Tati, I want my Tati. But I left him. How could I leave him?"

"He died, honey," Dad said. "You've told us he got sick and died. You didn't leave him, and he certainly didn't leave you."

"Yes, he did," Jamie insisted, choking. "He didn't know who I was. He looked like somebody else. His face, his arms, he was all covered with horrible sores and he smelled like rotten meat. He kept asking for more light, but when they opened the barracks shutters he couldn't stand it, he covered his eyes, and then he stopped talking."

Jamie got his voice under control and turned to lean back against his pillow, moving away from Dad's hands as he did so. Mom stroked his arm; the others looked on with expressions Jamie didn't want to see. Jamie covered his eyes with his hands to block them out and went on, "I thought he was asleep, but the other men said he wouldn't wake up again. They said I should say goodbye to him, but I didn't want him to go away; how could I say goodbye? So I hid in the corner of the barracks, and when morning came he was dead. He left me there all alone, so I left him first. But why should I be alive, when he's dead? When they're all dead, everyone but me?"

He started gasping, pulling in more breath and more. Mom drew his hands away from his face and said firmly, "Slow down. Just breathe normally, Jamie. In... now hold... now out. In... hold... out. That's it, keep it up, in... hold... out."

By the time Jamie's breathing had returned to normal, Ruby had shepherded the others out and it was only Mom and Dad in the room with him. Dad had snaked his hand between Jamie's neck and his pillow and was rubbing little circles where the back of his neck met his shoulders. Jamie flinched away, only fractionally, but it was enough to make Dad say, "Shall I leave you two alone?"

Jamie didn't answer, but a minute later Mom was the only one there. She went back to holding his hands. Eventually she said, "It sounds like typhus. Prison fever, they used to call it. Lice carry it between people in filthy, crowded conditions. It's what Anne Frank died of, in Belsen."

"I should have done something. I should have helped him."

"Sweetheart, without antibiotics, it's a death sentence. What could you possibly have done?"

"I left him. I didn't even stay with him."

"He was delirious; he didn't know you, you said."

Jamie shook his head, denying the reassurance. Mom sighed, thinking. Then she said, "Do you remember when Ruby came down with pneumonia, a little while after you first came here?"

Jamie focused on those early, confusing months in this house and recalled some added confusion: Ruby in the smaller guest room, a strange man with a black bag coming in to see her, an odd contraption he now realized must have been an oxygen tank, Ruby herself looking gray and drained with a thermometer sticking out of her mouth. "I remember," he croaked.

"Why didn't Celia help her?"

"Celia?" he said, startled. "She was just a little kid." He could see her on the floor next to Ruby's sickbed, crayons spread around her, coloring a picture of a red-haired doll, then proudly presenting it to

Ruby. She was wearing little black shoes with straps, and white socks with lace around the tops—it must have been a Sunday. "She cried," he remembered. "Ruby didn't open her eyes to see her picture."

Mom gave a little laugh. "I'd forgotten that picture," she said. "Raggedy Ann, wasn't it? Ruby kept it for years; I'd bet she still has it squirreled away somewhere. But at the time, she was just too sick to notice it. So why didn't Celia do something more useful for her?"

"She was a little kid," Jamie repeated. "There wasn't anything she could do."

"She's a year younger than you. Two years older then than you were when your father died. Do you remember what Joy was like when she was four?"

Jamie smiled. "She was obsessed with *The Little Prince*. She wore that scarf everywhere, and carried around her 'sheep in a box'."

"Could she have helped Ruby? Or your father? Or anyone at all?"

"All right, I see," Jamie admitted. "But it's different for me. I had been through… all those things. I knew… things."

"You knew suffering and death in a way our little girls didn't, thank God," Mom said. "But more than that, you didn't have the things they had. Coloring books and stories and sheep in a box: the links to sweet dreams and fantasies that keep little children connected to the life of the spirit."

"I had a sheep," Jamie said suddenly.

"I remember your mentioning it. Your 'shepsele'."

"It got left behind, the night we ran away. I left it."

"I'm sure you didn't mean to leave it."

"I didn't understand that I'd never see it again, that we'd never go back to our apartment again, never go home again."

"You've got a new home now."

"But my parents never did. They never found a home, ever again." Mom opened her mouth to speak but Jamie cut her off. "And don't talk to me about some home in the sky or some crap like that. It's not good enough. If that's all God has to offer, than God damn God."

She sighed. "I don't have any answers for you, Jamie. I only know that we have to make the best of what we have, to go forward because we can't change the past. The truth, the undeniable truth, is that you're here now, you have survived, you have a home, you have a family that loves you—you have a future. Don't you think your parents would have wanted that, more than anything in this world?"

Tears were leaking out of Jamie's eyes again. "Ok," he said. "Ok."

"Do you think you could sleep now?"

"Maybe."

As she helped him settle back and drew his covers over his shoulder, he said, "Could you ask Dad to come back in?"

She kissed his temple and went out. But when Dad came in and sat on the side of the bed, Jamie stayed curled away from him and could find no words to say.

After a while Dad said, "I would never try to replace him, you know. I can only do what I hope someone would do for you if you lost me. It's all right to miss him, and it's all right to love me."

Jamie let out a breath and let his knees relax a little. Dad slid down beside him, cupping himself around Jamie's back.

He was still there in the morning; someone had put a quilt over them both.

CHAPTER 36.

"Try it again," Mrs. Seixas said. "Raise your wrists higher and keep your fingers relaxed. It takes stamina to play Liszt; it also takes heart. Try to be less rigid."

Jamie attacked the *Piano Sonata in B Minor* again, trying to master the harsh, precise opening notes in the lower octaves sliding into rippling treble runs and thundering back down to dense, ominous chords, then overlaid with lyric melody and again to striding octaves and around once more to delicate meandering on the upper keys...

"I don't understand this at all," he said, breaking off in frustration. "It's all over the place. What does he mean by it? Are you sure this was written a hundred years ago? It seems more like some modern cr— er, nonsense."

The piano teacher's wrinkled lips turned down in a scowl at his near vulgarity, but her eyes twinkled understandingly. "It was met with a storm of controversy when he first performed it," she acknowledged. "It was ahead of its time. And there've been a number of theories about what he 'meant' by it: literary, mythological, psychological. For our purposes, let's just say he's expressing various emotions—an aspect of musicianship that tends to be absent in your repertoire." Her eyes were still twinkling.

Jamie sighed. "Did you ever consider that all these emotions are missing in more than my musical repertoire?"

"Nonsense," she said briskly, and smiled when his lifted eyebrow acknowledged her picking up on his word of a moment before. "It can't all be Bach and cerebral exercises," she went on.

"I don't see why not," he said, addressing himself to the keyboard again with an air of resignation.

"Actually, I think that's enough for this week," she said. "Work on it for next time. Your sister isn't due for her lesson for another fifteen minutes, and I've got rugelach to go with the tea."

The stout little woman bustled into her kitchen. Jamie ran a few arpeggios, then left the piano and settled on the slippery sofa in the stuffy, cluttered parlor. He got up to help Mrs. Seixas with the tea tray.

When they sat back with cups in hand, Jamie took a nibble of the flaky pastry filled with chopped nuts and raisins and pressed his lips together, gazing around the room. "Madeleines," he said.

She took the reference immediately. "My rugelach make you remember?"

He nodded. "Them, and this room." He looked around him at the piles of books on every flat surface, rucking up the tatted doilies underneath them; the faded sepia photographs on the floral-papered walls; the upholstered chairs set cheek-by-jowl across from the sofa, with the piecrust table set between holding the ornate silver tray and the simple pottery pot. "It reminds me of home," he said, and then gaped at himself. *Home, Hymie? You think of that flat across the gulf of world and time as home?*

But Mrs. Seixas was nodding. "I've wondered," she said, "whether any of it had stayed with you."

"It's been coming back lately," he said. "The past few years, anyway. And last week, you know we went down to Washington for that Prayer Pilgrimage for Peace—"

"Did you? Herman and I were there, too; we could have driven together."

"We took the charter bus. But standing there in front of the Lincoln Memorial with all those people, listening to Dr. King speak, it came to me that Civil Rights, the struggle for equality for Negroes here, is something I can take part in, do something about, even if what happened back there, back then, to us Jews, is out of my control. It changed something in me, made me feel less helpless."

"I remember when you first started coming for lessons," she said. "Eight years old and still as shy and scared as if you'd just come off the boat. Herman and I had been in this country since 'forty-one—he likes to say we turned out the lights, being the last Jews to leave Germany—and had settled in pretty well, but seeing you brought it all back."

Jamie noticed, for the first time in a long time, the traces of her origins in her vowels: *lahst, oll,* and in the crispness of her final "t's." "I remember, too," he said. "After three years, I had gotten used to the family and the house, but this place made me feel at home right away. That house—my house—is so big and quiet and clean; it frightened me at first, the space and the silence and the immaculate surfaces… not that I mean your house is dirty, just that—"

She raised a hand dismissively. "I understand," she said. "This place is a warren, I know. For Herman and me, the world is well lost as long as we have music and books. Do you know, the most serious quarrel we ever had was over whose set of Schiller we should take with us when we fled? Schiller." She shook her head ruefully. "Fleeing for our lives, but we couldn't leave our books behind. 'The good is the beautiful,' in a world of evil and ugliness."

"My parents, too," Jamie said. "But they couldn't take any books with them. My mother thought they'd come back; she asked the super to watch their things till it was all over. They waited too long to leave." It was the first time he'd ever said that aloud.

"So many did," she said, shaking her head. "It's hard to tear up your life and leave everything you know, every*one* you know, and to admit the world's gone mad. Don't blame them, *yingele.*" Her mouth twisted ruefully. "Don't tell Herman I used Yiddish," she said wryly. "He doesn't like reminders of my Litvak grandfather."

But Jamie was too stricken by what she'd said to spare a thought for the vagaries of Jewish ethnic snobberies. "I don't blame them," he protested, before registering that she'd used the only Yiddish he'd ever heard from her, and to call him a diminutive of what he used to call himself.

Der yingl: the boy. How his parents used to refer to him, speaking to each other. What the men called him in the camp. What he used to call himself. "I don't blame them," he said again.

"All right," she said. *Oll rightt.*

Chapter 37.

"Well, that was fast," Celia said with satisfaction as she put away the last of the dishes they'd just washed and Jamie finished wiping down the counters. "The advantages of a cold supper. That was a great idea you had, by the way, having the leftover fish and vegetables in a salad instead of reheating them."

Jamie nodded without speaking.

"I never had corn in a cold dish like that before," she went on, hanging up the damp dishtowel on the oven door. "How did you think of that?"

Jamie shrugged. "Food's food," he said. "I figured it wouldn't make any difference."

"I noticed you didn't pass up the tapioca pudding, though."

He nodded with a rueful grin; it was one of the few sweet desserts he actually liked. *Leave it to Celia to notice.* He turned to leave the kitchen but she put a hand on his arm. "You're worried about this kid they're bringing in, aren't you?"

There'd been a family meeting last night, when Mom and Dad and Ruby had informed them all that they were bringing in a new boy, a troubled thirteen-year-old who'd been seriously abused and was now in danger of being shunted into custodial care or even the juvenile justice system because he was thought too far gone to help, and too dangerous to keep with the other kids at Rolling Meadow.

186

"I keep thinking about David," Jamie admitted.

"We all are, I think. But we're older now, we know more about what's what. We'll be able to help the folks more than we could with him." Jamie had turned away as she spoke, but she circled around in front of him again and once more reached out to touch him lightly on the arm. "It'll be ok, Jamie. You'll see."

"Of course. If Miss Celia decrees it'll be ok, the universe will just have to snap into line," he said. But his tone was only sarcastic, not bitter, and she took it for the teasing he meant it as.

"So it shall be written; so it shall be done," she intoned, crossing her arms over her chest like Yul Brynner as Pharaoh in *The Ten Commandments* movie. Then she started toward the dining room. "Come on, they're waiting for us to start the reading, since we didn't have much time last night."

"I think I'll skip it tonight," he said. "I need to... think about everything."

Celia cocked her head to one side. "You're not enjoying *Till We Have Faces?* You don't really like Lewis, do you?"

"Not much," he admitted, "though this is better than the Narnia stuff."

"Maybe next time, you should pick the book."

Jamie snorted. "Yeah, you'll all love listening to *Principia Mathematica.*"

"Probably do us good," Celia laughed as she went out through the swinging door.

For a moment, Jamie was tempted to follow her, but the lure of solitude in his attic cabinet proved too strong and he made his way up the back stairs.

The evening had cooled down, but the attic was still hot and the narrow space under the eaves was stifling. Air hot enough to make him sweat usually made him feel loose and safe, but tonight he had trouble getting comfortable. His knees knocked against the low slanted ceiling, and his sleeping bag bunched up in lumps beneath him.

I'm getting too big for this, he realized. *Too bad, Hymie. Pretty soon you won't have any other place to be alone.*

At the family meeting, he'd asked whether the new kid—Steve, his name was—would be moving into his room the way David had. The answer had been yes, especially since this Steve had spent the past ten years isolated in a locked room by the cousin who'd taken him in when his parents were killed. Mom had said something about Jamie's "loving heart" that had made Jamie snort, but she'd repeated it more firmly.

He thought about that now. *I guess I do love some people now. The family, and Rima maybe, in a way. But some stranger?'* He considered what he knew about Steve from newspaper stories and what the folks had said. He'd been systematically tortured by this cousin, and had ended up killing him in self-defense. He didn't know how to be around people.

That gives us something in common, anyway. And I bet he's got food hang-ups, too.

But there was something else: another reason Jamie wasn't feeling the jealousy and fear of displacement he had over David. He looked at the question the way he did when he encountered a mathematical proposition that wasn't clear at first, picking around the edges looking for any element that did seem familiar and might lead him into the labyrinth of the less obvious.

David came in here full of piss and vinegar, ready to take us all on. Scared, sure, but covering it with bravado. It doesn't sound like this Steve will be like that. He's afraid of the other kids, Mom said. He's got plenty of nerve, he must have to have fought back against his cousin after all those years of abuse, but he doesn't know how to be with people.

That's it, he doesn't know how to be with people! Like me, especially back at the beginning...

Jamie thought that over for a while, then realized something else. *He knows. He knows how the world can be, the ugliness. How people can cause each other pain for the sheer love of doing it. The* Blockführer's *face, when he beat me that time, that slavering hungry lust on his face: I bet Steve has seen that expression.*

Suddenly the cabinet was too oppressive for Jamie to stand a minute longer. He unsnapped the door and crawled out into the attic space, then sat on an old trunk to finish his line of thought.

Maybe I can help this kid. Maybe I can finally do something for somebody else, instead of always being the one who needs something done. I can do better than I did for David, anyway. Like helping Laurie and Rob with algebra, but more: not just me being a brain, but helping this kid the way the others have helped me.

The thought was intoxicating. A little frightening, as it seemed to open up the possibility of new territory, of unknown opportunities, but overall exciting.

Jamie fidgeted on the trunk. He still wasn't at ease. Maybe he should go down to his room, enjoy the privacy while he still could. Or maybe... maybe what he really wanted was to rejoin the others.

He got up and headed for the living room.

Chapter 38.

For once, Jamie and Rima were propped against opposite doors of the car, just talking. The warehouse parking lot they sat in was dark and empty; the background noise of crickets and the plashing of nearby LeTort Creek was punctuated by the soft thump and swish of machinery from the Frog and Switch factory. They'd come here because it was isolated, thinking they'd be able to make out in peace without being interrupted the way they had at the potato chip factory. But they'd ended up talking instead; Jamie had been telling Rima about his new brother.

"I don't know what made me do it," Jamie said. "I just looked at him, this skinny, scared, angry kid, and I knew he needed that cabinet more than I did."

"I think it's great," Rima said. "And I think you're not giving yourself enough credit. It's not only that you let him have your special hiding place—it's that you don't need it yourself any more."

"I showed him my scars, too."

"You did? Wow. You really trust this kid, huh?"

Jamie hunched forward to see her face more clearly. "It's not that so much. I wanted him to trust me, to show me his. I knew he'd have them, but he always gets dressed in the bathroom... so do I, for that matter. But Rima, this little kid, he's been whipped and burned and starved and God knows what."

She made a soft sound of distress.

"Hey," Jamie said quickly, "don't let on I told you that, all right? I don't want him to think I would go around gossiping about it."

"No, of course not. He always leaves the room when I'm around, anyway."

"Yeah, he's scared of girls. He never saw anyone but that cousin of his, for ten years. He's scared of everybody, but girls especially. Girls and black people: he's having a hard time with Laurie, but they went for a walk today, so maybe that's getting better."

Rima put a hand on his knee. "You told me you had a hard time connecting to that other kid—was his name David?—but you seem to already have a feeling for this Steve."

"Hmm," Jamie said sardonically. "I bet he wouldn't think so, if you asked him. I've been pretty sharp with him since he came here. It's harder than I thought it would be, being open to somebody who's so… damaged. It feels dangerous, as though he might pull me back into that place in my head." *And I was so sure I was going to be able to help him,* he thought despairingly. *Who was I kidding?*

Jamie was silent for a minute, thinking about the revelation he'd had in the attic the night Mom told them Steve was coming. "It's that he knows," he said finally. Then, to her questioningly tilted head, "About the world, I mean. About how cruel people can be, how evil can strike you down out of the blue. I mean, here was this little boy, hardly more than a baby, living this ordinary life, and there's a car crash, and the next thing he knows, he's locked in a room all alone with nothing but a radio for company, and a sadist who comes in every night and tortures him. I let him bring one of our radios into the room; I don't want to feel like I'm also torturing him."

There was no moon; the only light came from the faint glow of the dashboard. He could see Rima shudder, though. Her grip on his knee tightened. The response made him feel oddly irritated. *Not the point,* he thought. *She's trying to be sympathetic, but she doesn't really get it in her gut, the way Steve does.*

His thought was interrupted by the splash of a car running through a puddle in the warehouse parking lot. It stopped behind them and a man got out. Jamie and Rima straightened up in their seats.

The man stepped up to the driver's side and shone a flashlight into their eyes. "What do you kids think you're doing here?" he said harshly.

"We're just talking… uh, officer?" Jamie said uncertainly; the man was not in uniform.

"Constable," the man corrected him. "Let me see your ID."

"ID?" Rima repeated disbelievingly. "What is this, Nazi Germany?"

Jamie froze, halfway through taking out his driver's license.

Rima, unheeding, kept arguing with the guy. "I don't even drive," she said. "What am I supposed to show you? My library card?"

"Don't get smart with me, miss."

"I'm not getting smart with you, I'm really asking. And please get that light out of my eyes."

The flashlight never wavered. "Just show me some ID before you get in real trouble."

Jamie pushed his driver's license back and pulled out his military ID from the Depot instead. *Maybe that will impress him.*

Instead, it seemed to infuriate him. "You're one of those army brats, huh?" he growled.

"Navy," Jamie said.

"Same difference. You're all the same, coming into our communities, getting cozy with our girls…"

"I've lived in this community since I was six!"

"…corrupting the morals of a minor…"

"I'm older than he is!" Rima exclaimed.

"Then you should be ashamed of yourself," the man countered illogically.

I'm getting tired of this, Jamie thought. *That time by the potato chip factory, now this. I'm not going to keep sitting down for it.*

He cut across the increasingly hostile dialogue. "May I have your name, Constable?"

"My name? What would you need my name for?"

"I'd like to see some form of identification from you, actually. We have only your word that you even have any right to question us."

"I could take you in right now, smart boy. How do you like them apples?"

"Take me in for what?"

"Trespassing," he said triumphantly.

Jamie tucked his ID back into his wallet. Turning the key in the ignition, he slipped the car into gear and started forward, just fast enough to knock the flashlight aside. He ignored the outraged cry of "Hey, you kids get back here right now or you're in real trouble!"

Jamie's heart was pounding so hard he thought it must be visible, and he could hardly force the breath in and out of his throat, but he kept on, out of the parking lot and through the quiet streets toward Rima's house. *This has to stop,* he told himself.

Rima was crying; oddly, that calmed him. "It's all right," he said. "That guy can't hurt us."

"What if he took your license number?" she said. "He could report us."

"Not if I report him first," Jamie said.

"What do you mean?"

"He's not allowed to do that, harass people like that, refuse to identify himself; he wasn't even in uniform."

"But how can you report him if you don't know who he is?"

"I'm not sure, but I bet my folks will know."

"You're going to tell them about this?"

Jamie pulled up in front of Rima's house. "You bet I am," he said.

"Aren't they going to be mad?"

He shrugged. "I don't see why, we weren't doing anything wrong. And even if they are, what difference does that make? The important thing is stopping this character from bullying people. Even if they're irritated at me—hell, even if they're furious at me—they'll still be on my side." Then it hit him. *It's the same way I can be on Steve's side: I can be his brother, even if I make mistakes with him. Even if I started off wrong, I can still fix it. Look at how things ended yesterday; I did help him.*

Rima leaned across and kissed him on the cheek. "You're really changing," she said. "I think your new brother is having a good influence on you, having somebody around who understands the kind of thing you've been through."

"Maybe so," Jamie said.

CHAPTER 39.

THURSDAY, AUGUST 22, 1957

There was a time, Jamie thought, *when I would have gone to my cabinet over this.* He stretched mentally, feeling for the boundaries of his confidence. *Am I sorry that I showed it to Steve, gave it to him as a refuge? No. I'm not sorry. It's been getting too small for me—in more ways than one.*

He drew a deep breath and closed the book he was failing to read. He swiveled his desk chair a little and looked around the guest room. He planned to cede the desk in their bedroom to Steve, too, having seen how nervous he was about starting school next week. This room was quieter, and there was enough space for him to spread his books out without encroaching on Steve or making their bedroom seem like an exploded library.

The room was fine; it was the conversation he knew was taking place downstairs that was distracting him and bringing up second thoughts about giving up the cabinet. He'd come upstairs to avoid it, thinking it would make him more nervous to listen in while his parents pursued the complaint against last night's mysterious constable, but not knowing what was going on was proving to be worse.

Also, sitting here alone was making him think about Steve and how badly he'd failed him in their conversation yesterday, and in the weeks before.

195

He pulled out a handkerchief and polished the lenses of his glasses, taking his time about it. He tightened the laces of his brown oxfords, noting that they could stand a polish. He aligned his papers with the edge of the desk, absently admiring the swirls of the fractals he'd been drawing, and laid his fountain pen perpendicular across the stack. Having run out of time-wasting maneuvers, he pushed himself out of the chair and made his way downstairs.

He hovered near the closed study door, listening to the steady rumble of Dad's voice, interspersed with occasional sharp comments from Mom. He raised his hand to the knob, then let it fall again and turned towards the living room.

Laurie was there, in the armchair by the window, watching Jamie over the top of a book. "What's up, Doc?" he asked with a grin that slid into a grimace of concern as Jamie came into the room and Laurie could see his face.

Jamie flapped a dismissive hand. "It's nothing, really," he said. "Rima and I got harassed by some guy claiming to be a constable last night; the folks are hot on the trail."

Laurie closed his book and set it on the deep windowsill beside him. "Don't you want to be in there with them?"

Jamie shrugged, dropping onto the long couch. "The idea makes me nervous," he admitted. "Part of me wants to see this guy get his, he was so obnoxious. But part of me is… this will sound stupid, but… scared. Like they're going to set something off, going after a cop."

"Like the SS will be at the door, next thing?" Laurie said.

"I told you it was stupid."

"I don't think it is at all. I know what it's like to be leery of some guy in a uniform with a gun. 'The policeman is your friend,'" he quoted mockingly. "Not yours and mine, though."

An idea struck Jamie. "God, if that had been you and Linda in the car last night—"

"Why do you think we never make out in cars? A black boy and a white girl? Trouble not only for us, but for the folks, too."

Jamie whistled through his teeth. "I think that's what makes me nervous here," he said. "It feels like I'm somehow putting them in danger."

"What kind of danger?"

"The kind where the Nazis come and get you, I guess." He looked at Laurie. "I remembered some stuff yesterday, talking to Steve. Where I got some of my scars; I knew that before, of course, but I showed them to him, and that made it come back, how they actually happened."

Laurie drew back in his chair, surprised. "You did? But you didn't... you know, I would have thought that would have brought on one of those nightmares. Or at least a flashback; did you have one of those?"

Now it was Jamie's turn to be surprised. "No, I didn't," he realized. "Talking to Steve made the memories come back, but I could handle them. It wasn't fun, but it didn't make me fall apart."

"That must have been some conversation."

"It was an awful conversation. I was terrible to him. I was afraid, on some level, that being around him would pull me back to where I was before, but talking to Rima last night, I didn't feel that way so much. I don't know that I won't be crappy to him again, though."

"Why?"

"Why? What do you mean, why? Isn't it obvious?"

"Oh, you mean because you're such an awful person?"

"Well, I'm not in the same league as Saint Laurie, I know that." Jamie escaped the hurt on his brother's face by pulling his glasses off.

He pinched the bridge of his nose and said, face turned downwards, "Don't pay any attention to me; I'm just jealous."

"Jealous of what? Or who?"

"Whom," Jamie said reflexively. They both laughed, and Jamie put his glasses back on, though he still didn't look at Laurie. "I saw you two through the window, walking up to the house. It made me…" He thought about what exactly the feeling had been. "It made me feel left out, the way I do with you and Robbie."

There was a silence, then Laurie said softly, "Rob and I never meant to make you feel left out." Jamie shrugged and Laurie went on, "The other day I heard you use a phrase: 'Zero sum game.' Love's not like that, you know, where there's only so much and the more people it's divided among the less there is for each. It's more like— like yeast in the bread Ruby makes on Shabbat. The more there is, the more the bread grows."

Jamie rolled his eyes, but he did feel better about it. He went over to the chess table and pulled the playing pieces out of the drawer, arranging them on the board as he thought over what Laurie had said. He tried to focus on the logic of the thought, rather than the mawkishness of the sentiment. *It's true that emotion is unquantifiable, not subject to either inflation or entropy; it can fluctuate in microcosm while maintaining a steady state.* He shook his head at his own flight into abstraction and came back to the concrete. *And I did help Steve in the end, even if I did snipe at him at first.*

The study door opened and Jamie craned around the corner to see Mom and Dad coming out. "I'm in here," he said.

They came into the living room and settled on one of the settees.

"He was off duty," Dad said. "He had no business interfering with you. And he absolutely is required to provide name and identification when asked."

"They stonewalled and covered their backsides—and his," Mom said, "but I think the message was received. He won't be bothering you any more. I thought of pressing for him to apologize to you both, but…"

"Oh, God, please, no," Jamie said hastily. "And thanks for doing what you did."

"On the other hand," Dad said, "you were in fact trespassing. If you want to spend time with Rima, do it at our house or hers from now on."

"Yes, sir," Jamie said.

"After all," Mom put in, "it's not as though you'd be doing anything you couldn't do here, anyway—right?"

"Of course, Mother." He managed an impudent grin, then said reluctantly, "But I'm still worried about that crack he made about the military. I don't want this to make any trouble for you, Dad."

Dad laughed. "Don't worry about that, son. I had a few words to say on that subject myself. In the first place, nobody in this neck of the woods is going to make trouble for anyone named McAlister; my family's lived here since Moses was a pup. In the second place, the War College is important to Carlisle's economy, and peaceful coexistence with military personnel is important to local law enforcement. In fact, my repeating that anti-military remark is what galvanized them into figuring out who this constable was and promising to put his feet to the fire."

Jamie breathed a little easier at that. "Well, thanks for going to bat for me," he said.

"That's what we're here for, sweetheart," Mom said.

They both came over and leaned in to kiss his cheeks, then waved at Laurie and disappeared back into the study.

"Feeling better?" Laurie said.

"Sure," Jamie answered. "I knew it would be ok, really, but it's a relief to know it for sure." What he didn't say was that he was suddenly filled with a surge of self-confidence. *Yes, it took the folks to follow up and fix things, but it started with me standing up for myself; I didn't just cave in to that guy.*

Laurie, though, was following a different train of thought. "Kinda cramp your style, though, having to limit your make-out action to the house. Linda and I have the excuse of studying together to go into the spare room, but—"

Jamie shrugged. "To tell you the truth, just lately we've been soft-pedaling that aspect of things." He gave Laurie a sidelong look. "I almost feel… relieved, like it's an excuse to cool things off a little."

Laurie nodded. "Well, good, then. Want to play some chess?"

"Sure," Jamie said.

Chapter 40.

Saturday, October 5, 1957

Another Yom Kippur had passed. Most of Jamie's family had, as usual, spent the day with him at services. Ruby had taken Steve home after the morning service; he'd done well staying in a crowded room listening to unfamiliar prayers, some of them not in English, but when he'd started to tremble in a fine thrum like the humming of a power cable, Mom had signaled to Ruby to take Steve away.

So the rest of the family came home for the break-the-fast meal rather than staying for the synagogue potluck.

Ruby met them at the door with Steve beside her. "Come on in," she said.

That's odd, Jamie thought.

On the thought, Dad said, "Ruby, what's happened? Is something wrong?"

"You haven't heard the news?" she said.

Jamie's stomach sank. *Oh, God, not another horrible race killing!*

But as they all pressed into the front hall, she said, "The Russians have put a satellite into orbit. Sputnik, they call it. It happened yesterday."

"Oh, my God," Mom moaned.

"The Soviet Union's in space before us?" Laurie said blankly.

"Now they can spy on us, shoot us…" Celia stopped, seeing the look of panic on Joy's face. "I'm sure Eisenhower's got some secret plan," she said reassuringly.

"Oh, yeah," Rob scoffed. "Old General Don't-Tell-Me-Your-Troubles is right on top of things."

"What do you think, Dad?" Beth said. "Should we be worried?"

"I think I have to make some calls," Dad said. He moved into the study and closed the door behind him.

"Well, come in and have some supper, anyway," Ruby said. "The world looks worse on an empty stomach."

In a few seconds, Jamie and Steve were the only ones left in the hallway.

"I don't even know what everybody's talking about," Steve said miserably. "What's a sat-a-whatever? And what's so bad about it?"

"It's a device that's orbiting—going around—the earth, way up high, higher than an airplane, up where there's no air. I don't know what this particular one can do, what kinds of tools they've built into it, but I'd bet it isn't much, not on this first one."

Jamie started for the dining room, Steve trailing behind. *He's trusting me enough to ask questions; keep talking.* "And people are upset because the Russians got there first, the Communists, and they're our enemies, but also because it's something really important in the history of the world, and we feel like America should be the one to do that kind of thing."

Answering Steve's questions made Jamie's own feelings crystallize. The tingling in his stomach wasn't anxiety or dread, it was excitement.

Dad came in behind them and everyone settled at the table. "I'll be going to meet with Max Johnson, the commandant over at the War College, after supper," Dad said. "They're going on alert till we know more about what's going on. But I don't think there's any immediate danger. They're saying this thing is less than eighty-five kilos and just a little bigger than a volleyball. It can't have much of a payload—"

"Eighty-five kilos!" Jamie interrupted. "That's getting on for two hundred pounds! Dad, that's *huge*. How did they manage it?"

The others were all staring at him. Jamie realized they were reacting to the awe and admiration in his tone. "Don't you get it?" he said to them. "This isn't just about the Cold War, this is something that's going to change the world. Man, I'm glad to be going to college early. I'll bet there's going to be more support for math and science students now."

Dad's shoulders relaxed a little. "That's the spirit," he said. "Now, how about we say grace and refuel?"

After supper, Jamie gravitated to the baby grand in the living room, looking for an outlet for the tumult of his feelings. He'd finally mastered the Liszt piano sonata, and soon lost himself in the flow of the music. He played the whole thing through, almost half an hour. As the final double bass chords diminished to silence, he heard a soft, "Wow," from beyond the raised lid of the piano.

He craned around it to see Steve on the armchair in the bay window.

"How'd he do that?" Steve asked.

"Do what?"

"That thing at the end, that jump. And the way it sounds, that's different."

"You mean this?" Jamie played the A minor, F major, B major progression. "The different sound you hear is called an augmented fourth—here, come look."

Steve came to stand behind him and leaned over the keyboard, propping a hand on the music rack.

"See," Jamie explained, demonstrating, "this is called a perfect fourth, and this is a perfect fifth. The augmented fourth is here, sort of in between, along with the diminished fifth." *Going too fast? No, he looks more interested than I've ever seen him.*

So Jamie went on, "And that 'jump' you heard, you're right, that's very unusual. People at the time—a hundred years ago—thought it was awful, you know."

"Can I try?" Steve breathed.

Jamie got up and let him sit on the stool. Steve tried to mimic Jamie's fingering; he got it wrong, of course, yet he was surprisingly close. *But then, it's pretty surprising he could hear the music so precisely and understand what was happening so well. Robbie said he liked music, but I had no idea...*

Jamie reached down to adjust Steve's fingers and the kid flinched, startling him. *It's just an impersonal correction, I wouldn't have thought it would make him nervous.*

The fine-boned, slender wrist was trembling ever so slightly, but Steve took a breath and lifted his hand from the keyboard, silently inviting Jamie to position it. Understanding blossomed in Jamie's head. *He doesn't flinch from touch the way I do, to hide from feelings; he does it because he's afraid of being physically hurt.*

An unaccustomed tenderness filled him, looking down on the blond head bent before him. "It'll be a while before you can play Liszt," he said, guiding him to the keys for the chord. "Why don't you ask the folks to set you up with lessons? Mrs. Seixas is very nice."

Steve shrank in on himself. "No," he said. "Robbie's teaching me guitar, that's enough. Besides, lessons cost money, right?"

"Right. So you're not worth spending money on?"

Jamie saw that, in Steve's mind, the question answered itself.

"You don't have to worry about that," he told the kid. "What do you think we keep them around for, except to spend money on us?"

The sarcasm went over Steve's head, as Jamie should have expected. "I thought it was to help us out, like when you had that trouble with that constable guy."

"Well, that's right, but this is kind of the same thing, isn't it? Just a different kind of help. Like when I go to college, I'm going to try for a math scholarship, but if I don't get one even with the impetus of this Sputnik business, they'll come up with the money somehow."

Steve slipped off the stool and stepped out of Jamie's immediate space, turning half away from him. "Yeah, but that's you," he said. "You're, like, some kind of genius or something. I'm nothing."

"Oh, right, poor you," Jamie scoffed. "Laying it on a little thick there, aren't you, kid?"

Steve's mouth gaped, then twisted into a rueful smile. "You think?" he said. "Everybody else gets all googly when I say stuff like that."

"I'm a tougher nut to crack," Jamie said. They grinned conspiratorially at each other, but it seemed to Jamie that they both knew there was a real underlying pain in Steve's joke, and a real concern in Jamie's.

"Let's go listen to your radio," Jamie said. "There's probably something about Sputnik on it; maybe we can even hear the satellite itself."

"It makes noise?" Steve asked.

"Well, it doesn't play Liszt," Jamie said. "But it probably broadcasts some sort of signal."

They headed for their bedroom, contentment filling Jamie's gut like an unfamiliar wine.

Chapter 41.

Wednesday, November 27, 1957

Ruby's great-nephew Henry Still had come from Philadelphia to spend Thanksgiving with them.

Jamie'd had a chance to size him up a little during the Monopoly game Laurie had dragooned him into joining this afternoon. Jamie had mostly been absorbed in applying some of the ideas from a book he'd been reading on game theory, but in analyzing how the various players mixed, and speculating on composite strategies, he had paid more attention to Henry than he otherwise might have.

He seemed ok; smart enough, and personable: a little jittery, but Jamie chalked that up to his being uncomfortable with people who employed his great-aunt. From what Laurie had said, none of Ruby's family understood her relationship with the McAlister family, or believed how much more than an employee or a servant she was to them.

In any case, Henry gradually relaxed as the afternoon wore on. He'd even flashed a grin during a negotiation between himself and Joy when Jamie had muttered, "Nash's Equilibrium."

"Only if she takes the deal," he'd said. "Otherwise, it's the Prisoners' Dilemma."

"In Monopoly? I don't see it," Jamie'd answered. Henry had shrugged and nodded, conceding the point. The others had looked puzzled, and Laurie seemed a little put out that Jamie evidently shared some area of interest with his "cousin" that didn't include him, but he visibly quashed the feeling and confined himself to asking mildly, "Want to share with the group?"

After five minutes of Henry and Jamie talking about monopoly versus monopsony and payoff matrices, Laurie had waved his hands in laughing defeat while the others clamored to resume the game. But Henry had leaned toward Laurie and said in an undertone, "You need to know this stuff if you're going to learn political strategy." Laurie had reached over and flicked Henry's forehead with his forefinger, the way he did with Jamie sometimes when he felt Jamie was getting too cerebral.

Now, with supper just over and Beth and Joy bustling around helping Ruby clear up as the rest moved into the living room, Henry seemed almost naturally part of the group. When Mom and Dad excused themselves to go do some paperwork in the study, the last of the tension seemed to go out of Henry's shoulders.

"So where's these here gals I heered tell of," he leered in a comic rustic accent.

"They'll be a-moseyin' in right peart," Laurie said in the same vein.

"I don't think you can be 'peart' while 'moseying,'" Jamie objected. "'Mosey' implies a leisurely, lazy sort of movement, while 'peart'—"

Laurie threw a sofa pillow at him. "Excuse my little brother," he said to Henry. "His brain's so big it spills out his ears sometimes; he can't help himself."

The doorbell rang before Jamie could think of a response. "The chick-mobile!" Rob shouted, and ran to answer.

Soon the girls were among them: Laurie's girlfriend, Linda, who'd driven them all; Rima, back from Franklin and Marshall for the holiday; Nancy, Robbie's girlfriend; and her friend Mary, obviously here for Henry.

"We should have invited our boyfriends," Beth said to Celia, popping out of the dining room to check on what was happening.

"Ray's at his grandparents' for Thanksgiving, you know that, Beth. You're just showing off that you finally have a boyfriend yourself. Too bad he lives in the back of beyond."

Beth murmured, "Plymouth Meeting's not so isolated, now that the Turnpike goes through it," as she disappeared back into the dining room to finish the cleanup, but she said it with a satisfied smirk and Jamie realized she really had just wanted an excuse to mention that she had a boyfriend, as of the past two weeks.

By now the girls had their coats off and Rima had come to stand by the settee where Jamie perched. "Come on," he said, patting the seat cushion beside him. "Tell me what college is like."

He'd seen her a couple of times since the beginning of the semester; F&M was close enough that she came home almost every other weekend. But this would be the first time they'd get to spend an evening together since she started.

She smiled and squeezed his hand as she sat down, but when he leaned to kiss her she turned her head ever so slightly so that his lips hit the crease beside her mouth. *Was that on purpose?* He tried to catch her eye, but she was looking across at Henry as Laurie introduced him to everyone.

"Did I hear someone mention college?" Henry asked her. "Where are you going?" and the conversation became general.

After a while, Celia put some music on the hi-fi and they moved the settees and the coffee table aside and kicked off their shoes to dance on the carpet. Shuffling to the syrupy strains of Debbie Reynolds crooning "Tammy," Jamie pressed against Rima, relishing the familiar, comforting contours of her ample curves. Beside them,

Henry was dancing with Nancy's friend Mary, who was giggling and blushing and generally acting like an idiot; Henry impassively turned and dipped and swung her in a much more accomplished mode than Jamie could, his slim body swaying to the beat, his intelligent face focused and intent.

Rima poked Jamie in the side. "Hey," she said softly. "You still with me?"

"Where else do you think I am?"

"I don't know, it felt like I lost you there for a minute. Listen, let's sit down, I want to talk."

They retreated to the long couch by the door as the record ended and the next one came on: Presley's "All Shook Up." Laurie laughingly opted out and disappeared with Linda to fetch refreshments, but Nancy and Rob and Henry and Mary threw themselves into it; Celia and Beth danced with each other.

"Boy's got rhythm," Jamie observed sardonically, hoping to get a rise out of Rima, but she refused to be deflected.

"I've been thinking," she said.

"Uh, oh."

She shot him a reproachful look and he settled down. She said, "We've never really talked about what you said that day behind the cafeteria, about you feeling what you wanted from me was more about comfort than sex."

"That's not exactly the way I'd put it, but yeah, ok," Jamie said, forcing himself to meet her eyes. "You said you'd have to think over how you felt about that, but then we seemed to just go on like before.'

She took his hand and stared down at their joined fingers. "It was easier to coast along, not making waves, just keeping the status quo. But since I've started college—moving away a little bit, and seeing how other couples interact—I've realized I don't want to just get by."

She brought her other hand around to cover their joined ones. "I deserve more, Jamie." Looking up and seeing his face, she said quickly, "I'm not breaking up with you."

"You're not?"

"Not exactly. Well, it depends on whether you can live with…. I'm saying, I still want to be with you, but I'm not going to hold myself to being with you exclusively. I'm going to look around, get to know other guys, see… see whether I'm attractive to anyone else." She finished in a whisper, but Jamie heard her loud and clear.

Or whether you're only good enough for a loser like me, Jamie thought bitterly, then quashed the thought. *You know that's not what she means.* He gave her a wry smile. "That seems fair," he said carefully, remembering what Laurie had said after the constable incident. "It's not a zero-sum game, after all."

Rima sighed. "It's not a game at all, Jamie."

Jamie was saved from answering when Steve came down the stairs behind them and into the room, drawn by the music, evidently. He perched on the ottoman by Jamie, smiling uncertainly. Linda and Laurie backed into the room through the swinging door to the dining room, carrying trays of snacks and drinks. Rima jumped up to help them; Jamie, with an effort, refrained from burying his head in his hands.

CHAPTER 42.

THURSDAY, NOVEMBER 28, 1957

L ate on Thanksgiving night, ready for bed, Jamie realized he'd left the latest *Life* magazine on the desk in the guest room where Henry was staying. *It's been half an hour since everyone headed upstairs; it can wait till morning.*

But he wanted to read it before he slept, and besides… something in him wanted to speak to the young man Laurie had started calling his cousin. Jamie reminded himself that Laurie had disliked him when he'd met him at Ruby's sister's in Philadelphia last year; he'd made an anti-Semitic remark and his grandfather had taken a strap to him for it. But they'd been writing to each other, and met again at the Prayer Pilgrimage for Freedom this spring. He'd seemed pleasant enough then and today. But that first time, he'd used the word "kike," Laurie had said. *So who's the real Henry?*

Mind made up, Jamie stepped across the hall from his room and rapped softly on the guest room door. It opened almost immediately, and Henry stood there expectantly, wearing only a pair of pajama bottoms slung low on his hips. His skin was a smooth medium brown, a little lighter than Laurie's; his chest hair was wiry but sparse, and narrowed to a tapering line as it disappeared into his waistband.

Henry shifted a little and Jamie realized he'd been staring. "Uh, sorry," he said. "Sorry to bother you. I left a magazine in here …" He trailed off.

Henry stepped aside and gestured him in. "That's ok," he said, "I wasn't asleep or anything."

As Jamie moved to the desk, Henry said, "Actually, I was hoping to get a chance to talk to you. Laurie said he told you what happened that time he visited us, when I got in trouble."

Jamie, turning with the magazine, involuntarily glanced down to those loose pajama pants. Horrified at himself, he dragged his eyes back up to Henry's face, feeling his own face flush with heat.

Henry barked a short laugh. "Guess you know just what kind of trouble I got in, huh?"

"I'm sorry, I didn't mean to… I mean, I'm not, uh…"

Henry was laughing outright now. "Geez, you're as bad as Laurie. I can't believe you people get so shook up over a simple walloping. Are you that scared of a little pain?"

Jamie felt the blood leave his face. "You don't want to know what I know about pain," he said coldly.

Henry sank back to perch on the edge of his bed. "Ok, fair enough," he said slowly. "Laurie told me you'd been through some pretty dark shit. But that's not the same ballpark, don't you see? It'd be like me sayin Papaw Still whalin my ass was like lynching. It's a whole different world."

Jamie leaned back against the desk and crossed his ankles, getting into the discussion. "A quantum difference in scale, yes, but on the same continuum, isn't it? Violence is violence."

"That's like sayin, 'Aspirin can kill you if you take too much, so don't take any—poison is poison.'"

Jamie shook his head. "I can't believe I'm the one bringing this up, but you're ignoring the emotional component. Violent behavior affects both the perpetrator and the victim; it desensitizes both, and begets more."

"Well, if we're gonna talk emotions, you're leavin out that my papaw loves me. And he was hurtin me a little to keep me from bigger hurt. I don't learn to control my mouth, I risk a lot more than some candy-ass white kid would."

An image burst into Jamie's mind: Tati pulling him back from the porch of Cousin Yankel's shul and slapping him hard across the face; he'd laughed at a kid on the street wearing a ridiculous outfit. *One of the Hitlerjügend, Hitler Youth,* he realized now. *Tati was afraid for me.*

"Jews, too," he said to Henry.

"Yeah, it's one of the things we have in common, one of the reasons Jews and Negroes are political allies."

"I know plenty of prejudiced Jews."

"I don't care how they feel about me, long as they vote in ways that benefit me, and mostly they do." Henry shrugged. "Anyway, that nasty word I used was more to do with flippin my wig that they were all goin ape over Laurie."

Jamie snorted. "I'm on your wavelength there, as Robbie would say."

Henry put his head to one side. "Turns out Laurie's a pretty nice guy, though."

"Yeah, he is. Listen, I better let you get some sleep, it's been a long day for you."

"Sure. Enjoy the magazine—some babe, huh?"

Confused, Jamie looked at it. There was a picture of some actress or something on the cover. He shrugged. "I guess. I'm interested in the article on the missile program, and the one on Sputnik. Which reminds me: where did you learn about game theory?"

"I'd been reading this guy von Neumann, and that led me to John Nash." Jamie noticed that Henry lost his sliding, Philadelphia-toned diction when he focused on an academic topic. "I've been thinking to use it in civil rights work, understanding how individuals interact in a group."

"You should try that new book by Luce and Raiffa," Jamie said. "It's a little more accessible, too—might appeal to Laurie more, if you want him to get into the subject."

Henry shook his head ruefully. "I'm rethinking that," he said. "Watching him with you all, I realized that he's got a natural instinct for grasping behavior and strategies." He rubbed his hands over his close-cropped head and leaned sideways against the pillows, tucking his long bare feet under the afghan folded across the bottom of the bed.

"I've been watching your whole family," he went on. "At dinner today, when Aunt Ruby stopped your little brother—Steve, is it?—from hiding turkey in his napkin, the kid flinched like she was going to bash him."

"He was starved and beaten for years," Jamie said stiffly. He backed up toward the door.

"I know, Laurie told me. And you, too, you had stuff like that happen, right?"

Jamie nodded.

Henry sat up again, hands clasped between his knees. "So they don't hit you, and you learn to communicate other ways."

"That's only part of it," Jamie said. "Anyway, I don't communicate much at all." He turned his eyes away from where Henry lounged half-naked on the bed. *I've got to get out of here.*

Henry seemed to pick up on his unease. He flapped his hands at Jamie as he got up off the bed. "Ok, thus endeth tonight's Jewish/Negro Summit Meeting on Violence in the Home and Society," he laughed. "You're excused." He clapped a hand on Jamie's shoulder as he closed the door behind him.

CHAPTER 43.

SATURDAY, FEBRUARY 27, 1958

Steve's adoption had been formally approved. The family had spent the evening gathered in the living room, singing and laughing and eating the carrot cake Ruby had made to mark the occasion. Jamie didn't care for the cake, and he wasn't much for singing, but he was able to enjoy the celebratory atmosphere.

Still, watching Steve shyly smiling at the others from where he sat on the floor at Rob's feet, Jamie couldn't help but wonder whether it were really going to be that simple. *His face looks ok, but his body seems wound tight as a spring. I wonder if anyone else notices that.* He glanced around and caught Mom's eye. *Yeah, I guess so,* he thought as she gave him a minute nod, then went back to watching Steve.

Dad, though, seemed to have his eye on Laurie more often than not. Laurie did seem a little abstracted, swaying to "Good Night, Irene," but losing the words and humming for some of it. He was sitting on a settee instead of his armchair by the window, and Celia, sitting next to him, seemed squeezed up a little closer than usual. *Something's going on there, too.*

Laurie had received a National Leadership Award at school recently. It carried a nice scholarship prize with it. *So he's all set for college, what could he have to fuss about? And Haverford accepted him already, while I haven't heard from MIT yet.* Jamie mentally shrugged. *No sense worrying about it, there's nothing I can do about whatever it is, I'm sure.*

Eventually, the evening drew to a close. Joy insisted on leading the family in three cheers for Steve, which seemed to both embarrass and please him, then they all headed to their rooms for the night.

Jamie was just saying his prayers when Steve came out of the bathroom. The kid got into bed but, instead of just turning off his light the way he usually did, he sat watching till Jamie was finished. Jamie remembered how David had challenged him over his reciting the Hebrew blessings and wondered whether Steve was about to give him grief over it.

Instead, the younger boy said seriously, "Does that help?"

Jamie considered pretending not to know what he meant, then rejected that idea. "It does," he said. "In that place—you know, the place where I was…"

Steve nodded. Since he and Jamie had shown each other their scars, they'd talked a few tentative times about what they'd experienced. Steve now knew what a concentration camp was, and that Jamie had been in one.

"So," Jamie continued, "there weren't any, like, holidays or anything, you understand. Aside from the fact there was nothing to celebrate, and nothing to eat beyond what barely kept us alive, nobody had any energy; the grownups came back to the barracks at night exhausted, hardly able to hold their heads up." Jamie shifted around to stare at the ceiling instead of Steve's intent face, remembering. "But a few people," he went on, "my Tati—my father—for instance, still said their prayers night and morning. And when he died, I kept on with it. It was something I remembered from Before, and it felt like a connection to him and Mamme."

"So it's not really about, like, God or whatever, at all?"

Jamie thought about it. "Yes and no," he said finally. "I'm not completely sure I believe in God. I mean, after all, if there's a God, why isn't he doing a better job of it?" He glanced across at Steve, who nodded in understanding.

"But still," Jamie went on, "there's… I don't know… Something there. Some*one*, maybe even, like the folks think. And keeping up the prayers is like keeping the communication lines open."

"Like maybe someday he'll pick up the phone?"

Jamie laughed. "Something like that."

There was a tap on the door, then Celia pushed it open a few inches. "Something's going on," she said. "Mom and Dad are in with Laurie. I think it's about the prom; he told me Dean Dunkelman is threatening Linda to keep them from going to it together. Anyway, he's crying."

She disappeared. Jamie and Steve looked at each other. *This is what it must be like when I have a nightmare and everybody comes,* Jamie thought. He swung his feet out of bed and put on his glasses. At the door, he looked back at Steve. "You coming? You're really a member of the family now, remember."

Steve drew his knees up to his chest. "What can I do?" he said. "I don't know how to help anybody."

"Neither do I," Jamie answered. "But we can be there."

"Oh," Steve said. "Oh, ok, I can do that." The two of them headed down the hall together.

CHAPTER 44.

SATURDAY, MARCH 15, 1958

Jamie and Beth were cleaning the TV room. He straightened magazines and cleared away clutter while she dusted the furniture. It was easy work, and made for easy talking.

They'd been discussing Laurie, and his problems with the school administration over his plan to take Linda to the prom. The whole family was worked up about it, and word had evidently gotten out beyond the family, since Laurie'd had a threatening call last night.

"It was supposedly anonymous," Beth was saying, "but Laurie told me this morning that he recognized the voice. It was somebody named Tank Lebo."

Jamie stopped rolling old newspapers for fireplace kindling, thinking about the muscular blond he'd stared at during dozens of track meets, and dreamed of as a Nazi more than once now. *Why is he in my head so often?* "What did he say?" he rasped.

"Nothing specific, just some nasty names and that Laurie 'better watch out' if he dared go to the dance with a white girl. I take it you know him?"

"We're not friends or anything, but I know who he is."

"You sound upset."

"Of course I'm upset," he snapped. "The guy's threatening my brother."

There was a silence as Beth calmly moved the ornaments on top of the television console cabinet so she could dust under them.

Jamie's mouth was dry. "Ok," he admitted, as though she'd accused him of something. He went back to rolling newspapers. "There is something about this particular guy that… that gets to me. If you could see him, you might understand."

"Is he especially unpleasant to look at?"

"He's beautiful." Jamie could have bitten his tongue. *Why did I say that?*

Beth, though, simply said, "Ah."

"What do you mean, 'Ah'?"

"Just that I imagine it would be upsetting, if his looks are so different from his manner. This whole business of looks is mysterious to me, you know—Laurie's skin, for instance, doesn't feel any different to me than yours or mine, but everyone who can see him seems to automatically think they know things about him because of it." She finished dusting the TV and moved on to the small bookcase under the window. "Do people think this Tank Lebo person is better than he acts because of the way he looks?"

Jamie stacked the rolled papers next to the door, ready to be stored by the fireplaces in the living room and study, and went on to straightening the cushions on the sofa and refolding the afghan over its back. "I suppose they do," he said. "Nobody really calls him on his crap, anyway. Of course, that's partly because they're afraid of him."

"Was he one of the people who bullied Steve in the playground that time after he first came to live with us?"

"No, that was Tom Varner and a couple of his sidekicks, another set of sterling characters."

Beth sighed. "There is a lot of ugliness in the world, I guess." Then she brightened a little. "But Steve's growing all the time, don't you think? The way he sang that song for Mom on her birthday this week, and even played the guitar, now that was something beautiful."

"Yeah, it was," Jamie agreed. "Hey, could you give me a hand here? This sofa got pushed out of place, I want to straighten it out again."

She came over to him. "Just hold that end down," he said. "Keep it from shifting while I move it from this end. Ok, that's got it, thanks."

Beth, dusting finished, went and sat on the wicker armchair while Jamie fetched up an empty coffee cup revealed by the shifting of the sofa. "There was that incident at the end of Mom's party, though," she said.

"The flashback, yeah," he agreed.

"Was that like what happens to you sometimes, when you seem to relive some horrible experience?"

"That's right. I never know what will trigger it, a sound or a glimpse of something" *like a flash of blond hair,* he thought, "will bring back an event I've tried not to think about."

"I couldn't tell what brought it back for Steve."

"It was Mom's necklace, Joy's present to her. It fell forward when she leaned over Steve to thank him for the song, and it's metal, so it triggered a memory of Steve's cousin beating him with the buckle end of his belt."

There was another silence, then Beth said, "We should spend more time with him. Well, I should, anyway—I guess you're with him a lot as it is."

"We don't talk much, though," Jamie said. "I probably should do something besides just read in the same room as him."

"Let's all go for a walk!"

"What, now? In the rain?" Jamie said disbelievingly, glancing out the window.

"I can hear it, it's just a drizzle, sissy," Beth teased. "Are you made of sugar?"

"I thought that was supposed to be you," he grumbled. "All right, you go get him while I put away this junk. But if I get pneumonia, you're taking care of me."

"Deal," she said, giggling. She ran lightly into the hall and up the front stairs as Jamie took the papers to the fireplaces and the mug to the kitchen. He shook his head resignedly at the dripping trees outside the back door and went to get his raincoat.

Chapter 45.

Jamie slipped into the house behind Steve and Rob, who were chattering away about Elvis having been drafted into the army. Laurie and Celia came in behind him, arguing over St. Patrick and whether American schools ought to be observing the supposed death date of a fifth-century bishop.

Jamie didn't care much about either topic. He and Beth had had a pleasant walk with Steve the other day, but it had been hard to find a subject of conversation in common, and the kid had seemed troubled and a little sulky.

He hung up his jacket, reveling in the warmth of the house after the chilly bluster outside, and turned to the stack of mail Ruby had set on the hall table. *I'm always the odd man out,* he thought as he sorted through the envelopes. *They don't even notice I'm not talking to them.*

There it was. His heart sank as he stared at the thin, narrow envelope with the MIT seal in the corner. "Science and Arts," it said, and at the bottom *"Mens et Manus." Mind and hand,* he translated to himself. *Not for me.* For a while, Jamie had thought he might have some control of his life, that his parents were right when they told him he could shape his own future. *The future's not mine, any more than the past was.*

Laurie's hand came to rest on his shoulder. He'd noticed after all. Jamie wished he hadn't.

"It came?" he breathed into Jamie's ear. The others were already thundering upstairs. Jamie reflexively crushed the envelope in his fist and thrust it into his shirt pocket. Laurie had been accepted at Haverford back in November, Early Decision. He didn't have anything to worry about.

Jamie shrugged the hand off. "Yeah, guess I'll have senior year in high school after all," he said as flatly as he could manage.

"Oh, shit, sweetheart," Laurie said.

Then Celia spoke; she must have come back down when she saw them standing there. "Oh, Jamie," she said. "The folks said you should apply to more than one school, this is just—"

Now he had no trouble controlling his voice. "Right," he snapped. "You all told me so. I screwed up again. Thanks for your support."

"I didn't mean that," she started, as Laurie protested over her, "Come on, you know that's not what…"

Cold air washed over them and the front door closed with a thud. "What's going on here?" Mom asked.

They moved aside to let her put her purse and gloves on the table and take off her hat. Laurie helped her off with her coat and hung it up as Celia said, "Jamie heard from MIT; he didn't get in."

Her shoulders slumped. "Oh, sweetie, I'm so sorry. Listen, come into the study and we can talk about—"

"There's nothing to talk about," he said, turning toward the stairs. "You were all right, I should have applied to other schools."

"Jamie, I'm sorry," Celia said. "I was commiserating with you, not trying to say it was your fault. I only—"

"Wait a minute," Laurie interrupted. "You just barely had time to pick up that envelope; I don't think it was even open. Have you actually read what they said?"

"I didn't have to," Jamie said tiredly. "It's too thin to be an acceptance. They would have sent other stuff with it. It has to be a rejection."

Mom heaved a deep sigh. "Jamie, for heaven's sake," she said. "Open it. Now."

Jamie closed his eyes and pressed his hand against his shirt pocket so the envelope folded into it crackled.

"Now," Mom repeated firmly.

Without looking at her, he plucked it out of his pocket and held it out. She took it out of his hand and he listened to the crackling as she tore it open without bothering to pick up the letter opener that lived on the hall table.

When he heard her sigh again, his heart shriveled and his head started to throb. All he wanted was to be alone. But then she was prodding at his hand with the damned thing.

"Read it," she said softly. "Sweetie, open your eyes and read it."

She's right. I have to face reality. Biting his lip, he shook out the creased paper. For a second, his brain couldn't make sense of the words. *"We are pleased to inform you..."* Pleased? *They're* pleased *to reject me?*

His eyes dropped to the next paragraph. *"...orientation packet and financial aid information will follow shortly."*

"What does it mean? I don't understand," he said, allowing his voice to shake a little now.

"It means you've been accepted," Mom said, voice still soft as though she thought he might bolt like a frightened bird.

Laurie and Celia had no such compunctions; they both yelped in delight. Laurie pummeled him on the shoulder while Celia grabbed him around the neck and kissed his ear before he could duck away. Rob and Steve had evidently been lurking on the stairs. They joined the scrum, then Joy came out of the TV room and Ruby appeared from the direction of the kitchen and Jamie was the center of exclaiming voices and petting hands.

He even enjoyed it for a minute, till he started feeling trapped and beleaguered. He turned his head toward Mom in wordless appeal, but behind her he could see the front door opening again. Dad was home.

His eyes searched the smiling group clustered around Jamie and settled on the paper still clutched in his hand. Then he strode forward, sweeping the others aside as he grasped Jamie and actually lifted him off his feet in a giant hug.

"Dad!" Jamie protested, laughing.

Dad put him down but didn't let go. "It's starting," he said. His tone was solemn, though his lips were still grinning wide.

"What's starting?"

"Your future," Dad said. "The world recognizing what you have to offer. This is just the first step."

Yes, Jamie thought, but he said, temporizing, "They didn't say anything about financial aid yet. It's awfully expensive, you know, $1300—that's even more than Harvard."

Dad's grin never wavered. "We'll figure it out," he said. "You're going, so don't try to weasel out of it."

"Aye, aye, Commander." Jamie used his mock salute to disengage from Dad's hands, then was rather sorry he'd done so.

"See to it, Mister," Dad said, and hugged him again. Then he stood him back at arm's length, hands on his shoulders. "You're our guided missile."

"What?" Jamie squeaked, to the laughter of the others.

"Last week they mothballed the *Wisconsin,*" Dad explained. "Our only battleship still on active service. I served on her once, when she'd already been reduced to an instruction ship for midshipmen. The days of those big, heavy dreadnoughts are over; tomorrow's need will be for speed and precision." He looked around at the family. "I'm not just talking about war. We've started into space; it's not only the Russians, it's mankind. Satellites, transistors, even those frozen tuna pies Ruby gets for lunch sometimes: the world is changing, and people like Jamie, people with the brains and focus to understand the changes and bring them forward, will be in the vanguard."

"Wow," Laurie said.

Ruby said, "Well, wherever he's going to be, he's going to need fuel for it. I made peanut butter cookies for y'all's afterschool snack. Come on in and sit down and I'll bring them out."

As the others trooped into the living room, Jamie opened his letter and read it through carefully. For the first time, he noticed the date at the top: March 14. *Pi!* he realized. *They sent the letters out on the date that's the same as the first three digits of pi. I'll bet they posted them at 1:59, too. Oh, I'm going to love this place!*

CHAPTER 46.

MONDAY, APRIL 28, 1958

Jamie surfaced from sleep like a swimmer out of deep water. The skin on his face felt tight and stretched, and his eyes were blurry even after he jammed on his glasses. *Crying*, he realized. *I've been crying.* But he couldn't remember a nightmare.

He said the morning blessing, then levered himself up onto his elbows and looked across at Steve. The kid was still asleep, curled up around Jamie's old teddy bear. At the sight, the events of last night came flooding back.

Jamie had gotten up in the middle of the night because Steve had sneaked out for the fourth night in a row. Steve had gone into the bathroom first and brought back towels that he'd stuffed under his blankets, but not before Jamie had caught the whiff of urine. That had been going on for several nights, too. So Jamie felt it was past time for him to alert the folks about it.

The three of them had found him up in the attic cubbyhole. Steve had reacted first with anger, then he'd tried to retreat into one of his trances, what Mom called hysterical conversion: his face had gone blank and his arms hung limp as his breathing slowed and his eyes closed.

When Mom had sharply called him back, and Dad had backed that up with coaxing, he'd gone into what Jamie thought of when he heard the word "hysteria"—screaming and crying and coughing out the fear and anger at the memories of his miserable past. He'd gasped out how he'd stabbed his cousin to death with the knife the man had threatened

227

to kill him with, and that now he was actually afraid Mom and Dad would try to kill him, literally kill him, for what he had done in his bed, and that then he'd have to kill them... but he didn't want to.

As he had done last night, Jamie shook his head at the burden this frail-looking kid bore. Jamie had similar scars, had experienced similar suffering, had even similarly been tormented by guilt. But his was the guilt of the survivor; he'd never had to kill someone, to take up a shiny, lethal instrument and drive it into resisting living flesh, to see the red blood pour out and the eyes dim—had the cousin had his eyes open?— and know that he'd ended a life, the life of the only person Steve knew in the whole, uncaring, unknown world.

Last night, after Steve had been calmed and cleaned up and tucked into his new-made bed, Jamie had searched out the stuffed bear Mom had given him when he first came to this house, that had almost replaced his shepseleh, his stuffed lamb left behind in another world. Then he'd lain on his bed and wept, as he'd not wept in waking memory. For years, his only tears had been the stuff of nightmares; these were the first he'd been able to shed for someone else, out of love and pity.

He could feel them prickling behind his eyes again as he looked at Steve, wound tightly in the covers he'd pulled out of their moorings to wrap around himself, the bear's head protruding just next to his own, his face soft and young-looking without the defensive vigilance it bore when he was awake and not singing. Jamie sat up and dropped his feet to the floor, staring at his newest brother's face.

He heard the door open softly behind him and quiet footsteps come into the room. Without turning, he said in a low voice, "I suppose we're late for school?"

"I called you in sick," Mom murmured. "Stretching the truth a little, but not too far—I don't think either one of you is in shape for classes today, and you didn't get to sleep till nearly dawn. In fact, I'm ditching work myself today; I told them we were having a family emergency."

Steve started to stir. Mom moved forward and perched on the edge of his bed, tenderly stroking the hair back from his forehead. She gave the bear a pat, too. She didn't look at Jamie, but he felt self-conscious and headed for the bathroom before she could start focusing some of that tenderness on him.

When he came back out, Steve was awake. "Try to tell us next time something's bothering you like that," Mom was saying. "Last night you said you realized we're on your side. Remember that. Even if you think whatever it is will make us angry, it won't make us stop loving you, or stop being on your side. Do you understand?"

Steve mumbled something into his chest. Mom evidently couldn't understand it, either, because she gently grasped his chin and raised his head. "What was that, sweetie?"

"Dad was so mad," he said.

That was true; Jamie had never seen him so furious. He'd smashed a knick-knack shelf with a music stand. Even Jamie had been a little scared, and Steve had been petrified.

Now Mom said, "You understand he wasn't mad at you, right? He was angry at what had been done to you."

"I know, he said so." But Steve didn't sound convinced. Jamie understood. Just seeing that Dad was capable of that kind of rage raised the question of whether it would ever be directed at one of them. It reminded him of the time Dad slapped Laurie. *Probably just as well Steve doesn't know about that. It was hard enough for me to get over, and I already trusted him.*

Mom sighed. "I suppose it will take you some time to get over that. I wish he hadn't done it, and so does he, but you know we're not perfect, Steve. We're all just doing the best we can."

Steve's chin had dropped back onto his chest. Mom gazed at him for a minute, then said in a different tone of voice, "I got something out of my files I thought you might like to see, to keep if you like." She reached into a pocket of her slacks and pulled out a newspaper clipping, folded in quarters.

Steve unfolded it and stared at it, uncomprehending.

Jamie could see enough from where he sat to know what it was. He remembered seeing it when the stories first started coming out about the "wild child" who'd been locked in a room for ten years and freed himself by killing his captor. It was a photograph of a young couple. He was wearing an ill-fitting tux, she was in a fluffy white dress, a short veil perched on her blonde head.

"It's your parents' wedding picture," Mom said. "It was published at the time they married, and the *Patriot* unearthed it when they printed the story about what happened to you."

Steve stared and stared, his mouth fallen open and his breath coming in soft little hitches. "Lovey," he whispered, and then again, "Lovey."

After a while, Mom got up. "You two go ahead and get dressed," she said. "Ruby's keeping some oatmeal hot in a double boiler for you. After breakfast, Steve, I'm going to take you over to Rolling Meadow for a special session with Mrs. French." She waited till Steve nodded abstractedly, then went out.

"I'll take the first shower," Jamie said. Steve nodded again.

When he came back out, the clipping had disappeared. Steve went into the bathroom; Jamie took off his bathrobe and got dressed. Then, the noise of the running water reassuring him that Steve was occupied, he started searching for the picture.

It was in the pocket of one of Steve's shirts in the closet, folded over and over into a square barely bigger than a matchbook. Jamie unfolded it and sat back on his bed, studying it as though it were some abstruse mathematical proposition he had to master.

The girl in the grainy picture was smiling tremulously, happy but uncertain, looking no older than Celia. The boy beside her was young, too, with a look Jamie at first took for grim determination, but after a few minutes' study decided was underlain with a barely contained fear.

Jamie's eyes dropped to the caption beneath the picture. *Rory and Lilian O'Riordan*, it read. *January 16, 1944.* Jamie's first thought was, *I wonder why he's not in uniform.* Then the significance for Steve registered. *He was born in July of that year, only six months later. She was already pregnant with him. I wonder if he's noticed?*

He was so involved in drinking in every detail that he didn't notice when the shower went off. Steve's outraged "Hey!" startled him so, he almost tore it.

Then Steve almost tore it, plucking it out of his hands. "It's mine," he said. "You can't have it. They're not your parents."

"I don't have one of my parents," Jamie said. "I don't have anything of theirs. I don't even really remember what they looked like."

"At least you remember them, though," Steve said. "You remember stuff they did with you, stuff they said to you. You know what I would give to have that?"

"Sorry," Jamie said. "I'm sorry. I just—I just wanted to—" He broke off, unable to articulate just what it was he wanted.

"Ok," Steve said. But he still stood there, arms akimbo, the refolded clipping clutched in his fist. Obviously, he wasn't going to put it away in front of Jamie. "No one gets to see them but me," he said fiercely.

"I understand," Jamie said, getting up. At the door, he turned back and said again, "I'm sorry."

Chapter 47.

"Tonight we're going to start a book that Jamie suggested," Mom said, settling into the big armchair beside the fireplace. "It's called *Fantasia Mathematica.*"

Celia squeaked. "I thought that was a joke," she said to Jamie, half laughing.

"No," he answered, "it was a joke when we talked in the kitchen that time. I said *Principia Mathematica,* which is a classic text by Isaac Newton. It revolutionized mathematical thinking and made modern physics possible, but even I wouldn't pick it for family reading night. No, this is a new book, a collection of stories and poems and essays with math themes, but it's supposed to be entertaining and accessible to—er, non-mathematicians."

"Dummies like us, you mean," Laurie said, but his tone was light, so Jamie nodded at him.

"Exactly," he said. Ruby, beside him on the long couch, gave him an admonitory whap on the back of the head.

The family settled in to listen. The first story, called "Young Archimedes," was by Aldous Huxley. Jamie had high hopes that a story by the author of the dystopian novel *Brave New World* would have the sort of sardonic incisiveness he enjoyed. But this story started slowly, with a lyrical description of the Italian countryside and

232

a leisurely telling of the English narrator's settling into a rented villa with his wife.

Jamie's mind was drifting when it was caught by a discussion of musical theory. "'The corruption of the best, I thought, is the worst,'" Mom read. "'Beethoven taught music to palpitate with his intellectual and spiritual passion. It has gone on palpitating ever since, but with the passion of inferior men... Mozart's melodies may be brilliant, memorable, infectious; but they don't palpitate, don't catch you between wind and water, don't send the listener off into erotic ecstasies.'"

Yes, Jamie thought, remembering the disastrous radio concert of the *Eroica* in this very room so long ago. *And that's why I like Mozart better.* He looked around the room. The others seemed caught up in the story. Steve looked confused, but rapt, his fine blond brows drawn together as he concentrated on the unfamiliar words. *I did this,* Jamie realized. *I brought something to the family that they wouldn't have had without me.*

As the evening drew on, though, he wasn't so sure this had been a good idea, where Steve was concerned, at least. The kid had been twitchy and out of sorts since his breakdown, and he still seemed almost afraid of Dad. As it became clear that the child in the story was being exploited by the adults in his life, Steve became more and more anxious. By the end, he was shivering, squeezed between Rob and Beth on the settee, though Rob's arm encircled his shoulders and Beth was stroking his hand.

"'On the innumerable brown and rosy roofs of the city the afternoon sunlight lay softly, sumptuously, and the towers were as though varnished and enameled with an old gold,'" Mom read. "'I thought of all the Men who had lived here and left the visible traces of their spirit and conceived extraordinary things. I thought of the dead child.'"

233

She drew a deep sigh and closed the book. "Well, that wasn't what I was expecting at all when I started," she said.

"I—I'm sorry," Jamie began uncertainly, his earlier triumph turning to ashes in his mouth.

"No, no," Mom said. "That wasn't a criticism, sweetie. It's a beautiful story, and I'm glad we read it." She opened the book again and riffled through some pages. "It looks as though the next story is meant to be comic," she said, "so that'll be a change of pace next week. And I'm enjoying reading something so different from our usual fare."

"I agree," Dad said. "I'd thought, from the title, that this was going to be more fantasy, and I was surprised since you've said you didn't much enjoy the Lewis and Tolkien the rest of us favor, but they've evidently used 'fantasia' in the musical sense, as a collection of themes or tunes that come together to make a harmonious whole."

"Tolkien's not so bad," Jamie said. "Anyway, there are some stories in this book that are fantasies in the way you're talking about, I think. And some that have more actual math in them; I just thought maybe I could show you all something about what I like."

Rob clapped him on the back as he passed on his way out of the room. "It was great," he said. "The story was, like, bluesville, but that geometry bit was a real gas."

Laurie chuckled, getting up from the armchair by the window. "And there you have it, sports fans," he said. "You're in like Flynn, Jamie; Robbie pronounces your choice 'a real gas'."

Everyone laughed, and there was a flurry of good-nights and bustling off to bed, but Jamie noticed that Steve had slipped out silently.

When he got up to the bedroom, he found that the kid was already in the bathroom. After he'd taken his own turn and gotten into bed, he looked over at the silent lump beside him.

He doesn't want to talk about it. I hate it when people nag at me about what I'm feeling when I clearly would rather be left alone. Besides, what could I do about it?

But he found that something had shifted in him since he had taken the plunge to tell the folks that he thought Steve was in trouble. Gathering his resolve, he said softly, "Are you all right?"

There was no sound or movement. Jamie was about to give up and address himself to his prayers when Steve suddenly pushed off the covers and sat up.

"He killed himself," he said shakily. "That kid in the story, he threw himself off the balcony, right? Why'd he do that? The rich lady was taking care of him, everything was nice for him. Why did he want to die? Why did he—" Steve's voice wavered. "—Why did he give up?"

Jamie swallowed, thinking fast. "It wasn't really what he wanted to do, being a musician, performing the way the lady wanted him to," he said carefully.

"He didn't want to do music?" Steve said incredulously. "But he was good at it."

"Yes, and he did like it, but it wasn't his real love. His real love was mathematics; that's where his genius lay, but the lady couldn't dress him up like a little doll and make herself important with him doing math. But that wasn't the biggest problem. The biggest problem was that he realized she wasn't what he thought she was, she didn't care about him the way he thought she would."

"Sometimes people are different than you think they're going to be," Steve whispered. "Bert was always the same. I mean, sometimes he was drunk and sometimes he wasn't, but he was always horrible. I don't know how to be around people who change around."

Ah. "Dad hasn't changed," he said. Steve gaped at him. "That is what you're worried about, isn't it? Seeing him get so mad that night? He's the same, you just saw part of him you hadn't seen before. I did, too, for that matter. But..." *Spit it out, Hymie.* "But he loves you. That kid in the story gave up partly because he thought everyone had abandoned him, no one cared about him any more. That's not you."

"It's not?"

"No. Dad cares about you; that's why he was so mad. And Mom cares about you, Robbie, Ruby, everybody." Jamie swallowed. "I care about you."

"Yeah?"

"Yeah."

Steve gave him an impish grin. "So sometimes people do change?"

Jamie threw his pillow at him.

Chapter 48.

T*he collar is not too tight, Hymie, it's your imagination,* Jamie told himself as Dad fussed with the bow tie on his rented tux and Mom tweaked the blue bow at the waist of Celia's bouffant white skirt.

He swallowed hard, fighting a rising panic. He was going to the prom as Laurie's girlfriend Linda's date, while Laurie took their sister Celia to avoid crossing swords with the bigoted dean of girls. Dean Dunkelman had threatened to write Linda a negative college rec if she went with Laurie.

Celia had come up with the idea when Jamie had mentioned that Rima was with her parents at Cape May. "So you won't be taking her to the prom," she'd said, "so you're free to take Linda."

It had never crossed Jamie's mind to go to the prom, with Rima or anyone else. Still, it had seemed like a neat way to circumvent Dean Dunkelman and her stupid prejudice. *And it's a chance to do something for Laurie.*

But now that it was upon him, he was filled with doubt and an undeniable undercurrent of fear. He'd be putting himself in the spotlight beside Laurie, becoming part of the focus of whatever hostile forces might be there. *Time to stop hiding,* he told himself bracingly, but his gut was not convinced. He drew on the little store of self-confidence standing up to that constable had given him, and straightened his back.

As they went out to Dad's Buick, followed by parental exhortations to take care and behave themselves, Jamie looked at the car's sleek black and white curves and pictured them the way they'd been two weeks ago, mottled and streaked with dirty yellow and gray, stinking from the rotten eggs someone had smeared all over the car.

They had all come out to clean the mess, wielding hose and sponges and the ice scraper on the gummy residue. Mom had been tightlipped and furious, Dad philosophical, Ruby inscrutable. Laurie had kept his head down as though he were ashamed, as though he had done it himself. Robbie and the girls were resolutely cheery, as though it were all just a practical joke. Only Steve had been shaking with fear, showing openly what Jamie was feeling secretly.

"Why?" Steve kept saying. "Why would somebody do this?" The adults tried to answer, to provide a context and soothe his fears, but the words and reassurances rang hollow.

Luckily, Steve never answered their phone—no one ever called him—so they were able to keep from him the fact that they were getting anonymous threatening calls. Jamie had fielded a couple; the one he suspected was from Tank Lebo again had consisted of a series of obscene and racist words, the other one just silence ending in a whispered, "Don't. Do. It."

Linda's family had gotten it even worse, Laurie had told Jamie. Her parents weren't native to the area; her father's name didn't carry the weight that Sean McAlister's reputation had around here.

But she and Laurie had both been determined not to let bigotry keep them from being together tonight, and the parents had reluctantly agreed in principle, and, once they heard it, then in practice, to this plan Celia had cooked up, and Jamie'd gone along with them. *What was I thinking?*

Now, all the way to the dance—picking Linda up, handing her the corsage, being polite to her parents, riding in the back seat to the school, following Laurie and Celia into the gym—he ran scenarios through his head. *What if they stare at us? What if they make remarks? What if they hiss and boo? What if... what if they attack us?*

Should he try to protect the girls? Should he try to protect Laurie? *How can I protect anyone?* What if he just ran? Could he ever look at himself in the mirror again? *But what if I get hurt? What if I get... killed?*

Don't be so dramatic, he told himself. But in his mind's eye, as they approached the gym, iron gates overlaid the doors: 'Jedem das seine.' *People are killed sometimes, for no good reason. They are.*

Then they were stepping in, and for an instant everything froze. *Relax, Hymie, they're not all staring at you.* But they were. At him with Linda, and Laurie and Celia behind them. Dunkelman glared at them from among the other chaperones at the punch table; dancers stared over each other's shoulders and giggled together. A few couples even stopped dead to gape. Jamie spotted Tank Lebo leaning in a corner, sneering.

Then they were on the dance floor. The band was belting out "Breathless" with more enthusiasm than skill, and Jamie was gyrating stiffly, eyes darting around the crowd.

Linda cleared her throat and brought his gaze back to her. Her pretty face was paler than usual, except for two spots of hectic color high on her round cheeks—a sharper pink than her dress. But her head was high and her lips firm as she said between her teeth, "Smile. You're at a dance, not an execution."

Jamie couldn't smile, but he did relax his mouth a little. *You agreed to do this, Hymie. Do it right.*

Things seemed to go fairly smoothly for a while after that. Laurie's dances with Linda were interspersed with ones with Celia, with that girl Mary, and with a couple of others. Jamie danced two or three times with Linda and twice with Celia; otherwise, he lurked on the sidelines, nursing a cup of punch he didn't really want and watching for trouble.

He tensed up at one point when a circle cleared on the floor around Laurie and Linda, but the motive seemed to be some kind of support; the watching faces were smiling or at least neutral. Except for Dean Dunkelman outside the circle—she was positively prune-faced with disapproval.

Another hour went by; Jamie tried not to check his watch too often. Then there was a little disturbance. Two other couples jostled Laurie and Linda on the floor. *Was that an accident?* It happened again. Laurie and Linda stopped dancing; the other two couples loomed over them menacingly.

Jamie pushed himself upright from the wall he'd been leaning on. Beside him, Celia stood up.

"Is that Tom Varner?" she said.

Shit. "Yes, it is. And his sidekick, the faithful Travis Thumper." But as they started forward, the dean of boys and Laurie's track coach got to the troublemakers and ejected them from the gym. There was a ripple of grumbling, on whose behalf Jamie couldn't tell, rumbling under a descant of nervous titters.

Then the band determinedly launched itself into the driving rhythms of Ritchie Valens's "Come on, Let's Go," and the dancing resumed. By now, Jamie and Celia had joined Linda and Laurie at the refreshments table, just in time to hear the coach growling at Laurie as though the whole incident had been his fault.

"Jamie, I need to sit down," Linda said, and Jamie escorted her back to the folding chairs, Laurie and Celia following.

When Jamie's heart had stopped pounding and his breath was even enough that he felt he could control his voice, he asked Linda to dance; he hardly knew what the music was at that point—something fast and loud—but he evidently acquitted himself satisfactorily. After it, he collapsed next to Celia with relief and prepared himself to relax while sitting out the next number.

Unfortunately, he immediately tightened up again when he saw that Laurie had guided Linda back onto the dance floor—for "The Stroll," of all things. Echoing his thought, Celia hissed, "Are they *crazy?* Why don't they just take an ad out in the paper?"

"The Stroll" was not a dance to be inconspicuous in. It was like an old-fashioned contra dance, with the dancers forming two lines while each couple in turn sashayed down the aisle between them. But they were of necessity not in very close contact as they "strolled" to the other end; maybe that was why no one reacted sharply.

As he drew in a tentative breath, Jamie became aware of someone standing next to him. Someone large. And blond. And male. Tank Lebo. Jamie leaped to his feet, then flushed as he tried to think of a reason for having done so. He sank back onto the seat.

Lebo had his own agenda, though. He half-pulled a silvery flask from his metallic blue jacket pocket and leaned confidingly toward Jamie. "Want a real drink?" he murmured. "Come on, egghead, live a little, why doncha. It's only a buck a shot. Whaddya have ta lose?"

He was leaning over Jamie, close enough that Jamie could see the blond stubble on his chiseled chin. His muscular thighs strained the fabric of the cheap black slacks he wore with the garish, shiny coat; he smelled of Old Spice aftershave, alcohol, and sweat. He filled the universe.

I have to make him back off, Jamie thought desperately. Or did he want him to come closer? *Why would I want him closer? I don't. I don't.*

Trying for a joking, friendly, neutral tone, Jamie said, "What do I have to lose? Let me see: my equilibrium, my good sense, my reputation, my freedom if I get arrested—in which case my early acceptance to MIT might be at risk—seems like I've got a lot to lose, actually." Lebo had reared back, so Jamie was able to sit up straighter as he went on, "Look at it logically: the risks far outweigh any potential benefit."

He dared a glance up and saw he'd gotten it wrong again. Lebo didn't look amused or impressed or intrigued. He looked disgusted, contemptuous.

Jamie tried to think of a way to retrieve the situation, but the big blond had already turned away and was busy with Laurie, who'd come up behind him, calling him "King Kong" and making offensive suggestions about under which circumstances he would allow him to drink from the flask.

"Get lost, Lebo," Laurie said in a tone he managed to keep light, but Jamie could hear the banked rage underneath. Maybe Lebo heard it, too. At any rate, he backed off and left them.

Then Celia was there, making some remark about Lebo being like a statue of a Greek god—beautiful physique, marble head.

With that, the dance seemed to be over. Jamie felt relieved, but oddly empty as they retrieved discarded shoes and jackets and made their way out of the gym. They all stopped on the outside steps for a bit, enjoying the cool and the quiet of the dark parking lot.

But as they moved down into it, tension came back over Jamie, an atavistic sense of danger lurking. The others didn't seem to feel it, but Jamie focused on the distinctive black and white of Dad's Buick, willing away the image of the iron gates that tried to interpose themselves between him and the safe haven. He quickened his steps, then slowed again as he realized Laurie was lagging behind.

Around them, other people were getting into their cars, laughing, calling to each other, slamming doors, but Jamie felt as though the four of them were in a special capsule, separated from the rest. No one spoke to them or looked at them, in any case.

So when Varner and Thumper stepped out from between the cars two over from theirs, it never occurred to Jamie that any of those bystanders would be of any use. Laurie muttered something to Linda that sent her running for the gym—to get adult help, Jamie assumed, though he didn't put much faith in that prospect, either.

Celia resisted Laurie's effort to get her to leave as well. Instead, she stepped up to Jamie and gave him one flaming look of determination and élan. Then she turned her shoulder to his; Laurie was already on his other side, and the three of them formed an outward-facing triangle, slowly rotating to keep watch all around them.

There only seemed to be those two, though, and they were momentarily stymied by the united triangular front. Then Varner lurched forward, swinging a two-foot length of chain, while Thumper raised his fists menacingly. But Jamie thought he looked a little less enthusiastic. *Maybe a weak spot there. Should we go on the offensive?*

Celia beat him to it. "What's the matter, jerks, your dates finally wise up and beat it out of here?"

Varner's mouth twisted into a sneer. "At least our dates are white," he said smugly.

Jamie heard his own voice speaking almost without his own volition. "Is that supposed to be a witty riposte, ape-man? How proud your parents must be."

That did it. Varner swung the chain, clipping Jamie on the cheek, then jumped him. *At least it made him too furious to keep using the chain,* Jamie had time to think. *Sun Tzu was right: "If your enemy is of a choleric temper, irritate him."*

Then there was no more time to think. He grabbed the chain-wielding hand with his own left and pushed it to one side. With his right, he sank his fist deep into the pit of Varner's stomach. It was surprisingly soft and yielding; it came to Jamie that he'd never seen anyone actually stand up to Varner.

It was over as suddenly as it had started. Varner was bent over, whooping and gasping for breath. Celia had grabbed the chain out of his hand and was coiling it up. Thumper was clutching his nose and cursing as blood seeped between his fingers. The skin on Laurie's forehead glistened in the moonlight, covered in blood evidently, but his expression was stunned rather than hurt; Jamie wondered whether the blood was Thumper's.

Out of nowhere, Dad's voice came. "That's enough, boys. The police are on their way."

He and Linda's dad seemed to have materialized out of thin air. Some other adults were coming out of the gym, Linda in the lead. The hoodlums fled. Linda ran to her father's arms, and he and Laurie had a brief exchange as she went off to the Markses' Ford.

Jamie's cheek was starting to sting, and he felt dizzy and sick as the adrenaline drained out of him. But underneath it all, a fierce triumph rose in his chest. *I did it. I stood up to them. I was not a victim. I did it.* We *did it.*

Celia looked a little shaky. Jamie caught her arm as she stumbled, and helped her into the Buick. Over the top of it, he could see Mom's Dodge. *Dad must have come in that. Deus ex machina.*

"Funny, doesn't look like a celestial chariot," he said, gratified to hear how steady his voice sounded.

Laurie agreed, and Dad explained that he and Linda's father had been there all evening, just in case something like this happened. Dean Dunkelman took that moment to put her two cents in, blaming Laurie for everything, naturally, and she and Dad got into it. Dad put her down handily, of course, then had a brief colloquy with Laurie before getting into Mom's car and driving off. It was all a distant buzz to Jamie.

Jamie started to get into the back seat of the Buick, then on second thought squeezed into the front next to Celia. Laurie bent forward in the driver's seat to look across her at him. "Should I swing by the hospital?" he asked. "Maybe you need stitches or something."

"Nah, it's not even bleeding any more," Jamie said. "I can hardly feel it now. My fist hurts worse, to tell you the truth. How about you? You've got blood all over your face."

"Not mine," Laurie said, confirming Jamie's speculation. "I think I broke Varner's nose, head-butting him. Couple of aspirin, I'll be fine. Cissy?"

"I'll be ok as soon as my heart stops pounding, which should be in a week or so," Celia said.

"Listen, I want to thank you guys," Laurie began.

Celia and Jamie cut him off simultaneously.

"Don't you dare," she said.

Jamie said, "We didn't do it for you. Not exactly. You know what I mean." *What's going on? I'm dithering.* He tried again. "I feel better than I have in a long time. Maybe ever."

"I know exactly what you mean," Celia said.

"I doubt it," Jamie answered.

She laughed as though he'd been joking, then squeezed his arm.

"Anyway," Laurie said.

"Yeah, ok," Celia conceded. "Maybe a little for you. We do love you, right, Jamie?"

"Right," he said.

Chapter 49.

Saturday, July 5, 1958: Part 1

Rima sat at the desk in the larger spare room, looking over at Jamie where he sprawled on the bed; he'd been reading Jacobson's latest collection in the "Lectures in Abstract Algebra" series when she came in. "Yes," she said. "I am breaking up with you."

Jamie didn't feel as bad as he'd thought he would, imagining this development. "Have you met somebody?" he asked.

"No," she said. "Well, yes, but not the way you mean." She shifted the wheeled desk chair back and forth for a minute, looking at him sidelong, then said, "I met somebody, but he's not boyfriend material. Not for me, anyway. Or for any girl."

Jamie's heart speeded up; he wondered why that was. "He's queer?" he said.

"He says 'gay,'" she answered. "But yes, he is."

Jamie sat up and drew his knees to his chest. "So what does that have to do with you and me?"

She stopped jiggling the chair around and stared down at her folded hands, then raised her plain, pleasant face to his. "Some things he said, some of the ways he is around me... Jamie, have you ever considered that you might be attracted to boys?"

"I don't know," he said sardonically. "It's hard to notice anyone with my hand up your blouse and my tongue down your throat." But a streak of blond hair flashed in his mind's eye, quick as the click of a camera shutter.

Her face kept its serious, concerned expression. "That's part of it," she said. "We talked about that, Fred—that's his name—and I. How sometimes you seem kind of... desperate."

Jamie felt himself flush in humiliation. "You said that to some other guy? About me?"

Now she looked impatient. "You're never going to meet him, what difference does that make? Stick to the point."

"Which is that you think I'm queer, or gay, or whatever you want to say, because I like making out with you? Not much of a testimonial for either of us, is it?"

"Jamie, be honest. You know we've been all around Robin's barn about this. You've blown hot and cold with me from the beginning." She chewed her lip, then seemed to make up her mind. "And I have made out with a couple of guys since we decided not to be exclusive—"

Since you *decided,* he thought bitterly, but she was still speaking. "—and it's just different. I'm not talking about technique or anything; it's hard to put my finger on it, but... they pay *attention* to me in a way you don't, they're *there.*"

"So I don't pay enough attention to the wonderful Rima Shapiro, queen of the universe, therefore I must be a homo."

She stood up and walked over to the bed. He shrank back without meaning to, which made her smile wryly. "Ok, this conversation is over for now," she said. "When you start making cracks calculated to drive me away, I know there's no more getting through to you. Just think about it, Jamie. I want what's best for you, I really do."

"And telling me I'm a social pariah and a pervert and an object of scorn and ridicule is what's best for me? Your usual penetrating judgment at work, I see." But she was already out the door.

He lay back, seething, trying not to panic. *What if it's true? What will I do? What can I do? Damn, damn, just when I'm about to go to college, to start my life—this would ruin everything. God damn Rima.*

But if it's true, it's not her fault, the other voice in his head put in, the one that always put him down, the one he hadn't been hearing lately. *It's nobody's fault but yours, Hymie. You're the one who's damaged goods, you've always known that.*

And part of you has known this was coming. Ever since the night that Steve broke down, when you started letting yourself feel, you've felt something like this coming on. This is one reason you didn't want to think about your feelings; you've been afraid to look at this.

"Jamie? Jamie, are you in here?" Beth's voice broke through the turmoil in his brain.

He thought about pretending not to be here, but she was already walking toward him. "Has something happened? I passed Rima on the stairs just now. I spoke to her, but she didn't answer. I think she was crying." She sat on the edge of the bed. "Are you all right?"

"No," he croaked. "I'm anything but all right." *She's only fifteen. I've got no right to lay this on her.* But she sat there calmly, eyes seemingly focused somewhere far beyond him, and eventually he ground out, "Rima thinks I'm queer."

Her brows creased. "Well, I suppose you're a little unusual, but she's known you a long time. Why would she say that now?"

"No, *queer.* You know." But obviously she didn't, so he tried again. "That I... I'm attracted to men." Her face was still serene and a little puzzled, so he added, "Sexually."

The wrinkles smoothed out as she understood. "Oh," she said. Then, "Are you?"

"I don't know. Maybe."

"How can you not know?"

"Maybe I don't want to know."

She shrugged. "I can see it might be awkward, but it's better to know the truth, isn't it?

"Not when the truth would ruin my life."

She smiled and lifted her eyebrows. "Aren't you being a little dramatic? It's not a crime to like your own sex."

"Of course it is! That's exactly what it is! I could go to prison!" He heard his voice rising as the implications struck home. He buried his face in his hands. "Maybe it's not true," he muttered into them, but in his head a thousand images and impressions were swirling around and clicking into place, one by one, forming a picture he couldn't avoid seeing. The feeling of comfort and safety he got surrounded by male arms, resting on a male chest. The stifling sensation when breasts pressed against him. His obsession with Tank Lebo. *Tank Lebo, God, he'd kill me if he even suspected.* Jamie groaned and looked up.

Beth's face had gone completely blank and calm, eyes and mouth closed. He knew that look; she was meditating, putting herself in some Quaker place of contemplation, waiting for inspiration. He waited with her, as if for a verdict.

Her eyes opened and she laid a hand on his chest. "I don't know what you should do," she said softly. "So you'd better talk to someone who does. You have to tell Mom and Dad."

Jamie knew she could feel his heart speed up under her hand. "No way," he said. "There is no way."

She only smiled. "You know I'm right," she said with quiet confidence. "I'll go with you if you want." She groped for his hand, found it, and tugged gently. "Come on."

"What, now?"

"Why not?"

He pulled his hand away. "No, I can't. Not yet. I'm not even sure it's true yet."

Her head cocked at the lie, but she didn't contradict him.

"Just give me a little time," he pleaded.

"It's not up to me to make you do anything," she said. "But you know I'm right."

"Just a little time," he repeated.

"Of course," she said, patting his hand.

She left the room, and Jamie fell back and contemplated the ruin of his life.

Chapter 50.

Saturday, July 5, 1958: Part 2

It had been raining on and off all day, but that hadn't made it feel cooler. Jamie was stifling in the guest room, and told himself that was why he couldn't concentrate on his reading. *Stop kidding yourself, Hymie. It'll be bedtime soon, and the day gone by without you doing what you know you have to. You got up the nerve to tell them about Steve that time; now the shoe's on the other foot, are you going to chicken out?*

He thought about Steve's courage, his refusal to collapse under the weight of the abuse and isolation he'd suffered, even to the point of striking down his oppressor. *And Mom and Dad helped him come to terms with that, once he could bring himself to let them help. So what does that tell you, Hymie?*

Gritting his teeth, he got up and made his way downstairs. The study was empty, so he circled the stairs and peeked into the TV room. There they were, watching Spike Jones singing—could it be? Yes—Christmas songs. The comic beeps and whistles that were Jones's specialty were underlain by the sound of the window air conditioner the folks had put in this summer; the sudden shock of dry, cool air made the skin on Jamie's arms rise up in goose bumps.

"What on earth is this?" he asked.

"Unmitigated drivel," Dad answered.

"We got lured in by the air conditioning," Mom agreed, "but I'm not sure it's worth the price."

"Well, if you're not really watching it, could I talk to you?"

"Of course," Mom said as Dad got up and switched the racket off.

Jamie was glad of the air conditioner's rumble; it seemed to ensure they'd not be overheard. He came around the end of the couch Mom and Dad shared and sat in the wicker chair against the side wall.

"I'm not sure how to start," he admitted, clasping his hands between his knees.

They looked at each other; Dad had an "I told you so" expression, Mom was smiling ruefully. "Maybe we can start for you," Dad said.

Jamie was stricken. *They already know?*

But then Dad said, "You've been worrying about what happened after the prom, haven't you? About fighting with those hoodlums." As Jamie's jaw dropped, Dad went on, "It's not unusual, son. The first experience you have with that sort of violence..."

"You think that was my first experience with violence?"

"Of course you've seen much worse than that," Mom put in, her tone understanding, "but to be actually involved in it is different. It's natural that you'd be upset."

Jamie was so surprised he felt a sort of vertigo. "Upset?" he repeated. "Why would I be upset? It's you Christians who worry about forgiving your enemies; I felt better than I ever have in my life when those thugs took off, and I helped make them do it."

"That's natural, too," Dad reassured him. "You shouldn't feel guilty if it gave you some satisfaction to—"

"Wait, wait, wait," Jamie said. "You're way off base. This isn't what I wanted to talk about at all."

"It isn't? Then what is it?" Mom asked.

Somehow, the confusion made it easier to say. "Rima thinks I'm a homo," he blurted.

That stopped them. Then Dad barked out an incredulous laugh. "What?" he said. "With the way you two carry on?" But Mom laid a quelling hand on his forearm, a speculative look on her face.

"That's what I said," Jamie answered Dad. "She said something about how I don't pay enough attention to her, or something." Dad sat back, looking thoughtful.

"Is that all there is to this?" Mom asked.

"No." Jamie pulled his ankle up onto the opposite knee and rubbed at the knobby bone under his sock. "When I'm with Rima, part of me feels the way I used to when I'd pretend not to be scared when strangers came up to me, how I'd force my face to stay straight and my feet to keep steady. For a long time, I thought it was because I wasn't sure I was ready to have sex—" He looked up at Dad, who nodded, remembering their conversation. "And the whole touching thing—" Mom nodded at this. Jamie grabbed his ankle in both hands. "The thing is, there's always been something else there. When I'm with her, or afterwards, in bed at night, I think about..."

They waited patiently, silent under the rattling air conditioner. "Tank Lebo," Jamie said finally.

Dad's brow drew down. "The runner?"

"Yes, he ran track against Laurie."

"But he's—" Mom began, and stopped.

"He's a brute," Jamie snapped. "A big, blond, Aryan brute."

Dad buried his face in his hands. "Like me," he said so softly Jamie almost missed it.

"Like you," Jamie agreed. "Except for the brute part, of course."

"Of course," Mom said with a wry smile. "So... you're thinking that Rima may be right about this?"

He nodded. "I talked about it a little with Beth, and I've been thinking about it all day. It makes more and more sense. Do you think it's true?"

"I can see that it might be," Mom said. "Let's not rush to conclusions, though. You know, a lot of boys experiment with different—"

"I haven't 'experimented,' Mom, that's the whole point. I've buried myself in Rima, almost literally." Suddenly, a sense of despair filled him like water filling a cup. "What am I going to do?" he groaned. "How am I going to deal with this?"

"We'll figure it out," Dad said. "We'll help you, son."

"How can you? If it's true, how can you even stand to be near me?" The thought he'd been fighting all day suddenly spilled over. "Is it because I'm a Jew, do you think?" he asked.

"What on earth do you mean?"

"You know, like Hitler said… weak, dirty, not a proper man."

For the first time in their conversation, Dad was gaping in horror.

"Oh, honey. It's got nothing whatsoever to do with your being Jewish. Do you think, say, sailors are weak and dirty and not proper men? Did you know that Churchill once said, 'The traditions of the British navy, sir, are rum, sodomy, and the lash'? Men on shipboard have been trying it on with each other for as long as there's been seafaring."

"That's not quite the same thing," Mom put in.

"I understand that. But everyone in the navy knows there are men who are drawn to that particular service precisely because it means being isolated in the exclusive company of other men for weeks or months at a time. The difference is not really important here. What I'm trying to say, son, is that your being homosexual wouldn't frighten or repel me."

"In any case," Mom put in, "anybody who thinks you're weak isn't paying attention."

"Just sick and twisted," Jamie said. "Come on, Mom," he went on as her mouth opened to protest. "Everybody knows perverts like me are sick. I bet it says so in that big book of yours, the one that describes the different kinds of mental illness."

"Yes, it does," she admitted. "But I don't know that I agree. It's very hard to tell how much of the problems homosexuals have are caused by the very people who are so busy telling them what's wrong with them. There's been some research lately that seems to indicate the phenomenon is much more common than people suppose, in any case."

Research, he thought, the word sending ripples of calm across the turmoil in his brain. "Research," he said aloud. "I could study about this, there must be books on it."

"Yes, there must be," Mom said. "I could make inquiries at work."

"No!" Jamie exclaimed in alarm. "Don't let anybody around here know."

"Confidentiality," Mom began, but he cut her off.

"I don't want anybody outside this room to know," he insisted. "It could ruin everything. What if MIT finds out I'm queer?"

There was a gasp from the door; Celia was standing there, still poised on one foot as she'd started to step into the room.

Jamie groaned. "Cissy, I swear to God," he said.

She quickly closed the door behind her and threw her hands up. "I won't say anything, I promise. I'm sorry I butted in, I just wanted to talk to Mom about—well, never mind, it's not important. Just... Really? Jamie, you really think you're... that way?"

Dad got up and put an arm around her. "This is still pretty new," he told her. "I don't think Jamie's ready to talk about it with you just yet."

"Too many people already know," Jamie said. "Beth. And Rima, she's the one who—"

"Kevin," Dad put in suddenly. "You need to talk to Kevin."

That's right, he's one, too, Jamie remembered. He nodded slowly, assimilating the idea. Kevin was someone he admired, someone he could trust, and also someone who'd been living with this… this disaster in his own life.

Dad went on, "You should think about talking to Laurie and Rob, too; they had some problems with this subject a while ago."

"I know about their 'problems,'" Jamie said. "It turned out not to be true about them, right? No, thanks, I don't think so."

Dad let go of Celia, who crossed over to the couch and started murmuring to Mom. He stepped up to Jamie and pulled him firmly into his strong arms, against his hard chest. "Whatever makes you comfortable," he said into Jamie's hair. "We're going to help you, and it's going to be all right."

Jamie hung on.

Chapter 5.1

From his seat on the couch, Jamie could see the Chicago River over the air conditioner in one of the long wood-shuttered windows of Uncle Kevin's apartment. The walls of the room were beige, the carpet tan flecked with green and coral. The furniture was upholstered in pale green shot with silver thread; coral throw pillows were scattered here and there. The energy of the room came from Uncle Kevin's paintings: huge abstract canvases in riotous colors, hung on the bland walls, propped in corners, leaning on the mantel of the fireplace with its shallow, pristine coal grate, now filled with a sheaf of dried milkweed pods and cattails.

Uncle Kevin, coming in with a loaded tray, noticed Jamie staring around him. "It used to be chartreuse and electric blue," he commented. "About knocked your brother Laurie's eyes out when he came here for me. Since then, I've gone for a more neutral background for my stuff. Cream?"

At Jamie's nod, he poured coffee from an angular steel pot with black lid and handle into an earthenware cup and saucer banded in dusky red and leaf green and handed it to Jamie with a matching creamer. "He changed my life that day," he went on, settling back into his armchair with his own coffee. "I had given up on any hope of ever setting eyes on my brother Sean again; connecting to a whole family that would welcome me into it had never entered my wildest dreams."

He put his cup and saucer down on the table next to him and leaned forward, elbows on his knees. He was wearing black slacks and a white shirt with a classic men's smoking jacket, maroon watered silk with black lapels, pointy-toed red Turkish slippers on his feet. "I know you're scared and confused," he said. "Just don't give up hope. Things can turn out better than you expect. And I'll do anything I can to help."

"Can you make this go away?"

"You know I can't."

"Then I don't see how you could possibly help me."

"I hope I can help you come to terms with your situation."

"My 'situation'? You mean discovering that I'm a pervert, an outlaw, a social pariah—without even having done anything? Come to terms with that?"

"Yes," the older man said evenly. "That's what I mean. You're not the first one to face this, you know. You're not even that unusual. Have you seen the Kinsey Report? More than a third of all men have had at least one homosexual experience."

"Well, that puts them one ahead of me," Jamie snapped. "Have you read Voltaire? If you try it once, you're a philosopher; twice, you're a sodomite. But I haven't tried it even once." He crossed his arms over his chest. "I have a girlfriend."

Kevin sat back, pursing his lips. "So why are you here?" he asked finally.

Good question, Jamie thought. *Why, if not to get his help? Where will snarling till you drive him away get you?*

He let his arms drop back into his lap. "Sorry," he said. "I'm a little on edge. I'm leaving for MIT next week and I still can't even think about this without going into a panic. I've been trying to research the subject, but there isn't much out there to go on. Mom's had better luck, but not being able to get a handle on this intellectually is making me crazy."

"I understand," Uncle Kevin said. "Let's just take it a step at a time. Can you tell me why you think you're homosexual, girlfriend notwithstanding?"

"It was my girlfriend who made me see it," Jamie admitted. He took a breath and pressed forward. "Because all the time I'm leaning into her soft curves, I'm thinking about hard bodies. Because I dream of men. Because I obsess about—about someone in my school, a boy. Because I've never been able to see a future for myself that includes any woman."

Uncle Kevin nodded judiciously. "Sounds about right," he said. "So you've made the first, most important, most difficult step: you've recognized yourself for who you are. And the second most important and difficult step, by the way: you've shared that knowledge with those nearest and dearest to you."

"Yeah, I'm sure they're thrilled, too. No doubt they'll visit me in the psych ward, or in jail."

Uncle Kevin's lips firmed as he sat up straight. For the first time, he reminded Jamie of Dad. "All right," he said. "A little bit of self-pity is understandable. God knows, this life is no picnic. But try to keep a little perspective here. I help run a sort of Underground Railroad for kids in your situation who've been thrown out by their families, sometimes after being beaten up, and left to live on the streets. Instead, your mother started researching and your father sent you to talk to his queer brother. Do you have any idea how rare that is?"

Jamie felt like crawling under the couch. "I know, I do. And I am grateful for it. My sisters were pretty good about it, too, the older two who heard. I dread telling the others, though; I don't think I can stand any more pity in my life. And yes, I know there are worse things than pity." He pulled his shoulders up around his ears, looking for a less fraught subject. "But that reminds me: they think I'm here to see the World's Fair exhibit at the Museum of Science and Industry. I guess I'd better go so I have something to tell them."

"I know," Uncle Kevin said, following his lead. "Sean told me. We'll go tomorrow. One of the perks of having my own gallery and having no one to answer to: I can visit museums on weekdays when they're less crowded, even in summer. My usual haunt is the Art Institute, though—I'm counting on you to explain to this long-haired aesthete what's going on in the great world."

"'There is no great world at all, only a little earth, for ever isolated from the rest of the little solar system.'"

Uncle Kevin smiled. "And fools—how does it go?—'confuse "great," which has no meaning whatsoever, with "good," which means salvation.' *The Longest Journey*. Forster is one of us, you know."

Jamie was confused. "E. M. Forster is a Jew?"

Uncle Kevin smiled gently. "No more than I am. No, not Jewish: homosexual."

"Really?"

"That's the word among the cognoscenti. There are rumors of a novel, written years ago and hidden away. Now that the Wolfenden report over there has recommended that homosexuality not be treated as a crime, especially in the wake of the scandal over Alan Turing, maybe Forster will be free to come out."

"'Come out'?"

"Into society, like a debutante. The Germans have done a lot of work on how important that is."

"The *Germans* have?" Jamie exclaimed in disbelief. "Hitler murdered homos!"

"This was before the Nazi regime. And they've picked it up again since. Some of the most progressive work on our community is being done there."

"'Our community'? Queers are a community, now?"

"A group of people with similar characteristics and common interests," Uncle Kevin said mildly. "What would you call it?"

"A bunch of freaks and outcasts," Jamie said flatly. "You know, kids in my school had been taught enough about prejudice that they were mostly ashamed to use words like 'nigger' or 'kike,' but they didn't have any trouble with 'nancy boy' or 'fruit' or 'pansy' or 'fairy' or—"

"Yes, I know the words," Uncle Kevin interrupted. "That's part of what our *community* has to work on, to make them just as ashamed to say them."

Jamie shook his head, scoffing. "Did you hear what happened last week? The Air Force sent up a rocket probe that was supposed to explore the moon. It exploded, but now they've created a new agency that focuses on space exploration, separate from the regular military. NASA, they're calling it. National Aeronautics and Space Administration. There will be huge opportunities for people with science and math skills. Think they'll hire queers?"

Jamie pushed his glasses back on his head and rubbed his hands over his face. "I'm not making any 'debut' any time soon," he said. "I'm staying squarely in hiding, like a skeleton in a closet."

"Like Anne Frank in her 'Annex'?" Uncle Kevin suggested. "Have you seen this?" He leaned forward to the kidney-shaped glass coffee table between them, pushed aside the Sunday *Sun Times,* and revealed the latest issue of *Life* magazine. Beside the picture of the dark-haired girl and a page of her famous diary, the cover blurb read, "What Happened After End of Anne Frank's Diary: Exclusive Story Tells of Her Tragedy."

Jamie picked up the magazine and stared at the cover without opening it. "So what's your point?" he asked. "They murdered her, if you remember."

"I remember, and so do you. So does just about everyone in the civilized world. And that's my point: her life has had meaning for millions of people."

"And millions of other people died, just like her," Jamie began, when his eye caught a smaller, stapled-together publication that had been at the bottom of the pile on the table. "What's that?" he asked in astonishment.

He picked it up in trembling fingers. *Mattachine Review*, it was called. He skimmed the list of contents in disbelief.

"It has NOT passed yet - But Britons Keep Talking About [the] Wolfenden Report," "Homosexuals in a Related Culture: A Brief Investigation," "Doctor Urges Review Of Sex Deviate Laws"—a whole series of articles and essays on topics related to homosexuality and homosexuals, with profiles, book reviews, letters, travel notes— "What is this?" he asked again.

"A couple of guys in California started the society a few years ago," Uncle Kevin answered. "They called it 'mattachine' after some medieval Italians who danced in masks, keeping their identities hidden. There are chapters all over the country now. I told you we were a community."

He got up and started clearing away the coffee things. "You'll meet some of us tonight; I've invited a few friends over. I'd take you out, but if we got picked up I could get nailed for contributing to the delinquency of a minor."

Jamie gave a short, sardonic laugh. "That's ok," he said. "I'll help with whatever you're fixing, if you give me explicit instructions—I'm not much of a cook."

"Can you wrap bacon around chicken livers and water chestnuts for rumaki?"

"Er, actually…"

Uncle Kevin set the coffee tray down on the pass-through counter to his kitchenette and bonked himself on the head with a fist. "Oh, damn, Jamie, I'm sorry, I forgot. All right, skip the bacon, would you mind cutting up some carrots and celery for the onion dip?"

"That I can do," Jamie agreed.

That night, shifting to get comfortable on the sofa, Jamie spotted the *Mattachine Review* on the coffee table and picked it up again. He settled back in the crisp percale sheets Uncle Kevin had given him and leafed through the pages, thinking about the supper party.

Most of the guests had been Uncle Kevin's age, though there were a few teenagers and men in their twenties. But they'd all been extravagant, flamboyant… *effeminate,* Jamie thought reluctantly. They'd made loud jokes with broad gestures and high, shrieking laughs—putting it on a little for Jamie, he recognized, but it still made him ill at ease. This was not a world he felt comfortable in, nor did he especially want to become comfortable in it. He wanted a world of quiet men with narrow ties and pen-protector shields in their shirt pockets, a world of order and predictability where the inspiration was cerebral and the innovations were scientific.

Still, seeing a little of Uncle Kevin's circle—his *community*—did make Jamie feel that there were possibilities beyond any he'd considered when he thought of his own future. He put the magazine down, took off his glasses and switched off the table lamp, letting in the silvery light of the half moon hanging over the river to the west. He punched his pillow and turned it over, said his prayers, and composed himself for sleep.

When he woke, the room was pitch dark and a stranger's hand grasped his shoulder. He cried out and flailed in panic, still half in the nightmare, in the camp and the fear.

"It's all right, you're all right, son," said a half-familiar voice softly. Jamie fell into what felt like familiar arms.

"Dad?" he whispered.

"It's Kevin, Jamie," came the answer. The arms moved to a firmer purchase and Jamie started to relax.

Then a wave of revulsion washed over him and he tried to push away, but the arms only held him tighter.

"Jamie," Uncle Kevin said, more sharply now. "Jamie, stop. Listen to me. Are you listening?"

Jamie nodded against the broad chest.

"I'm going to hold you till you stop shaking," Uncle Kevin said. "We are not going to fuck, understand?" Jamie jerked at the unexpected crudity, but it got through to some place of fear inside him and he started to relax. "You're my nephew, and you're thirty years younger than I am. I'm bent, I'm not twisted. I'm not into teenagers. I'm just going to hold you till you feel calmer, all right?"

"All right," Jamie whispered.

CHAPTER 52.

SATURDAY, OCTOBER 25, 1958

J amie had been on the bus all night. The other ten MIT students who'd decided to go to the march on Washington for school integration were all asleep, hunched uncomfortably in their seats or leaning on each other, but Jamie was too keyed up to do more than doze intermittently.

He knew Laurie would be coming out from Haverford to meet him and join in the march. He was on edge about that; would Laurie sense something different about him? Would the folks or one of the girls have told him? When they'd dropped Laurie off on the Haverford campus in September, on the way to delivering Jamie to the 30th Street Station in Philadelphia for the long train trek to Boston, Laurie had kissed him goodbye in the parking lot. Jamie had felt that impress on his cheek like a brand for hours afterwards.

Of course, it wasn't visible to anyone else—and Jamie himself was almost invisible on the MIT campus, to his relief. Still, he'd navigated the first few weeks of school on mental tiptoe, fearing that a wrong word or look or gesture would somehow proclaim his secret to the world and end his life before it began.

If not for that fear, he would be as close to happy as he'd ever been. Classes were challenging, for the first time in his life, but not overwhelming. His dorm room in East Campus was pleasant and old-fashioned enough, with its exposed ductwork and electric wiring in pipes running down the walls, to feel homey.

Above all, his roommate, a slight young man of mixed Chinese/Jamaican/Jewish heritage, was compatible: brilliant, shy, and reticent. They'd spent the first week, after brief introductions, nodding to each other night and morning as the roommate—Joel See-Hu, a name that, he said, quickly sorted the wheat from the chaff as people did or did not refrain from making obvious jokes—navigated up or down the bunk bed ladder past Jamie.

On the third night, Joel had chimed a soft "Amen" to Jamie's murmured prayer; by the fifth night, he was reciting it with him. Jamie stifled both the fellow-feeling and the curiosity this engendered; he was afraid to get too involved lest his secret somehow escape his control.

But yesterday he'd ventured to say, as they jockeyed around each other at the room's sink alcove, "By the way, I'll be gone this weekend; I'm going to that demonstration in Washington for school integration."

Joel had turned toward him, wide doe-eyes looking oddly hurt as he said, "If I'd known, I'd have gone, too."

"Oh." Jamie stared at him, nonplussed. There was a spot of toothpaste on Joel's chin. "You'd have been interested in this 'asinine escapade'?" he said finally, referring to comments made by Southern students.

Joel had extended a slim tobacco-brown hand. "Did you think I'd be less interested than you?"

"You don't have to be a Negro to be interested in equal education," Jamie had snapped.

Joel had turned back to the sink, rinsing the toothpaste off his chin after a glance in the mirror. "You're right," he'd said softly. "I'm sorry. It's my own responsibility to get involved."

"I'm sorry, too," Jamie had said. "Next time I'll let you know."

They'd nodded at each other in the mirror, then fallen back into their usual silence.

Now Jamie wished he had his taciturn but familiar roommate beside him as the bus pulled in to Washington's Union Station. The other ten MIT students seemed to know each other, and were upperclassmen in any case. Jamie hovered uncertainly on the edge of the group as the leader, a white senior Jamie had the impression was also Jewish, discussed their planned delegation to the White House later in the day.

A hand grasped his elbow from behind. Thinking of warnings he'd heard about big city pickpockets, Jamie swung around with his fist up, only to find himself engulfed in a massive hug. "Damn," Laurie said. "Hold on there, Marshall Dillon. I know you're feeling your oats after wiping the parking lot with those hoods last spring, but it's me you're squaring up to here."

Jamie felt himself flush but didn't allow himself to squirm out of his brother's arms, not wanting to make the other MIT students— who'd turned to stare at the large black man hugging him—think there was anything wrong. *And there isn't anything wrong as far as he knows, so get a grip on yourself, Hymie.*

But he couldn't help remembering how, last night on the bus, someone had been reading James Baldwin's *Notes of a Native Son.* Someone else had said, "Why are you reading that faggot?" to general nods of agreement. Jamie had been stunned that such a powerful voice for civil rights could be so easily dismissed because of his sexual bent.

"Um, this is my brother," he said to the gaping faces around them now.

"Adopted brother," Laurie said gently. They almost never used that word about each other, but Jamie could see it was necessary in this context. Expressions were still stunned as Laurie said, "Laurence

McAlister," and offered his hand, but they all shook with him, if rather dazedly.

"Anyway," Laurie went on, "hope you don't mind if I take this guy off with me. We've got some catching up to do."

"No, that's ok," the leader said. "We have to get going ourselves. We don't want to miss Dr. King's speech."

To their surprise, Laurie's expression grew grave. "That's right, you guys have been on the bus all night—you won't have heard. Dr. King was stabbed yesterday. His wife is speaking in his place."

Amongst the exclamations of shock and dismay, someone said, "God damned white supremacists! Is he going to be ok?"

"Actually," Laurie said, "it was a black woman. She just came up to him at a book signing in New York and stabbed him in the chest. No word yet on how he is, but I think it's pretty bad."

They immediately started conferring on how this might affect their chances of getting to see President Eisenhower.

Laurie drew Jamie aside a little. "Do you want to go with them?" he asked in an undertone. "I don't want to cramp your style here."

"No, that's ok," Jamie told him. "I'm not really part of that group, and I'd rather grab some time with you."

He felt self conscious at Laurie's obvious pleasure. *He wouldn't be so happy to be with me if he knew the truth.* But as they walked toward the car that Laurie said some other Haverford students had come in, Jamie's other internal voice said, *Uncle Kevin can talk about community, but I've got family to stand with me.*

After the march, while the others were occupied with the delegation to the White House, Jamie and Laurie ducked into a diner for a cup of coffee. The place was jammed with other marchers, but the warm fug was a pleasant contrast to the brisk fall day and a party of white students made a point of stepping aside for Laurie, so before long they were contentedly sipping in a corner booth.

Jamie unwound the gray and crimson muffler Mom had knitted in MIT colors from around his neck; Laurie was doing the same with the scarlet and black Haverford one she'd made for him. "Snap," they said together, and smiled at each other.

Looking across at his brother, Jamie reflected that in the short time they'd been apart, he'd already forgotten how large Laurie was. *Maybe it's from being around Joel so much, since he's so slight.* That led to another thought.

"Mrs. King looked awfully small up there on the podium, didn't she? I don't think I've ever seen her before."

Laurie nodded. "Part of it was that fur coat she was wearing, I think. It dwarfed her a little. But good for her to have the guts to take his place today, after what happened."

"Was that her own speech, or did she just give his?"

"I don't know. I wasn't paying that much attention, to tell you the truth. I just kept thinking how bizarre it was, that it was a black woman who did that to her husband. Even if she was crazy like they're saying, why pick on another Negro?"

"I've been reading an article for one of my courses by some guy called Kurt Lewin. He was a prof at MIT before he died. The Research Center for Group Dynamics was his baby. He was a psychologist, but he sets out his ideas more like a real scientist would."

Laurie wagged a finger at him, chuckling. "Don't let Mom hear you say psychology isn't a real science."

Jamie smiled ruefully. "You know what I mean, though. With Lewin, it's not all about your lousy toilet training or whatever, but something he calls 'group dynamics.' He's a German Jew who came here in the early '30s, and one of the things that interests him is how some Jews can hate their own identity and try to squelch any resemblance they have to other Jews. Maybe this woman who stabbed King—odd name, I heard someone say it..."

"Izola Curry," Laurie put in.

"Right. So maybe there was some twisted thing like that, hating herself because she's black, that helped drive her to what she did."

Laurie thoughtfully twirled a napkin on the table with a long finger as he thought. "Sometimes when I'm around other black people and they're, I don't know, playing loud music or lounging around not doing anything useful, I start feeling—not superior, exactly, but like I'm not like them, like I don't want white people to think we're all like that." With a grimace, he crumpled the napkin. "Pretty stupid. I know white people who do those things all the time, some of them in my own family."

"Speaking of the family, where are they today?"

Laurie shrugged. "They had other things to do. I told them not to bother this time."

Jamie just stared at him.

After a minute, Laurie said slowly, "I think being away from home is making me feel... it's hard to pin down, but... like the whole race thing is my issue. Mine, not theirs. Not that it's such a great thing to have to deal with, but that it is my thing to deal with." He looked up and added quickly, "I don't mean you. You're different. I mean, you know about prejudice yourself, you've experienced it yourself, being part of a group other people look down on."

You have no idea, Jamie thought. Aloud he said, "That's a little selfish, isn't it?"

Laurie sat back. "Selfish?"

"They want to be part of all this, too. I don't mean they're dying to travel on some smelly bus so they can catch a glimpse of Harry Belafonte and drink lousy coffee in a crowded diner, but part of the changes that are coming, that people like Dr. King are leading the country to. It's their country too, after all, and they want to make it better as much as we do. Besides," he scratched the back of his neck self-consciously, "they l-er, care about you. You can't just seal yourself off from that as if you were in some kind of Faraday cage."

Laurie, who'd been nodding as he listened, grinned at Jamie. "Ok, what's a Faraday cage, genius?"

"It's a kind of shield that sets up an electrical field that keeps other electromagnetic impulses from getting past it. It's a little more complicated than that, but basically, if you're inside one, for instance, a lightning strike couldn't hurt you."

"Isn't that a good thing?"

"Sure, for some uses. They use them to protect delicate electronic instruments. But for people, I'm not so sure. Don't put yourself in an isolation booth, Laurie. Take a chance on the lightning."

Jamie quaked a little at his own words. *Listen to me, giving advice on not closing yourself off.*

But Laurie reached across and gripped his hand. "Message received," he said. He let go and started shifting out of the booth. "Let's blow this joint. I'll walk you back to the bus station and you can tell me about these courses you're taking that are giving you all the answers to the mysteries of life."

"I wish," Jamie laughed, and followed him out.

CHAPTER 53.

THURSDAY, NOVEMBER 27, 1958

"Did you want any more to eat, James?" Joel's father asked.

Jamie considered once again explaining that the name "Jamie" was an approximation of the Yiddish "Hymie" that in turn derived from his actual name, the Hebrew "Chaim," but dismissed the notion when his, "No, thank you, Dr. See-Hu," garnered no more response than a curt nod and an abrupt exodus of the older man from the table.

This was proving to be the least fraught Thanksgiving Jamie could remember. Dinner had been prepared by a hired woman the day before; the three men had reheated everything in the oven and eaten it in the modest apartment kitchen without ceremony.

Still, Jamie felt a pang as he rose and started clearing the table and scraping the plates when Joel said, "Never mind those, Graciela will do them in the morning." Oddly enough, the absence of clean-up chores made Jamie more homesick than the silent, Spartan meal had. The long-distance call from the family this afternoon had been awkward, with Joel and his father in earshot so that Jamie felt even less inclined than usual to respond to his parents' expressions of affection and his siblings' jocularity.

Now Joel's voice came from behind him again. "Come on, I want to show you that book of Newman's I was telling you about. I can't believe you haven't read it; it's much better than that anti-Semite

Bell's stuff. Newman puts math writings from over two thousand years in the context of history and philosophy. You're going to love it."

Jamie followed him through the living room with its picture window staring at another equally undistinguished one opposite, across the tiny foyer, and into the second of the two bedrooms. Joel's room was hung with more stark pictures like those in the living room—silverpoints, Dr. See-Hu had called them. Black lines on white backgrounds showed a minimalist seascape, a hunchbacked beggar, a head of a dark-bearded man in a turban. The only spots of color in the room were a blood-crimson poster of the Hitchcock movie *Vertigo* and the faded blue and red on Joel's well-worn Roy Rogers bedspread.

Jamie would have been self-conscious at having such a remnant of childhood still on display, but Joel didn't seem to notice as the two boys sat side by side on his bed with their knees against the trundle that had been pulled into the center of the room for Jamie. Joel showed Jamie the book he'd spoken of, and they were soon absorbed in a conversation far removed from idle observations on décor, though Jamie was uneasily aware of the warmth of Joel's thigh against his.

After a while, Jamie moved across to his own bed so they could talk face to face without the distraction of touch. They had moved on by that time, from Bertrand Russell's "Definition of Number" in the Newman book to talking about Russell's political activism. That led to a conversation about the Civil Rights movement and the rally Jamie had gone to.

"There were ten thousand people there," Jamie said, "and the MIT delegation included Harry Belafonte, but Eisenhower still wouldn't see them. Ike went golfing instead, and they wouldn't even let our group into the White House to present their list of demands to his secretary."

"I read that Governor Faubus claims anybody for desegregation is a Communist," Joel said, shaking his head.

"Yeah, the man who closed high schools in Alabama rather than let blacks in, a fine example of American ideals. Some of our students aren't any better, though. Did you see that quote in the school paper saying that black schools were on a lower level than white ones because of 'basic qualities of the Negro race'? My brother Laurie's one of the smartest guys I know."

"Hey, you don't have to convince me," Joel said wryly. "At least the tone in *The Tech* was friendlier after the march. That guy Friedland is right, MIT needs to get more involved."

"*We* need to get more involved," Jamie corrected him. Joel nodded.

Eventually, Joel went out to use the bathroom. Jamie stretched out a crick in his neck and glanced at Joel's alarm clock. "Man," he said when Joel came back in. "It's after midnight. Where's your dad?"

Joel shrugged. "Asleep, I imagine. He usually goes to bed around ten." Looking at Jamie's expression, he said defensively, "Did you want him to tuck us in and tell us a bedtime story?"

Jamie waved a hand dismissively. "Pass," he laughed. Still, it did seem a little... cold, his disappearing without a word that way. No wonder Joel was so quiet, growing up with this distant man.

Squelching another wave of homesickness, Jamie grabbed his pajamas from his suitcase on the floor and took his own turn in the bathroom. By the time he came back, Joel was in bed with the light off.

Jamie made his way to the trundle bed, feeling his way through the shadows, got in, set his glasses just under the bed where he could reach them but wouldn't step on them if he got up in the dark, put on his yarmulke, and composed his mind for prayer. As he had started doing in the dorm, Joel murmured the Hebrew bedtime blessing along with Jamie.

In the intimacy of this boyhood bedroom, Jamie finally felt free to ask, "Are you actually Jewish? I mean, your father doesn't seem to be…"

"No, he's an atheist," Joel said softly across the darkness. "My mother was. Is, I mean. I did some Jewish stuff with her before she left, and more with her parents. I still go to my grandparents' for Passover. That's mostly where I see Mom." There was a silence, then he went on, "So I feel kind of ambivalent about Judaism, because I associate it with her, and she… she went away."

They both fell silent. As Joel's breathing slowed and steadied in sleep, Jamie chewed over their conversations and the mix of feelings churning in his gut over his absent family, the march and his own involvement in the Movement, and Laurie himself.

Why am I so afraid for him to find out about me? he wondered. *These days we get along pretty well—ever since I helped him out with algebra, in fact. And he seems not to mind or even care particularly that Uncle Kevin is queer. The others know, after all, except for the kids.*

The trundle bed squeaked and rattled as he turned over, facing away from Joel's recumbent figure. Here, less than three feet away from Joel, he was much more aware of his presence than in their dorm bunk beds where he was out of sight and on another level. Jamie was aware of Joel's every twitch and sigh. On the wall in front of him, the white lettering on the crimson *Vertigo* poster seemed to float in the dim glow from the streetlight outside the window.

He wrenched his thoughts back from his hyperawareness of Joel and back to the problem of why he was so nervous over telling Laurie his new realization about himself when the other members of his family had already accepted it.

But the girls are girls, and Mom's a psychologist who's used to dealing with people who are... different, and Dad is, well, Dad. Laurie was important to Jamie in a different way from the others, he realized. *Maybe because we're the two oldest, or because he was there after I came to America and Dad had to go back on duty, or maybe just because even when we squabble, I know he really loves me. I couldn't stand to lose that.*

You won't lose that, Hymie, he told himself firmly. *He won't go ape over this, as Robbie would say. Just tell him. At Christmas. I'll tell him then.*

He turned back toward Joel, closed his eyes, and slept at last.

CHAPTER 54.

MONDAY, DECEMBER 8, 1958

Jamie sat coiled on his lower bunk in East Campus, tight as a wound spring. The sun had set and there was no visible moon, but Jamie hadn't moved to turn the lights on. He flinched and squinted as Joel came in and flipped the old-fashioned switch.

"Did you fall asleep?" he asked, surprised. "You missed dinner."

"Not hungry," Jamie said, uncoiling enough to turn in to the shadow of the upper bunk.

Joel came farther into the room and Jamie remembered too late that his books were still on his desk in their neat end-of-study night configuration rather than strapped up for carrying.

"You didn't go to class?" Joel said, in the same tone he might have used if told the earth had reversed its polarity.

Jamie sighed and turned back toward him. "I'm waiting for a phone call," he said. Then, as Joel hovered uncertainly, he swung his legs off the bed and scrubbed his hands over his face, dislodging his glasses so they fell on the floor. Before he could reach down, Joel had snatched them up and was proffering them in a move that brought him into Jamie's space, closer than either of them usually ventured.

Jamie took them with a nod of thanks and put them on, but Joel still stood there, almost touching him, wide dark eyes searching his anxiously.

"Sit down and I'll tell you," Jamie said, capitulating.

277

Once Joel was safely across the room in his own desk chair, Jamie began. "You remember how I told you that most of the kids in my family are adopted, and the youngest one had only been with us for about a year and a half? Well, something I didn't tell you is that he—Steve—had been locked up in a room before he came to us." He stopped, overwhelmed by the thought as he hadn't been when he'd first heard about it, before he actually knew Steve.

Joel's brow furrowed. "Locked up—like, whenever he came home from school?"

"Locked up, as in all day and all night for ten years, from the time he was three. No school, no friends, no other human being but this cousin he was left with when his parents were killed, if you can call him a human being. He was let out sometimes in the evenings to clean, and then the cousin would torture him." He glanced up. "He's got scars as bad as mine."

Joel flushed; they'd never acknowledged that, living together and sharing a communal bathroom, they'd seen more of each other's bodies than either was comfortable with. But he only said, "That's horrible." Then, after a pause, "So, the phone call?"

"Oh, right. Well, one night—I don't know why that night particularly—this Bert character was threatening Steve with a knife, and… I guess he was drunk; Steve got it away from him and stabbed him in the throat."

"Jesus, that was in the papers, wasn't it? I think I remember seeing something about that, but I didn't pay much attention. Actually, I tried not to dwell on it."

"I know how you feel. Anyway, he ended up in this psychiatric facility for troubled kids my mom works at, and she took a liking to him and brought him home, and he got along ok with everyone, and we adopted him."

"So, happy ending."

"Far as it goes. But then Mom's supervisor got agitated because she'd gone against him when he wanted to put Steve in the juvenile offender unit so he wouldn't have what he thought would be a disaster on his books, and he pushed to have Steve charged with Bert's murder. The hearing's today, I'm just waiting to—"

As if on cue, there was a knock on the door. "Phone for McAlister," a voice called.

Jamie jumped up so fast he rapped his head on the bottom of the upper bunk. Ignoring the pain, he ran for the hall phone. Then, when he had it, for a second he couldn't speak.

He must have been breathing hard, though, because after only a few seconds Mom's voice said, "Jamie? Is that you? It's ok, sweetheart, everything's ok."

He blew out a gust of air. "It went all right?" he repeated.

"Yes," she said. "The judge declared it self-defense and—" Her voice had been calm, but she suddenly started sobbing.

There was a rustling noise, then Dad's voice. "Your mother's been holding herself—and Steve, and all the rest of us—together by sheer strength of will the past few days," he said. "I think the relief just hit her."

Jamie couldn't speak. His knees were shaking and there were iron gates in his mind's eye. *Jedem das seine,* the sign still said. *You get what you deserve.* Steve didn't deserve to be treated like a murderer. *So do I? Just for surviving?* Jamie couldn't tell, couldn't decide, couldn't think.

After a minute, Dad spoke again. "It's all right, son. I'm here, your mother's here, Steve is going to be fine. We're all going to be here waiting for you when you get home in a couple of weeks. I'm so sorry you're all alone there for this; I should have insisted you cut the semester short, but I know you didn't want to. But you'll be home soon and we'll all be together again." His voice was deep and calm and sure.

279

Jamie's heart slowed to a more reasonable rate and he was able to force some air into his lungs, but he still couldn't really talk. "Dad," he croaked, hardly above a whisper. "Dad." The receiver started to slip from his hand.

Another hand, a slim brown one, entered his field of vision and gently took the phone from him. He hadn't even realized Joel had followed him out of the room.

"Sir," Joel said into the phone, "this is Jamie's roommate, Joel See-Hu. He's a little shaken up right now, but he's going to be all right. I'll look after him."

He listened for a minute, then smiled thinly. "It's not a problem," he said. Then, "Yes, sir, I'll tell him."

He hung up, took Jamie's elbow, and guided him back to their room. Jamie sank onto Joel's desk chair, which was closer to the door than his; his knees had finally given out.

"He said to remind you that they love you," Joel told Jamie. "And they'll call after supper when they light the menorah."

Jamie nodded, silent tears running down his face. Joel stood at his shoulder with a hand on his arm, facing the other way. Finally he reached out a foot and hooked Jamie's chair over so he could sit on it without moving his hand away, still with his face turned aside.

It might have been half an hour before Jamie was able to pull himself together. He mopped his cheeks with a tissue from Joel's desk, then said, "I should tell you, I'll probably have a nightmare tonight."

"About that," Joel said, gesturing toward Jamie's arm where they both knew the concentration camp tattoo marred the skin with the numbers of Jamie's broken life.

"Yes."

Joel shrugged. "Nightmares don't scare me," he said. He turned to meet Jamie's eyes for the first time. "You don't scare me."

Jamie drew a deep breath. "Well, maybe this will scare you," he said. "If I—if I wake up screaming, I'll need…"

"You'll need?" Joel prompted.

"Someone to, to, h- uh, touch, er, put a hand maybe—"

Joel's hand on Jamie's arm tightened, then released as he got up. "I get it," he said softly. "I can do that, don't worry about it."

He poked Jamie on the shoulder. "Come on, let's go to Elsie's and get you a roast beef sandwich. My treat."

Chapter 55.

Sunday, December 22, 1958

Jamie had come home for the holiday on Friday; Laurie had arrived only last night. Tense at the thought of carrying out his resolution to tell Laurie his secret, Jamie had opted out of the family sing that arose, and been snippy with him later, an attitude Laurie had returned in spades. That may have fed the screaming, spewing nightmare he'd had afterwards; in any case, once the family had put his pieces back together, he'd flinched from Laurie's kiss on the forehead as though pierced by a needle. Still, the dread he felt about talking to his brother kept being swept back by surges of optimism.

Uncle Kevin had written to Jamie several times during the semester, urging him to take Laurie into his confidence, amongst other advice. He seemed to think Laurie would be able to handle it; he also thought it was important for Jamie to learn to trust his own instincts. Jamie wasn't sure those two pieces of advice were entirely compatible.

He'd also advised Jamie to pay attention to his own reactions to the people around him, which sounded simple but actually went against the grain of his usual preoccupations. He'd tried, though, noticing how the girls and boys of the student body affected him.

The girls left him cold, for the most part, though there was one young woman in Professor Mueller's physics class who reminded him of Rima. He almost spoke to her once, but realized the yearning he felt toward her reminded him of his occasional attempts at eating the sweet, rich desserts his siblings liked: the brief pleasure of the taste and comfort at being like the others never balanced out the sick discomfort that followed.

It mirrored the discomfort he felt at things he sometimes saw scrawled on men's room walls: crude drawings and obscene slogans that both fascinated and terrified him.

Watching other boys at the Field Day activities or milling around at the Tech Show, though, he found himself silently cataloguing their physical attributes, noting a muscular arm here, a broad chest there, the slope of a cheekbone or the shape of a mouth. There was no use trying to deny it any more; male bodies appealed to him the way plain food did, a nourishment he needed the way he needed bread, no matter what Laurie might think about it.

Now Laurie was sitting on the bed in the spare room where Jamie had retreated to pretend to study, nattering away about Haverford while Jamie sat at the desk and tried to screw up his courage to tell him what he now knew about himself.

Do it, he urged himself. Jump, Hymie. You're alone in the house with him while everyone else is at that stupid movie. You'll never get a better chance. Just tell him.

But what if he hates me?

He's never hated you for anything you've ever done or said before.

But this isn't about something I'm doing, this is about something I am. What if he just can't handle it?

What if he can't? That's his problem, isn't it? You are what you are, you can't change that. He can change his attitude, and if he won't, that's on him.

Am I, though? Am I really so sure that's what I am?

Yes.

Yes, he thought again, with something almost like excitement swelling in his chest as a new aspect of the realization sank in. Ever since the conversation with Rima last summer, he'd been focusing on the problems and challenges, the sheer specter of impending catastrophe, of the revelation she'd brought him.

But sitting here listening to Laurie in the same room where Rima had shattered his own understanding of himself, he suddenly realized there was another side to this. It came to him that he'd felt a shift deep in his core, a movement of his self image and all his perceptions of the world and his place in it, that actually left him more confident and freer than he'd ever been in his life.

Having his parents and the girls be so accepting had been a marvelous boon that helped him overcome his initial panic. Spending time with Uncle Kevin and meeting his friends had eased his fears of being a social pariah. Getting through his first semester at MIT had let him see that he would still be able to cope with the day-to-day demands of ordinary life without bringing disaster down on his own head.

The rest is up to me. If Laurie or anybody else rejects me because of who I am, that will be terribly sad, but it won't make any difference to the reality. And the reality is, I feel better on some level now because I know this is right. I don't have to search for the truth about myself, I only have to accept the truth that I know in my soul.

Feeling as though a stone that had been grating inside him for most of his life had suddenly shifted into place and settled where it belonged, he closed his eyes and said abruptly, "I'm queer."

Laurie stopped talking and froze with his mouth still in a grin that would have looked comic if there had been anything in Jamie capable of humor at the moment. Then he snapped it closed and sat there for a moment looking as though he'd swallowed a frog.

When he did speak, what he said was not at all the sort of thing Jamie had been expecting. There was neither condemnation nor affirmation, just a sort of astonished curiosity. He wanted to know about Rima, about Mom and Dad, about how Jamie had been coping all by himself.

"You didn't think they were going to give you a hard time about it, did you?" he asked.

That made Jamie laugh and cover his own face. "Hard time, yeah, that's one way of putting it." Then he made himself look at Laurie again. "And you?"

But Laurie was off again, talking about that day they'd looked at the *Playboy* together, talking about what psychologists did or didn't think about homosexuality, about whether Mom did or didn't agree with them, about Uncle Kevin, about what Jamie's life would be like.

"He says it's a hard life," Laurie said.

Jamie shrugged. "That's what the folks say, too. Can't be helped; my life is my life. Mom wants me to get therapy, but I don't feel like I'm sick, I just feel scared about what might lie ahead."

"Mom doesn't think homos are sick."

"Everybody else in the world does. Sick or criminal. Or both. That's what she thinks therapy will help, dealing with how people are going to look at me."

"Man, I'm sorry about that. Is there anything I can do to help? No, stupid question. Well, maybe I can stop making sarcastic remarks that tip you into nightmares. You'd think I'd've learned that by now."

This was so far from what Jamie had been thinking that it surprised him out of his reflective mode and into his habitual sarcasm. "Yeah, always about you, isn't it? Don't you think you're a little dark to be the fair-haired boy?"

Laurie seemed to find that amusing, even reassuring. He got up and took a step toward Jamie, saying, "Hey, this'll give you a chuckle. My suitemate at Haverford thought you and I were a couple 'cause I kissed you goodbye."

This is it, Jamie thought. *This is where I find out how alone I'm about to be.* He came to his feet and took a few steps away from Laurie. His brother followed, but stopped at arm's length away.

Jamie took a breath and plunged. "At least no one around here will want to touch me again, that's one benefit."

"No such luck, bubeleh," Laurie said. As Jamie thought, *Sure, easy for him to say, but he hasn't really thought about it,* Laurie went on, "So because I'm heterosexual, you think when I kiss, say, Cissy, I'm coming on to her?"

"It's not the same thing," Jamie said. "I don't know how to explain it to you."

"Lucky for you, you don't have to." Laurie pulled Jamie into a hug, kissed the side of his head, and whispered, "You are my brother. I love you. If it makes you nervous to be close to me, get over it. If it makes you hot, get over yourself. I draw the line at incest."

Jamie hung on tight, his face hidden. *I could do it alone if I had to,* he told himself. *But I don't have to. They're not going to let me be alone, not any of them.*

Chapter 56.

"You might have told me it was your birthday," Joel said.

Jamie looked up in mild surprise from the package from home he was opening. "Why? Were you planning to bake me a cake?"

"Do you always have to be so snide?"

"Yes. Do you always have to play with that stupid toy?"

"Yup," Joel said, balancing the Slinky on one palm and flipping its end onto the other. "They're fascinating. It's Hooke's Law, look. The oscillation is governed by the harmonic motion till it reaches equilibrium." He demonstrated by holding the coiled spring aloft, then started slinging it in accordion coils from one hand to the other. "The mass is governed by the force of gravity and the constant of the spring."

"Uh, huh," Jamie said, only half listening as he pulled tissue paper from the gift box and lifted out the garment inside. "Oh, my God. Look at this. Elastic-waist pants. My mother thinks I'm ten years old."

Joel glanced over. "They're not so bad. Nice color, anyway."

"They're black."

"Right."

Jamie shrugged. "Fine. You like 'em, they're yours."

"Are you kidding? They're your present from your mother."

"One of them. She and Dad sent me some books, too."

"You know what my mother sent me for my last birthday? A baseball mitt."

"I didn't know you played baseball."

"I don't."

"Oh." Jamie watched as Joel put down the Slinky and reached for Jamie's birthday slacks. When Joel stood and undid his fly, Jamie turned his eyes away and opened his present from Celia: Huxley's *Brave New World Revisited.*

A movement caught the corner of his eye; Joel had jostled the desk getting his jeans off and the Slinky toppled off. Reflexively, Jamie leaned forward and caught it before it hit the floor, then raised his head to find himself with his nose inches away from Joel's bare, lightly furred thigh. *Like a peach,* he thought, and for an instant had the mad desire to take a bite out of it.

Then the combined scents of Dial soap and male musk hit the back of his palate and seemed to strike straight into his brain. He reared away, heart pounding.

"Um, they're too long and a little too tight," Joel said. His voice was shaky.

Jamie glanced up to see his roommate's face had flushed to a dark ruddiness. He hunched his shoulders up around his own hot cheeks and said, "Listen, I'm going to hit the head."

He took enough time in the bathroom to be sure Joel would have changed back into his own jeans. As he returned to their room, trying to erase the—incident, or whatever it was, he said, "What about your dad?"

Joel, who was rummaging in his narrow closet, pulled his head out. "What about him?"

"What did he give you for your birthday?"

"Oh. Uh, a copy of Landau's *Classical Theory of Fields.*"

"Our Physics course book?"

"Yeah."

Into the bleak silence that developed, Jamie raised the last unopened package from the pile on his bed. "This is from Ruby," he said. "Bet you anything it's for sharing."

"Sharing? Oh, Ruby's the, the woman who works for your family, right? So it's something to eat?"

Jamie thought about trying to describe the complex and subtle nuances of his relationship with Ruby, then dismissed the idea as too difficult and not his kind of conversation in any case.

"Right," he said, ripping the brown paper off the taped-shut square tin. He peeled off the tape and pried up the lid to reveal a loaf of Ruby's stollen, which she called coffee cake, redolent of cinnamon and rum. A little cloud of its powdered sugar topping had puffed up when the lid opened; as he breathed it in, it hit his palate right where the scent of Joel's thigh had.

He cleared his throat. "Want some?"

"Sure," Joel said, dropping into his desk chair. "So this is your birthday cake?"

"I don't like real sweet stuff," Jamie said defensively.

Joel only nodded. "Should we, like, put candles on it or something?"

Jamie snorted, palming the little box of candles Ruby had tucked in with the tin and shoving the wrapping paper over it on the bed. He gouged out chunks of the cake with his pocket knife and he and Joel munched them in silence.

When they finished, Joel went over to the sink and filled their tooth glasses with water. He handed Jamie his, settled back at his desk to take a gulp from his own, then with a look that Jamie recognized as trying to be casual, pulled out a pack of Marlboro filters.

He ripped the cellophane off the red and white package, opened the top, and after a couple of false starts managed to pull out a cigarette. He tapped its end on his thumbnail a few times, still affecting an air of nonchalance.

Jamie's jaw had fallen slack with surprise. Now he tightened it up to say sardonically, "It's filtered, hep cat."

Joel looked a little wounded. "I know that."

Jamie shook his head. "Tamping it on your thumb is supposed to pack the tobacco down so it doesn't come off on your lip. You don't need to do it if there's a filter."

"Oh." Joel looked at the cigarette uncertainly.

Jamie sighed. "In any case, you can't smoke in here."

"I can't? Why not?"

"Besides the fact that it would make the place smell like an ashtray and the other fact that, knowing you, you'd probably fall asleep over one and set fire to the place, my lungs can't take it."

Joel's hands, that had begun fiddling with a book of matches, froze. After a minute, he carefully set matches and cigarettes on the desk. "Because of...?" He gestured toward Jamie's arm, the one with the numbers tattooed on it.

"Right. My lungs were damaged."

"Really? How?" Then, when Jamie didn't answer immediately, "I'm sorry. You don't have to say if you don't want to talk about it."

"It's not that, it's that I don't know."

"How can you not know?"

"I don't remember much about... all that."

Joel stared. "Don't you want to know? There must be ways of finding out what happened to you."

"I suppose. Maybe." Jamie packed the stollen back into its tin.

Suddenly the simultaneous sharpening of his senses and blurring of his surroundings warned him a flashback was coming on, the first one in years. But the scene he found himself plunged into was brief and without violence. He was sitting on the edge of the barracks bunk, nibbling a hard crust that the skeletal man crouching in front of him, a stranger to Jamie, had just handed him from his own meager ration. The man was staring at him as though he wanted to climb into Jamie's brain. "Remember," he said. "I give you my food so that you will live, and remember."

He snapped back into awareness of the warm MIT dorm room, and the spice and mild sweetness of Ruby's cake lingering on his tongue, and Joel's anxious face staring at him.

There was no sound in the room but a hollow knocking in the heating pipes, then Joel said hesitantly, "Your name. Jamie. It doesn't seem like—"

"Chaim," Jamie said. "It was Chaim Metzger."

"Oh, ok."

They looked at each other across the room, then Joel said, "Can I have some more of that cake?"

"Sure," Jamie said.

Chapter 57.

Saturday, April 25, 1959

"You missed a spot," Ruby said.

"I haven't finished yet," Jamie huffed, though in fact he'd thought the windowpane he was working on was pretty well done. He turned the wad of crumpled newspaper to a dry patch and scrunched it into the corner of the glass.

He could hear Dad and Celia's voices around the corner of the house, taking down more storm windows. *This house is like Theseus's ship, or maybe a Heraclitean wave,* he reflected. *Its parts are constantly being replaced and repaired and relocated and cleaned, but in its whole presence it's stable, secure and unchanging.*

Working on it, as usual, calmed and centered him. He'd been oddly discommoded by driving by himself to services this morning, only nodding at the Epsteins across the sanctuary. The Shapiros had been there, too, on one of their rare forays to the synagogue, in honor of Passover week. Rima had smiled and given him a quick hug, but then gone on with her parents to their favored seats at the back. Afterwards, Jamie had eschewed the refreshments served by that day's bar mitzvah boy's family and hurried home without speaking to anyone.

Now he settled into the familiar rhythms of working quietly with Ruby, reveling in the quiet and the feeling of satisfaction as windows started to sparkle under their hands.

"Do you have the vinegar over there?" she asked.

"Here." He handed her the bottle, stretching over the desk between them. Steve's remedial English homework sat in the middle of it. "How's the kid doing?" he asked. Steve had been in bed with the flu ever since the first seder, three nights ago.

"He's better," Ruby said. "I chased him outside. It's such a beautiful day, and he's been cooped up in here."

"Being outside makes him nervous," Jamie observed mildly.

"Being outside is good for him," Ruby responded tartly. She leaned out the window to work on the outside of the glass.

Jamie stuck his head out his own window and grinned at her. "You're the mother of us all," he said.

"You have a perfectly good mother already," she scoffed.

"Yes, she's—she's our heart mother. You're our home mother."

He pulled his head back into the house, embarrassed at having said something so sentimental. Ruby stayed suspended half outside, but she'd stopped moving.

He took a fresh sheet of newsprint, crumpled it, and thrust his torso back through the window frame. He avoided looking directly at her, but he could tell Ruby was still staring at where he'd disappeared and now reappeared. After a minute, she went back to washing.

An hour later, she called a halt. "This is your holiday," she said. "You've done more than enough."

"I don't mind it," he said. "I actually kind of enjoy it."

"I know that, or I wouldn't have asked you to help. But I'll get Joy to finish up with me next weekend; Steve should be well enough to lend a hand, too, and he likes cleaning even more than you do."

Jamie started gathering up used newspaper and cramming it into the trash bag they'd been carrying from room to room. "I thought Mom didn't want to encourage that," he said. "Since it's a result of how that cousin treated him, the only times he got to be out of that room."

"I know," she said, pulling off the kerchief she'd bound around her head. She pursed her lips. "Sometimes your mother thinks too much."

A lock of her hair, disarranged from her usual careful coif, hung against her neck, thick and twisted. Jamie stared at it, fascinated, then reached forward a finger to make it swing free. "It's like a little Slinky," he said.

She reared back. "My hair is stinky?"

"No, I said Slinky. You know, those spring toys that you can make go down stairs and stuff?"

If anything, she looked more stricken. She clutched at the errant lock, then quickly crammed her hair back into the kerchief.

"It's ok, Ruby," he said. "It doesn't look bad or anything. It looks—interesting." *Something's wrong. What have I said?* She'd turned her back on him; he edged around the bed in Mom and Dad's room, where they'd ended up, and looked anxiously into her face.

"Ruby?" To his horror, he saw her lips were trembling. Then she pressed them closed and flared her nostrils, visibly getting herself back into control.

"Bring the trash outside, please, child," she said briskly. "I'll clear up the rest of this truck."

He almost took the easy out she was offering, but his brain couldn't stop worrying at the problem. *Hair, Slinky, spring… springy… Oh.*

"Ruby," he said as they left the room, keeping his voice as dispassionate and neutral as possible, "it's about the keratin in your hair, and the shape of it. Each hair is flatter along one axis than the other, so it forms a natural helix—er, a coil. A spiral. So does the metal in a Slinky. That's all I meant."

She didn't look convinced, so he tried again, cudgeling his memory for the theory. "Listen, hair curls because disulfide bonds form with weaker hydrogen bonds between the hairs, so they stick in curves. Your straightening iron breaks the hydrogen bonds so they re-form straighter, but moisture gets in there and makes them snap back."

"I work so hard to have good hair," she said, shoulders slumping.

Jamie couldn't believe what he was hearing. "'Good'—you mean, hair more like white people's? Ah, Ruby, you know better than that."

"Yes, I suppose I do," she said. She shook her head as though shedding the subject. "Now come on down to the kitchen, I'll make you a sandwich."

"I can't have bread," he said. "Passover, remember?"

"Oh, that's right. Funny way to celebrate a holiday."

He followed her down the back stairs into the kitchen, carrying the bucket with the rags and vinegar bottle in one hand and the trash bag in the other. Once he'd disposed of those, he pulled out a box of matzo and a jar of gefilte fish and assembled himself a snack while Ruby made a sandwich for her own lunch with chicken from last night's Shabbat dinner.

"It's a reminder of origins," he said, picking up the conversation as he slid into the breakfast nook bench across from her. "The escape from Egypt, freedom from slavery."

"I know, I know," she said. "The old folks used to sing about that." She looked up from her sandwich. "I know it's important to you, being Jewish," she said. "But don't you believe in Jesus, even a little tiny bit?"

"No," he said. "Not even a little tiny bit. In fact, given what your people have suffered from so-called Christians, just like mine, I'm a little puzzled as to why you do."

"Oh, don't give me that old story," she said. She took another bite and chewed, gazing over his shoulder thoughtfully. Jamie said a blessing on the matzo, spread horseradish on his fish, and forked up a mouthful.

"I was raised African Methodist Episcopal," she said. "I turned Catholic after I came here, to please old Mrs. Mac. But there was always Jesus. It had nothing to do with history, or theology, or anything in the brain. It was as simple as knowing who your parents are; Jesus is always just there, whenever I think about him."

"I don't know who my parents are," Jamie said. "They're not there when I think about them, and Jesus isn't, either."

Her eyes narrowed in a skeptical look. "That's not so," she said. "Seanie told me you'd remembered your father, how he died in that place."

"Yeah, that's what I remember about him: how he died."

She kept that keen regard trained on him till, with a sigh, he relented. "All right, I remember some other things, too. But nothing about my mother, not after she screamed at me to hide when they came for us."

"Isn't there some way to find out what happened to her?"

He shifted uneasily on the bench. "Maybe. But why should I?" He gave her a sardonic smile. "You think if I find her, I'm going to find Jesus?"

"I think you're going to find what happens to boys who give me sass if you're not careful," she snapped.

"Ok, ok, keep your shirt on," he laughed, holding his hands up in surrender. Ruby had been known to smack a misbehaving kid on occasion, but she'd never hit Jamie and he hardly thought she was going to start now. Still, she had a formidable temper and he didn't want to aggravate her, especially after his blunder over her hair.

Stop defending, just tell her. "It scares me to think about her," he admitted. "Besides, I already have two mothers."

As she stood up and stacked their empty plates, she leaned to put a hand on his shoulder. "We all need to know our roots, child," she said softly. "Don't be scared, your mother and I will still be here."

He put a hand over hers. "I know," he said. "I'll think about it."

Chapter 58.

Wednesday, June 24, 1959

"C'mon, Jamie, please? Pretty please with sugar on top?" Joy was jiggling up and down in the doorway to the larger spare room as though she had to go to the bathroom, which only served to irritate Jamie more than he already was.

"I'm *busy,*" he snapped for the third time. "Ask one of the others. Or go by yourself; you have a bike."

"They're all busy, I told you that," she said. "And it's no fun swimming alone."

So I'm her last resort. Typical. He shook his head and swiveled to face the desk again.

"You never do anything with me," she said. Her voice had lost the babyish whine she'd been affecting; she actually sounded serious.

He turned his head to stare at her. "That's ridiculous," he said. "I do things with you all the time. We went to that rally in Washington to hear Dr. King, for instance. And last summer we must have gone to the pool half a dozen times, at least. And there was the Labor Day Intercultural picnic, and—"

"That's all family stuff," she interrupted. "I mean things that are just you and me together. You've never done that, not even once, in my whole entire life."

That can't be true. But he couldn't think of anything to refute it. To deflect the discomfort this caused, he said sourly, "You're always tagging after Laurie. He's your favorite, everyone knows that." He hadn't realized it himself till just now, or that he resented it.

Instead of being distracted by this, Joy looked at him more closely than before, coming into the room and moving so the sunny window was at her shoulder instead of in her eyes. She chewed her lower lip for a minute, then said, "You know what Mom always says: instead of focusing on who's to blame, focus on the solution. We won't get to know each other better unless we do stuff together, so let's start."

He snorted. "Nice try. You're still just angling for a ride to the Post pool. If Rima's dog could drive, you'd be asking him."

She gave a brief smile at the image. "Maybe at the beginning," she admitted. "But now I'm getting the bit between my teeth. You're going to do something with me; I'm going to keep pestering you till you do."

"All right," he said. "Get a book. You can come in here and read with me."

She rolled her eyes. "You got a hope. No, we're going outside. It's a gorgeous day, and you never get any fresh air. You're all white and slimy, like that celery Ruby gets that's been growing underground."

"I am not slimy."

"Figuratively."

"My, my, such a big word."

"See? You don't know me. I've got lots of them. Come on, I'll tell you a few more on the way to the pool."

He sighed. "I really am busy, Joy. I have to grade a pile of papers for my professor. It's my summer job."

"You can do it later, when the sun's not out."

"It's my *job,*" he repeated as patiently as he could.

Her eyes went past him to the surface of the desk. "You're reading the paper!" she exclaimed. "You're not working at all!"

"Just taking a break." But it sounded feeble even to himself. He tried again. "Look, Joy, there was something that was upsetting me in it."

She cocked her head to one side and raised an eyebrow.

Jamie rubbed his forehead. Would she understand? *Only one way to find out.* "The Brits released Klaus Fuchs from prison yesterday."

"Who's that? Some bad guy?"

"He's a mathematical physicist who was involved with the Manhattan Project, you know, the atom bomb inventors. He passed secrets to the Soviets."

"And you're upset they let him out?"

"I'm upset he only served nine years; they executed the Rosenbergs for less. But he's not a Jew. He gets to go back to Germany and have an academic career and probably a nice long life."

"Establishment, part of the in-crowd." She nodded. "Not like the ones 'who passed through universities with radiant cool eyes, hallucinating Arkansas and Blake-light tragedy among the scholars of war.'"

Jamie's mouth fell open as he spun his chair to face her. *"What?"* he squawked.

She rolled her eyes again. "It's a poem," she said. "By Allen Ginsberg."

"I know what it is, I've read 'Howl' a million times. I want to know what you're doing reading it. And if you roll your eyes at me another time I'm going to dunk your head under once we get to that pool."

She used both hands to pull her eyelids apart and goggle at him. "You knew I liked poetry, didn't you? What, did you think I was just reading Longfellow and Edward Lear?"

"And maybe Robert Burns," he admitted. *She's right, I really don't know her. But still...* "Do Mom and Dad know you're reading Beat poets?" he demanded.

"Geez, Jamie, I am fifteen years old, you know, not twelve. Besides, did they ever try to stop you reading whatever you wanted to?"

"No, but that's different."

"Because I'm a girl? Or because you're so smart?" She leaned forward and poked him in the side.

"You're pretty smart, too," he said, "...for a girl." He dodged her outraged lunge and scooted toward the door.

"Where do you think you're going? Come back here and fight like a man, you coward!"

"Going to find my bathing trunks. I can't dunk you in the pool in my clothes, can I? Maybe you're not as smart as I thought."

He could hear her all the way into his bedroom, still laughing like a loon. The sound was unaccountably pleasing.

Chapter 59.

Thursday, August 20, 1959

"Man, I don't think I've ever seen you cry before, except from a nightmare," Laurie said.

They had come out onto the screened porch to enjoy the relative cool of the evening, after listening to Steve sing his first original song to the family. It was called "Bright, Warm Home" and it had struck chords in Jamie that were still reverberating.

"I wasn't the only one in tears. You weren't exactly Leonidas the Spartan yourself." *Don't be so defensive, Hymie,* he scolded himself.

But Laurie only chuckled a little, then said seriously, "My tears come a lot easier than yours. They don't mean as much."

"Quod erat non demonstrandum," Jamie said. "Your conclusion doesn't follow from your premise."

"To get back to my point?" Laurie suggested.

"It got to me," Jamie admitted. "Not only the song itself—that plaintive tune and the longing of the lyrics and the contentment at the end—but the fact that he would sing it to us, that he would share those feelings."

"It was brave of him; he's come a long way," Laurie agreed. "And he evidently got to some of your feelings, too."

Jamie was glad it was dark on the porch. He shifted on the wicker chair and said resolutely to Laurie's silhouette, "We had a good talk a while ago."

"I heard about that from Celia. She was pretty broken up that she blew the gaff on you."

"I wasn't too pleased with her at the time, but it was probably just as well. I got to talk to Steve about…" He gulped and stopped talking. "Maybe I shouldn't say," he said finally. "Not my sec—er, story."

"Oh, come on, you can tell me. Are you saying that Steve's queer, too? Do you mind me saying 'queer'?"

"No, I don't mind, and no, Steve's not. It was about that cousin of his."

Even in the dark, Jamie could sense Laurie's dawning horror. "He was molested?" he whispered.

Jamie hunched over and crossed his arms over his stomach. "You know that's not—I mean, being queer doesn't mean—it's not the same thing, going after little boys."

"I do know that," Laurie said. "But I guess Steve didn't."

"Right. We had a good talk about it, though." He couldn't see Laurie's expression, but he thought he could imagine it. "Yeah, we talked. Me, Mr. Communication. Hugged and everything."

Laurie reached a hand to Jamie's ankle where it rested on the opposite knee. He gave it a brief squeeze. "So you're doing ok with all that?"

"'Doing ok' would be putting it a little high. I'm working on it. It's hard, though; there are so many pitfalls."

"I know. I heard some people talking at that rally last spring, complaining about Bayard Rustin being so involved in civil rights activity. They're afraid that, since he was arrested for homosexual activity, he'll be a distraction or undermine the credibility of the Movement."

"It's everywhere. Uncle Kevin sent me some stuff to read, about the Army expelling homos now, even if they fought in World War II.

Did you hear, they fired a guy for that who was an astronomer in the Army map service? " *Jewish, too.* He shrugged off the thought and got back to the point. "Like he was going to seduce the stars out of the sky, or sneak homosexual bat signals into the maps. Now we can't get federal jobs because they're afraid we'll be blackmailed into giving away secrets or something."

"Kind of circular thinking, isn't it? If they didn't make such a fuss about it, there wouldn't be anything to blackmail you over."

"Surely you don't expect the government to be rational?"

"Sorry, lost my head there for a minute. So, Kevin's been helpful?"

"Yeah, we've been writing back and forth. I'm going to see him next week."

"You'll love his apartment; the chartreuse rug will blow your eyes out."

"Actually, he's redecorated since you saw it. More neutral colors now."

There was a silence from Laurie that Jamie couldn't decipher at first. Then it hit him. Before he could think of a story to cover his gaffe, Laurie said mildly, "I thought you told me at Christmas that you'd only written to him. So when did you have a chance to go there?"

"Last summer," Jamie admitted. "I wasn't ready to talk about it at Christmas. I didn't want to get into all the things I realized while I was with him, about myself and what the future might hold for me. I guess I'm still not ready to talk about it, exactly, but I somehow don't mind you knowing about it any more."

"I think you've come a long way, too."

"How about you? I gather things didn't go so well between you and Linda in the Adirondacks last month."

"We're not a couple any more," Laurie said, "though we'll always be good friends. And we had a good conversation about how to deal with hateful people without getting filled with hate ourselves."

"You worry too much about how the jerks of the world are going to feel if you put them down."

"And you worry too little, which makes me worry about you. It's like what we said that day I broke the pitcher, you remember? I guess you didn't know that about yourself then, that you liked guys, but the principle's the same—focus on what you want to have happen, rather than how to get back at people who hurt you. It's the main reason, I guess, that Linda and I can still be friends, in a way: instead of focusing on the ways we've let each other down, or can't be what we wanted to be for each other, we're trying to look to the future, to the way we want to be able to be now that we're not together."

Jamie tried to picture it. He rubbed his chin, feeling the roughness of his evening stubble. Then he took a breath and said, "I always wondered—"

"What?"

"Did you ever sleep with her? Never mind, never mind, too personal. Who you have sex with is your own business. You don't have to tell me."

Laurie laughed briefly. "Since I've only ever had sex with my right hand and the mattress, there's not much to tell."

"Really?"

"Really. Why? Did you and Rima—"

"No. Nor anybody else." *And I never even think about Tank Lebo any more. Was it his being so obnoxious at the prom that blew the bloom off the rose? Or is it what happened after, standing up to those other hoods, so I don't feel like I need some Aryan brute to save me any more? Take the violence out of sex-and-violence, and that leaves...* "I've been thinking about it a lot lately, though," he said to Laurie.

"Yeah, thinking'll do you in every time. There's this girl at Bryn Mawr I've been noticing…"

"Just noticing?"

"Well, I'm under orders now from Linda to speak to her, so I guess I will. Anybody you've got your eye on?"

"No," Jamie said, though an image of Joel flitted through his mind, elusive but evocative as a memory of honey on the tongue.

"It must be scary," Laurie said.

"It is."

They sat in silence for a few minutes, then Laurie pulled himself out of his chair with a creak of rattan. "I guess I'll hit the sack," he said. "Night, then."

"Good night."

Laurie brushed a hand over the top of Jamie's head as he passed and disappeared into the kitchen. Jamie could hear him murmuring a few words to Ruby. Then the light through the window of Ruby's sitting room beside him went off, and the one in her bedroom came on. He heard the rustle and splash of her washing and brushing her teeth for the night, then her lights went off.

Jamie sat on in the dark, listening to the sounds of the soft summer night.

Chapter 60.

"So, how many smoots long is this bridge again?" Joel asked.

"Three hundred sixty-four point four, plus or minus an ear," Jamie said.

Last fall there'd been a fraternity stunt in which Lambda Chi Alpha had used their shortest pledge, a guy named Oliver Smoot, to measure the Harvard Bridge, which carried Massachusetts Avenue from Boston proper to Cambridge. They'd laid him down, marked the distance, and then moved him to the next spot, over and over to the end. The painted stripes demarcating the five-foot seven-inch lengths were still visible on the pavement.

Jamie shook his head, half in amusement, half in scorn; while he'd been involved in planning to go to the march for school integration, these guys had been wasting time and energy on a prank. On the other hand, it was kind of funny, and it didn't do anyone any harm.

"Did you ever think about pledging a fraternity?" he asked Joel as they moved off the bridge and onto the footpath along the Charles River.

"Nah," Joel said. "I don't have time for that stuff. Besides, I'm not—you know, I'm not exactly the world's most social guy. You?"

"Pretty much the same," Jamie admitted. "Anyway , there's a lot of discrimination in those groups, I hear."

"Well, you could have pledged ZBT, that's a Jewish frat, right?"

The sun glinting off the river was warm. Jamie loosened the tie he'd worn to tea with Dean and Mrs. Fassett and slung his jacket over his shoulder. "They accept non-Jews now, but yes." That hadn't been the sort of discrimination he'd been thinking about, in any case.

They stopped strolling for a minute to watch some racing shells shoot past on the ruffled water, the coxes' voices calling instructions carried to them on the breeze. Jamie stared as the rowers bent and flexed and straightened, their bodies lithe in their shorts and sleeveless shirts, gleaming with sweat, muscles bunching and rippling.

"The manifold uses of a fulcrum," Joel remarked, pulling Jamie out of what was becoming a rapt fascination.

"Um, right," Jamie said, not able at the moment to think of an intelligent reply. To cover his flustered feeling, he suggested, "Let's sit down a minute," and led the way across the grass to a concrete bench. *Great move, Einstein,* he thought exasperatedly as soon as they were seated. *Now you're stuck in one place.*

He turned his eyes away from the rowers, back toward the medallioned arches of the bridge and the red cupola of the Harvard clock tower beyond. He could sense Joel watching him from the other end of the bench.

"Is there anything wrong?" Joel asked. "Yesterday in class, you confused a Fibonacci sequence with Mersenne primes; that was an elementary mistake, not like you. In fact, ever since we came back to school this fall, you've seemed a little off. Don't you like it here any more?"

"No, I love it here," Jamie said in surprise. "It's a beautiful place full of smart people who appreciate intelligence in other people. And to tell you the truth, the fact that there are so many Jews here makes me feel safe. Years ago, I was obsessed with the Rosenbergs, with how the Establishment turned against them, and I've wondered, since

NASA was founded, whether, even after all this time, there would be repercussions against Jews there." *And homosexuals,* he thought but did not say. "Anyway, here at MIT they value brains no matter who has them. I've never felt so at home—when I wasn't actually at home. I mean with my family."

Joel huddled into himself a little, drawing his feet in under the bench and folding his arms across his body.

Another smooth move, Hymie. Now you've made him feel bad about not having a real family.

But when Joel spoke, turning his face away from Jamie, what he said—so softly it was almost lost on the drifting air—was, "So it's me, then."

"What's you?" Jamie said blankly. *Oh, God, does he suspect I feel attracted to him?*

"What's making you act so cold and distant. You're sorry you agreed to room with me again this year."

"No—" Jamie began, but Joel straightened up, turned toward him, and spoke strongly over him.

"It's all right," he said. "I'm a big boy, you don't have to worry about me. We can go to the housing office and request a transfer. Or I will, I know you like that room. They won't let you keep a double on your own, I guess, so you'll have to take a chance on some random assignee, but at least you won't have me hanging around, and—"

"Stop! Stop, no, you've got the wrong end of the stick entirely!"

"I do?"

"Yes, it's me! I'm the one who—I mean, I wanted to leave you some room, not crowd you."

Now Joel looked bewildered. "Crowd me? What on earth are you talking about? The room's the same size it was last year."

"I don't mean physically. Or, I guess, in a sense I do mean physically, but that's not..." *Remember what Uncle Kevin said on your visit last month: if you can't be yourself with your friends, you can't be yourself. There's only one way out of this tangle, and you know it. Cut straight through.* Jamie closed his eyes and pushed forward. "There's something I've been keeping from you. Well, keeping from everyone outside my family, but I owe it to you especially to tell you, and I've been afraid to and that's why I've seemed distant."

He pulled his glasses off and wrapped his fingers around them, clutching till the frames seemed to cut into his hand. "The truth is," he said, "I'm queer; I'm a homosexual."

He wasn't sure whether the vertigo that washed over him was from fear or exhilaration; maybe it was both. *This must be what it feels like to jump out of an airplane. Now I wonder whether the parachute's going to open.*

He cracked his eyelids a slit and peered sideways. Joel's face was down almost on his knees; both his hands were wrapped over the back of his head. He was rocking back and forth and making an odd little keening noise.

No, no parachute. Ok, dead-stick landing then. "Now it's my turn to say, don't worry about me. I understand this is a shock, and I'm sorry if you feel like I misled you. I should have told you before you agreed to room with me again. For what it's worth, I could promise you that I won't, you know, try any funny business with you."

Joel stopped rocking and making that sound. After a moment he unlaced his hands and raised his head. He shot one quick glance at Jamie, then directed his eyes forward to the river. Still looking ahead, he said, "I know you won't. It's all right. We can—we can just be friends and keep living together. I mean, where would I find another study partner as good as you?"

310

Jamie's mouth twitched in recognition of the attempt at sarcastic humor, while his chest ballooned in relief. *A soft landing after all.* But he couldn't refrain from saying, "You're sure you don't mind?"

"Are you planning to attack me in the night?"

"No. I already said that."

"Then no, I don't mind. Come on, let's get going. We have prep to do for Dr. Mueller."

"Right," Jamie said. "Priorities."

He stood up, and they started down the path toward their dorm.

Chapter 61.

Saturday, January 2, 1960

J amie was holed up in the spare room, taking a break from the Christmas-Hanukkah extravaganza that had been inundating the rest of the house for a week. He was reading a book called, *The Homosexual in America: A Subjective Approach.* The author was given as Donald Webster Cory, but Jamie suspected that was a pseudonym.

There was a knock on the door, and Celia's voice: "Jamie, are you in there? Can I come in?"

Suppressing a sigh, Jamie sat up on the bed. *I owe her a conversation, it might as well be now.* "Come on in," he said.

She made a sympathetic face at him as she perched on the end of the bed by his feet. "I know you really want to be alone," she said, "but I never seem to get a chance to talk to you with nobody around. They'll all be trooping up to get ready for bed soon, and I thought I'd catch you first."

"It's ok," he said, sinking back against the pillow. "I wanted to thank you for this book, anyway." She'd slipped it to him as a sort of auxiliary Hanukkah present, late on Christmas night.

Now she said, "I found it in a peculiar little bookstore near Barnard."

"I bet it was peculiar," he said. "Queer, even."

"Well, if it was, that didn't keep the guy behind the counter from giving me the fish eye when I handed it to him."

"I can imagine. It was nice of you to do that for me."

She shrugged. "It was the least I could do, after the way I messed up this summer, letting it out to Steve. I know you said you're not still mad at me about that, but—"

"I'm really not," he said quickly, hoping to stave off yet another apology. "I told you, it worked out well; I got to talk to Steve about some things that were bothering him. And to tell you the truth, the more people who find out—I mean, who find out and don't have a fit about it—the easier it gets for me to deal with it myself, and talk about it to other people. I told my roommate this fall."

She pulled a foot up onto the mattress and rested her chin on her knee, looking at him with bright eyes. "I take it he didn't 'have a fit'?"

"Not even a small seizure. A few spasms before he got used to the idea, but since then he seems to be going out of his way to be nice to me, I guess to reassure me that he's not going to go off the deep end. I do have to keep in mind that most people won't be so cool about it, though," he said, patting the book cover reflectively.

"But everybody in the family knows now."

"Yeah. I wrote to Joy; she wrote me back with a list of homosexual poets I should read."

They both chuckled fondly.

Jamie shifted up onto an elbow. "I hear Laurie's got a new squeeze. Steve said there was some flap when she visited here?"

"Yeah, Rob referred to Laurie as a gorilla, and Julia went ballistic. Laurie managed to calm her down, though, and Robbie gave her a taste of his patented manic charm, and I told her it was a prerequisite to membership in this family, being a little weird."

"But you liked her?"

"I did. She's smart and she's gorgeous and she's evidently crazy about Laurie. A little touchy about the black stuff, but that's understandable; I gather she's never known many white people."

"So Laurie's finally got a black girlfriend, after all those years with Linda."

"Yeah, he said it's a different ballgame, having someone he doesn't have to explain certain things to, someone who understands where he is from the get-go."

Jamie sat all the way up, feeling as though a little rubber hammer had just bonked him on the forehead. *That's Joel. He gets so much: the Jewish thing, yes, but the math and science part of me, too. To hell with the blond Aryans who keep haunting my dreams; to hell with Tank Lebo. It's Joel I want.* It had never been so clear to him before.

It had been months, he realized, since he'd seen one of those blond flashes in his mind's eye—not since he'd had the talk with Steve about his being gay, and about the difference between that and Steve's experience being molested by his cousin, and about the way they'd both suffered. And he hadn't thought about Tank Lebo since he told Joel his secret. No, his truth; it wasn't really a secret any more, not from anyone who mattered to him.

Earlier today, Dad had talked to Steve about his drinking problem, and that he'd never be able to use alcohol safely. *That's an irreducible fact for Steve, but for me, progress is possible. I'm not going to be drawn to blond brutes for the rest of my life; I've already stopped thinking about Lebo. I don't have a disease or a disability: I am a homosexual.*

He suddenly became aware of Celia again. She had dropped her foot to the floor, leaned forward, and waved her hand in front of his face. "Earth to Jamie," she said.

He gave her his full attention. "Sorry," he said. "Just got distracted thinking about—er, the nature of sexual attraction." *Thinking about who matters to me. And Joel matters to me.*

"As part of your researches?" Celia said. "How's that going, anyway?"

Jamie turned his attention back to the conversation. "It turns out there's not much published to research with. Mom's been looking at stuff like the Kinsey Report and Masters and Johnson, but there are methodological problems, she says, and the only conclusion she's come to is that it's commoner than people think, and there's no way to 'cure' it."

"I guess it's kind of hard for you to do research on it without letting anyone at MIT know what you're doing."

"Yes, to say nothing of the fact that I have piles of course work to do in any case. I get this magazine Uncle Kevin told me about, called *The Mattachine Review;* it comes in the proverbial plain brown wrapper. The other guys in the dorm, except for my roommate, think it's porn."

Celia snorted and got off the bed with him as he moved over to the desk and shoved aside the stack of papers there to reveal the little stapled publication. She took it from him and sank cross-legged to the floor. "'Incest, A Consistent Social Taboo,'" she read. "Damn, and here I had my sights set on a secret love nest with Joy."

"Freak," he said genially. "I'll get you a subscription to *The Ladder.*"

"What's that?"

"It's the newsletter for the Daughters of Bilitis."

"Sounds like a poetry club."

"It's meant to. But it's an organization for lesbians." He plopped onto the desk chair and gazed at her consideringly. "You don't really think you might be one, do you, Cissy?"

She raised her head from the magazine, shaking her dark, smooth hair back out of her face. "No," she said. "In fact, at Barnard, mixing with guys from Columbia and other New York schools, for the first time I'm meeting men who aren't scared off by a woman with brains. And there nobody, by the way, calls me 'Cissy'."

He hadn't realized she had been hurt by being rejected for her own intelligence. *I have things in common with her that I'd never noticed, too. Suddenly, I feel as if I can see everyone more clearly, make connections I've been afraid to make before.* "Sorry," he said for the third time in this conversation. "I didn't know being called Cissy bothered you."

"It doesn't exactly bother me, it's just that it makes me feel like a little kid; specifically like a little sister."

"Biology is destiny," he said solemnly.

"Oh, well, if you're going to start quoting Freud at me, we're going to have a problem," she laughed.

She raised a hand and he pulled her to her feet, using the counterweight to lever himself out of the chair at the same time. The movement brought them to a stand with only a couple of inches between them. Jamie backed against the desk a little.

She raised an eyebrow with a knowing look. "It von't help you, chikki," she said in a comic half-Transylvanian, half-Yiddish accent. "I vant to drink your blod. Or give you a hug, at least."

But she stayed where she was till he gave a theatrical sigh. "All right," he said, quoting Mom, "'Nobody knows what I suffer.'"

She came back with a favorite phrase of Dad's: "Did you ever consider taking your troubles to a policeman?"

"Right," he said flatly. "Especially the ones with the little double esses on their collars."

Then, at the stricken look that started to come over her face, he said, "Sorry, I didn't mean that as a deflection. So hug me already, if you must."

"I must," she said, and did.

CHAPTER 62.

SUNDAY, APRIL 24, 1960

Jamie fled into the dorm room, Joel on his heels. His shivering was caused by more than the chilly sleet they'd just run through, but Joel attended to that aspect first, pulling off Jamie's sodden gray trench coat and flinging it into the sink, unwinding his gray and crimson muffler and hanging it over the mirror, bringing back a towel for his hair and—when Jamie didn't move to use it—scrubbing it over Jamie's head himself, then crouching in front of Jamie where he sat on the edge of his bed and chafing Jamie's hands between his own. He did all this while still in his own short yellow slicker, shiny with wet.

They had been to a campus showing of the movie *The Diary of Anne Frank*. Jamie had avoided seeing it when it came out in commercial theaters last spring. Reading the book had been hard enough; he didn't think he could bear the immediacy of the images. But today was Yom Hashoah, Holocaust Remembrance Day. He'd wanted to acknowledge it in some way, especially now, with Laurie down in Nashville sitting in at segregated lunch counters; Jamie felt that the least he could do was confront the terrors of his own past while his brother fought the demons of the current struggle.

He'd known that the story line wouldn't actually bring the characters to the concentration camp where most of them had died; he wasn't afraid the movie would have harrowing scenes like the ones he'd read about appearing in the documentary film *Night and Fog*.

He'd read Ann Frank's diary, after all, and thought he could deal with the relatively mild depiction of their years hiding in a Dutch attic.

It was hearing the sirens that brought him down. Once, as a child, he'd been thrown into a two-day silence by a passing Carlisle Hospital ambulance, but he'd eventually learned to endure the singular wail of an American siren. It had been fifteen years since he'd heard the distinctive, insistent, ominous two-note cry of a European police siren; the sound of it in the movie had cloven into his brain like lightning.

He'd clutched Joel's hand, heedless of any possible onlookers or even of what Joel himself would think of him. Joel had held it hard and brought his other hand over to cover it, then gripped Jamie's arm and helped him out of his seat and out of the room, sidling past knees in the row of folding chairs and stepping over and around the overflow of students who sat on the floor.

Now he said anxiously, "Are you all right now, Jamie? A little better, at least? I'm sorry I pushed to go to that, I didn't mean for you to get upset, I should have realized—"

"No," Jamie croaked, pulling one of his hands away to grip Joel's shoulder. "It was good that I went." Joel still looked doubtful, so Jamie tried to explain. "You know, in the camp, they called the walking dead, the ones who had given up, Musselmen. I don't know why; maybe because they were so weak from starvation and exhaustion that they'd fall down, like Muslims at prayer. But even when I was little, I knew I didn't want to become one of them. I used to stay away from them, as though I could catch what they had. I don't want to be dead inside, even if it hurts to remember."

He gave Joel's shoulder a little push. "Get out of that jacket. I don't want to be responsible for you getting pneumonia."

"You know that's an old wives' tale, getting sick from being cold and wet," Joel said, but he got up and hung up his jacket and Jamie's and dried his own hair.

"It may be an old wives' tale, but my mother always says that maybe the old wives knew something the professionals haven't figured out yet. My mother's good at focusing on what actually works instead of getting beguiled by the theoretical all the time."

"It always comes back to that family of yours, doesn't it?"

"I suppose it does." *The family makes you strong, Hymie.* Jamie toed off his soaking shoes and walked over to one of the heating pipes. Wrapping his hands around it for warmth, he stared into the blowy night outside the window.

"You know," he said to the glass, "I had one of my nightmares while I was at home for Passover. About my brother Laurie."

"The one who's demonstrating down South?"

"Right. I dreamed they were lynching him, but it was there, at Buchenwald. The camp was named for the beech trees in the forest outside the fence, you know. They called it the singing forest, because of the screams of the people they hanged there."

Joel came to stand beside him, leaning a hand on the windowsill and facing Jamie sideways. "How could they scream if they had ropes around their necks?"

"The hangman—Sommer, his name is; it struck me when I read about him when they finally arrested him a couple of years ago, that his name should mean 'summer' when it was always so cold— Sommer didn't hang them by the necks. He tied their wrists behind their backs and hanged them from them. It took them a long time to die, and they screamed almost to the end."

Jamie was breathing hard; he leaned his head against the blistery old paint of the window frame, waiting for the dizziness to pass. *I haven't had one of those dreams in, what is it, almost two years, since that night at Uncle Kevin's. I thought I was done with them. Won't I ever be done with them?* He felt Joel's grip on his arm again, then the pull as he was drawn into his roommate's arms. *Let yourself have some comfort, Hymie,* he told himself, and willed his clenched shoulders, his constricted chest, to relax. *This is just like being hugged by Dad, or Laurie; this is safe.*

But when he finally sighed and raised his head to thank Joel for the assistance, Joel leaned up and kissed him softly on the mouth.

All the voices in Jamie's head fell silent. There was a roaring in his ears, drowning out the memory of sirens. He stared at Joel's thin brown face, his liquid dark eyes, his expressive, shapely lips...

Lips that quivered now, as Joel stammered, "I, I, I'm sorry, I didn't mean to, I know you don't think of me that way, I just—"

Jamie bent his head and kissed him back. He suddenly remembered learning to ride a bicycle. He hadn't been on one in years, but he remembered what it was like the first time he'd done it successfully: the giddy triumph of the accomplishment, but also the astonishment that what had seemed so hard suddenly felt so natural; the way his body had reveled in his newfound sense of balance and control came back to him now, with Joel in his arms and their lips locked together.

He ventured an exploratory tongue, and Joel's mouth opened eagerly to his. Joel tasted of coffee and Chapstick and a warm, salty-sweetness that was all his own. After a minute, though, Jamie felt a return of his habitual self-doubt.

He pulled his head back. "Was that all right?" he asked hesitantly.

Joel tilted forward till his forehead rested on Jamie's chest. "Oh, God, yes," he breathed.

Then he pushed away a little and went on, "That day by the river, when you told me about—about yourself, I wanted so much to tell you about me, but I couldn't; I've never told anybody, and I was so scared. I told myself I didn't have to be scared of you, obviously I didn't, but…"

"I understand," Jamie said. He drew Joel over to sit beside him on the lower bunk, thigh pressed to thigh.

"Then," Joel went on, "I kept trying to show you how I felt, doing little things for you; pretty feeble, I guess, since you never responded, but I thought it just meant you weren't… attracted to me that way, and you were just letting me down easy—"

Jamie barked a short laugh. "I never let anyone down easy," he said. "You should know that by now. But I just thought you were the one being nice, showing me you would still be my friend even though I was *one*."

"'One'?"

"It's sort of code among queers, my Uncle Kevin told me, just to say, 'I'm one,' or 'he's one.' There's even an organization and a magazine called that; they won a Supreme Court case a little while ago, that said the post office couldn't refuse to deliver it as obscene just because it was about homosexuality."

"God, you know something about everything, don't you?"

"I deal with fear by research," Jamie said. "Safer than, say, actually confronting issues."

"I think it's a great way of confronting your fears. It's one of the things I lo-like about you. I don't confront mine at all; I just wait and repress them and eventually something snaps. Like tonight, seeing how you felt about the movie, I just couldn't keep my distance any more."

"Well, I'm not complaining, but I don't quite see the connection."

"You're always so strong—" Joel began. Then, at Jamie's disbelieving gape, he went on, "You always seem so together, so self-contained—"

"Except when I wake up screaming," Jamie interjected.

Joel only nodded. "Except when you wake up screaming," he agreed. "Or like tonight, when something hits you from your past. It just reminded me that you've got needs, too, and that maybe I can…" His voice tapered off.

Jamie cleared his throat and shifted slightly away; Joel did the same, till they were sitting about six inches apart. "The thing is," Jamie said, "I don't know how ready I am for, uh, anything more than, uh," he gestured obscurely toward the window where they'd kissed.

Joel seemed to understand; Jamie thought the sigh he gave was disappointment. But when he looked at him sidelong, he saw from his face that it was relief. "Me neither," Joel said. "Let's just be this," he in turn lifted a hand toward the window, "for a while."

He turned to face Jamie more fully. "One thing, though," he said. "From now on, I'm calling you Chaim."

"I don't mind," Jamie said.

Chapter 63.

"That was amazing," Joel said.

Jamie had just finished playing the Liszt *Piano Sonata in B Major* on the living room baby grand. The emotional music seemed to be a way to communicate to Joel something of what he couldn't say in words. It felt strange to have Joel here in the house, out of the MIT context. Jamie had never invited friends over, growing up, the way the other kids did—*except for Steve, the other misfit*. He mentally shook himself. *Stop that. You have a friend here now. And besides, there was Rima…*

Rima was supposed to come over after supper, and Jamie was nervous about that. *Talk about mixing worlds.* But so far, Joel's visit had gone well. The family seemed to like him, and he them.

Laurie had Julia, the girlfriend who'd replaced Linda, here for the week. Their experiences in Nashville had evidently cemented their relationship. Julia's gregarious personality and interest in civil rights issues had engaged Joel and helped him over his initial shyness on being plunged into the heady mix of talk, laughter, affection, music, and seemingly constant activity that was the McAlister style.

This was the first the two of them had been alone together since Joel arrived two days ago. Suddenly at a loss for conversation, Jamie had retreated into the Liszt; now that was over, he wondered what on earth he'd thought he and Joel could spend their time on without homework or the occasional light make-out session to fall back on.

Joel did seem impressed by Jamie's piano playing, though. He came to stand behind him, looking over his shoulder at the sheet music Jamie almost didn't need any more.

"Do you read music?" Jamie asked. "I don't even know whether you play an instrument."

"I played violin as a kid," Joel said. "But when my parents heard from my teacher that I wasn't going to be the next Yehudi Menuhin, they lost interest, and so did I. You obviously stuck to it."

Jamie slipped into one of his favorite Bach Inventions, the E Minor, as they talked. "I've always found it relaxing," he said. "It's like math, only without the calculations."

"I've heard that," Joel said. "You can analyze it using abstract algebra, right?"

"Right," Jamie agreed. "Have you read Lewin's transformational theory? It's really an expansion of set theory. You can describe just intonation—the way the note frequencies are related by whole number ratios—as the basis of an abelian group."

Joy drifted in from the dining room, looking disconsolate. She stared at them for a minute; Jamie thought of asking her if there was anything wrong, but she only nodded at them abstractedly and made her way out of the room and up the stairs.

Jamie had lost the thread of conversation. He closed the piano lid and pushed back the stool, which brought him up against Joel's legs. He leaned his head back against Joel's stomach and said, "What do you feel like doing?"

The look on Joel's face, turned down toward Jamie's, was the one he wore back at MIT when he was about to suggest a necking session.

Before he had a chance to say anything, though, Ruby's voice came from the doorway. "Dinner's going to be soon," she said. "Your father just put the burgers on the grill."

Jamie straightened up, trying not to look flustered. He knew Ruby was not happy about his homosexuality, though she hadn't said anything directly to him about it; he didn't want to flaunt it in front of her and hurt her feelings by making her think he did it to twit her. "Ok," he said. "We'll go wash up."

An hour later, Joel was helping him brush the pie crumbs off the table in the screened porch. To the sounds of Rob and Steve helping Ruby in the kitchen, Joel said, "My God, what a meal. I'm surprised you're not the size of a hippo, eating like this all your life."

"Not all my life," Jamie said mildly.

"Oh, you know what I mean." Then he stood and stared at Jamie in the twilight, stricken. "But that's the point, isn't it? I mean, you were on the verge of starvation so long—that's why you don't eat much now, isn't it?"

"More or less, yeah. At least now I can face a meal like today's without wanting to run away, though."

Joel handed the crumber across to Jamie, who put it down on a side table, and the two of them folded the cloth.

"What do you want us to do with the tablecloth, Ruby?" Jamie called toward the kitchen.

Ruby came to the screen door. "Just leave it on the side table," she said. "We'll use it again tomorrow."

"I was just saying," Joel said to her, "that was a wonderful meal, ma'am. I haven't eaten like that since last time I was with my Jamaican relatives, and then the food was so spicy I had to eat about a quart of peach ice cream just to put out the fire."

Ruby chuckled. "Thank you," she said. "I'm glad to hear you keep in touch with your roots." She shot a monitory glance at Jamie.

"Ruby," he said, "I hear you. I've *heard* you, ok?"

She sniffed and disappeared back into the kitchen.

"What was that about?" Joel asked in an undertone as they settled on the garden bench outside the porch, waiting for the fireworks to start.

"Ruby thinks I should do something about finding out what happened to my mother," Jamie said. "My birth mother, I mean."

"I think that, too."

"I know. It's funny, though," he lowered his voice. "Being with you is making things come back to me, but in a way that doesn't hurt the way flashbacks did when I used to have them. And telling you about my nightmare; I never told anyone outside the family about them before. It all makes me feel like I might be able to deal with finding out about my mother. It's not that I don't want to; I just don't know where to start."

"How about the Red Cross?" Joel said. "They have a service for helping war refugees reconnect."

"Who's reconnecting? You and me?" Rima let the porch door bang behind her and made her way across the grass to them.

Jamie and Joel both stood up; Rima held her hand out to Joel, who shook it. "So this must be the famous Joel," she said.

"And you're the famous Rima."

"That's me." Her smile flashed white in the deepening dusk.

They turned back to the bench; Jamie and Joel started to sit at either end. With an impatient gesture, Rima pushed them aside to take one end herself, leaving them to squeeze in together.

"So, you two doing it yet?" she asked confidentially.

"Holy God," Joel yelped.

"Rima, behave yourself," Jamie said firmly. "We're not talking about that."

"Damn," Rima said unrepentantly. "Ok, then what are we talking about? How's Laurie? Did he get back all right from deepest darkest Dixieland?"

"Yes, he's fine. He and Julia are around here somewhere; they disappeared after dinner."

"I can't *imagine* what they might be doing," she said with a leer.

"God, you're incorrigible. Get your mind out of the gutter."

"All right, all right. I suppose you just sit around talking about civil rights."

"Actually, yes," Joel said. "I had a great conversation with Julia last night, while you were helping with the dishes, Chaim."

"Chaim?" Rima whispered to Jamie.

He shrugged. The name Chaim still seemed alien to him, someone else's name. *Life. Chaim means "life." That's not me.*

Joel was still talking. "Everything they're doing for civil rights; I'd like to get more involved in that. I know you've been to a few rallies and such, Chaim, and I want to start doing that kind of thing, too. Helping counteract prejudice against Negroes like Laurie and Julia and me is a way of making sure that the kind of thing that happened to Jews in Europe doesn't happen again. And even—" He stopped.

"'And even'?" Rima prodded.

Joel ducked his head. "Well," he said softly, "this may sound crazy, but I thought, maybe even someday there could be a movement for equal rights for people like Chaim and me."

"Hmm," Rima said. "I never thought about that being the same sort of thing. But I guess I can see it happening. What do you think, Jamie?"

"I suppose it's possible," Jamie said. "Maybe."

CHAPTER 64.

SATURDAY, AUGUST 13, 1960

Steve and Rob's musical career had really taken off while Jamie had been away at MIT. From performing in friends' basements they'd played at school events, then such venues around the area as bar mitzvah and confirmation parties and War College and Navy Depot celebrations. Then they'd made a demo disk with Steve's "Bright, Warm Home" on the A side, and now they had a bona fide agent.

His name was Wolfowitz ("Call me Wolfie") and Jamie detested him after barely a minute in his presence. He had exactly the sort of oily, cold-eyed pushiness that anti-Semites liked to attribute to all Jews.

Mom and Dad were evidently not that impressed with him, either. They were now ensconced in the study, having a confab over some proposal of Wolfie's they weren't happy with. Steve had run upstairs, looking on the verge of tears. Rob had brought Wolfie here, into the living room, where Jamie had been peacefully reading the papers.

Wolfie got out a silver lighter and flicked it open, leaning forward with his omnipresent stogie in his mouth.

Jamie looked at him out of the corner of his eye, wondering if he'd have to be the one to say something. *Evidently not.*

Before Jamie could speak, Rob said, "You can't light that in here."

"Eh?" Wolfie paused, blinking.

"No smoking in the house—my brother's lungs were damaged when he was little."

Wolfie gaped at him. "No smo— you mean, people can't even smoke cigarettes in here?"

"That's right, no smoking."

Wolfie shook his head. "Surprised you people have any friends at all. So what's the big deal with your brother, little asthma or something?"

"We don't really know what happened. Just the doctor says his lungs are damaged."

"How could you not know what happened?"

I am in the room here, you know. Jamie sighed, put down the newspaper he was reading, and rolled up his left sleeve. "You're Jewish, too, right?" he said to Wolfie. "You know what this means."

Wolfie peered at the numbers on Jamie's arm. "How old are you, kid?" he asked, reaching out abruptly, ignoring Jamie's reflexive jerk away. "Eighteen? Nineteen? How did a four-year-old survive Auschwitz?"

"Buchenwald," Jamie said.

"Auschwitz," Wolfie repeated.

"You think you know better than I do where I was?"

"I think I know they only used tattoos at Auschwitz," Wolfie insisted. "Maybe you went to Buchenwald later, but you were at Auschwitz, kid. You don't remember?"

I don't remember. How could I not remember?

"Jedem das seine," Jamie said. "You get what you deserve."

Wolfie stared at him. "They really did a number on you, kid. Who told you that's what it means?"

"I don't remember who. I remember somebody shouting it at me, in Yiddish. I can still hear him: *Jedem das seine, ir bakumen vos ir fardinen.*"

"A kapo, maybe," Wolfie said. "Toeing the Nazi line. It should have been, *'Tsu yeder zayn eygn.'*"

"So what does it really mean?" Rob put in.

Still looking at Jamie, Wolfie said, "To each his own."

Jamie gaped at him, stunned. The slogan that had governed his life turned on its head. He wasn't to blame for anything. He was his own person, his fate was his own.

Then Dad came out of the study and invited Wolfie back in. Rob ran upstairs to fetch Steve. Jamie took the opportunity to escape to the larger spare room.

His head was reeling from what Wolfie had said: reality shifted and blurred, and he could make no sense of it. *Jedem das Seine,* the watchwords on the gates of his mind: there was no way that memory could be false, even if his understanding of them had been. He'd seen them as he looked out the back of the jeep in the convoy that drove them away after liberation, and in his mind's eye ever since. The words on the gates of Auschwitz were *Arbeit Macht Frei,* "Work Sets You Free." He was certain he'd never seen them, except in books.

And yet, Wolfie was so sure. Could it be that an entire horrendous episode had vanished from his memory, and his mother with it? And could it be that he'd always misunderstood what those words meant, that had loomed so large in his head? That he'd taken the word of his tormentors and made it his own watchword? Jamie closed the spare room door behind him, wishing he could shut out the turmoil Wolfie's words had set loose.

Lying on the desk was Jamie's translation of Jean Cayrol's *'Chant d' Espoir,"* "Song of Hope," from a collection of poetry the writer composed after surviving the Matthausen-Gusen concentration camp. Joy had told Jamie about him; he'd heard the name before then, but only as the author of the script for *Night and Fog*, the French documentary about the Holocaust.

Once he saw the poem, though, he'd been stirred by the little he could decipher on sight. He'd gathered the scraps of French he still remembered from his time in the orphanage and the textbook French he'd studied in high school and begun teasing out the meaning.

He sat down and focused on it now; he was almost finished. Most of the poem was about hope and rebirth, the quotidian reality of basic, simple things concentration camp inmates lacked and yearned for: bread, flowers, freedom, fruit, light. Gradually, the last few lines yielded up their essence:

When we can say in our prayers
The damned names of our prisons
Then we will move, brothers
In step with the living.

Jamie put his head down on the desk. *The damned names of our prisons*, he thought. *Auschwitz. Auschwitz. Mamme. Ruby was right; Joel is right. They're all right, everyone who wants me to remember. That's why I survived, so I could remember. As soon as I get back to Boston, I'm going to the Red Cross.*

CHAPTER 65.

SATURDAY, OCTOBER 22, 1960: PART 1

Jamie shut himself into the phone booth, ignoring the pervasive urine smell and the rumble of traffic down Commonwealth Avenue a few feet away. This call couldn't wait, and it couldn't be made in the dorm hallway.

It seemed to take forever to get enough quarters for the long-distance call through the slot; he kept dropping them, scraping them back off the filthy floor with shaking fingers, trying again.

It wasn't hard to remember the number, though. Mom had given it to him years ago, saying, "You can call whenever you need me. If I'm with a patient, I won't be able to pick up right away, so let it ring four times, hang up, then call again and ring once. I'll call you back as soon as I can. If I'm out on the ward and can't hear my phone, just keep trying: I'll be there for you."

He'd never had to use it, but more than once when he was little the thought had comforted him, that she was no farther away than the phone. Today was Saturday; she was most likely right at her desk, doing paperwork. He recited the number to the long-distance operator, then jiggled with impatience waiting for the signal to go through.

But when she answered on the second ring, "This is Dr. McAlister, can I help you?" the words fled as so often before and he stood there, frozen in silence.

It only took a few seconds of the crackling static of the long distance line before she said, in a different tone of voice, "Jamie? Is that you?"

A simple question. He could answer that, couldn't he? But he couldn't.

She took an audible breath and said, "Hymele?"

Close enough. "Yes," he croaked.

"All right, my darling. Breathe. Are you breathing?"

Was he? "I am now."

"Good. Just take your time and keep breathing."

He breathed, swallowed, closed his eyes and centered himself. "My mother," he said.

"Tell me."

The familiar command seemed to free his vocal chords. "At the Red Cross, they had the records. Just a few lines, names, places, dates—but they brought it all back. It was raining."

"There in Boston?"

"No, there. On the platform. We were standing there, Tati and Mamme and me, and it was raining."

"How did that feel?"

"It felt wonderful. We'd been crammed into a train car, I don't know how long, no food, no water, people crying, Tati and Mamme taking turns holding me so I wouldn't get trampled. Now there was room to breathe, and water on my face. I opened my mouth and let the raindrops fall in."

"What happened next?"

"There was a lot of shouting, and men with guns, and big dogs—*Schäferhunden*. That's when I started to get scared." He leaned his forehead against the glass of the phone booth, remembering. "They divided everyone up, the men and the women. Mamme took my hand. We started to walk away with all the other women and little kids. Then all of a sudden…" He froze again.

"You left her?" Mom said.

"No," he whispered. "She pushed me away. She pushed me towards Tati. She said, she said—"

"What did she say?"

"Chaye."

"Your name, your Hebrew name?"

"Not quite. I think at the time, that's what I thought it was. Then I thought it was just *chai,* life, like on my square in the family quilt. But I can hear the sound she made, and now I know Hebrew verbs. It's the imperative."

"The imperative?"

"A command. 'Live,' she told me." His breath was coming in soft hitches now, though his eyes were dry.

The line was silent, then Mom said, "And you did. You did what she told you to, my darling."

"It was the gas chamber, you understand? They were taking the women and the other little kids to be killed."

"I understand."

"But I found Tati and they shaved our heads and tattooed our arms and gave us gray clothes to wear. Mamme must have been ash on the wind by the time they shipped us on to Buchenwald."

"Shipped you?"

"On a train, in open cars. It got really cold. People froze to death, I think. Tati kept me under his shirt, against his chest." Jamie felt wrapped in a pall of wretchedness now. "That's all I remember, till the barracks," he finished.

"And you lived."

"And I lived." *But it's not enough. I'm alive, but why? For what purpose?* "What do I do now?" he asked her.

"Anything in the whole world that you want to do," she said. "But for right now, go be with someone. Where's Joel?"

"Back at the dorm. We're supposed to have dinner together."

"So go have dinner. Be alive. We'll talk again tomorrow."

"Ok. Tell Dad, will you?"

"Of course."

He hesitated, then asked, "Why do I feel so awful?"

"It's an awful thing to remember, much as you wanted and needed to remember it. It's going to take a while to work through. It's like any other new set of knowledge: you need to pore over it, ponder it, decide what it's going to mean for you. Just remember that we're here and that we love you."

"Ok. All right. Good bye."

CHAPTER 66.

SATURDAY, OCTOBER 22, 1960: PART 2

It was a brisk, clear day. The colors of the leaves of a New England fall were spectacular. The sun shone in through the common room windows where Jamie's dorm mates were planning a Halloween party. Jamie wished the whole lot of them and the jolly, rational, hopeful world they inhabited would disappear down a deep hole.

Instead, I'm the one in a hole.

The conversation with Mom had pulled him back into the present world, but it didn't feel as though he fit there anymore. He needed to connect to someone. *That's why she told you to find Joel,* he realized. In his present mood, her perceptiveness irritated him.

He burst into his room and slammed the door behind him. Joel, he saw to his annoyance, had left Jamie's desk lamp on. He snapped it off with a snarl. *He's so thoughtless, so careless, going out and leaving this on. And where's he gone, anyway? We were supposed to have supper together. He's never here when I need him.*

That was so patently untrue it gave him pause. *Calm down, Hymie. It's not his fault.* He thumped his briefcase onto the desk and turned around. *That's funny, he usually makes up his bunk before he leaves. He must have been in a hurry for some reason. Maybe that's why—* Suddenly, he realized the lump of bedclothes on the upper bunk was shaking. Joel was in there, having wrapped himself up the way Steve did when life in the free air became too much to bear.

336

"Joel?" he said uncertainly. "What's wrong?"

He half expected Joel to roll himself tighter into hiding, the way Steve would. Instead, he flung the covers aside with a wail and rolled straight off the bunk bed without bothering with the ladder, landing lightly on his feet and plunging for Jamie.

He buried his head in Jamie's chest and sobbed. Jamie's irritation vanished; he was half blind with panic, but resolved to stand firm for Joel. "What?" he demanded, and then more softly, "What? What is it, sweetheart?"

He heard Laurie's familiar endearment come out of his own mouth with something like horror, which was mirrored by Joel as he raised his blotchy face to look at Jamie. Or maybe not horror; amazement, certainly, and maybe a little wonder, but fear, too.

"Jamie?" he whispered.

"Oh, so now I'm Jamie again. What, did I lose my romantic Jewish credentials while I was out?"

"It's just, I can't... being Jewish is so... and then on top of that..."

"You realize you're not making any sense, right?"

Joel nodded miserably. Jamie turned him, still with an arm around his shoulders, and propelled him over to the lower bunk. Joel sat down on the edge of it, but Jamie leaned over and picked up his stocking feet, swiveling him so he was lying at full length. He pulled his own shoes off, dropped his jacket on the floor, yanked Joel's quilt off the top bunk, and crawled in beside him, covering them both.

Pulling Joel into his arms with his head against his shoulder, as Dad had done for Jamie so many times, he said softly, "Now, tell me."

Joel, breath still hitching a little, said, "I was reading."

"Always a dangerous idea."

"It was that Shirer book that just came out, you know, *The Rise and Fall of the Third Reich?*"

"I know; I was planning to read it after you."

"It's so horrible, Jamie. I knew it would be, naturally, but seeing the whole weight of it all in one book, the descriptions and the photographs, and—Auschwitz, Jamie, there are pictures of bodies being bulldozed into pits."

"Did any of them look like me?" Jamie asked wryly.

"They all looked like you. That's the thing, Jamie, Chaim, I kept seeing your face on all of them, thinking of you while I read the descriptions of the starvation and the beatings and the torture." He pulled away just far enough to look up into Jamie's face. "Wait a minute, what do you mean, did they look like you?"

"Maybe you saw my mother. I was at the Red Cross today; the report came in. It's definite: she was separated from Tati and me right off the transport and sent directly to the gas chamber. We were processed and then shipped out with a labor detachment to Buchenwald. God knows why they didn't kill me, too, but there were several of us little boys who survived, so they must have thought we'd be some use. But Buchenwald was huge, and not as well organized as Auschwitz; they must have lost track of me, after Tati and the other men started hiding me. He never talked to me about what happened to Mamme. I suppose he couldn't bear to, but I wish he had, Joel. I wish he had."

Now it was Jamie's turn to cry. He didn't sob the way Joel had, but the tears washed down his face and Joel started kissing them off. He stopped with a stricken look and buried his face in Jamie's chest again.

Jamie gently jostled him off and pushed him onto his back, then leaned over him, propped on one arm. "You already knew about what happened in the camps, though. That's not what had you so upset. Tell me." *I'm turning into Mom,* he thought.

Joel turned his head aside. Jamie took his chin in hand and turned it back. "Tell me," he repeated firmly. *There are worse things to turn into.*

Joel gulped and said, "It says... he says... Shirer... every time he mentions the homosexuals in the camps, he calls them perverts; it's as though he thinks they deserved to be there, as though they weren't victims, too."

He raised his hands to cover his face, then pushed away Jamie's supporting arm so that he fell back. Propped on an elbow, he looked down at Jamie in turn and said fiercely, "I'm a homo and a Jew, and black on top of that. Everybody in the world wants to kill me."

"I don't want to kill you," Jamie said with sudden decision. "I love you."

"You—"

"I love you, and I don't believe I've ever said that particular English sentence before. I love you, and what's more, I want to make love to you. Do you want that, too?"

Joel nodded. Jamie pressed him. "Are you sure? We don't have to, if you're not ready, or not ever, really, if that's not your thing—"

"Can you reach my bunk from here?"

"Um, I think so."

"Stick your hand up under my pillow."

Jamie did so, and felt something that he gripped and dragged back down. It was a tube of K-Y jelly. He gaped at Joel. "How long has that been up there?"

"All semester. I've been hoping... I take it you know what to do with it?"

"Never fear," Jamie said. "I read a book."

Later, Joel raised a drowsy head, face still marked with the residue of his earlier breakdown. "Do you suppose it's possible to actually die of embarrassment?" he asked.

"Evidently not," said Jamie drily, "or I'd have expired about five minutes ago."

Joel snorted. "Shall we stomp around and do manly things for a while? Kick a ball around the grass or go out and shoot something furry in the woods or maybe pick a fight with some guys?"

Jamie laughed. In his head, iron gates swung open. At his side, Joel said uncertainly, "Chaim? I mean, Jamie?"

There had been another survivor looking for answers at the Red Cross office, an old man in a yarmulke who'd glanced over at the papers Jamie was reading and then up into his face with something like wonder.

"You were there?" he'd asked. And then, at Jamie's nod, he'd grasped his arm. "*Der Yingl,*" he'd breathed. "You're *der Yingl.* You lived!"

What are the chances? his sardonic inner voice had said. *It's some other boy he saw, some other barracks he was in.*

So what? he'd answered, pushing the voice away. *It's still true, what he says. I lived. I lived to remember, like that man who gave me the bread told me to. Sha already, be quiet and leave me alone.* This time, he'd somehow thought the voices would obey.

"Yes," he'd said to the old man. "I was *der yingl.* And I lived. I lived to remember."

"Chaim," he said now to Joel, "My name is Chaim."